THE FARTHER ADVENTURES OF ROBINSON CRUSOE

broadview editions
series editor: Martin R. Boyne

THE FARTHER ADVENTURES OF ROBINSON CRUSOE

Daniel Defoe

edited by John Richetti and Rivka Swenson

broadview editions

BROADVIEW PRESS
Peterborough, Ontario, Canada

Founded in 1985, Broadview Press is a fully independent academic publishing house owned by approximately twenty-five shareholders—almost all of whom are either Broadview employees or Broadview authors. Broadview is supported by a collaboration with Trent University, a liberal arts university located in Peterborough, Ontario—the city where Broadview was founded and continues to operate. Broadview is committed to environmentally responsible publishing and fair business practices.

Library and Archives Canada Cataloguing in Publication

Title: The farther adventures of Robinson Crusoe / Daniel Defoe ; edited by John Richetti and Rivka Swenson.
Names: Defoe, Daniel, 1661?-1731, author | Richetti, John J., editor | Swenson, Rivka, 1973- editor
Series: Broadview editions.
Description: Series statement: Broadview editions | Includes bibliographical references.
Identifiers: Canadiana (print) 20240465148 | Canadiana (ebook) 20240465172 | ISBN 9781554811151 (softcover) | ISBN 9781770489769 (PDF) | ISBN 9781460409008 (EPUB)
Subjects: LCSH: Defoe, Daniel, 1661?-1731—Criticism and interpretation. | LCSH: English fiction—18th century—History and criticism. | LCGFT: Novels.
Classification: LCC PR3404 .F37 2024 | DDC 823/.5—dc23

Broadview Editions
The Broadview Editions series is an effort to represent the ever-evolving canon of texts in the disciplines of literary studies, history, philosophy, and political theory. A distinguishing feature of the series is the inclusion of primary source documents contemporaneous with the work.

Advisory editor for this volume: Michel Pharand

Broadview Press handles its own distribution in Canada and the United States:
PO Box 1243, Peterborough, Ontario K9J 7H5, Canada
555 Riverwalk Parkway, Tonawanda, NY 14150, USA
Tel: (705) 482-5915
email: customerservice@broadviewpress.com

Broadview Press acknowledges the financial support of the Government of Canada for our publishing activities.

Canada

Cover design and typesetting: George Kirkpatrick

PRINTED IN CANADA

Contents

Acknowledgements

For help with technical matters early in our process, we would like to thank Brian Kirk at the University of Pennsylvania. For able research and editing assistance, we would like to thank the following graduate students: Drew Scheler (University of Virginia); Ciera Higginbotham, Hannah Kilgore, and Meredith Spencer (Virginia Commonwealth University). Globally, we would like to thank Marjorie Mather, Martin Boyne, and Michel Pharand, editors extraordinaire at Broadview Press, along with the press's external readers whose comments helped to shape this edition.

Introduction

Daniel Defoe (c. 1660–1731) and his contemporary eighteenth-century readers considered the novel you see before you to be "Part II" in the adventures of the eponymous protagonist Robinson Crusoe. Part I, published in London by William Taylor on 25 April 1719, is the novel that modern readers know simply as *Robinson Crusoe.*[1] Part II, entitled *Farther Adventures*, or, as it was originally called, *The Farther Adventures of Robinson Crusoe: Being the Second and Last Part of his Life, And of the Strange Surprizing Accounts of his Travels Round three Parts of the Globe*, was published on 20 August 1719, a scant four months after Part I. It was a preconceived sequel, the first half of which was summarized in Crusoe's concluding address to the reader at the end of Part I. The shift from the island to Crusoe's truly *farther* adventures halfway through Part II constituted a "transformation" that "for its contemporary audience ... was no less appealing" than the island story, as Steve Clark and Yukari Yoshihara point out ("Introduction" 3). Yet today's readers typically do not even know of Part II's existence—an issue we seek to help remedy, especially considering the wealth of fresh critical attention that the novel has received in the past two decades, as evidenced by the Works Cited and Select Bibliography section that closes this book.[2]

During its time, however, Part II, *The Farther Adventures*, was perceived as integral to an intended whole and was immediately and sustainedly popular as such. Four new editions appeared in short order (seven by 1747). Subsequently, the two Parts were almost always reprinted together as a *single* volume in most

1 Full original title of Part I: *The Life and Strange Surprizing Adventures of Robinson Crusoe, Of York, Mariner: Who lived Eight and Twenty Years, all alone in an uninhabited Island on the Coast of AMERICA, near the Mouth of the Great River of OROONOQUE; Having been cast on Shore by Shipwreck, wherein all the Men perished but himself. WITH An Account how he was at last as strangely deliver'd by PYRATES.* Quotations in this introduction from Part I are from a modern edition that bears the title we know the book by today: *Robinson Crusoe* (1719), edited by John Richetti.

2 Our teaching edition complements the larger variety of modern editions, of which there are two. The first is *The Farther Adventures of Robinson Crusoe*, edited by W.R. Owens, while the second is *The Farther Adventures of Robinson Crusoe: The Stoke Newington Edition*, edited by Maximillian E. Novak et al.

English and European translations until the end of the nineteenth century. In fact, the holistic printing of Crusoe's story did not really decline until after World War I. From that point forward, for reasons perhaps tied to global and domestic events that dampened the resonance of Part II with readers (as argued by Melissa Free)[1] who perhaps desired to experience a more manageably self-contained tale, the drop-off of holistic editions was steep.[2] But until that time, indeed for more than two hundred years after its first appearance, Crusoe's story was encountered by generations of readers as *one* text in *two* Parts; the second novel was understood to constitute a clear and substantial continuation of the protagonist's story. In short, the history of Defoe's most famous fictional character extends over two volumes, a history—and a revolution of character, reached recursively but surely, as we shall see—that remains incomplete until the end of Part II.[3]

Crusoe introduces himself in the opening sentence of *Robinson Crusoe* as an entity who is susceptible to being changed by outside influence but is also potentially able to induce change in others—or even, perhaps, to claim an identity regardless of the dynamics of influence. "I was called Robinson Kreutznaer; but by the usual Corruption of Words in England, we are now called, nay we call ourselves, and write our Name Crusoe, and so my Companions always called me" (5), the protagonist explains, thus signaling the ability of Englishness to change what it encounters. This admission serves as a formally unifying paratext for the two Parts of the story, but it is meaningfully modified by Crusoe's statement in the inaugural sentence of Part II that "*what is bred in the Bone will not go out of the Flesh*" (p. 19). What we see across the two Parts, ultimately, is a shift from Crusoe's need to change-others-lest-he-be-changed in Part I to a developing security in the boundaries

1 Free speculates that the plunge was tied to postwar publishers' reluctance to print, and/or readers' reluctance to read, a narrative that might seem to undercut fantasies of British unity or authority (political, cultural, or otherwise) abroad.

2 In the introduction to the Pickering & Chatto edition of *The Farther Adventures*, Owens dates the decline of the dual edition to a period between 1920 and 1980, when fewer than twenty-five percent of the 190 editions included Part II (16–17).

3 By contrast, the 1720 Part III, *Serious Reflections During the Life and Surprising Adventures of Robinson Crusoe*, usually was not published with Parts I and II and is not properly a part of the "history" but rather functions as a meditative and instructional addendum. For this reason, Crusoe notes at the end of Part I that he is at the "middle" of his tale.

of the self—a confidence in an essential self that cannot be corrupted despite external influence—that paradoxically allows him to finally develop some respect for others' boundaries, too.

Part I shows a Crusoe who is driven to selectively collect, organize, and transform the world (practically and in narrative terms). Ruled by an eat-or-be-eaten philosophy, Crusoe in Part I can well stand as an emblem of the English colonial mind of the time. He shores up his identity not simply by defining himself in binary relation to an Other but by expanding the range of the self: incorporating, digesting, and changing the world around him. In Part I, Crusoe uses his corrupting English influence to rename Friday, bequeath him an English identity, English clothes, and English ways, and thereby pass on to him what Crusoe calls the *story* of Englishness.

This process of Crusoe's self-becoming in Part I, which proceeds haltingly and recursively but reaches new levels of fruition with the domestication of Friday, is initially enabled by Crusoe's use of his parrot Poll as a kind of interlocutor: Poll learns to "ask" Crusoe questions such as "*how did I come here? and where had I been*?" (114), and Poll's parroting enables Crusoe to begin fashioning his identity through story. The process is complete (for the purposes of Part I) when Crusoe relates his digested story to the island's European newcomers (and by extension to us, with much of his revisionary writerly process laid bare in his frequent comments about rearrangement, truncation, and omission). At last, by way of these conveyances, Crusoe stops losing himself to fear and becomes the confident figure that he spends most of Part I writing himself towards. He becomes a man who can enter a dark cave (literally and figuratively) without stopping to question his ability to take charge and make use of what's there.

The first half of Part II pursues continuity of character—and a teasing resonance with Defoe's extra-novelistic writerly pursuits—as Crusoe returns to the island to help the nascent community adopt his organizational and transformational narrative strategies in order to form a self-supporting union. As can be gleaned from the material brought together by Defoe's biographers (the most extensive biographies are by Paula Backscheider and Maximillian Novak) and the material in our Appendices (Defoe's letters from Scotland in Appendix A and his essays on trade in Appendix B), the entrepreneurial Defoe had some things in common with his protagonist: indeed, Defoe's writing about national polity, like his writing about trade, often feels as if it could have been written by Crusoe. Like Crusoe, Defoe was a writer, at once prolific and self-reflexive; just as Crusoe in Part I alludes explicitly and often to the constructed nature of his "story" as he restructures his autobiography "in miniature, or by abridgement" (155), Defoe wrote overtly about his own real-life willingness to manipulate reality at will and thus forge a "story of Union"—as a paid political propagandist supporting the 1707 Act of Union—that would inspire readers to embrace a particular vision of national unity in their hearts.[1] Like Crusoe coaching the islanders in the first half of Part II, Defoe as propagandist tries to use language to stabilize and unify a fractured island community around a common cause of self-preservation. Indeed, much of the language about nation-building in the first half of Part II resonates with Defoe's propaganda in support of the Union in his personal letters, his copious political pamphlets, his prospective *A History of the Union of Great Britain* (advertised before the Union was achieved), and his retrospective *A Tour thro' the Whole Island of Great Britain.* Duplicating Defoe's warning in the *History* that Britons "have the same Enemies, and the same Friends, and in Probability must have the same Duration" (v), Crusoe insists that the islanders "must destroy the [external enemies], or be all of them destroy'd themselves" (p. 119). We glimpse in Crusoe's efforts to unify the society a window onto what Defoe labored to write into being for the island of Great Britain, a project that he understood as involving a certain privileging of English and Protestant values.[2]

The first half of Part II thus works at the generic intersection of allegory and fantasy; indeed, Defoe's statement in the later *Serious Reflections of Robinson Crusoe* (Part III) about the Crusoe story's status as an "allegory" of a real man's life (whether Defoe's or the anthropomorphized figure of the nation) is suggestive in this context: "there is a man alive, and well known too, the actions of whose life are the just subject of these volumes ...; and to this I set my name" (51). As such, *The Farther Adventures* extends and complicates the first novel's themes and formal aspects by returning to and fulfilling (before it bankrupts) the original theme of

1 See Swenson, *Essential Scots* 26–66.

2 The project of Union was a centuries-long project, involving, notably, before Defoe's time, England's annexing of Wales in 1284, the Act of Union of 1536 that incorporated Wales to England (thus forming "Britain"), the 1603 Union of Crowns that brought the three kingdoms (Scotland, England, Wales) together under one monarch, and England's longstanding attempts to incorporate Scotland (as it had Wales) to form Great Britain; Ireland, meanwhile, was akin to a colony in Defoe's time, as the United Kingdom was not formed until 1800.

unity. We observe that the islanders establish an avowedly indissoluble "union of friendship" between Protestants, Catholics, and, so to speak, pre-Christians; bound by their common fear "of being eaten up like Beef or Mutton," they eventually became "good Friends, for common Danger … had effectually reconcil'd them" (p. 90). Crusoe and his helpers "shew'd them the Necessity of it, so plainly, that they all came in to it" (p. 119), into an "entire Friendship and Union" (p. 130). A kind of counter to Defoe's own difficult experiences in promoting national unity off the page, the islanders' union is achieved easily, with "[voluntary] Consent" from all parties (p. 139).

It helps that the Catholic priest suppresses specifically Catholic doctrine and practice in deference to Crusoe's Protestantism. Crusoe is pleased that the priest is "bound … under [my] government," "and therefore, [he] shall not … enter into any Debates on the Point of Religion in which we may not agree" (pp. 134–35), a point that holds true for the island's Spanish Catholics as well. Crusoe tells the priest he is happy to let him possess his "different Opinion" (p. 135) so long as he does not express it, and Crusoe declares that he "wish[es] all the Clergy of the *Roman* Church were blest with such Moderation" (p. 155). In a novel published just four years after the 1715 Jacobite Rebellion that originated in Scotland and intended to radically undo the terms and the tenor of the new Union by setting a Catholic king on the throne, we see fulfilled Defoe's own fantasy about the ideal primacy of English Protestant practice and doctrine in Great Britain. The deal is sealed with the baptizing and renaming of women, and their marriages to the European men, at which point Crusoe is triumphant: "Having thus brought the Affair of the Island to a narrow Compass, I was preparing to go," he announces (p. 164). The marriages are officiated on 1 May (we know this because Crusoe returned to the island on 10 April, stayed twenty-five days, and left not more than four days after the marriages), a clear allusion to the 1 May 1707 Act of Union, right at the structural center of the novel.[1]

With these symbolic marriages, Crusoe is freed to seek the new. The second half of *Farther Adventures* might almost seem to be a new novel, as Crusoe forcefully leaves behind not just the literal island but the very *subject* of it. He does so forcefully, calling attention several times to the break. If the part of the novel up to Crusoe's leave-taking is an allegory of a fantasy about British

1 See Swenson, *Essential Scots* 51–58, and "*Robinson Crusoe*" 25–27.

Union, the part that follows represents a kind of personal fantasy for Defoe, who felt compelled to keep plugging away at supporting the national narrative despite his confession in his periodical publication *The Review* that he was tired of doing so, since "Indeed it is the Fate of all poor Authors that ever did or shall write; the World will never relish a long Story."[1] Crusoe insists happily, "I have now done with the Island" (p. 175). Drawn back to the subject once again, he repeats himself several pages later: "I have now done with my Island, and all Manner of Discourse about it; and who ever reads the rest of my Memorandum's, would do well to turn his Thoughts entirely from it" (p. 182). Not quite two full pages hence, after his expression of guilt over not returning to the island, he affirms, for the third and final time, "they that will have any more of me, must be content to follow me thro' a new Variety of Follies, Hardships, and wild Adventures" (p. 184). The repetition calls attention to how difficult it is for Crusoe to let the subject go, but it also emphasizes his stubborn resolve not to "return" to the island either literally or narratively. As Robert Markley ("Defoe and the Problem") and Lincoln Faller elucidate, the island is a failed experiment. Emphasizing the turn, Friday is disposed of as a "subject," too; he disappears from the novel almost immediately after Crusoe's party leaves the island. Indeed, the human treasure who once gleamed in all his naked, consumable splendor now falls victim to enemy fire: he is mooned, shot with arrows, and buried at sea.[2]

Part II veers global, and we see Crusoe tested by new challenges. What readers remember from the first novel is the island, but of course there are diverse scenes and events before and after that lengthy episode (e.g., Crusoe's time as a slave in Morocco, his escape and travel along the western African shore, his life in Brazil, his endeavors as a tobacco and nascent sugar planter, his trip home over the Pyrenees while battling ravenous wolves), a pattern that resumes in the second half of Part II. Crusoe (part ethnographer, part quasi-anthropologist, part Enlightenment philosopher, part mercenary connoisseur) collects more experiences and things and enumerates them for readers in list after list, even as we witness the collapse of the colonial-imperial fantasy, from the horrors of Indigenous/colonial relations (rape, torture, massacre) to the relative horror of a world—as Crusoe traverses

---

1 See discussion in Davis 26.

2 See Stuchiner, "The Death of Friday," on the implications of Friday's fate on the development of Crusoe's character.

China, Mongolia, and Siberia—that does not bend easily or at all to Crusoe's will.

Crusoe's need to know who he is by replicating himself in the world around him goes increasingly unmet amid adventures that come thick and fast in an array of new settings (Madagascar, the Indian Bay of Bengal, southeast Asia). His Eurocentrism is on full display in China: "What are their Buildings," he observes in a long disquisition, "to the Pallaces and Royal Buildings of *Europe*? What their Trade, to the universal Commerce of *England*, *Holland*, *France* and *Spain*? What are their Cities to ours, for Wealth, Strength, Gaiety of Apparel, rich Furniture, and an infinite Variety?" (p. 237). Crusoe protests too much; there is nothing here he can bend to his will, and much that threatens to influence him instead. Indeed, from the beginning of the China/Mongolia section of his travels, Crusoe makes it clear that his descriptions of these places are subordinate to his "own Story," yet he foregrounds the difficulty he has in centering the narrative on himself. At one point, he pauses from his descriptions of new sights to remind himself that he must occupy the center of his narrative: "But I am no more to describe People than Countries, any farther than my own Story comes to be concern'd in them" (p. 269). However, despite asserting that he will "say very little of all the mighty Places, desart Countrys, and numerous People, I have yet to pass thro'" (p. 239), he says quite a bit. Seemingly, his experiences of the East threaten to undo all the shoring-up, all the self-mastery and narrative mastery, that he wrote himself towards in Part I and the first half of Part II. No wonder Christopher Borsing describes the second half of Part II as "a narrative of empire unravelling" (24).

Arguably, Crusoe achieves some personal growth (in response to the existential challenges of China, Mongolia, and Siberia) in Part II. If the first half of Part II shows some fleeting hints of his potential to appreciate cultural difference (e.g., upon observing Friday's reunion with his father upon the return from England that "if the same filial Affection was to be found in Christians to their Parents, in our Part of the World, one would be tempted to say, there would hardly ha' been any Need of the fifth Commandment" [p. 70]), then the second half enlarges upon those examples. Indeed, Crusoe's descriptions of "China ware," as we will see, serve as a window into the potentially inspirational crisis his wandering now affords him, and these descriptions resonate with and expand upon the wonder he experienced in the first half of Part II while viewing and describing Will Atkins's marvelous basket-work basket-house that was made not by Atkins but by "the savages"—a structure that inspired the island community to build a whole basket-work city that is self-supporting and impermeable.

Now in China, Crusoe is impressed by the self-contained, impermeable, and unified aspect of the China ware, as well as its aesthetic display, and the relevant passage is worth quoting in full because of what it says about his new (limited) capacity to appreciate cultural difference:

> I had seen one Thing which was not to be seen in all the World beside.... a House all made of *China* Ware.... The Outside, which the Sun shone hot upon, was glazed, and look'd very well, perfect white, and painted with blue Figures, as the large *China* Ware in England is painted, and hard as if it had been burnt: As to the Inside, all the Walls, instead of Wainscot, were lin'd up with harden'd and painted Tiles, like the little square Tiles, we call Galley Tiles in *England*, all made of the finest China, and the Figures exceeding fine indeed, with extraordinary Variety of Colours, mix'd with Gold. (p. 245)

In spite of himself, Crusoe is awed by this display of aesthetic and practical unity, hence the prolix nature of the long descriptive passage. Indeed, the vibrancy of the passage can be taken as prime evidence of Noriyuki Harada's argument that Asian contexts are surprisingly vitalizing forces within pre-1800s English prose fiction.[1] The harmony of parts is seamless and absolute, with

> many Tiles making but one Figure, but joyn'd so fially, the Mortar being made of the same Earth, that it was very hard to see where the Tiles met: The Floors of the Rooms were of the same Composition, ... as hard as Stone, and smooth, but not burnt and painted, except some smaller Rooms like Closets, which were all as it were pav'd with the same Tile; the Ceilings, and ... all the plaistering Work in the whole House were of the same Earth; and after all, the Roof was cover'd with Tiles of the same.... (p. 247)

---

1 Although Harada does not discuss the China ware house itself, see Harada.

Overwhelmed (as denoted by the extent of the description in a novel largely lacking physical description), he continues begrudgingly:

> This was a *China*-Ware-house indeed, truly and litterally to be call'd so, and had I not been upon the Journey, I could have staid some Days to see and examine the Particulars of it; they told me there were Fountains and Fish-ponds in the Garden, all pav'd at the Bottom and Sides with the same and fine Statues set up in Rows on the Walks, entirely form'd of the *Porcellain* Earth, and burnt whole.
>
> As this is one of the singularities of *China*, so they may be allow'd to excel in it.... This odd Sight kept me two Hours behind the Caravan.... (p. 247)

He is so taken with this wonder that he almost gets left behind. As Scott Nowka argues, the China ware passages are expressive of a kind of existential crisis for the protagonist. There is nothing Crusoe—he who labored over a retinue of ugly and often useless clay pots in Part II—can do in the face of such beautiful self-containment; there is nowhere for him to insert himself or "improve" anything, and we see some potential for his progressive development as a result.

Alas, Crusoe's development is halting and recursive, such that the begrudging equanimity he felt in Peking is soon forgotten. As the caravan approaches the Muscovite dominions, he finds himself drawn disturbingly to violence; in a passage discussed by Christopher Loar (chap. 3), Crusoe shows himself possessed again by the urge to destroy that which he cannot revise. Specifically, he comes across a Pagan idol in a Tartar village that infuriates him to the point of losing all reason (recalling some of Defoe's hyperbolic accusations of Paganism in Scotland in his travel narrative *A Tour thro' the Whole Island of Great Britain* (1724–26).[1] Impotently, Crusoe cuts off the idol's bonnet with his sword and returns a few nights later to blow it up: "we saw it burn into a meer Block or Log of Wood" (p. 264). This is Crusoe at his worst, once again.

But Crusoe soon moderates his crisis as he absorbs and accepts the shock of unassailable difference. That is, he realizes in due course that any efforts to force himself further upon this new

1 *A Tour* is in large part an assessment (in Scotland and in northern England especially), and a pessimistic one at that, of the successes and failures of the Act of Union of 1707. See Swenson, *Essential Scots* 58–66.

setting would be pointless, for "[n]ot a Town or City we pass'd thro', but had their Pagods, their Idols, and their Temples, and ignorant People worshipping, even the Works of their own Hands" (p. 256). Notably, Crusoe finally accepts the spectacle of difference: "I thought ... that as we came nearer to *Europe* we should find the Country better peopled, and the People more civiliz'd, but I found my self mistaken in both..., for Rudeness of Manners, Idolatry, and Multi-theism no People in the World ever went beyond them" (p. 269). Leaving behind the reactive hysteria that caused him to destroy the first Tartar idol, he simply accepts the leather houses, obscurely gendered populace, underground living systems, and ubiquitous Pagan idols he now encounters in these last legs of his travel:

> They are all cloth'd in Skins of Beasts, and their Houses are built of the same: You know not a Man from a Woman, neither by the Ruggedness of their Countenances or their Cloths; and in the Winter, when the Ground is cover'd with Snow, they live under Ground in Houses like Vaults, which have Cavities going from one to another.
>
> If the *Tartars* had their *Cham-Chi-Thaungu* for a whole Village or Country, these had Idols in every Hut and in every Cave. (p. 269)

Crusoe is thus pushed by his expanded experiences of the world to change himself (trading phobia for acceptance) rather than the world around him; no more idols are destroyed. He puts on more furs, to ward off the cold, and moves along. This is simply not an attitude that the Crusoe of Part I could have possessed.

As Crusoe prepares to sail from the Russian port of Arch-Angel to England, a series of conversations in Tobolski, Siberia, with an exiled Russian prince shows his developing willingness to let others' stories proceed as they will, without annexation or incorporation to his own story. He tells the prince about his time alone on the island and is startled when the prince says "with a Sigh" that he would never have abandoned that kind of isolated life (p. 273). Crusoe is even more shocked that the prince cannot be convinced to let Crusoe return him to his Muscovy roots and take up the royal mantle of his birthright; instead, the prince says "that he found more Felicity in the Retirement he seem'd to be banish'd to there, than ever he found in the highest Authority he enjoy'd in the court of his Master the Czar" (p. 273). The prince dismisses the pursuit of "our Ambition, our particular Pride, our Avarice, our Vanity, and our Sensuality" (p. 274). Satisfied in himself, he tells Crusoe that he is happier in his banishment than those who have "the full Possession of all the Wealth and Power that they (the Banish'd) had left behind them" (p. 274). The ruminative conversation between the two men, in a narrative that is marked primarily by swashbuckling adventure, martial action, and commercial enumeration, is powerfully rendered, calling attention to Crusoe's new willingness to define himself by something other than the ability to remake the world around him in his own image. That is, he is able to engage others without needing to change them or fear he will be swallowed up by them.

In its quiet seriousness and attention to emotional interchange, the dialogue between the two men is like nothing else in the book, or in Part I for that matter, and is important for what it reveals about Crusoe's capacity for personal growth:

> He heard me very attentively, and look'd earnestly on me all the while I spoke, nay, I could see in his very Face, that what I said put his Spirits into an exceeding Ferment; his Colour frequently chang'd, his Eyes look'd red...; nor could he immediately answer me...; but after he had paus'd a little he embrac'd me, and said, ... Did you believe I spoke my very Soul to you, and that I had really obtain'd that Degree of Felicity here, that had plac'd me above all that the World could give me, or do for me? ... Dear Sir, let me remain in this blessed Confinement, banish'd from the Crimes of Life, rather than purchase a Shew of Freedom, at the Expence of the Liberty of my Reason.... O be not my Friend and my Tempter both together. (p. 278)

The passage continues, and the prince's quietism, his moral and philosophical rejection of the world of power, evokes a serenity that counters Crusoe's aggressively acquisitive drive. Indeed, the scene constitutes a quiet retraction of the book's main thematic trajectory, a devaluation of Crusoe's triumphant transformation from forlorn castaway on his island to master of his fate, a deep thematic questioning of Crusoe's remaking of himself into the hero of his adventurous life. This is not to say that the prince's example transforms Crusoe into something else entirely; what is bred in the bone does not simply disappear. But Crusoe allows the prince to have his own truth and his own narrative way.

The men accept each other's different trajectories and exchange gifts at their parting, showing an equality of engagement that is further expressive of Crusoe's progressive development as a character. The colonial Crusoe of Part I gave the gift of Englishness to Friday without accepting any cultural complications in return. And he gave the gift of his story to the island's newcomers (and, as the faux-editor says in the preface to Part I, while seeing Friday's service to him as no gift or exchange but rather his colonial due). The dialogue opens up something in Crusoe, such that he leaves off pressuring the prince to come away with him; Crusoe does not need to "save" or remaster or re-father the prince, does not need him to change course at his urging. The prince bolsters Crusoe's sense of himself as a stable entity and identity, not unlike the seamlessly mortared porcelain China house, a person who "[carries his]whole Estate about [himself]" (p. 204)—that is, a being that can potentially engage others without needing to change them or be "swallowed up" himself.

Next, Part II offers a kind of thematic corrective to Crusoe's characteristic callousness and a direct contrast to his dismissive treatment of Friday's father in Part I. Leaving the prince, Crusoe promises, "I would shew my Respect to him, by my Concern for his Son" (p. 280). And so he does: he agrees to give the prince's son passage to Vienna. Notably, he follows through on that promise, again a departure from tradition, as his islanders (who wrote and begged him to return to the island and bring them back to their own homelands, to no avail, as he tells us now) well know.

In the final pages of Part II, Crusoe must travel cautiously to avoid the local Tartar marauders, and the old hysterical Crusoe of Part I threatens to surface. Crusoe is recursively shocked upon "enter[ing] Europe" and finding no "evident Alteration in the People" but instead "very little Difference" from "*Mongul Tartary*": "the People [are] mostly Pagans, ... their Houses and Towns full of Idols, and their Way of Living, wholly barbarous, except in the Cities as above, and the Villages near them; where they are Christians, as they call themselves, of the *Greek* Church, but have their Religion mingled with so many Reliques of Superstition, that it is scarce to be known in some Places from meer Sorcery and Witchcraft" (p. 282). Within Europe itself, Crusoe is thus confronted with the crisis of hybridity. He imagines he will be "plunder'd and robb'd, and perhaps murder'd by a Troop of Thieves; of what Country they were ... I am yet at a Loss to know" (p. 282). He is on the verge of panic, using language that recalls the Crusoe of Part I: "now I confess I gave my self over for lost" (p. 284). Unlike his partner, he is less concerned with the prospect of losing "all that I had" than with "the Thoughts of falling into the Hands of such *Barbarians*, at the latter End of my Journey, after so many Difficulties and Hazards as I had gone thro'; and even in Sight of our Port, where we expected Safety and Deliverance" (p. 284). Young Crusoe could not have said it better.

Ultimately, however, Crusoe does *not* panic. He consults with the young lord and the pilot as his group works together to "escape" both the real danger and the existential psychic threat that would have sent young Crusoe into a swoon for days. And, with that, there are no more adventures. The final sentences encompass in brief the sea voyage by a ship from Hamburg that takes Crusoe to the Elbe River on the North Sea in Germany, where he and his partner make a great profit on their goods from China and Siberia. Crusoe's share amounts to £3,475, 17 shillings, 3 pence, including "about six hundred Pounds worth of Diamonds which I had purchas'd at *Bengal*" (p. 286). From Hamburg, Crusoe goes by land to The Hague, and thence to London by sea, arriving on 10 January 1705, "having been gone from *England* ten Years and nine Months" (p. 287). Crusoe can now more confidently say he "[carries his] whole Estate about [himself]" (p. 204), having finally achieved an ontological security that does not demand incorporating others (other people, other stories) to his will.

Thus one way to understand Part II is to see it as a study of recursive personal growth. Crusoe retains his relish for adventure and acquisition until the end, but he also demonstrates a new willingness to engage in fair exchange, honor the boundaries of others' stories instead of enfolding them within the pale of his own influence and narration, and tolerate some manner of fundamental difference (be it cultural, philosophical, or aesthetic) without dissolving in fear or forcing his way. In the end, he no longer harbors fear that the self will be corrupted, and, in turn, he somewhat eschews his old "English" propensity to corrupt that which he comes into contact with. These revolutions of self mark a personal triumph no less notable than the huge amount of economic wealth that Crusoe's travels garner otherwise.

Daniel Defoe: A Brief Chronology

1660	Restoration of Stuart monarchy: Charles II's return to England.
1660/61	Daniel Foe born in London to James and Alice Foe (date unknown).
1662	The Act of Uniformity requires conformity in religious services to the Church of England's *Book of Common Prayer*; office-holders must be members. The Foes follow Reverend Samuel Annesley, leaving the Church as dissenters.
1664	The Conventicle Act forbids Nonconformist worship in groups of more than five.
1664–67	Second Anglo-Dutch War: Dutch ships come up the Thames, devastating the English fleet.
1665–66	The Great Plague (in London, over 70,000 are killed) and the Great Fire of London (most of the wooden old city is destroyed).
c. 1671– c. 1679	Attends Reverend James Fisher's school at Dorking, Surrey, and then Reverend Charles Morton's Dissenting Academy at Newington Green, north of London.
c. 1683	Is established as a wholesale hosiery merchant and lives near the Royal Exchange, in Cornhill.
1684	Weds Mary Tuffley; receives a dowry of £3,700 (equivalent to almost a million dollars today).
1685	Monmouth's Rebellion: Foe joins the failed rebellion against James II headed by one of Charles II's illegitimate sons, the Duke of Monmouth.
1685–92	Is a successful businessman, with various ventures (e.g., wine, tobacco), and may have traveled extensively on business in England and the Continent.
1688	Glorious Revolution: James II abdicates the throne and is followed into exile, in France, by English Catholics and by Scots; the Dutch Prince William of Orange is invited to rule as William III of England, with James's daughter Mary as queen.
1691?	Foe's first published poem, *A New Discovery of an Old Intreague* (pro-Williamite and anti-Jacobite), appears sometime before 17 January. (His earlier poems, in

The Meditations, a twenty-three-page manuscript with the flavor both of biblical exegesis and of personal narrative, were written in 1681 but not published until 1946.)

1692 Is bankrupt for the first time, declaring a bankruptcy of £17,000 (equivalent to about four to five million dollars today); he is imprisoned for debt.

1694 Establishes a brick and tile factory at Tilbury, Essex.

1695 Daniel Foe begins styling himself "Defoe."

1697 Defoe's first published book appears: *An Essay on Projects*, containing radical social and economic propositions.

1697–1701 Is an agent for William III in England and Scotland; he ratchets up what will be a year-long practice of writing essays that decry religious-political factionalism.

1701 Publishes *The True-Born Englishman*, a poem satirizing English xenophobia and defending William III.

1702 William III dies; Queen Anne, James II's daughter, succeeds him on the throne.

Defoe publishes *The Shortest Way with the Dissenters*, a satiric attack on High Church extremists.

1703 Arrested for writing *The Shortest Way with the Dissenters*, charged with sedition, committed to Newgate Prison, and sentenced to stand in the pillory for three days. While he is in prison, his brick and tile factory fails: bankrupt again. Released from Newgate due to Robert Harley's influence as the Speaker of the House.

Publishes poems *Reformation of Manners*, *More Reformation*, *A Hymn to the Pillory*, and an authorized collection of his writings, *A True Collection of the Writings of the Author of The True-Born Englishman* (a second volume in 1705).

1704 Publishes the poem *An Elegy on the Author of the True-Born Englishman. With an Essay on the Late Storm*; in the latter, he sees weather as a providential national omen.

1704–13 Works for the government again, acting as spy, propagandist, and political journalist for Harley and other ministers; publishes a pro-government newssheet, *The Review*, as often as thrice weekly; his essays decry political-religious factionalism, condemn Jacobitism, and encourage readers to think of themselves as part of a personified national body; he travels in England and Scotland to promote Union, both before and after the Act's passage. (Defoe's essays, developing the metaphor of the nation as a body, a man, in conflict with itself, variously assure the English that the Union will privilege Englishness and assure the Scots that the Union will favor both countries equally; his private letters expose his personal investment in the former argument.)

1705 Celebrates Marlborough in his poem *The Double Welcome* and indirectly in his science-fiction–flavored prose work *The Consolidator*.

1706 Publishes poem *A Hymn to the Peace*, on the theme of harmony, Union, and Whig progress.

Publishes the epic poem *Jure Divino: A Satyr. In Twelve Books*, a brew of political theory, philosophical inquiry, intellectual complexity, and critical theory about literature and art. Reason (to which the poem is dedicated) and Liberty stop tyranny's progress; the epic ends with an optimistic paeon to William III and Anne.

Publishes *Caledonia: A Poem in Honour of Scotland, and the Scots Nation*; the poem suggests that Scotland can improve itself by assimilating with England, and by lending its energies to a new pan-British cause.

Begins advertising for *A History of the Union of Great Britain*, although the Union has not yet passed.

1707 Publishes poem *A Scots Poem: Or A New-years Gift, From a Native of the Universe, To His Fellow-Animals in Albania* (Scotland), which modifies and extends the themes of *Caledonia*.

1 May: Act of Union of England and Scotland: England, Scotland, and Wales are united to form Great Britain.

1709 Publishes *A History of the Union of Great Britain*, explicitly manipulating the historical narrative in order to assert both the desirability and inevitability of the 1707 Union. Bringing the narrative up to the present day and styling Defoe himself as the "Author" of the "Story of Union," the *History* describes ongoing resistance to Union and presents itself as a deliberate attempt to use narrative itself in order to bring about a desired end.

1711 Founding of South Sea Company.

1713–14 Arrested several times for debt and for his political writings, but released through government influence.

1715 Publishes *The Family Instructor*, the first of his conduct books.

Jacobite Rebellion in support of James II's son, "James III," the "Old Pretender."

1719 Publishes *Robinson Crusoe* and *The Farther Adventures of Robinson Crusoe*; the scenarios and the language of the latter echo Defoe's voluminous writings on national matters.

Shortly after publication of *The Farther Adventures*, Charles Gildon lambasts Defoe and *Crusoe* alike in a satirical pamphlet, *The Life and Strange Surprising Adventures of D— De F—, of London, Hosier.*

1720 Publishes *Captain Singleton*, *Memoirs of a Cavalier*, and *Serious Reflections During the Life and Surprising Adventures of Robinson Crusoe*; the latter asserts that the Crusoe story is an allegory, or an allegorical history, of the life of a real man well known to readers. The insistence has been variously received as everything from a hollow defense to an allusion of the body/man of the nation as described in Defoe's political writings.

South Sea Bubble: South Sea Company fails.

1721 Robert Walpole appointed First Lord of the Treasury and Chancellor of the Exchequer.

1722 Publishes *A Journal of the Plague Year*, *Moll Flanders*, and *Colonel Jack*.

1723 *The True-Born Englishman* and *Jure Divino* are praised, and identified as poems that have the respect of respectable people, by Giles Jacob in *The Poetical Register*.

1724 Publishes *Roxana*, *A General History of the Pyrates*, *A Tour Thro' the Whole Island of Great Britain* (3 volumes, 1724–26); the latter, in large part a charting of the failures and successes of the Union, builds on Defoe's early political metaphors of the nation as a growing child and emphasizes Scotland's success at influencing England while escaping English influence.

1725 Already the author of numerous essays on trade, publishes *The Complete English Tradesman* (volume I).

1726 Publishes *Mere Nature Delineated* and *The Political History of the Devil*.

1727 Publishes *Conjugal Lewdness*, *An Essay on the History and Reality of Apparitions*, *A New Family Instructor*, and *The Complete English Tradesman* (volume II).

1728 Publishes *Augusta Triumphans*, *A Plan of the English Commerce*.

1729 Writes *The Compleat English Gentleman* (not published until 1890).

1731 Daniel Defoe dies on 24 April, in Ropemaker's Alley, London, in debt and hiding from creditors. When his wife died a year and a half later, his library was sold; the catalogue is both diverse and deep, including, for instance, around sixty volumes about the new science and around 150 volumes about travel, maps, and geography.

A Note on the Text

The first edition of *The Farther Adventures of Robinson Crusoe: Being the Second and Last Part of his Life, And of the Strange Surprizing Accounts of his Travels Round three Parts of the Globe* was printed on 20 August 1719 by William Taylor at the Sign of the Ship in Paternoster Row, not quite four months after the publication of the first Crusoe novel. We take the first issue of that first edition as our copy-text (BL G131276), due to Defoe's known participation in its publication. Of the subsequent editions that appeared within Defoe's lifetime (almost all of which, after 1726, appeared under a single cover with the first novel, a tradition that was maintained in the majority until well into the twentieth century), their variants are not typically significant and, moreover, as they do not appear to have been directed by Defoe, are unlikely to be of interest to readers here. We have also trodden lightly with respect to our copy-text. That is, we have taken the copy text as it is, in order to preserve for the novel's modern readers the strangeness of period in which the novel first appeared; we have maintained the nominalizations, italicizations, and spelling variations in all cases where the meaning is not elusive.

Glossaries

Definitions are given for terms, usages, and locations that appear more than once in the text (single usages are accompanied by footnote instead), as denoted by an asterisk (*).

1. Unusual or Archaic Terms

accident: Unexpected incident.
adultery: According to moral theology, any sexual relations, other than those between two people who are married to each other.
affected/affecting: Profoundly mentally affected by; profoundly mentally affecting.
amaz'd: Amazed, the quality of being lost in a maze; stunned, confused, bewildered.
antick: One who is grotesquely animated.
aqua-vitæ: Distilled liquor.
artificer(s): Inventor(s), craftsman, fiction-maker(s).
aukward(ly): Incongruous. Unfamiliar, strange.
backward(s)/backwardness: Reluctant; reluctance.
bad: Bade, requested.
Bedlam: Bethlehem Royal Hospital, London; lunatic asylum and favored tourist site at the time.
bisket cake: Hard, flat, twice-baked flour-and-water cakes that could be stored for a long time.
burnt: Porcelain that has been fired, or cured, in a kiln.
callico(es): Plain-woven fabric(s) of unbleached cotton, coarser than muslin, finer than canvas.
carriage: Bearing, deportment.
character: To "give a character" is to describe what a person is like and convey their reputation.
China ware(s): Chinese ware(s), especially blue and white porcelain, exported in huge quantities from Nanjing to Europe in the 1600s and 1700s.
cholick: Colic, from the Greek for "relating to the colon," is a pain that begins and ends suddenly, due to internal muscular contractions (of the colon or otherwise) as the body attempts to force out an obstruction.
Church of Rome: Roman Catholic Church.
clerk: In English parish churches, a lay officer who assisted the clergyman.

comely: Attractive.
compass: A span or stretch (of time or space). Alternatively, to surround, enclose, encompass.
cordial: Pleasant-tasting medicine.
corn: In British usage of the time, any cereal plant, e.g., wheat, rye, barley.
dainty/dainties: Delicacy/delicacies.
damask: Woven fabric, patterned on both sides.
deal board: A pine or fir table top.
distemper: Ongoing illness.
distracted: Mentally ill, mentally disordered; dangerously detached from reality.
divert(ing): Entertain(ing).
dram: Small drink of whisky or some other liquor.
draught: Draft, here meaning a single act of drinking.
dressing/dressed: Cooking and/or or preparing food for cooking; cooked and/or prepared food for cooking.
East-India Company: Chartered in 1600 to trade with the East Indies, the Company came to dominate trade with the Indian sub-continent and the Persian Gulf area and east and southeast Asia. Eventually, with its private armies, the company ruled much of India from 1757 to 1858.
ecclesiastic(k): Priest.
engine(s): Instrument(s), driving force(s).
equipage: Coach and horses, sometimes with liveried servants.
extasy, extasies: Manic delight.
extravagancy, extravagancies: Emotional excesses, outbursts.
extremity, extremities: Extreme, dire situation(s); the outer limits of what is bearable.
fancy/fancy'd/fancying: Here, synonymous with the imagination; imagined, imagining.
fain: Glad, gladly, or to "desire to," depending on the usage.
farthing: A quarter of an old penny; symbolically, the least amount possible.
flag(s): Grass reed(s).
forrage: Food for horses; fodder, provender; dried plant stuffs.
hallowed or hallo'd/hallowing: Hollered; hollering.
heretick(s): One with beliefs at odds with accepted religious doctrine.
hogshead: Large cask, holding around 64 gallons.
husbandry: Cultivation of crops, animals; management of natural resources.
indifferent: Mediocre.

ingenious/ingeniously: Inventive, or intelligent; inventively, or intelligently.

insensible: Physically or mentally unaware, but usually meant in a more extreme sense, i.e., unnaturally incapable of being affected (as in being unmoved by the suffering of others).

lusty: Healthy, strong.

mandarin: General designation for Chinese government officials.

meer(ly): Complete(ly).

milch: Milk.

moidores: Portuguese gold coins, each worth twenty-seven shillings.

Mongul Tartars: Mongol Tartars or Tatars, a nomadic people living in what is now northwestern Mongolia, some of whom became part of Ghengis Khan's Mongol armies (in the early thirteenth century) that invaded Russia and Hungary and became known as Tartars or Tatars.

out-rageous: Wild.

(within the) pale: A pale is a fence, border, or boundary.

pallisado: Stout fence made of stakes.

Papist: Roman Catholic.

passion: State or outburst of strong emotion.

pec(c)une: Money, from the Latin pecunia.

petition: Request.

pitch: Sticky, dark, resinous substance, hard and waterproof when cold, made by distilling tar or petroleum.

pocket-book: Pocket-sized notebook, carried as such.

Popish: Roman Catholic.

profligate: Debauched, licentious, dissolute.

providence: Divine foresight and guidance.

providential/providentially: Divinely guided; happening through the workings of a Christian god's Providence (favorable term).

pumps: Low-cut shoes without fastenings.

refractory: Obstinate, unmanageable.

relish: Great enjoyment, or to enjoy greatly, depending on the usage.

rogue(s)/roguery: Dishonest, unprincipled person(s); acts of dishonesty or other villainy.

Roman: Roman Catholic.

sable: Sables are martens in the weasel family which inhabit forests, especially in Russia from the Ural Mountains throughout Siberia.

say O: Praise god, pray to god.
scruple(s): Schemes.
sensible: Physically or mentally aware, often meant in a more extreme sense, i.e., sensitively and acutely aware, emotionally responsive (as in being affected by the experiences of other people).
sensibly (affected): Emotionally affected, usually visibly so.
shilling: One shilling was worth one twentieth of a pound, or twelve pence.
smith: A blacksmith, a metal-worker.
sober: Serious, solemn.
stuffs: Woolen fabric.
suffer(ed)/suffering: Allow(ed) / allowing.
sweet-meats: Sugary delicacies of any kind.
taffaty: Taffeta, silk cloth.
tallow: Rendered animal fat.
transport(ed): Overwhelmed emotional state.
vapours: Gloomy imaginative states. Older clinical term, still popular in the early 1700s for describing disordered states: "Exhalations supposed to be developed within the organs of the body (esp. the stomach) and to have an injurious effect upon the body" (*OED*).
victual(s)/victualed: Noun, food (or other provisions); verb, fed (supplied or given other provisions).
viz.: That is, namely.
wench: May indicate a young woman or a prostitute, depending on the context.
whether: Variant of whither: where.
without: Outside.

2. Nautical and Military Terms

antient: National ensign or flag.
bark: Any small vessel propelled by sails or oars. Alternatively, "barque," a square-rigged sailing ship.
boatswain: On a ship, the most senior-ranked member of the deck department.
cockswain: Person in charge of steering the ship.
cutlash: Cutlass.
broad-side: Broadside, simultaneous firing of all the guns on one side of a warship.
equipage: Coach and horses, sometimes with liveried servants.

fuzee(s): Flintlock musket(s).
(perspective) glass: Early telescope with a magnifying glass and angled mirror.
halberd (or halbert): Weapon, consisting of a battle-axe and spear mounted on a pole.
hanger(s): Short sword(s) that hung from the belt.
jonk: A junk, or a Chinese sailing vessel. Flat-bottomed, with square prow and lug-sails.
jury fore-mast: A jury mast is a temporary one, fashioned to replace one lost at sea.
league(s): One marine league is three nautical miles (or 3.452 miles).
(the) line: Equator.
long-boat: The biggest boat carried by a sailing ship, used for provisions and as the principal lifeboat, with a mast and sails, and, sometimes, a mounted gun in the bow.
magazine: A store of ammunition, arms.
main-top-mast: Mast raised above the lower main mast.
pinnace (ship's pinnace): A small boat used as a tender to larger vessels.
pole-ax(e)(s): Axe with a hammer-face opposite the blade, typically used to slaughter cattle.
powder: Gunpowder.
(give no) quarter: Give no shelter, no mercy; technically, the refusal to spare the life of an opponent in exchange for unconditional surrender.
quarter/quarterdeck: The stern side of the main mast on the upper deck of a sailing ship, usually the officers' command-deck.
quarter-staff/quarter-stave: Long wooden staffs, typically tipped with iron.
scymitar/scymetar: Scimitar, a curved sword with a sharp edge on the convex side.
sloop: A single-masted, fore-and-aft-rigged sailing boat, framed and ready for finishing.
steerage: The ship's part closest to the rudder, immediately below the main deck; prior to the eighteenth century, the ship was steered from there.
wild-fire: Flammable mixture, easy to light, difficult to put out.
yard-arm: The outer end of the spar crossing the mast; the flag was hung from there, as were people at sea.

3. Geographical Locations

Bay of All Saints: Baía De Todos Os Santos, a sheltered bay of the Atlantic Ocean on the eastern coast of Brazil.

(the) **Brasils:** Brazil, and the subdivided provinces thereof.

Coremandel/Coromandel: South-eastern coast of the Indian sub-continent, between Cape Comorin and False Divi Point.

East-Indies: East Indies, broadly the lands of south and south-east Asia.

Formosa: Now Taiwan, off China's coast.

Macao: Now Macau. In southeastern China on the South China Sea, a trading port leased by the Portuguese from the Chinese empire.

Maderas: Madeiras, a Portuguese archipelago in the North Atlantic.

Martinico: Martinique.

New-found Land: Newfoundland.

Pecking: Peking (now Beijing) was the capital of the Chinese empire.

Siheilka: Shilka, Siberia.

Sur(r)at(te): A city in the East Indian state of Gujarat where the English East India company operated in the 1600s.

Tartary: That part of Central Asia from the Caspian Sea to the Pacific, inhabited by Mongols, Tartars, and Turks, many of them descended from Genghis Khan, who conquered much of Asia and eastern Europe.

Tonquin: Now Vietnam.

West-Indies: West Indies, the Caribbean.

THE FARTHER ADVENTURES OF ROBINSON CRUSOE

THE PREFACE.

The Success the former Part of this Work has met with in the World,[1] *has yet been no other than is acknowledg'd to be due to the surprising Variety of the Subject, and to the agreeable Manner of the Performance.*

All the Endeavours of envious People to reproach it with being a Romance,[2] *to search it for Errors in Geography, Inconsistency in the Relation, and Contradictions in the Fact, have proved abortive, and as impotent as malicious.*[3]

The just Application of every Incident, the religious and useful Inferences drawn from every Part, are so many Testimonies to the good Design of making it publick,[4] *and must legitimate all the Part that may be call'd Invention, or Parable in the Story.*[5]

The Second Part,[6] *if the Editor's Opinion may pass, is (contrary*

---

1 *The Life and Strange Surprizing Adventures of Robinson Crusoe* (1719) appeared on 25 April. Second, third, and fourth editions appeared on 9 May, 4 June, and 7 August. The sequel, *The Farther Adventures*, some of its plot previewed by the last paragraphs of the first novel, appeared immediately thereafter, on 20 August. See Hutchins. Starting in 1726 with the fifth edition of *Farther Adventures* and the seventh edition of *Crusoe*, novel and sequel were commonly published—until the twentieth century—in a single volume as "Robinson Crusoe, Parts 1 and 2." *Serious Reflections during the Life and Surprising Adventures of Robinson Crusoe* (1720), or Part III of what critics have loosely called the "Crusoe Trilogy," is a kind of meditative addendum that was less successful.

2 Here not only fiction, but poorly designed fiction.

3 See Charles Gildon's satirical denouncement in *The Life and Strange Surprizing Adventures of Mr. D— DeF—, of London, Hosier.* The pamphlet features an encounter between Crusoe, Friday, and a drunken "Defoe"; "Defoe" is literally forced to eat his words (the pages of his book). The accompanying "Epistle to Daniel D'foe the Reputed Author of Robinson Crusoe" accuses Defoe of theological absurdity and superstition, and the "Postscript" carries the mocking critique to conclusion.

4 Defoe echoes the preface to *Crusoe*: "the story of" a "private man's adventures [...] worth making publick" (3). See John Richetti's edition of *Robinson Crusoe*, from which all quotations from that novel are taken.

5 The preface to *Crusoe* claims that the story is "a just History of Fact" without "any Appearance of Fiction in it" (3). The preface to *Serious Reflections* claims that "the fable is always made for the moral, not the moral for the fable," and that the story is not an "Invention" but is rather "Allegorical" and "also Historical." Moreover, "there is a Man alive, and well known too, ... to whom all or most Part of the Story most directly alludes, ... and to this I set my Name" (51).

6 The Second Part, or Part II, is *Farther Adventures*, which is, as its subtitle says, "the Second and Last Part OF HIS LIFE."

to the Usage of Second Parts),[1] *every Way as entertaining as the First, contains as strange and surprising Incidents, and as great a Variety of them; nor is the Application less serious, or suitable; and doubtless will, to the sober,* as well as ingenious* Reader, be every way as profitable and diverting;*[2] *and this makes the abridging this Work, as scandalous, as it is knavish and ridiculous,*[3] *seeing, while to shorten the Book, that they may seem to reduce the Value, they strip it of all those Reflections, as well religious as moral, which are not only the greatest Beautys of the Work, but are calculated for the infinite Advantage of the Reader.*

By this they leave the Work naked of its brightest Ornaments; and if they would, at the same Time pretend, that the Author has supply'd the Story out of his Invention, they take from it the Improvement, which alone recommends that Invention to wise and good Men.

The Injury these Men do the Proprietor[4] *of this Work, is a Practice all honest Men abhor; and he believes he may challenge them to shew the Difference between that and Robbing on the Highway, or breaking open a House.*

If they can't shew any Difference in the Crime, they will find it hard to shew why there should be any Difference in the Punishment: And he will answer for it, that nothing shall be wanting,[5] *on his Part, to do them Justice.*[6]

---

1 Contrary to what is customary or usual, as respecting those sequels that are not as good their predecessors.

2 Useful (*utile*) and entertaining (*dulce*). The preface to *Crusoe* makes a similar claim about the reader's opportunity for "instruction" and "diversion" (3).

3 A cheap abridgement of *Crusoe* was published by T. Cox (two shillings, as opposed to five for Defoe's *Crusoe*) in August 1719. Cox omitted many of the moral, philosophical, and religious reflections. See Owens's edition of *Farther Adventures of Robinson Crusoe* 200nn6–7.

4 William Taylor, the printer of Parts I and II (novel, sequel), held the copyrights.

5 Nothing shall be lacking.

6 To sue them for damages. Defoe attacks all pirated editions. Taylor, Defoe's printer, complained in an advertisement in *The St. James Post* (7 August 1719) about Cox's abridgement; the advertisement was printed after the preface in the first edition of *Farther Adventures*. Taylor began a lawsuit against Cox, who responded in *The Flying Post* on 29 October 1719, and hinted that the abridgment had been arranged by Defoe himself because of a financial quarrel with the publisher over payment for *Farther Adventures*. By 1720 Cox was dead; the case went unresolved. See Hutchins 141–45.

THE FARTHER

ADVENTURES

OF

ROBINSON CRUSOE;

Being the Second and Last Part

OF HIS

LIFE,

And of the STRANGE SURPRIZING

ACCOUNTS of his TRAVELS

Round three Parts of the Globe.

Written by Himself.

To which is added a Map of the World, in which is

Delineated the Voyages of *ROBINSON CRUSOE.*

LONDON: Printed for W. TAYLOR at the

Ship in *Pater-Noster Row.* MDCCXIX

A Map of the World on which Is Delineated the Voyage of Robinson Crusoe[1]

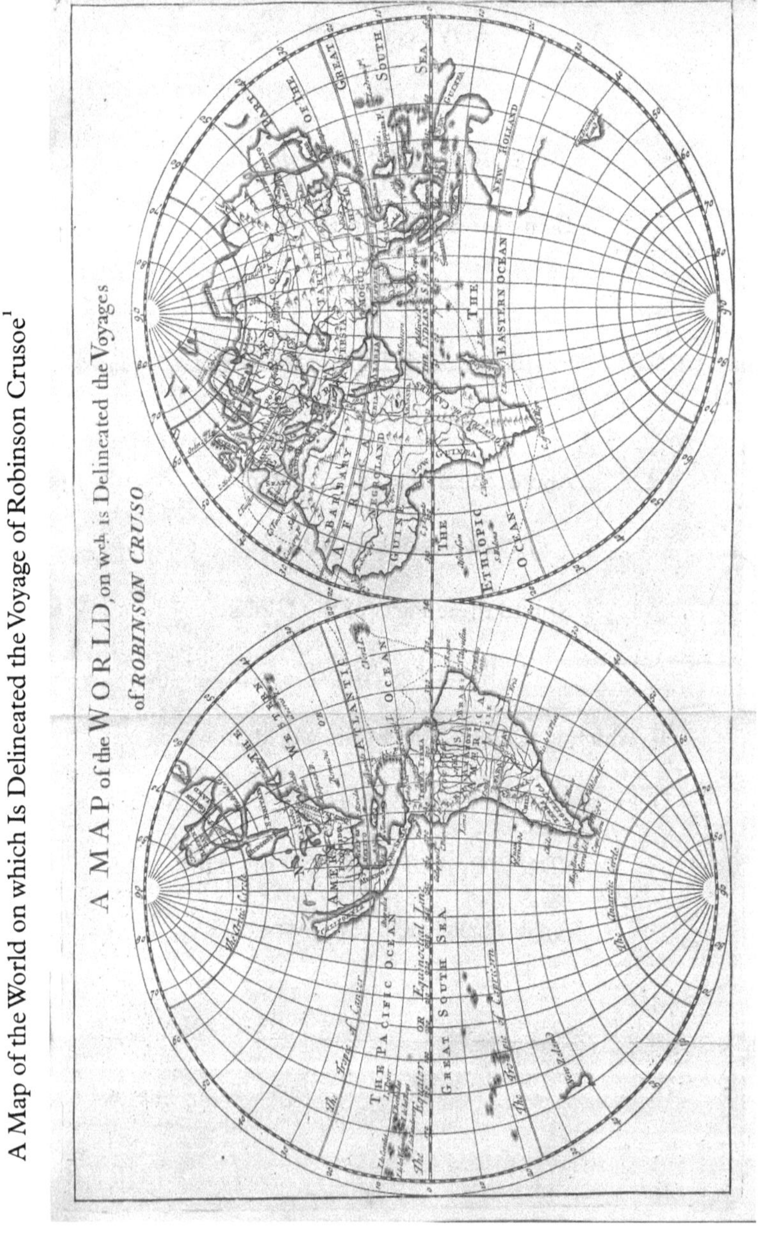

1 The map's first appearance was in the fourth edition of *Robinson Crusoe*. Image courtesy of Houghton Library, Harvard University.

THE FARTHER ADVENTURES OF ROBINSON CRUSOE, &C.

That homely[1] Proverb used on so many Occasions in *England*, *viz.* * *That what is bred in the Bone will not go out of the Flesh*,[2] was never more verify'd, than in the Story of my Life. Any one would think, that after thirty-five Years Affliction, and a Variety of unhappy Circumstances, which few Men, if any ever, went thro' before, and after near seven Years of Peace and Enjoyment in the Fulness of all Things;[3] grown old, and when, *if ever*, it might be allowed me to have had Experience of every State of middle Life,[4] and to know which was most adapted to make a Man compleatly happy: I say, after all this, any one would have thought that the native Propensity to rambling,[5] which I gave an Account of in my first Setting out into the World, to have been so predominate[6] in my Thoughts, should be worn out, the volatile Part be fully evacuated, or at least condens'd, and I might at 61 Years of Age[7] have been a little enclin'd to stay at Home, and have done venturing Life and Fortune any more.

Nay farther, the common Motive of foreign Adventures was taken away in me; for I had no Fortune to make, I had nothing to seek: If I had gain'd ten thousand Pound, I had been no richer; for I had already sufficient for me, and for those I had to leave it to; and that I had was visibly encreasing; for having no great Family,[8] I could not spend the Income of what I had, unless I would set up for an expensive Way of Living, such as a great Family, Servants, Equipage,* Gayety,[9] and *the like*, which were Things I had no

---

1 Familiar, well-known.

2 From a medieval Latin proverb: *osse radicatum raro de carne recedit* (that which is rooted in the bone rarely comes out from the flesh).

3 Crusoe first went to sea thirty-five years ago (spending twenty-eight years, two months, and nineteen days as a castaway). The seven years since have been peaceful.

4 At the beginning of Part I (i.e., *Crusoe*), Crusoe's father encourages him to stay home and be content with "the middle-state" or "the upper station of low life," neither too high nor too low (6).

5 Crusoe claims an in-born or fundamental disposition toward leaving home to seek variety, which here coincides with his obsession about returning to his old island.

6 Predominant.

7 In Part I, we learn that he was born on 30 September 1632, so *Farther Adventures* begins in 1693.

8 Not part of the upper social circle.

9 Ostentatious dress.

Notion of, or Inclination to; so that I had nothing indeed to do, but to sit still, and fully enjoy what I had got, and see it encrease daily upon my Hands.

Yet all these Things had no Effect upon me, or at least, not enough to resist the strong inclination I had to go Abroad again, which hung about me like a chronical Distemper;* particularly the Desire of seeing my new Plantation in the Island, and the Colony I left there, run in my Head continually. I dream'd of it all Night, and my Imagination run upon it all Day; it was uppermost in all my Thoughts, and my Fancy* work'd so steadily and strongly upon it, that I talk'd of it in my Sleep; in short, nothing could remove it out of my Mind; it even broke so violently into all my Discourses, that it made my Conversation tiresome; for I could talk of nothing else, all my Discourse run into it, even to Impertinence, and I saw it my self.

I have often heard Persons of good Judgment say, That all the Stirr People make in the World about Ghosts and Apparitions, is owing to the Strength of Imagination, and the powerful Operation of Fancy in their Minds; that there is no such Thing as a Spirit appearing, or a Ghost walking, *and the like*: That Peoples poreing affectionately upon the past Conversation of their deceas'd Friends, so realizes it to them, that they are capable of fancying upon some extraordinary Circumstances, that they see them; talk to them, and are answered by them, when, in Truth, there is nothing but Shadow and Vapour in the Thing; and they really know nothing of the Matter.

For my Part, I know not to this Hour, whether there are any such Things as real Apparitions, Spectres, or walking of People after they are dead,[1] or whether there is any Thing in the Stories they tell us of that Kind, more than the Product of Vapours,* sick Minds, and wandring Fancies; But this I know, that my Imagination work'd up to such a Height, and brought me into such Extasies* of Vapours, or what else I may call it, that I actually suppos'd my self, often-times upon the Spot, at my old Castle behind the Trees; saw my old *Spaniard*, *Friday*'s Father, and the reprobate Sailors I left upon the Island; nay, I fancy'd I talk'd with them, and look'd at them so steadily, tho' I was broad awake, as at Persons just before me; and this I did till I often frighted my self

1 Defoe published a ghost story, the pamphlet *The Apparition of Mrs. Veal* (1706). See also his *Essay on the History and Reality of Apparitions* (1727).

with the Images my Fancy represented to me: One Time in my Sleep I had the Villany of the 3 Pyrate Sailors so lively related to me by the first *Spaniard* and *Friday*'s Father, that it was surprizing; they told me how they barbarously attempted to murder all the *Spaniards*, and that they set Fire to the Provisions they had laid up, on Purpose to distress and starve them, Things that I had never heard of, and that indeed were never all of them true in Fact: But it was so warm in my Imagination, and so realiz'd to me, that to the Hour I saw them, I could not be perswaded, but that it was or would be true; also how I resented it, when the *Spaniard* complain'd to me, and how I brought them to Justice, try'd them before me, and order'd them all three to be hang'd: What there was really in this, shall be seen in its Place:[1] For however I came to form such Things in my Dream, and what secret Converse of Spirits injected it,[2] yet there was very much of it true. I say, I own, that this Dream had nothing in it literally and specifically true: But the general Part was so true, the base villanious Behaviour of these three harden'd Rogues* was such, and had been so much worse than all I can describe, that the Dream had too much Similitude of the Fact, and as I would afterwards have punished them severely; so if I had hang'd them all, I had been much in the Right, and should ha' been justifiable both by the Laws of God and Man.

But to return to my Story; in this Kind of Temper I had liv'd some Years, I had no Enjoyment of my Life, no pleasant Hours, no agreeable Diversion, but what had some Thing or other of this in it; so that my Wife, who saw my Mind so wholly bent upon it, told me very seriously one Night, That she believ'd there was some secret powerful Impulse of Providence* upon me, which had determin'd me to go thither again; and that she found nothing hindred my going, but my being engag'd to a Wife and Children. She told me that it was true she could not think of parting with me; but as she was assur'd, that if she was dead, it would be the first Thing I would do: So as it seem'd to her, that the Thing was determin'd above,[3] she would not be the only Obstruction; for if

---

1 I.e., the following pages will show the extent to which the dream reflects reality.

2 As in other works—e.g., *Crusoe*, "A Vision of the Angelick World" (in *Serious Reflections*), and *A History of the Union of Great Britain*—the possibility of supernatural, divine, or Providential communication via the waking or sleeping imagination is raised and affirmed.

3 Determined by god, guided by Providence.

I thought fit, and resolv'd to go—here she found me very intent upon her Words, and that I look'd very earnestly at her; so that it a little disorder'd her, and she stopp'd. I ask'd her, Why she did not go on, and say out what she was going to say? But I perceiv'd her Heart was too full, and some Tears stood in her Eyes: Speak out my Dear, said I, Are you willing I should go? No, *says she very affectionately*, I am far from willing: But if you are resolv'd to go, says she, and rather than I will be the only Hinderance, I will go with you; for tho' I think it a most preposterous Thing for one of your Years, and in your Condition, yet if it must be, said she again weeping, I won't leave you; for if it be of Heaven, you must do it. There is no resisting it; and if Heaven makes it your Duty to go, he will also make it mine to go with you, or otherwise dispose of me, that I may not obstruct it.

This affectionate Behaviour of my Wife's brought me a little out of the Vapours, and I began to consider what I was a doing; I corrected my wandring Fancy, and began to argue with my self sedately, what Business I had after threescore Years, and after such a Life of tedious Sufferings and Disasters, and closed in so happy and easy a Manner, I say, what Business I had to rush into new Hazards, and put my self upon Adventures, fit only for Youth and Poverty to run into.

With those Thoughts, I considered my new Engagement, that I had a Wife, one Child born, and my Wife then great with Child of another;[1] that I had all the World could give me, and had no Need to seek Hazards for Gain; that I was declining in Years, and ought to think rather of leaving what I had gain'd, than of seeking to encrease it; that as to what my Wife had said, of its being an Impulse from Heaven, and that it should be my Duty to go, I had no Notion of that; so after many of these Cogitations, I struggled with the Power of my Imagination, reason'd my self out of it, *as I believe People may always do in like Cases, if they will*; and, in a Word, I conquer'd it; compos'd my self[2] with such Arguments as occurr'd to my Thought, and which my present Condition furnish'd me plentifully with, and particularly, as the most effectual Method, I resolv'd to divert* my self with other Things, and to engage in some Business that might effectually tye me up from any more Excursions of this Kind; for I found that Thing return

1 The second of three; in the closing paragraphs of Part I, we are told the couple "had three children, two sons and one daughter" (240).

2 Here, Crusoe describes consciousness as a matter of will, of self-composure.

upon me chiefly when I was idle, had nothing to do, or any Thing of Moment immediately before me.

To this Purpose I bought a little Farm in the County of *Bedford*,[1] and resolv'd to remove my self thither. I had a little convenient House upon it, and the Land about it I found was capable of great Improvement, and that it was many Ways suited to my Inclination, which delighted in Cultivating, Managing, Planting, and Improving of Land; and particularly, being an Inland County, I was remov'd from conversing among Ships, Sailors, and Things relating to the remote Part of the World.

In a Word, I went down to my Farm, settled my Family, bought me Ploughs, Harrows, a Cart, Wagon, Horses, Cows, Sheep; and setting seriously to Work, became in one half Year, a meer* Country Gentleman; my Thoughts were entirely taken up in managing my Servants, cultivating the Ground, Enclosing, Planting, *&c.* and I liv'd, as I thought, the most agreeable Life that Nature was capable of directing, or that a Man always bred to Misfortunes was capable of being retreated to.

I farm'd upon my own Land, I had no Rent to pay, was limited by no Articles;[2] I could pull up or cut down as I pleased: What I planted, was for my self, and what I improved, was for my Family; and having thus left off the Thoughts of Wandring, I had not the least Discomfort in any Part of Life, as to this World. Now I thought indeed, that I enjoy'd the middle State of Life, that my Father so early recommended to me, and liv'd a kind of heavenly Life, something like what is described by the Poet upon the Subject of a Country Life.

Free from Vices, free from Care,
Age has no Pain, and Youth no Snare.[3]

But in the Middle of all this Felicity, one Blow from unforeseen Providence unhing'd me at once; and not only made a Breach upon me inevitable and incurable, but drove me, by its Consequences, into a deep Relapse into the wandring Disposition, which, as I may say, being born in my very Blood, soon recover'd its hold of me, and like the Returns of a violent Distemper, came

---

1 Bedfordshire, about fifty miles northeast of London.

2 Legal or contractual limitations.

3 Concluding lines from James Hart's song "The Country Life," published in John Playford's *Choice Ayres and Songs to Sing to the Therobo-Lute, or Bass Viol* (1683).

on with an irresistible Force upon me; so that nothing could make any more Impression upon me.[1] This Blow was the Loss of my Wife.

It is not my Business here to write an Elegy upon my Wife, give a Character* of her particular Virtues, and make my Court to the Sex by the Flattery of a Funeral Sermon.[2] She was, in a few Words, the Stay of all my Affairs, the Centre of all my Enterprizes, the Engine,* that by her Prudence reduc'd me to that happy Compass* I was in, from the most extravagant and ruinous Project that flutter'd in my Head, as above; and did more to guide my rambling Genius,[3] than a Mother's Tears, a Father's Instructions, a Friend's Counsel, or all my own reasoning Powers could do. I was happy in listening to her Tears, and in being mov'd by her Entreaties, and to the last Degree desolate and dislocated in the World by the Loss of her.

When she was gone, the World look'd aukwardly* round me; I was as much a Stranger in it, in my Thoughts, as I was in the *Brasils,** when I went first on Shore there; and as much alone, except as to the Assistance of Servants, as I was in my Island. I knew neither what to do, or what not to do. I saw the World busy round me, one Part labouring for Bread, and the other Part squandring in vile Excesses or empty Pleasures, equally miserable, because the End they propos'd still fled from them; for the Man of Pleasure every Day surfeited of his Vice, and heap'd up Work for Sorrow and Repentance; and the Men of Labour spent their Strength in daily Struggles for Bread to maintain the vital Strength they labour'd with, so living in a daily Circulation of Sorrow, living but to work, and working but to live, as if daily Bread were the only End of wearisome Life, and a wearisome Life the only Occasion of daily Bread.

This put me in Mind of the Life I liv'd in my Kingdom, the Island; where I suffer'd* no more Corn* to grow, because I did

---

1 His native desire to leave home has reasserted itself. Defoe, in *Mere Nature Delineated* (1726), echoes John Locke's metaphors of the mind, describing how the mind or soul may initially be "as a Lump of soft Wax, which is always ready to receive any Impression; but if harden'd, grow callous, and stubborn, and like what we call Sealing-Wax, obstinately refuse the Impression of the Seal, unless melted, and reduced by the Force of Fire; that is to say, Unless moulded and temper'd to Instruction" (60–61).

2 From Part I, all we know of the marriage is that "I marry'd and that not either to my disadvantage or dissatisfaction" (240).

3 Fundamental spirit or character.

not want it; and bred no more Goats, because I had no more Use for them: Where the Money lay in the Drawer 'till it grew mouldy, and had scarce the Favour to be look'd upon in 20 Years.[1]

All these Things, had I improv'd them as I ought to have done, and as Reason and Religion had dictated to me, would have taught me to search farther than human Enjoyments for a full Felicity, and that there was something which certainly was the Reason and End of Life, superiour to all these Things, and which was either to be possess'd, or at least hop'd for on this Side the Grave.

But my Sage Counsellor was gone, I was like a Ship without a Pilot, that could only run afore the Wind: My Thoughts run all away again into the old Affair, my Head quite was turn'd with the Whimsies of foreign Adventures, and all the pleasant innocent Amusements of my Farm, and my Garden, my Cattel, and my Family, which before entirely possest me, were nothing to me, had no Relish,* and were like Musick to one that has no Ear, or Food to one that has no Taste: In a Word, I resolv'd to leave off House-keeping, lett my Farm,[2] and return to *London*; and in a few Months after, I did so.

When I came to *London*, I was still as uneasy as I was before, I had no Relish to the Place, no Employment in it, nothing to do but to saunter about like an idle Person, of whom it may be said, he is perfectly useless in God's Creation; and it is not one Farthing* Matter to the rest of his Kind, whether he be dead or alive. This also was the Life, which of all Circumstances of Life was the most my Aversion, who had been all my Days used to an active Life; and I would often say to my self, *A State of Idleness is the very Dregs of Life*; and indeed I thought I was much more suitably employ'd, when I was 26 Days a making me a Deal Board.*

It was now the beginning of the Year 1693,[3] when my Nephew, who as I had observ'd before I had brought up to the Sea, and had made him Commander of a Ship, was come Home from a short Voyage to *Bilboa*,[4] being the first he had made; and he came to me,

---

1 A reference to the moment when Crusoe finds in the wrecked ship a store of money, and, after soliloquizing on its worthlessness, decides to keep it. See *Crusoe* 47.

2 Rented it out.

3 At the end of Part I, Crusoe describes how he set up his nephew as a private trader in 1694. See *Crusoe* 240. (Until 1752, dates in England reflected the then-official Julian calendar system, with a 25 March New Year's Day, as well as the Gregorian system.)

4 Bilbao, in northeastern Spain, near the Bay of Biscay.

and told me, that some Merchants of his Acquaintance had been proposing to him to go a Voyage for them to the *East Indies* and to *China*, as private Traders:[1] And now Uncle, says he, if you will go to Sea with me, I'll engage to land you upon your old Habitation in the Island, for we are to touch at the *Brasils*.

Nothing can be a greater Demonstration of a future State, and of the Existence of an invisible World, than the Concurrence of second Causes, with the Ideas of Things, which we form in our Minds,[2] perfectly reserv'd, and not communicated to any in the World.

My Nephew knew nothing how far my Distemper of Wandring was return'd upon me, and I knew nothing of what he had in his Thoughts to say, when that very Morning before he came to me, I had in a great deal of Confusion of Thought, and revolving every Part of my Circumstances in my Mind, come to this Resolution, *viz.* That I would go to *Lisbon*, and consult with my old Sea-Captain; and so if it was rational and practicable, I would go and see the Island[3] again, and see what was become of my People there. I had pleas'd my self with the Thoughts of peopling the Place, and carrying Inhabitants from hence, getting a Patent for the Possession,[4] and I know not what; when in the Middle of all this, in comes my Nephew, as I have said, with his Project of carrying me thither, in his Way to the *East Indies*.

I paus'd a while at his Words, and looking steadily at him, *What Devil*, said I, *sent you of this unlucky Errand?* My Nephew star'd as if he had been frighted at first; but perceiving I was not much displeas'd with the Proposal, he recover'd himself. I hope it may not be an unlucky Proposal, Sir, says he, I dare say you would be pleas'd to see your new Colony there, where you once reigned with more Felicity, than most of your Brother Monarchs in the World.

In a Word, the Scheme hit so exactly with my Temper, that is to say, the Prepossession I was under, and of which I have said so much, that I told him in few Words, if he agreed with the

---

1 Quasi-illegal traders who ignored the monopoly granted to the East India Company in 1600 for trading in the East Indies.

2 Crusoe observes that the ordinary, observable phenomena of second causes (which he holds as the working-through of first causes, i.e., of divine will)—in this case his nephew's invitation—conveniently concurs with his desire to return to the island.

3 In Part I, the unnamed island is termed "The Island of Despair."

4 Englishmen could obtain a royal patent from the king allowing them to take possession of land in the New World.

Merchants, I would go with him: But I told him, I would not promise to go any farther than my own Island. Why Sir, says he, you don't want to be left there again, I hope? Why, said I, can you not take me up again in your Return? He told me, it could not be possible, that the Merchants would allow him to come that Way with a loaden Ship of such value, it being a Month's Sail out of his Way, and might be three or four: Besides, Sir, if I should miscarry, said he, and not return at all, then you would be just reduced to the Condition you were in before.

This was very rational; but we both found out a Remedy for it, which was to carry a framed Sloop* on board the Ship, which being taken in Pieces, and shipp'd on board the Ship, might by the Help of some Carpenters, who we agreed to carry with us, be setup again in the Island, and finish'd, fit to go to Sea in a few Days.

I was not long resolving; for indeed the Importunities of my Nephew join'd in so effectually with my Inclination, that nothing could oppose me: On the other hand, my Wife being dead, I had no Body concern'd themselves so much for me, as to perswade me one Way or other, except my ancient good Friend the Widow,[1] who earnestly struggled with me to consider my Years, my easy Circumstances, and the needless Hazards of a long Voyage; and above all, my young Children: But it was all to no Purpose, I had an irresistible Desire to the Voyage; and I told her, I thought there was something so uncommon in the Impressions I had upon my Mind for the Voyage, that it would be a kind of resisting Providence, if I should attempt to stay at Home; after which, she ceas'd her Expostulations, and join'd with me, not only in making Provision for my Voyage, but also in settling my Family Affairs for my Absence, and providing for the Education of my Children.

In Order to this, I made my Will, and settled the Estate I had, in such a Manner for my Children, and placed in such Hands, that I was perfectly easy and satisfy'd they would have Justice done them, whatever might befal me; and for their Education, I left it wholly to my Widow, with a sufficient Maintenence[2] to her self for

---

1 In Part I, the widow of the English captain of the ship Crusoe sails on when he is captured and becomes a slave in Salee, in Morocco. When Crusoe arrives in Brazil on a Portuguese ship, he sends her (by way of the Portuguese captain) the money he has accumulated. She invests it for him, and when he at last many years later returns to England, he speaks of her as his "principal guide, and privy councellor" (238).

2 That is, an allowance for the widow's support.

her Care: All which she richly deserv'd; for no Mother could have taken more Care in their Education, or understand it better; and as she liv'd 'till I came Home,[1] I also liv'd to thank her for it.

My Nephew was ready to sail about the Beginning of *January* 1694–5,[2] and I with my Man *Friday* went on board in the *Downs*[3] the 8th, having besides that Sloop which I mention'd above, a very considerable Cargo of all Kinds of necessary Things for my Colony, which if I did not find in good Condition, I resolv'd to leave so.

First, I carry'd with me some Servants, who I purpos'd to place there, as Inhabitants, or at least to set on Work there upon my own Account while I stay'd, and either to leave them there, or carry them forward as they should appear willing; particularly, I carry'd two Carpenters, a Smith,* and a very handy ingenious Fellow, who was a Cooper[4] by Trade, but was also a general Mechanick; for he was dexterous at making Wheels, and Hand-Mills to grind Corn, was a good Turner,[5] and a good Pot-Maker; he also made any Thing that was proper to make of Earth, or of Wood; in a Word, we call'd him, *Our Jack of all Trades.*

With these I carry'd a Taylor, who had offer'd himself to go Passenger to the *East Indies* with my Nephew, but afterwards consented to stay on our New Plantation, and prov'd a most necessary handy Fellow, as could be desir'd, in many other Businesses, besides that of this Trade; for as I observ'd formerly, Necessity arms us for all Employments.

My Cargo, as near as I can collect, for I have not kept an Account of the Particulars, consisted of a sufficient Quantity of Linnen, and some thin *English* Stuffs* for cloathing the *Spaniards* that I expected to find there, and enough of them, as by my Calculation might comfortably supply them for seven Years; if I remember right, the Matterials I carry'd for cloathing them with, Gloves, Hats, Shoes, Stockings, and all such Things as they could want for wearing, amounted to above 200 Pounds, including some Beds, Bedding, and Houshold-Stuff, particularly Kitchen-Utensils, with Pots, Kettles, Peuter,[6] Brass, *&c.* and near a hundred

1 Crusoe foreshadows the end-point of narrative.

2 Prior to 1752, dates that fell between 31 December and 25 March were frequently given according to two dates, the Julian and Gregorian.

3 An anchorage in the southern North Sea near the English Channel, off the eastern Kent coast in southern England.

4 Maker of staved wooden vessels, such as tubs and barrels, held together by wood or metal hoops.

5 Maker of wooden furniture by way of a foot-powered treadle lathe.

6 Pewter.

Pound more in Iron-Work, Nails, Tools of every Kind, Staples, Hooks, Hinges, and every necessary Thing I could think of.

I carry'd also an hundred spare Arms, Muskets, and Fuzees,* besides some Pistols, a considerable Quantity of Shot of all Sizes, and two Pieces of Brass Canon; and because I knew not what Time, and what Extremities* I was providing for, I carry'd an hundred Barrels of Powder,* besides Swords, Cutlasses, and the Iron Part of some Pikes, and Halberts;* so that in short we had a large Magazine* of all Sorts of Stores; and I made my Nephew carry two small Quarter-Deck* Guns more than he wanted for his Ship, to leave behind, if there was Occasion; that when we came there, we might build a Fort, and mann it against all Sorts of Enemies: And indeed, I at first thought there was Need enough for it all, and much more, if we hop'd to maintain our Possession of the Island, as shall be seen in the Course of that Story.

I had not such bad Luck in this Voyage as I had been used to meet with; and therefore shall have the less Occasion to interrupt the Reader,[1] who perhaps may be impatient to hear how Matters went with my Colony; yet some odd Accidents,* cross Winds, and bad Weather happen'd, on this first setting out, which made the Voyage longer than I expected it at first; and I who had never made but one Voyage, (*viz.*) *my first Voyage to Guinea*,[2] in which I might be said to come back again, as the Voyage was at first design'd, began to think the same ill Fate[3] still attended me; and that I was born to be never contented with being on Shore, and yet to be always unfortunate at Sea.

Contrary Winds first put us to the Northward, and we were oblig'd to put in at *Galway* in *Ireland*, where we lay Wind-bound two and twenty Days; but we had this Satisfaction with the Disaster, that Provisions were here exceeding cheap, and in the utmost Plenty; so that while we lay here, we never touch'd the Ship's Stores, but rather added to them; here also I took in several live Hogs, and two Cows, and Calves, which I resolv'd, if I had a good Passage, to put on Shore in my Island, but we found Occasion to dispose otherwise of them.

We set out the 5th of *February* from *Ireland*, and had a very fair Gale of Wind for some Days, as I remember, it might be about the 20th of *February* in the Evening late, when the Mate having

---

1 The first of many nods toward the reader.

2 See *Crusoe* 15–16.

3 In the early pages of Part I, Crusoe frequently blames a fatal impetus, or fate, for both his inclinations and his condition.

the Watch, came into the Round-house,[1] and told us, he saw a Flash of Fire, and heard a Gun fir'd, and while he was telling us of it, a Boy came in, and told us the Boatswain* heard another. This made us all run out upon the Quarter-Deck, where for a while we heard nothing, but in a few Minutes we saw a very great Light, and found that there was some very terrible Fire at a Distance; immediately we had Recourse to our Reckonings,[2] in which we all agreed, that there could be no Land that Way, in which the Fire show'd it self, no not for 500 Leagues,* for it appear'd at W.N.W. Upon this we concluded it must be some Ship on Fire at Sea; and as by our hearing the Noise of Guns just before, we concluded it could not be far off: We stood[3] directly towards it, and were presently satisfy'd we should discover it, because the farther we sail'd the greater the Light appear'd, tho' the Weather being haizy, we could not perceive any Thing but the Light for a while; in about half an Hour's Sailing, the Wind being fair for us, tho' not much of it, and the Weather clearing up a little, we could plainly discern that it was a great Ship on fire in the Middle of the Sea.

I was most sensibly* touch'd with this Disaster, tho' not at all acquainted with the Persons engaged in it; I presently recollected my former Circumstances, and in what Condition I was in, when taken up by the *Portugal* Captain;[4] and how much more deplorable the Circumstances of the poor Creatures belonging to this Ship must be, if they had no other Ship in Company with them: Upon this I immediately order'd, that five Guns should be fir'd, one soon after another, that, if possible, we might give Notice to them, that there was Help for them at hand, and that they might endeavour to save themselves in their Boat; for tho' we could see the Flame of the Ship, yet they, it being Night, could see nothing of us.

We lay by some Time upon this, only driving as the Burning Ship drove, waiting for Day-Light; when on a sudden, to our great Terror, tho' we had Reason to expect it, the Ship blew up in the Air; and immediately, that is to say, in a few Minutes, all the Fire was out, that is to say, the rest of the Ship sunk: This was a terrible, and indeed an afflicting Sight, for the Sake of the poor Men,

---

1 Cabin on the quarter-deck.

2 Calculations of the ship's geographical location.

3 Steered.

4 Crusoe is referring to the Portuguese captain who rescues him and the boy Xury off the African coast in Part I after an escape from Moorish slavery.

who I concluded must be either all destroy'd in the Ship, or be in the utmost Distress in their Boat in the Middle of the Ocean, which at present, by Reason it was dark, I could not see: However, to direct them as well as I could, I caused Lights to be hung out in all the Parts of the Ship where we could, and which we had Lanthorns[1] for, and kept firing Guns all the Night long, letting them know by this, that there was a Ship not far off.

About 8 a Clock in the Morning we discover'd the Ship's Boats by the Help of our Perspective Glasses,* found there were two of them, both throng'd with People, and deep in the Water: We perceived they row'd, the Wind being against them, that they saw our Ship, and did their utmost to make us see them.

We immediately spread our Antient* to let them know we saw them, and hung a Waft[2] out as a Signal for them to come on Board, and then made more Sail, standing directly to them. In little more than half an Hour we came up with them, and in a Word took them all in, being no less than sixty four, Men, Women, and Children, for there were a great many Passengers.

Upon the whole, we found it was a *French* Merchant Ship of 300 Ton, homeward bound from *Quebeck*, in the River of *Canada*. The Master gave us a long Account of the Distress of his Ship, how the Fire began in the Steerage* by the Negligence of the Steersman; but on his crying out for Help, was, as every body thought, entirely put out, when they found that some Sparks of the first Fire had gotten into some Part of the Ship, so difficult to come at, that they could not effectually quench it, till getting in between the Timbers, and within the Ceiling of the Ship, it proceeded into the Hold, and master'd all the Skill, and all the Application they were able to exert.

They had no more to do then but to get into their Boats, which to their great Comfort were pretty large, being their Long-Boat,* and a great Shalloup,[3] besides a small Skiff[4] which was of no great Service to them, other than to get some fresh Water and Provisions into her, after they had secur'd their Lives from the Fire. They had indeed small Hope of their Lives by getting into these Boats at that Distance from any Land, only, as they said well, that they were escap'd from the Fire, and had a Possibility

---

1 Lanterns.

2 Flag.

3 Small, open boat fitted with oars or sails, although here probably signifying a large undecked boat with a single mast.

4 A little boat.

that some Ship might happen to be at Sea, and might take them in. They had Sails, Oars, and a Compass, and were preparing to make the best of their Way back to *New-found Land*,* the Wind blowing pretty fair, for it blew an easy Gale at S.E. by E. They had as much Provisions and Water, as with sparing it so as to be next door to starving, might support them about Twelve Days; in which, if they had no bad Weather, and no contrary Winds, the Captain said, he hop'd he might get to the Banks of *New-found Land*, and might perhaps take some Fish to sustain them till they might go on Shore. But there were so many Chances against them in all these Cases; such as, Storms to overset and founder them, Rains and Cold to benumb and perish their Limbs, contrary Winds to keep them out and starve them, that it must have been next to miraculous if they had escap'd.

In the midst of their Consultations, every one being hopeless and ready to despair, the Captain with Tears in his Eyes told me, they were on a sudden surpriz'd with the Joy of hearing a Gun fire, and after that four more, these were the five Guns which I caused to be fired at first seeing the Light: This reviv'd their Hearts, and gave them the Notice, which, *as above*, I desir'd it should, (*viz.*) that there was a Ship at hand for their Help.

It was upon the hearing these Guns, that they took down their Masts and Sails; the Sound coming from the Windward, they resolv'd to lye by 'till Morning. Some Time after this, hearing no more Guns, they fir'd three Muskets, one a considerable While after another; but these, the Wind being contrary, we never heard.

Some Time after that again they were still more agreeably surpriz'd with seeing our Lights, and hearing the Guns, which, as I have said, I caus'd to be fir'd all the rest of the Night; this set them to work with their Oars to keep their Boats a-head, at least, that we might the sooner come up with them; and at last to their inexpressible Joy, they found we saw them.

It is impossible for me to express the several Gestures, the strange Extasies, the Variety of Postures which these poor deliver'd People run into to express the Joy of their Souls at so unexpected a Deliverance; Grief and Fear are easily described; Sighs, Tears, Groans, and a very few Motions of the Head and Hands make up the Sum of its Variety: But an Excess of Joy, a Surprize of Joy has a Thousand Extravagancies* in it; there were some in Tears, some raging, and tearing themselves; as if they had been in the greatest Agonies of Sorrow, some stark-raving and downright lunatick, some ran about the Ship stamping with their Feet, others wringing their Hands; some were dancing, some singing, some laughing, more crying; many quite dumb, not able to speak a Word; others sick and vomiting, several swooning, and ready to faint; and a few were Crossing themselves, and giving God Thanks.

I would not wrong them neither, there might be many that were thankful afterward, but the Passion* was too strong for them at first, and they were not able to master it, they were thrown into Extasies and a Kind of Frenzy, and it was but a very few that were compos'd and serious in their joy.

Perhaps the Case may have some Addition to it from the particular Circumstance of that Nation they belong'd to, I mean the *French*, whose Temper is allow'd to be more volatile, more passionate, and more sprightly, and their Spirits more fluid than in other Nations.[1] I am not Philosopher enough to determine the Cause, but nothing I had ever seen before came up to it: The Extasies poor *Friday*, my trusty *Savage*, was in when he found his Father in the Boat, came the nearest to it, and the Surprize of the Master and his two Companions, who I deliver'd from the Villains that set them on Shore in the Island, came a little Way towards it, but nothing was to compare to this, either that I saw in *Friday*, or any where else in my Life.

It is further observable, that these Extravagancies did not shew themselves in that different Manner I have mention'd in different Persons only: But all the Variety would appear in a short Succession of Moments in one and the same Person. A Man that we saw this Minute dumb, and as it were stupid and confounded, should the next Minute be dancing and hallowing* like an Antick;* and the next Moment be tearing his Hair, or pulling his Cloaths to Pieces, and stamping them under his Feet, like a mad Man; a few Moments after that, we should have him all in Tears, then sick, then swooning, and had not immediate Help been had, would, in a few Moments more have been dead; and thus it was not with one or two, or ten or twenty, but with the greatest Part of them; and if I remember right, our Surgeon was oblig'd to let above thirty of them Blood.[2]

---

1 Defoe's poem *The True-Born Englishman* describes France's supposed national characteristics: "Ungovern'd passion settled first in France, / Where mankind lives in haste, and thrives by chance; / A dancing nation, fickle and untrue."

2 Opening veins to let blood was a common medical treatment for diverse ailments of body and mind, whether done by surgeons or semi-professionally by barbers.

There were two Priests among them, one an old Man, and the other a young Man; and that which was strangest was, that the oldest Man was the worst. As soon as he set his Foot on board our Ship, and saw himself safe, he dropt down stone-dead, not the least Sign of Life could be perceiv'd in him; our Surgeon immediately apply'd proper Remedies to recover him, and was the only Man in the Ship that believ'd he was not dead; at length he open'd a Vein in his Arm, having first chaff'd and rubb'd the Part so as to warm it as much as possible: Upon this the Blood which only dropp'd at first, flow'd something freely; in three Minutes after, the Man open'd his Eyes, and about a quarter of an Hour after that he spoke, grew better, and quite well; after the Blood was stopp'd he walk'd about, told us he was perfectly well, took a Dram* of Cordial* which the Surgeon gave him, and was what we call'd Come to himself; about a quarter of an Hour after they came running into the Cabbin to the Surgeon, who was bleeding a *French* Woman that had fainted, and told him the Priest was gone stark-mad; it seems he had begun to revolve[1] the Change of his Circumstance, and again this put him into an Extasy of Joy, his Spirits whirl'd about faster than the Vessels could convey them; the Blood grew hot and feverish, and the Man was as fit for *Bedlam** as any Creature that ever was in it; the Surgeon would not bleed him again in that Condition, but gave him something to dose and put him to sleep, which after some Time operated upon him, and he wak'd the next Morning perfectly compos'd, and well.

The younger Priest behav'd with great Command of his Passions, and was really an Example of a serious well-govern'd Mind; at his first coming on board the Ship, he threw himself flat on his Face, prostrating himself in Thankfulness for his Deliverance, in which I unhappily and unseasonably disturb'd him, really thinking he had been in a Swoon; but he spake calmly, thank'd me, told me, he was giving God Thanks for his Deliverance, and begg'd me to leave him a few Moments, and that next to his Maker he would give me Thanks also.

I was heartily sorry that I disturb'd him, and not only left him, but kept others from interrupting him also; he continued in that Posture about three Minutes, or little more, after I left him, then came to me, as he had said he would, and with a great deal of Seriousness and Affection, but with Tears in his Eyes, thank'd me that had, under God, given him and so many miserable Creatures their Lives: I told him, I had no Room to move him to thank God

1 Realize.

for it, rather than me, but I added, that it was nothing but what Reason and Humanity dictated to all Men, and that we had as much Reason as he to give Thanks to God who had bless'd us so far as to make us the Instruments of his Mercy to so many of his Creatures.

After this the young Priest apply'd himself to his Country-Folks; labour'd to compose them; perswaded, entreated, argued, reason'd with them, and did his utmost to keep them within the Exercise of their Reason, and with some he had Success, tho' others were for a Time out of all Government[1] of themselves.

I cannot help committing this to Writing, as perhaps it may be useful to those into whose Hands it may fall, for the guiding themselves in all the Extravagancies of their Passions; for if an Excess of Joy can carry Men out to such a Length beyond the Reach of their Reason, what will not the Extravagancies of Anger, Rage, and a provok'd Mind carry us to? and indeed here I saw Reason for keeping an exceeding Watch over our Passions of every Kind, as well those of Joy and Satisfaction, as those of Sorrow and Anger.

We were something disordered by these Extravagancies among our new Guests for the first Day, but when they had been retir'd, Lodgings provided for them as well as our Ship would allow, and they had slept heartily, as most of them did, they were quite another Sort of People the next Day.

Nothing of good Manners or civil Acknowledgments for the Kindness shewn them was wanting; the *French*, 'tis known, are naturally apt enough to exceed that Way. The Captain and one of the Priests came to me the next Day, and desiring to speak with me and my Nephew, the Commander began to consult with us what should be done with them; and first they told us, that as we had saved their Lives, so all they had was little enough for a Return to us for that Kindness received. The Captain said, they had saved some Money and some Things of Value in their Boats, catch'd hastily up out of the Flames, and if we would accept it they were ordered to make an Offer of it all to us; they only desired to be set on Shore somewhere in our way, where if possible they might get Passage to *France*.

My Nephew was for accepting their Money at first Word, and to consider what to do with them afterwards; but I over-rul'd him in that part, for I knew what it was to be set on Shore in a strange Country; and if the *Portugal* Captain that took me up at Sea had

1 Out of control.

serv'd me so, and took all I had for my Deliverance, I must have starv'd, or have been as much a Slave at the *Brasils* as I had been in *Barbary*;[1] the meer being sold to a *Mahometan*[2] excepted; and perhaps a *Portuguese* is not much a better Master than a *Turk*, if not in some Cases a much worse.

I therefore told the *French* Captain that we had taken them up in their Distress, it was true; but that it was our Duty to do so as we were Fellow-Creatures, and as we would desire to be so deliver'd if we were in the like or any other Extremity; that we had done nothing for them but what we believed they would have done for us, if we had been in their Case, and they in ours; but that we took them up to save them, not to plunder them; and it would be a most barbarous thing to take that little from them which they saved out of the Fire, and then set them on Shore and leave them; that this would be first to save them from Death, and then kill them our selves; save them from drowning, and abandon them to starving; and therefore I would not let the least thing be taken from them: As to setting them on Shore, I told them indeed that was an exceeding Difficulty to us, for that the Ship was bound to the *East-Indies*,* and tho' we were driven out of our Course to the Westward a very great way, and perhaps was directed by Heaven on Purpose for their Deliverance, yet it was impossible for us wilfully to change our Voyage on this particular Account, nor could my Nephew, the Captain, answer it to the Freighters, with whom he was under Charter-Party[3] to pursue his Voyage by the Way of *Brasils*, and all I knew we could do for them, was to put our selves in the Way of meeting with other Ships homeward bound from the *West-Indies*,* and get them Passage if possible to *England* or *France*.

The first Part of the Proposal was so generous and kind they could not but be very thankful for it, but they were in a very great Consternation, especially the Passengers, at the Notion of being carry'd away to the *East-Indies*, and they then entreated me, that seeing I was driven so far to the Westward before I met with them, I would at least keep on the same Course to the Banks of *New-found Land*, where it was probable I might meet with some Ship or Sloop that they might hire to carry them back to *Canada* from whence they came.

---

1 Young Crusoe is captured at sea by pirates and is enslaved in Sallee, in Morocco.

2 Follower of Muhammed/Islam.

3 Contract between ship owner and merchant, whereby a ship is hired to convey goods on a specific voyage, or for a defined period.

I thought this was but a reasonable Request on their Part, and therefore I enclin'd to agree to it, for indeed I consider'd, that to carry this whole Company to the *East-Indies*, would not only be an intollerable Severity upon the poor People, but would be ruining our whole Voyage by devouring all our Provisions; so I thought it no Breach of Charter-Party, but what an unforeseen Accident made absolutely necessary to us, and in which no one could say we were to blame, for the Laws of God and Nature would have forbid that we should refuse to take up two Boats full of People in such a Distress'd Condition, and the nature of the Thing as well respecting our selves as the poor People, oblig'd us to set them on Shore some where or other for their Deliverance; so I consented that we would carry them to *New-found Land*, if Wind and Weather would permit, and if not, that I would carry them to *Martinico** in the *West-Indies*.

The Wind continued fresh Easterly, but the Weather pretty good, and as the Winds had continued in the Points between N.E. and S.E. a long time, we missed several Opportunities of sending them to *France*; for we met several Ships bound to *Europe*, whereof two were *French* from St. *Christopher*'s,[1] but they had been so long beating up against the Wind, that they durst take in no Passengers for fear of wanting Provisions for the Voyage, as well for themselves as for those they should take in; so we were obliged to go on. It was about a Week after this that we made the Banks of *New-found Land*, where to shorten my Story, we put all our *French* People on Board a Bark,* which they hir'd at Sea there, to put them on Shore, and afterwards to carry them to *France* if they could get Provision to victual* themselves with. When, I say, all the *French* went on Shore, I should remember that the young Priest I spoke of, hearing we were bound to the *East-Indies*, desired to go the Voyage with us, and to be set on Shore on the Coast of *Coromandel*,* which I readily agreed to, for I wonderfully lik'd the Man, and had very good Reason, as will appear afterwards; also four of the Seamen entered themselves on our Ship, and proved very useful Fellows.

From hence we directed our Course for the *West-Indies*, steering away S. and S. by E. for about twenty Days together, sometimes little or no Wind at all, when we met with another Subject for our Humanity[2] to work upon, almost as deplorable as that before.

---

1 Island in the West Indies, now St. Kitts.

2 Our empathy, our emotions.

It was in the Latitude of 27 Degrees 5 Minutes North, and the 19th Day of *March* 1694–5, when we 'spy'd a Sail, our Course S.E. and by S. we soon perceiv'd it was a large Vessel, and that she[1] bore up to us, but could not at first know what to make of her, till after coming a little nearer, we found she had lost her Main-top-mast,* Fore-mast[2] and Boltsprit,[3] and presently she fired a Gun as a signal of Distress; the Weather was pretty good, Wind at N.N.W. a fresh Gale, and we soon came to speak with her.

We found her a Ship of *Bristol*, bound home from *Barbadoes*, but had been blown out of the Road[4] at *Barbadoes* a few Days before she was ready to sail, by a terrible Hurricane, while the Captain and Chief Mate were both gone on Shore, so that beside the Terror of the Storm, they were but in an indifferent* Case for good Artists[5] to bring the Ship home: They had been already nine Weeks at Sea, and had met with another terrible Storm after the Hurricane was over, which had blown them quite out of their Knowledge to the Westward, and in which they lost their Masts, as above; they told us they expected to have seen the *Bahama* Islands, but were then driven away again to the South East by a strong Gale of Wind at N.N.W. the same that blew now, and having no Sails to work the Ship with but a main Course,[6] and a kind of square Sail upon a Jury Fore-mast,* which they had set up, they could not lye near the Wind, but were endeavouring to stand away for the *Canaries*.[7]

But that which was worst of all, was, that they were almost starv'd for want of Provisions, besides the Fatigues they had undergone; their Bread and Flesh was quite gone, they had not one Ounce left in the Ship, and had had none for eleven Days; the only Relief they had, was, their Water was not all spent, and they had about half a Barrel of Flower[8] left; they had Sugar enough; some Succads[9] or Sweet-meats* they had at first, but they were devour'd, and they had seven Casks of Rum.

---

1 The ship.

2 The forward lower mast.

3 Bowsprit, a spar extending forward from the stem of a sailing ship.

4 Sheltered stretch of water, near shore, where vessels lie safely anchored.

5 Skilled mariners like the captain and chief mate.

6 The sails that hang from the lower yards of the mast, in this case the main mast.

7 The Canary Islands, an archipelago off the northwest coast of Africa, part of Spain.

8 Flour.

9 Type of sweetmeat: candied fruits or vegetables.

There was a Youth and his Mother and a Maid-Servant on Board, who were going Passengers, and thinking the Ship was ready to sail, unhappily came on Board the Evening before the Hurricane began, and having no Provisions of their own left, they were in a more deplorable Condition than the rest, for the Seamen being reduced to such an extreme Necessity themselves had no Compassion, we may be sure, for the poor Passengers, and they were indeed in a Condition that their Misery is very hard to describe.

I had, perhaps, not known this Part if my Curiosity had not led me, the Weather being fair and the Wind abated, to go on Board the Ship: The Second Mate who upon this Occasion commanded the Ship, had been on Board our Ship, and he told me indeed they had three Passengers in the great Cabbin, that they were in a deplorable Condition, nay, says he, I believe they are dead for I have heard nothing of them for above two Days, and I was afraid to enquire after them, said he, for I had nothing to relieve them with.

We immediately apply'd our selves to give them what Relief we could spare; and indeed I had so far over-ruled Things with my Nephew, that I would have victual'd them, tho' we had gone away to *Virginia*, or any Part of the Coast of *America*, to have supply'd our selves, but there was no Necessity for that.

But now they were in a new Danger; for they were afraid of eating too much, even of that little we gave them; the Mate or Commander brought six Men with him in his Boat, but these poor Wretches look'd like Skeletons, and were so weak, they could hardly sit to their Oars: The Mate himself was very ill, and half starv'd; for he declar'd he had reserv'd nothing from the Men, and went Share and Share alike with them in every Bit they eat.

I caution'd him to eat sparingly, but set Meat before him immediately, and he had not eaten three Mouthfuls before he began to be Sick, and out of Order; so he stopt a while, and our Surgeon mix'd him up something with some Broth, which he said would be to him both Food and Physick; and after he had taken it, he grew better. In the mean Time, I forgot not the Men; I order'd Victuals to be given them, and the poor Creatures rather devour'd than eat it; they were so exceeding hungry, that they were in a kind ravenous, and had no Command of themselves; and two of them eat with so much Greediness, that they were in Danger of their Lives the next Morning.

The Sight of these Peoples Distress was very moving to me, and brought to Mind what I had a terrible Prospect of at my first coming on Shore in the Island, where I had neither the least Mouthful of Food, or any Prospect of procuring any; besides the hourly Apprehension I had of being made the Food of other Creatures: But all the while the Mate was thus relating to me the miserable Condition of the Ship's Company, I could not put out of my Thought the Story he had told me of the three poor Creatures in the Great Cabbin, (*viz.*) the Mother, her Son, and the Maid-servant, who he had heard nothing of for two or three Days, and who he seem'd to confess they had wholly neglected, their own Extremities being so great; by which I understood, that they had really given them no Food at all, and that therefore they must be perish'd, and be all lying dead perhaps on the Floor, or Deck of the Cabbin.

As I therefore kept the Mate, whom we then called Captain, on board with his Men to refresh them, so I also forgot not the starving Crew that were left on board, but order'd my own Boat to go on board the Ship, and with my Mate and twelve Men to carry them a Sack of Bread, and four or five Pieces of Beef to boil. Our Surgeon charg'd the Men to cause the Meat to be boil'd while they stay'd, and to keep Guard in the Cook-Room, to prevent the Men taking it to eat raw, or taking it out of the Pot before it was well boil'd, and then to give every Man but a very little at a Time; and by this Caution he preserv'd the Men, who would otherwise ha' kill'd themselves with that very Food that was given them, on Purpose to save their Lives.

At the same Time, I order'd the Mate to go into the Great Cabbin, and see what Condition the poor Passengers were in, and if they were alive, to comfort them, and give them what Refreshment was proper; and the Surgeon gave him a large Pitcher with some of the prepar'd Broth which he had given the Mate that was on board, and which he did not question would restore them gradually.

I was not satisfy'd with this, but as I said above, having a great Mind to see the Scene of Misery, which I knew the Ship it self would present me with, in a more lively Manner than I could have it by Report, I took the Captain of the Ship, as we now call'd him, with me, and went my self a little after in their Boat.

I found the poor Men on board almost in a Tumult to get the Victuals out of the Boyler before it was ready: But my Mate observ'd his Order, and kept a good Guard at the Cook-Room Door, and the Man he plac'd there, after using all possible Persuasion to have Patience, kept them off by Force: However, he caused some Bisket Cakes* to be dipp'd in the Pot, and soften'd with the Liquor of the Meat, which they call Brewes,[1] and gave them every one, one, to stay their Stomachs, and told them it was for their own Safety that he was oblig'd to give them but a little at a Time: But it was all in vain; and had I not come on board, and their own Commander and Officers with me, and with good Words, and some Threats also of giving them no more, I believe they would have broke into the Cook-Room by Force, and tore the Meat out of the Furnace: For Words are indeed of very small Force to a hungry Belly: However we pacify'd them, and fed them gradually and cautiously for the first Time, and the next Time gave them more, and at last fill'd their Bellies, and the Men did well enough.

But the Misery of the poor Passengers in the Cabbin, was of another Nature, and far beyond the rest; for as first the Ship's Company had so little for themselves, it was but too true that they had at first kept them very low, and at last totally neglected them; so that for six or seven Days, it might be said, they had really had no Food at all, and for several Days before very little. The poor Mother, who as the Men reported, was a Woman of good Sense and good Breeding, had spar'd all she could get, so affectionately for her Son, that at last she entirely sunk under it: And when the Mate of our Ship went in, she sat upon the Floor or Deck, with her Back up against the Sides, between two Chairs, which were lash'd fast, and her Head sunk in between her Shoulders, like a Corpse, tho' not quite dead. My Mate said all he could to revive and encourage her, and with a Spoon put some Broth into her Mouth; she open'd her Lips, and lifted up one Hand, but could not speak; yet she understood what he said, and made Signs to him, intimating, that it was too late for her, but pointed to her Child, as if she would have said, they should take Care of him.

However, the Mate, who was exceedingly mov'd with the Sight, endeavour'd to get some of the Broth into her Mouth; and as he said, got two or three Spoonfuls down, tho' I question whether he could be sure of it or not: But it was too late, and she dy'd the same Night.

The Youth who was preserved at the Price of his most affectionate Mother's Life, was not so far gone, yet he lay in a Cabbin-bed as one stretch'd out, with hardly any Life left in him; he had a Piece of an old Glove in his Mouth having eaten up the rest of it; however being young and having more Strength than his Mother, the Mate got something down his Throat and he began sensibly

1 Broth-soaked bread.

to revive, tho' by giving him some time after but two or three Spoonfuls extraordinary[1] he was very sick and brought it up again.

But the next Care was the poor Maid, she lay all along upon the Deck hard by her Mistress, and just like one that had fallen down with an Apoplexy[2] and struggled for Life: Her Limbs were distorted, one of her Hands was clasp'd round the Frame of a Chair, and she grip'd it so hard that we could not easily make her let go; her other Arm lay over her Head, and her Feet lay both together set fast against the Frame of the Cabbin Table; in short, she lay just like one in the last Agonies of Death, and yet she was alive too.

The poor Creature was not only starv'd with Hunger, and terrify'd with the Thoughts of Death, but as the Men told us afterwards, was broken-hearted for her Mistress, who she saw dying for two or three Days before, and who she lov'd most tenderly.

We knew not what to do with this poor Girl, for when our Surgeon, who was a Man of very great Knowledge and Experience, had with great Application recover'd her as to Life; he had her upon his Hand as to her Senses,[3] for she was little less than distracted* for a considerable time after, as shall appear presently.

Whoever shall read these *Memorandums* must be desir'd to consider, that Visits at Sea are not like a Journey into the Country, where sometimes People stay a Week or a Fortnight at a Place. Our Business was to relieve this distressed Ship's Crew, but not to lie by for them; and tho' they were willing to steer the same Course with us for some Days, yet we could carry no Sail to keep Pace with a Ship that had no Masts; however, as their Captain begg'd of us to help him to set up a Main Top-Mast, and a Kind of a Top-Mast to his Jury Fore-Mast, we did, as it were lie by him for three or four Days, and then having given him five Barrels of Beef, a Barrel of Pork, two Hogsheads* of Bisket, and a Proportion of Peas, Flower, and what other Things we could spare; and taking three Casks of Sugar, some Rum, and some Pieces of Eight of[4] them for Satisfaction, we left them, taking on board with us, at their own earnest Request, the Priest,[5] the Youth, and the Maid, and all their Goods.

---

1 Bigger than usual.

2 Older usage, unconscious or incapacitated, as from a stroke.

3 He was responsible for attending to her mental state.

4 From.

5 There is no previous mention of a priest, aside from the one who joined Crusoe's ship after being rescued earlier; presumably the rescued priest boarded the ship to minister to their needs and now re-boards Crusoe's own vessel.

The young Lad was about seventeen Years of Age, a pretty, well-bred modest, and sensible* Youth, greatly dejected with the Loss of his Mother, and as it seems had lost his Father but a few Months before at *Barbadoes*. He begg'd of the Surgeon to speak to me to take him out of the Ship, for he said the cruel Fellows had murther'd his Mother; *and indeed so they had*, that is to say *passively*; for they might ha' spar'd a small Sustenance to the poor helpless Widow, that might have preserv'd her Life, tho' it had been but just to keep her alive. But Hunger knows no Friend, no Relation, no Justice, no Right, and therefore is remorseless, and capable of no Compassion.

The Surgeon told him how far we were going, and how it would carry him away from all his Friends, and put him perhaps in as bad Circumstances almost as those we found him in; that is to say, starving in the World. He said he matter'd not whether* he went, if he was but delivered from the terrible Crew he was among: That the Captain (by which he meant me, for he could know nothing of my Nephew) had sav'd his Life, and he was sure would not hurt him; and as for the Maid, he was sure if she came to herself, she would be very thankful for it, let us carry them where we would. The Surgeon represented the Case so affectionately to me, that I yielded, and we took them both on board with all their Goods, except eleven Hogsheads of Sugar, which could not be removed or come at, and as the Youth had a Bill of Lading[1] for them, I made his Commander sign a Writing, obliging himself to go as soon as he came to *Bristol* to one Mr. *Rogers* a Merchant there, to whom the Youth said he was related, and to deliver a Letter which I wrote to him, and all the Goods he had belonging to the deceased Widow; which I suppose was not done, for I could never learn that the Ship came to *Bristol*, but was, as is most probable, lost at Sea, being in so disabled a Condition and so far from any Land, that I am of Opinion, the first Storm she met with afterwards, she might founder in the Sea, for she was leaky, and had Damage in her Hold when we met with her.

I was now in the Latitude of 19 Deg. 32 Min. and had hitherto had a tolerable Voyage as to Weather, tho' at first the Winds had been contrary. I shall trouble no Body with the little Incidents of Wind, Weather, Currents, &c. on the rest of our Voyage; but shortening my Story for the sake of what is to follow, shall observe that I came to my old Habitation, the Island, on the 10th of *April*

1 Legal document between the shipper of goods and the carrier, detailing the type, quantity, and destination of the goods.

1695: It was with no small Difficulty that I found the Place; for as I came to it, and went from it before, on the South and East Side of the Island, and having no Chart for the Coast, nor any Land-Mark, I did not know it when I saw it, or know whether I saw it or no.

We beat about a great while, and went on Shore on several Islands on the Mouth of the great River *Oronooque*,[1] but none for my Purpose. Only this I learn'd by my Coasting the Shore, that I was under one great Mistake before, *viz.* that the Continent which I thought I saw, from the Island I liv'd in, was really no Continent, but a long Island, or rather a Ridge of Islands, reaching from one to the other Side of the extended Mouth of that great River, and that the Savages who came to my Island, were not properly those which we call *Caribbees*, but Islanders,[2] and other Barbarians of the same kind, who inhabited something nearer to our Side than the rest.

In short, I visited several of these Islands to no Purpose; some I found were inhabited, and some were not. On one of them I found some *Spaniards*, and thought they had liv'd there, but speaking with them, found they had a Sloop lay in a small Creek hard by, and they came thither to make Salt,[3] and to catch some Pearl Muscles[4] if they could, but that they belong'd to the Isle *de Trinidad*, which lay farther North in the Latitude of 10 and 11 Degrees.

But at last coasting from one Island to another, sometimes with the Ship, sometimes with the *French* Mans Shallop,[5] which we had found a convenient Boat, and therefore kept her with their very good Will; at length I came fair on the South Side of my Island, and I presently knew the very Countenance[6] of the Place; so I brought the Ship safe to an Anchor, Broadside with the little Creek where was my old Habitation.

As soon as I saw the Place, I call'd for *Friday*, and ask'd him if he knew where he was? He look'd about a little, and presently clapping his Hands, cry'd; *O yes, O there, O yes, O there*, pointing to our old Habitation, and fell a dancing and capering like a mad

---

1 The Orinoco, one of the largest rivers in South America, 1,330 miles long, flows through Venezuela into the Atlantic.

2 Here Defoe equates Carib with South American.

3 By evaporating seawater.

4 Freshwater mussels.

5 Alternative spelling of "shalloup," or small boat.

6 Face.

Fellow, and I had much ado to keep him from jumping into the Sea, to swim ashore to the Place.

Well, *Friday*, says I, do you think we shall find any Body here or no? And what do you think, shall we see your Father? The Fellow stood mute as a Stock[1] a good while, but when I nam'd his Father, the poor affectionate Creature look'd dejected, and I could see the Tears run down his Face very plentifully. What is the Matter, *Friday*, says I? Are you troubled because you may see your Father? No, no, *says he*, shaking his Head, no see him more, no ever more see again; *why so*, said I *Friday, how do you know that?* O no, O no, says *Friday*, he long ago die, long ago; he much old Man. Well, well, *says I*, *Friday*, you don't know; but shall we see any one else then? The Fellow, it seems, had better Eyes than I, and he points just to the Hill above my old House; and tho' we lay half a League off, he cries out, we see! we see! yes, we see much Men there, and there, and there. I look'd, but I could see no body, no not with a Perspective Glass, which was, I suppose, because I could not hit the Place, for the Fellow was right, as I found upon Enquiry the next Day, and there was five or six Men altogether, stood to look at the Ship, not knowing what to think of us.

As soon as *Friday* had told me he saw People, I caus'd the *English* Antient to be spread, and fir'd three guns, to give them notice we were Friends, and in about half a Quarter of an Hour after, we perceiv'd a Smoke rise from the Side of the Creek, so I immediately order'd a Boat out, taking *Friday* with me, and hanging out a white Flag, or Flag of Truce, I went directly on Shore, taking with me the young Fryer I mention'd, to whom I had told the whole Story of my living there, and the manner of it, and every Particular both of my self, and those I left there; and who was on that Account extremely desirous to go with me. We had besides about sixteen Men very well arm'd, if we had found any new Guests there which we did not know of; but we had no Need of Weapons.

As we went on Shore upon the Tide of Flood, near high Water, we row'd directly into the Creek, and the first Man I fix'd my Eye upon, was the *Spaniard* whose Life I had sav'd,[2] and who I knew by his Face perfectly well; as to his Habit I shall describe it afterwards. I order'd no body to go on Shore at first but my self, but there was no keeping *Friday* in the Boat; for the affectionate Creature had spy'd his Father at a Distance, a good Way off of the

1 Log or other substantial chunk of wood.

2 In Part I.

Spaniards, where indeed I saw nothing of him; and if they had not let him go on Shore, he would have jump'd into the Sea. He was no sooner on Shore, but he flew away to his Father like an Arrow out of a Bow. It would have made any Man have shed Tears in Spight of the firmest Resolution, to have seen the first Transports* of this poor Fellow's Joy when he came to his Father; how he embrac'd him, kiss'd him, strok'd his Face, took him up in his Arms, set him down upon a Tree, and lay down by him, then stood and look'd at him, as any one would look at a strange Picture, for a Quarter of an Hour together; then lie down on the Ground, and stroke his Legs, and kiss them, and then get up again, and stare at him; one would ha' thought the Fellow bewitch'd: But it would ha' made a Dog laugh to see how the next Day his Passion run out another Way: In the Morning he walk'd along the Shore, to and again, with his Father several Hours, always leading him by the Hand, as if he had been a Lady; and every now and then he would come to fetch something or other for him to the Boat, either a Lump of Sugar, or a Dram, a Bisket Cake, or something or other that was good. In the Afternoon his Frolicks run another Way; for then he would set the old Man down upon the Ground, and dance about him, and make a thousand antick Postures and Gestures; and all the while he did this, he would be talking to him, and telling him one Story or another of his Travels, and of what had happen'd to him Abroad, to divert him. In short, if the same filial Affection was to be found in Christians to their Parents, in our Part of the World, one would be tempted to say, there would hardly ha' been any Need of the fifth Commandment.

But this is a Digression; I return to my Landing: It would be endless to take Notice of all the Ceremonies and Civilities that the *Spaniards* receiv'd me with. The first *Spaniard*, who, as I said, I knew very well, was he who's Life I had sav'd; he came towards the Boat, attended by one more, carrying a Flag of Truce also; and he did not only not know me at first, but he had no Thoughts, no Notion of its being me that was come, 'till I spoke to him: Seignior, said I in *Portuguese*, Do you not know me? At which he spoke not a Word; but giving his Musket to the Man that was with him, threw his Arms abroad; and saying something in *Spanish*, that I did not perfectly hear, comes forward, and embrac'd me, telling me he was inexcusable, not to know that Face again, that he had once seen, as of an Angel from Heaven sent to save his Life: He said Abundance of very handsome Things, as a well bred *Spaniard* always knows how, and then beckoning to the Person that attended him, bad* him go and call out his Comrades. He then ask'd me, if I would walk to my old Habitation, where he would give me Possession of my own House again, and where I should see there had been but mean Improvements; so I walk'd along with him; but alas I could no more find the Place again, than if I had never been there; for they had planted so many Trees, and plac'd them in such a Posture, so thick and close to one another; and in ten Years Time they were grown so big, that *in short* the Place was inaccessible, except by such Windings and blind Ways, as they themselves only, who made them, could find.

I ask'd them what put them upon all these Fortifications? He told me, I would say there was Need enough of it, when they had given me an Account how they had pass'd their Time since their Arriving in the Island; especially after they had the Misfortune to find that I was gone; he told me, he could not but have some Satisfaction in my good Fortune, when he heard that I was gone away in a good Ship, and to my Satisfaction; and that he had often-times a strong Persuasion, that one Time or other he should see me again: But nothing that ever befel him in his Life, he said, was so surprizing and afflicting to him at first, as the Disappointment he was under when he came back to the Island, and found I was not there.

As to the three Barbarians (so he call'd them) that were left behind, and of whom he said he had a long Story to tell me; the *Spaniards* all thought themselves much better among the Savages,[1] only that their Number was so small. And, says he, had they been strong enough, we had been all long ago in Purgatory; and with that he cross'd himself on the Breast: But Sir, says he, I hope you will not be displeas'd, when I shall tell you how forc'd by Necessity we were oblig'd, for our own Preservation to disarm them, and make them our Subjects, who would not be content with being moderately our Masters, but would be our Murtherers. I answer'd, I was heartily afraid of it when I left them there; and nothing troubled me at my parting from the Island, but that they were not come back, that I might have put them in Possession of every Thing first, and left the other in a State of Subjection, as they deserv'd: But if they had reduc'd them to it, I was very glad, and should be very far from finding any Fault with it; for I knew they were a Parcel of refractory,* ungovern'd Villains, and were fit for any manner of Mischief.

---

1 In Defoe's poem *The True-Born Englishman* (1701), the Spanish are described as prideful: "PRIDE, the first peer, and president of hell, / To his share, Spain, the largest province fell."

While I was saying this, came the Man whom he had sent back, and with him eleven Men more: In the Dress[1] they were in, it was impossible to guess what Nation they were of: But he made all clear both to them and to me. First he turn'd to me, and pointing to them, said, These, Sir, are some of the Gentlemen who owe their Lives to you; and then turning to them, and pointing to me, he let them know who I was; upon which they all came up one by one, not as if they had been Sailors and ordinary Fellows, and I the like, but really, as if they had been Ambassadors of Noblemen, and I a Monarch or a great Conqueror; their Behaviour was to the last Degree obliging and courteous, and yet mix'd with a manly, majestick Gravity, which very well became them; and in short, they had so much more Manners than I, that I scarce knew how to receive their Civilities, much less how to return them in Kind.

The History of their coming to, and Conduct in the Island, after my going away, is so very remarkable, and has so many Incidents, which the former Part of my Relation[2] will help to understand, and which will in most of the Particulars, refer to that Account I have already given, that I cannot but commit them with great Delight to the reading of those that come after me.

I shall no longer trouble the Story with a Relation in the first Person, which will put me to the Expence of ten Thousand *said I's*, and *said he's*, and he *told me's*, and I *told him's*, and the like, but I shall collect the Facts Historically, as near as I can gather them out of my Memory from what they related to me, and from what I met with in my conversing with them and with the Place.

In order to do this succinctly, and as intelligibly as I can, I must go back to the Circumstance in which I left the Island, and in which the Persons were, of whom I am to speak. And first, it is necessary to repeat, that I had sent away *Friday*'s Father and the *Spaniard*, the two whose Lives I had rescued from the Savages, I say, I had sent them away in a large Canoe to the Main, *as I then thought it*, to fetch over the *Spaniard*'s Companions who he had left behind him, in order to save them from the like Calamity that he had been in; and in order to succour[3] them for the present, and that, if possible, we might together find some Way for our Deliverance afterward.

When I sent them away, I had no visible Appearance of, or the least room to hope for my own Deliverance any more than I had

1 Clothing, attire.
2 Part I, or *Robinson Crusoe*.
3 Help.

twenty Year before, much less had I any fore Knowledge of what afterward happened, I mean of an *English* Ship coming on Shore there to fetch me off; and it could not but be a very great Surprize to them when they came back, not only to find that I was gone, but to find three Strangers left on the Spot, possess'd of all that I had left behind me, which would otherwise have been their own.

The first Thing, however, which I enquir'd into, that I might begin where I left off, was of their own Part; and I desir'd he would give me a particular Account of his Voyage back to his Countrymen with the Boat, when I sent him to fetch them over: He told me there was little Variety in that Part, for nothing remarkable happen'd to them on the Way, they having very calm Weather, and a smooth Sea; for his Countrymen it could not be doubted, he said, but that they were overjoy'd to see him: (It seems he was the principal Man among them, the Captain of the Vessel they had been shipwreck'd in, having been dead some Time) they were, *he said*, the more surpriz'd to see him, because they knew that he was fallen into the Hands of the Savages, who, they were satisfy'd, would devour him as they did all the rest of the Prisoners, that when he told them the Story of his Deliverance, and in what Manner he was furnish'd for carrying them away, it was like a Dream to them; and their Astonishment, they said, was something like that of *Joseph*'s Brethren, when he told them who he was, and told them the Story of his Exaltation in *Pharaoh*'s Court:[1] But when he shewed them the Arms, the Powder, the Ball,[2] and the Provisions that he brought them for their Journey or Voyage, they were restor'd to themselves, took a just Share of the Joy of their Deliverance, and immediately prepar'd to come away with him.

Their first Business was to get Canoes; and in this they were obliged not to stick so much upon the honest Part of it, but to trespass upon their friendly Savages, and to borrow two large Canoes or Periagua's,[3] on Pretence of going out a fishing, or for Pleasure.

In these they came away the next Morning, it seems they wanted no Time to get themselves ready; for they had no Baggage,

---

1 See Genesis 37–50 for the Joseph story, and especially Genesis 45:3, when Joseph reveals himself at Pharaoh's court to his treacherous brothers who sold him into slavery.

2 Weaponry.

3 Small canoe or seacraft, from the Spanish *piragua* (which comes, in turn, from the Carib word for a dugout).

neither Cloaths or Provisions, or any Thing in the World, but what they had on them, and a few Roots to eat, of which they used to make their Bread.

They were in all three Weeks absent, and in that Time, unluckily for them, I had the Occasion offer'd for my Escape, as I mention'd in my other Part, and to get off from the Island, leaving three of the most impudent, hardn'd, ungovern'd, disagreeable Villains behind me, that any Man could desire to meet with, to the poor *Spaniards* great Grief and Disappointment, you may be sure.

The only just Thing the Rogues did, was, That when the *Spaniards* came on Shore, they gave my Letter to them, and gave them Provisions and other Relief, as I had ordered them to do, also they gave them the long Paper of Directions which I had left with them, containing the particular Methods which I took for managing every Part of my Life there, the Way how I baked my Bread, bred up tame Goats, and planted my Corn, how I cur'd my Grapes, made my Pots, and, in a Word, every Thing I did, all this being written down, they gave to the *Spaniards*, two of whom understood *English* well enough; nor did they refuse to accommodate the *Spaniards* with every Thing else, for they agreed very well for some Time; they gave them an equal Admission into the House, or Cave, and they began to live very sociably, and the Head *Spaniard*, who had seen pretty much of my Methods, and *Friday*'s Father together, manag'd all their Affairs; for, as for the *English* Men, they did nothing but ramble about the Island, shoot Parrots, and ketch Tortoises, and when they came home at Night, the *Spaniards* provided their Suppers for them.[1]

The *Spaniards* would have been satisfy'd with this, would the other but have let them alone, which, however, they could not find in their Hearts to do long; but, like the Dog in the Manger, they would not eat themselves, and would not let others eat neither:[2] The Differences nevertheless, were at first but trivial, and such as are not worth relating; but at last, it broke out into open War, and it begun with all the Rudeness and Insolence that can be imagin'd, without Reason, without Provocation, contrary to Nature, and indeed, to common Sense; and tho' it is true the first Relation of it came from the *Spaniards* themselves, who I may call

---

1 By contrast, in *The True-Born Englishman*, the Spanish are "lazy" and "haughty," apt therefore to "starve."

2 The proverbial phrase comes from a traditional fable, sometimes attributed to Aesop, about a dog in a manger who rejects the grain but will not allow the ox to have it, either.

the Accusers, yet when I came to examine the Fellows, they could not deny a Word of it.

But before I come to the Particular of this Part, I must supply a Defect in my former Relation, and this was, that I forgot to set down among the rest, that just as we were weighing the Anchor to set Sail, there happen'd a little Quarrel on board our Ship, which I was afraid once would have turn'd to a second Mutiny; nor was it appeas'd, 'till the Captain rouzing up his Courage, and taking us all to his Assistance, parted them by Force, and making two of the most refractory Fellows Prisoners, he laid them in Irons,[1] and as they had been active in the former Disorders, and let fall some ugly dangerous Words the second Time, he threaten'd to carry them in Irons to *England*, and have them hang'd there for Mutiny, and running away with the Ship.

This, it seems, tho' the Captain did not intend to do it, frighted some other Men in the Ship, and some of them had put it into the Heads of the rest, that the Captain only gave them good Words for the present, till they should come to some *English* Port, and that then they should be all put into Jayl, and Tryed for their Lives.

The Mate got Intelligence of this, and acquainted us with it; upon which it was desir'd, that I, who still pass'd for a great Man among them, should go down with the Mate, and satisfy the Men, and tell them, that they might be assur'd, if they behav'd well the rest of the Voyage, all they had done for the Time past should be pardon'd. So I went, and after passing *my Honour*'s Word to them, they appear'd easy; and the more so, when I caused the two Men who were in Irons to be released, and forgiven.

But this Mutiny had brought us to an Anchor for that Night, the Wind also falling calm, next Morning we found, that our two Men who had been laid in Irons, had stole each of them a Musket, and some other Weapons, what Powder or Shot they had, we know not; and had taken the Ship's Pinnace,* which was not yet hal'd[2] up, and ran away with her to their Companions in Roguery on Shore.

As soon as we found this, I order'd the Long-Boat on Shore, with twelve Men and the Mate, and away they went to seek the Rogues, but they could neither find them, or any of the rest; for they all fled into the Woods when they saw the Boat coming on Shore. The Mate was once resolv'd, in Justice to their Roguery, to have destroy'd their Plantations, burnt all their Houshold-Stuff

---

1 Shackles.

2 Hauled.

and Furniture, and left them to shift without it; but having no Order, he let it all alone, left every Thing as they found it, and bringing the Pinnace away, came on board without them.

These two Men made their Number five, but the other three Villains were so much wickeder than these, that after they had been 2 or 3 Days together, they turn'd their two New-Comers out of Doors to shift for themselves, and would have nothing to do with them, nor could they for a good while be perswaded to give them any Food; as for the *Spaniards* they were not yet come.

When the *Spaniards* came first on Shore, the Business began to go forward; the *Spaniards* would have persuaded the three *English* Brutes to have taken in their two Country-men again, that, as they said, they might be all one Family; but they would not hear of it: So the two poor Fellows liv'd by themselves, and finding nothing but Industry and Application would make them live comfortably, they pitch'd their Tents on the *North* Shore of the Island, but a little more to the *West*, to be out of the Danger of the Savages, who always landed on the *East* Parts of the Island.

Here they built them two Huts, one to lodge in, and the other to lay up their Magazines and Stores in, and the *Spaniards* having given them some Corn for Seed, and especially some of the Peas which I had left them, they dug, and planted, and enclosed, after the Pattern I had set for them all, and began to live pretty well; their first Crop of Corn was on the Ground, and tho' it was but a little Bit of Land which they had dug up at first, having had but a little Time, yet it was enough to relieve them, and find them with Bread and other Eatables; and one of the Fellows being the Cook's Mate of the Ship, was very ready at making Soup, Puddings,[1] and such other Preparations, as the Rice, and the Milk, and such little Flesh as they got, furnish'd him to do.

They were going on in this little thriving Posture when the three unnatural Rogues, their own Country-men too, in meer Humour, and to insult them, came and bully'd them, and told them, the Island was theirs, that the Governor, meaning me, had given them Possession of it, and no Body else had any Right to it, and damn 'em, they should build no Houses upon their Ground, unless they would pay them Rent for them.

The two Men thought they had jested at first, ask'd them to come in and sit down, and see what fine Houses they were that they had built, and tell them what Rent they demanded, and

---

1 Boiled dishes that typically contained suet, flour, egg, and any measure of savory or sweet ingredients.

one of them merrily told them, if they were Ground-Landlords, he hoped, if they built Tenements[1] upon their Land, and made Improvements, they would, according to the Custom of Landlords, grant them a long Lease, and bid them go fetch a Scrivener[2] to draw the Writings.[3] One of the three damning and raging, told them, they should see they were not in Jest, and going to a little Place at a Distance, where the honest Men had made a Fire to dress* their Victuals, he takes a Fire-brand, and claps it to the Out-side of their Hut, and very fairly set it on Fire, and it would have been all burnt down in a few Minutes, if one of the two had not run to the Fellow, thrust him away, and trod the Fire out with his Feet, and that not without some Difficulty too.

The Fellow was in such a Rage at the honest Man's thrusting him away, that he return'd upon him with a Pole he had in his Hand, and had not the Man avoided the Blow very nimbly, and run into the Hut, he had ended his Days at once; his Comrade seeing the Danger they were both in, run in after him, and immediately they came both out with their Muskets, and the Man that was first struck at with the Pole knock'd the Fellow down, that begun the Quarrel, with the Stock of his Musket, and that before the other two could come to help him, and then seeing the rest come at them, they stood together, and presenting the other Ends of their Pieces to them, bad them stand off.

The other had Fire-Arms with them too, but one of the two honest Men, bolder than his Comrade, and made desperate by his Danger, told them, if they offer'd to move Hand or Foot they were dead Men, and boldly commanded them to lay down their Arms: They did not indeed lay down their Arms, but seeing him so resolute, it brought them to a Parley,[4] and they consented to take their wounded Man with them, and be gone; and indeed it seems the Fellow was wounded sufficiently with the Blow; however, they were much in the wrong, since they had the Advantage, that they did not disarm them effectually, as they might have done, and have gone immediately to the *Spaniards*, and given them an Account how the Rogues had treated them; for the three Villains studied nothing but Revenge, and every Day gave them some Intimation that they did so.

But not to crowd this Part with an Account of the lesser Part

---

1 Dwelling-buildings.

2 Professional scribe.

3 Contracts.

4 Negotiating conference between opposing parties.

of their Rogueries, such as treading down their Corn, shooting three young Kids,[1] and a She-Goat, which the poor Men had got to breed up tame for their Store; and, in a word, plaguing them Night and Day in this Manner, it forced the two Men to such a Desperation, that they resolv'd to fight them all three the first Time they had a fair Opportunity; in Order to this they resolv'd to go to the Castle, as they call'd it, that was my old Dwelling, where the three Rogues and the *Spaniards* all liv'd together, at that Time intending to have a fair Battle, and the *Spaniards* should stand by to see fair Play; so they got up in the Morning before Day, and came to the Place, and call'd the *English* Men by their Names, telling a *Spaniard*, that answer'd, that that they wanted to speak with them.

It happen'd, that the Day before two of the *Spaniards* having been in the Woods, had seen one of the two *English* Men, who, for Distinction, I call the *Honest Men*, and he had made a sad Complaint to the *Spaniards*, of the barbarous Usage they had met with from their three Countrymen, and how they had ruin'd their Plantation, and destroy'd their Corn, that they had labour'd so hard to bring forward, and kill'd the Milch*-Goat and their three Kids, which was all they had provided for their Sustenance, and that if he and his Friends, meaning the *Spaniards*, did not assist them again, they should be starved. When the *Spaniards* came home at Night, and they were all at Supper, he took the Freedom to reprove the three *English* Men, tho' in very gentle and mannerly Terms, and ask'd them, How they could be so cruel, they being harmless inoffensive Fellows, and that they were only putting themselves in a way to subsist by their Labour, and that it had cost them a great deal of Pains to bring things to such Perfection as they had?

One of the *English* Men return'd very briskly, what had they to do there? That they came on Shore without Leave, and they should not Plant or Build upon the Island, it was none of their Ground. Why, says the *Spaniard* very calmly, Seignior Inglese, *they must not starve*? The *English* Man reply'd like a true rough-hewn Tarpaulin,[2] they might Starve and be Damn'd, they should not Plant nor Build. But what must they do then, Seignior, said the *Spaniard*? Another of the Brutes return'd, do! D---m 'em, they should be Servants and work for them. But how can you expect that of them, says the *Spaniard*, they are not bought with your Money; you have no Right to make them Servants; The *English* Man answer'd, the Island was theirs, the Governour had given it

1 Young goats.

2 Waterproof canvas; also a nickname for a sailor, often shortened to "tar."

to them, and no Man had any thing to do there but themselves; and with that swore by his Maker, that they would go and burn all their new Huts, they should build none upon their Land.

Why, Seignior, says the *Spaniard*, by the same Rule we must be your Servants too? Ay, says the bold Dog, and so you shall too, before we have done with you, mixing two or three G---d Dame's in the proper Intervals of his Speech; the *Spaniard* only smil'd at that, and made him no Answer: However, this little Discourse had heated them, and starting up, one says to the other, I think it was he they call'd *Will. Atkins*,[1] Come *Jack*, let us go and have t'other Brush with them; we'll demolish their Castle, I'll warrant you, they shall plant no Colony in our Dominions.

Upon this, they went all Trooping away, with every Man a Gun, a Pistol, and a Sword, and mutter'd some insolent Things among themselves of what they would do to the *Spaniards* too, when Opportunity offer'd, but the *Spaniards* it seems did not so perfectly understand them, as to know all the Particulars, only, that in general, they threatned them hard for taking the two *English* Mens Part.

Whether they went, or how they bestow'd their time that Evening, the *Spaniards* said, they did not know; but it seems they wandred about the Country, part of the Night, and then lying down in the Place which I used to call my Bower, they were weary and over-slept themselves. The Case was this, they had resolv'd to stay till Mid-night, and so to take the two poor Men when they were asleep, and as they acknowledg'd afterwards, intended to set Fire to their Huts while they were in them, and either burn them in them, or murther them as they came out, and as Malice seldom sleeps very sound, it was very strange they should not have been kept waking.[2]

However, as the two Men had also a Design upon them, as I have said, tho' a much fairer one than that of Burning and Murthering, it happen'd, and very luckily for them all, that they were up and gone abroad, before the bloody-minded Rogues came to their Huts.

When they came there and found the Men gone, *Atkins*, who it seems was the forwardest Man, call'd out to his Comrades, ha

---

1 This is the first mention of Atkins in *Farther Adventures*; his eventual reformation and his example as such prove crucial to forming the island's community. In *Crusoe*, Atkins prevents a mutiny by lying well and impressing Crusoe with his facility at such verbal manipulation: "[t]hough this was all a fiction of his own, yet it had its desired effect" (211).

2 Awake.

Jack, here's the Nest, but D——m 'em the Birds are flown; they mused a while to think what should be the Occasion of their being gone abroad so soon, and suggested presently that the *Spaniards* had given them Notice of it, and with that they shook Hands, and swore to one another that they would be reveng'd of the *Spaniards*; as soon as they had made this bloody Bargain they fell to work with the poor Men's Habitation, they did not set Fire indeed to any thing, but they pull'd down both their little Houses, and pull'd them so Limb from Limb, that they left not the least Stick standing; or scarce any Sign on the Ground where they stood; they tore all their little collected Houshold Stuff in Pieces, and threw every Thing about in such a manner, that the poor Men afterwards found some of their Things a Mile off their Habitation.

When they had done this, they pull'd up all the young Trees, the poor Men had planted, pull'd up an Enclosure they had made to secure their Cattle and their Corn; and in a Word, sack'd and plunder'd every thing, as compleatly as a Hoord of *Tartars*[1] would have done.

The two Men were at this Juncture gone to find them out, and had resolved to fight them where-ever they had been, tho' they were but two to three: So that had they met, there certainly would have been blood shed among them, for they were all very stout resolute Fellows, to give them their due.

But Providence took more Care to keep them assunder, than they themselves could do to meet; for, as if they had dog'd one another, when the three were gone thither, the two were here; and afterwards when the two went back to find them, the three were come to the old Habitation again; we shall see their differing Conduct presently: When the three came back like furious Creatures flush'd with the Rage which the Work they had been about had put them into, they came up to the *Spaniards*, and told them what they had done, by way of Scoff and Bravado; and one of them stepping up to one of the *Spaniards*, as if they had been a Couple of Boys at Play, takes hold of his Hat, as it was upon his Head, and giving it a twirle about, fleering[2] in his Face, says

1 Properly, *Tatars*: notoriously fierce central Asian people of Mongol descent who in the thirteenth century, under Genghis Khan (1162–1227), dominated a large portion of Asia and eastern Europe. "Tatar" became "Tartar" in common parlance; Tartarus was the lowest pit of Hell in Greek and Roman mythology. In Defoe's *The True-Born Englishman*, "poverty" makes "the Tartar" desperate.

2 Sneering.

he to him, *And you*, Seignior, Jack Spaniard, *shall have the same Sauce, if you do not mend your Manners*: The *Spaniard*, who tho' a quiet civil Man, was as brave as a Man could be desir'd to be, and withall a strong well-made Man, look'd steadily at him for a good while, and then having no Weapon in his Hand, stept gravely up to him, and with one blow of his Fist knock'd him down, as an Ox is fell'd with a Pole-Axe,* at which one of the Rogues, insolent as the first, fir'd his Pistol at the *Spaniard* immediately; he miss'd his Body indeed, for the Bullets went thro' his Hair, but one of them touch'd the tip of his Ear, and he bled pretty much: The Blood made the *Spaniard* believe, he was more hurt then he really was, and that put him into some Heat, for before, he acted all in a perfect Calm; but now resolving to go thro' with his Work, he stoop'd to take the Fellows Musket who he had knock'd down, and was just going to shoot the Man, and had fir'd at him, when the rest of the *Spaniards* being in the Cave came out, and calling to him not to shoot, they step'd in, secur'd the other two, and took their Arms from them.

When they were thus disarm'd, and found they had made all the *Spaniards* their Enemies, as well as their own Countrymen, they began to cool, and giving the *Spaniards* better Words, would have had their Arms again; but the *Spaniards* considering the Feud that was between them and the other two *English* Men, and that it would be the best Method they could take to keep them from killing one another, told them, they would do them no harm, and if they would live peaceably, they would be very willing to assist and sociate[1] with them, as they did before; but that they could not think of giving them their Arms again, while they appear'd so resolv'd to do Mischief with them to their own Countrymen, and had even threatned them all to make them their Servants.

The Rogues were now no more capable to hear Reason, than to act Reason, and being refus'd their Arms, they went raving away and raging like mad Men, threatning what they would do, tho' they had no Fire-Arms. But the *Spaniards* despising their Threatning, told them they should take Care how they offer'd any Injury to their Plantation or Cattle, for if they did, they would shoot them as they would do ravenous Beasts, wherever they found them, and if they fell into their Hands alive, they should certainly be hang'd. However, this was far from cooling them, but away they went raging and swearing like Furies[2] of Hell. As

1 Associate with.

2 Goddesses of vengeance in Greek mythology.

soon as they were gone, came back the two Men in Passion and Rage enough also, tho' of another Kind; for having been at their Plantation, and finding it all demolish'd and destroy'd, as above, it will easily be suppos'd they had Provocation enough; they could scarce have Room to tell their Tale, the *Spaniards* were so eager to tell them theirs; and it was strange enough to find three Men thus bully nineteen, and receive no Punishment at all.

The *Spaniards* indeed despised them, and especially having thus disarm'd them, made light of all their Threatnings; but the two *English* Men resolv'd to have their Remedy against them, what Pain soever it cost to find them out.

But the *Spaniards* interpos'd here too, and told them, that as they had disarm'd them, they could not consent that they (the Two) should persue them with Fire-Arms and perhaps kill them; but said the grave *Spaniard*, who was their Governour, we will endeavour to make them do you Justice if you will leave it to us, for as there is no doubt but they will come to us again when their Passion is over, being not able to subsist without our Assistance, we promise you to make no Peace with them, without having a full Satisfaction for you; upon this Condition we hope you will promise to use no Violence with them, other than in your own Defence.

The two *English* Men yielded to this very awkwardly, and with great reluctance, but the *Spaniards* protested, they did it only to keep them from Blood-shed, and to make all easy at last; for said they, We are not so many of us, here is room enough for us all, and it is great Pity we should not be all good Friends; at length they did consent and waited for the Issue of the thing, living for some Days with the *Spaniards*, for their own Habitation was destroy'd.

In about five Days time the three Vagrants, tyr'd with Wandring, and almost starv'd with Hunger, having chiefly liv'd on Turtles Eggs all that while, came back to the Grove, and finding my *Spaniard*, who, as I have said, was the Governour, and two more with him, walking by the Side of the Creek; they came up in a very submissive humble Manner, and begg'd to be receiv'd again into the Family. The *Spaniards* used them civilly, but told them, they had acted so unnaturally by their Countrymen, and so very grosly by them (the *Spaniards*) that they could not come to any Conclusion without consulting the two *English* Men and the rest; but however, they would go to them and discourse about it, and they should know in half an Hour. It may be guess'd, that they were very hard put to it, for it seems, as they were to wait this half Hour for an Answer, they begg'd they would send them out some Bread in the mean Time, which he did, and sent them at the same

Time a large Piece of Goats Flesh, and a broil'd Parrot, which they eat very heartily, for they were hungry enough.

After half an Hours Consultation they were call'd in, and a long Debate had among them, their two Countrymen charging them with the Ruin of all their Labour, and a Design to murther them; all which they own'd before, and therefore could not deny now; upon the whole, the *Spaniard* acted the Moderator between them, and as they had oblig'd the two *English* Men not to hurt the three while they were naked[1] and unarm'd, so they now oblig'd the three to go and build their Fellows two Huts, one of the same, and the other of larger Dimensions, than they were before; to fence their Ground again where they had pull'd up the Fences, plant Trees in the Room of those pull'd up, dig up the Land again for planting Corn, where they had spoil'd it; and in a Word, to restore every Thing in the same State as they found it, as near as they could, for entirely it could not be, the Season for the Corn, and the Growth of the Trees, and Hedges, not being possible to be recover'd.

Well, they submitted to all this, and as they had Plenty of Provisions given them all the while, they grew very orderly, and the whole Society began to live pleasantly and agreeably together, only that these three Fellows could never be persuaded to work, I mean for themselves, except now and then a little, just as they pleased; however, the *Spaniards* told them plainly, that if they would but live sociably and friendly together, and study in the whole the Good of the Plantation, they would be content to work for them, and let them walk about and be as idle as they pleas'd; and thus having liv'd pretty well together for a Month or two, the *Spaniards* gave them Arms again, and gave them Liberty to go abroad with them as before.

It was not above a Week after they had these Arms and went abroad, but the ungrateful Creatures began to be as Insolent and Troublesome as before; but however, an Accident happening presently upon this, which endanger'd the Safety of them all, they were oblig'd to lay by all private Resentments, and look to the Preservation of their Lives.[2]

---

1 Defenseless.

2 The idea of different groups banding together against external threat was a great theme of Defoe's when writing about the relationship between different groups in Great Britain; he drew on this theme in writing about the problem of political and religious factionalism in England in his newspaper *The Review* (1704–13) and in writing about the problem of Anglo-Scottish enmity in his pro-British *History of the Union* (1709).

It happen'd one Night, that the *Spaniard* Governour, as I call him, that is to say, the *Spaniard*, whose Life I had sav'd, who was now the Captain, or Leader, or Governour of the rest, found himself very uneasy in the Night, and could by no Means get any Sleep; he was perfectly well in Body, as he told me the Story, only found his Thoughts tumultuous, his Mind run upon Men fighting, and killing of one another, but was broad awake, and could not by any Means get any Sleep; in short, he lay a great while, but growing more and more uneasy, he resolv'd to rise: As they lay, being so many of them, upon Goat-skins, laid thick upon such Couches and Pads, as they made for themselves, not in Hammocks and Ship-Beds, as I did, who was but one, so they had little to do, when they were willing to rise, but to get up upon their Feet, and perhaps put on a Coat, such as it was, and their Pumps,* and they were ready for going any Way that their Thoughts guided them.

Being thus gotten up, he look'd out, but being dark, he could see little or nothing, and besides the Trees which I had planted, as in my former Account is described, and which were now grown tall intercepted his Sight, so that he could only look up, and see that it was a clear Star-light Night, and hearing no Noise, he return'd and laid him down again; but it was all one, he could not sleep, nor could he compose himself to any Thing like Rest, but his Thoughts were to the last Degree uneasy, and yet he knew not for what.

Having made some Noise with rising and walking about, going out and coming in, another of them wak'd, and calling, ask'd, who it was that was up? The Governour told him, how it had been with him. Say you so, says the other *Spaniard*, such Things are not to be slighted, I assure; there is certainly some Mischief working, says he, near us, and presently he asked him where are the *English* Men? They are all in their Huts, says he, safe enough. It seems, the *Spaniards* had kept Possession of the main Appartment, and had made a Place where the three *English* Men, since their last Mutiny always quarter'd[1] by themselves, and could not come at the rest. Well, says the *Spaniard*, there is something in it, I am persuaded from my own Experience; I am satisfy'd our Spirits embodied, have a Converse with, and receive Intelligence from the Spirits unembodied and inhabiting the invisible World,[2] and this friendly

1 Stayed in a group.

2 Similarly, in Part I, Crusoe evinces belief in the idea that a power beyond the human speaks to him through urges and through dreams, manifesting as his own inclinations and as a strange concurrence of

Notice is given for our Advantage, if we know how to make use of it. Come, says he, let us go out and look abroad, and if we find nothing at all in it to justify the Trouble, I'll tell you a Story to the Purpose, that shall convince you of the Justice of my proposing it.

In a word, they went out, to go up to the top of the Hill, where I us'd to go, but they being strong and in good Company, not alone, as I was, us'd none of my Cautions,[1] to go up by the Ladder, and then pulling it up after them, to go up a second Stage to the Top, but were going round thro' the Grove unconcern'd and unwary, when they were surpriz'd with seeing a Light, as of Fire, a very little Way off from them, and hearing the Voices of Men, not of one, or two, but of a great Number.

In all the Discoveries I had made of the Savages landing on the Island, it was my constant Care to prevent them making the least Discovery of there being any Inhabitant upon the Place; and when by any Occasion they came to know it, they felt it so effectually, that they that got away, were scarce able to give any Account of it, for we disappear'd as soon as possible, nor did ever any that had seen me, escape to tell any one else, except it was the three Savages in our last Encounter, who jump'd into the Boat, of whom I mention'd, that I was afraid they should go Home and bring more Help.[2]

Whether it was the Consequence of the Escape of those Men, that so great a Number came now together, or whether they came ignorantly and by Accident on their usual bloody Errand, they could not it seems understand; but whatever it was, it had been their Business, either to have conceal'd themselves, as not to have seen them at all, much less to have let the Savages have seen that there were any Inhabitants in the Place, or to have fallen upon them so effectually, as that not a Man of them should have escap'd, which could only have been by getting in between them and their Boats; but this Presence of Mind was

---

dates attached to important events in his life. The power of the invisible world is an ongoing theme for Defoe, especially in his book-length treatises *Essay on the History and Reality of Apparitions* (1727) and *Serious Reflections* (1720), particularly the long section in the latter entitled "A Vision of the Angelick World," which cites the invisible world's "Power of conversing among us, and particularly with Spirits embodied, and can by Dreams, Impulses and strong Aversions move our Thoughts." See Defoe, *Satire, Fantasy and Writings on the Supernatural* 67–68.

1 Given in Part I.

2 See Part I, where Crusoe says four escaped, but one of them was wounded, perhaps fatally (186–87).

wanting to them, which was the Ruin of their Tranquillity for a great while.

We need not doubt, but that the Governour and the Man with him, surpriz'd with this Sight, run back immediately, and rais'd their Fellows, giving them an Account of the imminent Danger they were all in; and they again as readily took the Alarm, but it was impossible to persuade them to stay close within where they were, but that they must run all out to see how things stood.

While it was dark indeed, they were well enough, and they had Opportunity enough for some Hours to view them by the Light of three Fires they had made at a Distance from one another; what they were doing they knew not, and what to do themselves they knew not. For, first, the Enemy were too many; and secondly, they did not keep together, but were divided into several Parties, and were on Shore in several Places.

The *Spaniards* were in no small Consternation at this Sight, and as they found that the Fellows ran straggling all over the Shore, they made no Doubt, but first or last, some of them would chop in upon[1] their Habitation, or upon some other Place, where they would see the Token of Inhabitants, and they were in great perplexity also for fear of their Flock of Goats, which would have been little less than starving them, if they should have been destroy'd; so the first Thing they resolv'd upon, was to dispatch three Men away before it was Light, *viz.* two *Spaniards* and one *English* Man to drive all the Goats away to the great Valley where the Cave was, and if Need were, to drive them into the very Cave it self.[2]

Could they have seen the Savages all together in one Body, and at any Distance from their Canoes, they resolv'd, if they had been an Hundred of them, to have attack'd them; but that could not be obtain'd, for they were some of them two Miles off from the other, and, as it appear'd afterwards, were of two different Nations.

And after having mused a great while on the Course they should take, and beaten their Brains in considering their present Circumstances, they resolv'd at last, while it was dark, to send the old Savage, *Friday*'s Father, out as a Spy, to learn, if possible, something concerning them, what they came for, and what they intended to do; the old Man readily undertook it, and stripping

1 Stumble upon.

2 Not Crusoe's old habitation, but the cave in Part I inside which Crusoe confronts his fears, buries an old, dying he-goat, and shelters the naked Friday after the latter's salvation.

himself quite Naked, as most of the Savages were, away he went: after he had been gone an Hour or two, he brings Word, that he had been among them undiscover'd, that he found they were two Parties, and of two several Nations who had War with one another, and had had a great Battle in their own Country, and that both Sides having had several Prisoners taken in the Fight, they were by meer Chance landed all in the same Island; for the devouring their Prisoners[1] and making Merry; but their coming so by Chance to the same Place had spoil'd all their Mirth; that they were in a great Rage at one another, and that they were so near, that he believ'd they would fight again, as soon as Day-light began to appear, but he did not perceive that they had any Notion of any Body's being on the Island but themselves. He had hardly made an End of telling his Story, when they could perceive, by the unusual Noise they made, that the two little Armies were engag'd in a bloody Fight.

Friday's Father used all the Arguments he could to persuade our People to lie close, and not be seen; he told them their Safety consisted in it, and that they had nothing to do but lie still, and the Savages would kill one another to their Hands,[2] and then the rest would go away; and it was so to a tittle. But it was impossible to prevail, especially upon the *English* Men, their Curiosity was so importunate upon their Prudentials, that they must run out and see the Battle: However, they used some Caution too, (*viz.*) they did not go openly, just by their own Dwelling, but went farther into the Woods, and plac'd themselves to Advantage, where they might securely see them manage the Fight, and as they thought, not to be seen by them, but it seems the Savages did see them, as we shall find hereafter.

The Battle was very fierce, and if I might believe the *English* Men, one of them said, he could perceive, that some of them were Men of great Bravery, of invincible Spirits, and of great Policy in guiding the Fight. The Battle, they said, held two Hours, before they could guess which Party would be beaten; but then that Party which was nearest our Peoples Habitation, began to appear weakest, and after some Time more, some of them began to fly; and

1 In Part 1, the natives who arrive on Crusoe's island are cannibals. The modern word *cannibal* derives from the Spanish word for West Indies native (*Caribale* or *Canibale*); whether the Caribs actually practiced cannibalism is unknown, but the conflation of terms by early-modern writers enabled imperial powers to justify their conquest of native peoples.

2 Easily, without the Spaniards and Englishmen having to do anything.

this put our Men again into a great Consternation, least any of those that fled should run into the Grove before their Dwelling for shelter, and thereby involuntarily discover the Place; and that by Consequence the Pursuers should do the like in search for them. Upon this they resolv'd that they would stand Arm'd within the Wall, and whoever came into the Grove, they should sally out over the Wall and kill them; so that if possible, not one should return to give an Account of it; they order'd also, that it should be done with their Swords, or by knocking them down with the Stock of the Musket, but not by shooting them, for fear of the Noise.

As they expected, it fell out; three of the routed Army fled for Life, and, crossing the Creek, ran directly into the Place, not in the least knowing whether they went, but running as into a thick Wood for Shelter; the Scout they kept to look abroad, gave Notice of this within, with this Addition, to our Mens great Satisfaction (*viz.*) That the Conquerors had not pursued them, or seen which Way they were gone; upon this, the *Spaniard* Governour, a Man of Humanity, would not suffer them to kill the three Fugitives, but sending three Men out by the Top of the Hill, order'd them to go round and come in behind them, surprize and take them Prisoners, which was done; the Residue of the conquer'd People fled to their Canoes and got off to Sea; the Victors retir'd, made no Pursuit or very little, but drawing themselves into a Body together, gave two great skreaming Shouts, which they suppos'd was by way of Triumph, and so the Fight ended: And the same Day, about three a Clock in the Afternoon, they also march'd to their Canoes, and thus the *Spaniards* had their Island again free to themselves, their Fright was over, and they saw no Savages in several Years after.

After they were all gone, the *Spaniards* came out of their Den, and viewing the Field of Battle, they found about two and thirty dead Men upon the Spot; some were kill'd with great long Arrows, some of which were found sticking in their Bodies; but most of them were kill'd with their great Wooden Swords, sixteen or seventeen of which they found in the Field of Battle; and as many Bows, with a great many Arrows: These Swords were strange great unweildy Things, and they must be very strong Men that us'd them: Most of those Men that were kill'd with them, had their Heads mash'd to pieces, as we may say, or as we call it in *English*, their Brains knock'd out, and several their Arms and Legs broken; so that it's evident they fight with inexpressible Rage and Fury. We found not one wounded Man that was not stone dead; for either they stay by their Enemy till they have quite kill'd him, or they carry all the wounded Men, that are not quite dead, away with them.

This Deliverance tam'd our *English* Men for a great while; the Sight had fill'd them with Horror, and the Consequences appear'd terrible to the last Degree, even to them, if ever they should fall into the Hands of those Creatures, who would not only kill them as Enemies, but kill them for Food, as we kill our Cattle. And they profess'd to me, that the Thoughts of being eaten up like Beef or Mutton, tho' it was suppos'd it was not to be till they were dead, had something in it so horrible, that it nauseated their very Stomachs, made them sick when they thought of it, and fill'd their Minds with such unusual Terror, that they were not themselves for some Weeks after.[1]

This, as I said, tam'd even the three *English* Brutes I have been speaking of; and for a great while after they were very tractable, and went about the common Business of their whole Society well enough; planted, sow'd, reap'd, and begun to be all naturalliz'd to the Country. But some time after this, they fell all into such Measures, which brought them into a great deal of Trouble.

They had taken three Prisoners, as I had observ'd, and these three being lusty* stout young Fellows, they made them Servants, and taught them to work for them; and as Slaves they did well enough; but they did not take their Measures with them as I did by my Man *Friday*, (*viz.*) to begin with them upon the Principle of having sav'd their Lives, and then instruct them in the rational Principles of Life, much less of Religion, civilizing and reducing them by kind Usage and affectionate Arguings;[2] but as they gave them their Food every Day, so they gave them their Work too, and

---

1 In Part I, the theme of being devoured looms large, characteristic of Crusoe's eat-or-be-eaten approach to the world, both literally and culturally. Dozens of times, Crusoe refers explicitly to his fear of being eaten, swallowed, consumed, or devoured (the latter term arises some three dozen times on its own), whether by animals, other people, the ocean, the earth, or his own fear. In the *History of the Union* and other propaganda writing, Defoe expanded the theme of being cannibalistically devoured at a symbolic political level, in discussing both the English and Scottish fears of being consumed by one another in a national Union.

2 Crusoe's sentiments here chime with Defoe's own recommendations for a peaceful national Anglo-Scottish Union. In his *History of the Union*, Defoe wrote that previous attempts at Union had been "force[d]" by the English upon the Scots and that a new strategy was crucial, i.e., a "voluntary" Union not brought about by "Tricking, and Sharping" (7:140).

kept them fully employ'd in Drudgery enough; but they fail'd in this, by it, that they never had them to assist them and fight for them, as I had my Man *Friday*, who was as true to me as the very Flesh upon my Bones.

But to come to the Family Part, being all now good Friends, for common Danger, as I said above, had effectually reconcil'd them, they began to consider their general Circumstances; and the first Thing that came under their Consideration was, Whether, seeing the Savages particularly haunted that Side of the Island, and that there were more remote and retir'd Parts of it equally adapted to their Way of Living, and manifestly to their Advantage, they should not rather remove their Habitation, and plant in some more proper Place for their Security, and especially for the Security of their Cattle and Corn?

Upon this, after long Debate, it was concluded, That they would not remove their Habitation; because, that some Time or other, they thought they might hear from their Governour again, meaning me; and if I should send any one to seek them, I should be sure to direct them to that Side, where, if they should find the Place demolish'd, they would conclude the Savages had kill'd us all, and we were gone, and so our Supply[1] would go too.

But as to their Corn and Cattle, they agreed to remove them into the Valley where my Cave was, where the Land was as proper for both, and where indeed there was Land enough: However, upon second Thought, they alter'd one Part of that Resolution too, and resolv'd only to remove Part of their Cattle thither, and plant Part of their Corn there; and so if one Part was destroy'd, the other might be sav'd: And one Part of Prudence they used, which it was very well they did, *viz.* That they never trusted those three Savages, which they had Prisoners, with knowing any Thing of the Plantation they had made in that Valley, or of any Cattle they had there; much less of the Cave there, which they kept in Case of Necessity, as a safe Retreat, and whither they carry'd also the two Barrels of Powder, which I had sent them at my coming away.

But however, they resolv'd not to change their Habitation, yet they agreed, that as I had carefully cover'd it first with a Wall or Fortification, and then with a Grove of Trees; so seeing their Safety consisted entirely in their being conceal'd, of which they were now fully convinc'd, they set to Work to cover and conceal the Place yet more effectually than before; to this Purpose, as I

1 Relief, deliverance.

had planted Trees, or rather thrust in Stakes, which in Time all grew up to be Trees for some good Distance before the Entrance into my Apartment; they went on in the same Manner, and fill'd up the rest of that whole Space of Ground from the Trees I had set, quite down to the Side of the Creek, where, as I said, I landed my Floats,[1] and even into the very Ouze where the Tide flow'd, not so much as leaving any Place to land, or any Sign that there had been any Landing thereabout; these Stakes also, being of a Wood very forward to grow, as I have noted formerly, they took Care to have generally very much larger and taller than those which I had planted; and as they grew apace, so they planted them so very thick and close together, that when they had been three or four Years grown, there was no piercing with the Eye any considerable Way into the Plantation: And as for that Part which I had planted, the Trees were grown as thick as a Man's Thigh; and among them they placed so many other short ones, and so thick, that, in a Word, it stood like a Pallisado,* a quarter of a Mile thick, and it was next to impossible to penetrate it, but with a little Army to cut it all down; for a little Dog could hardly get between the Trees, they stood so close.

But this was not all; for they did the same by all the Ground to the Right-hand, and to the Left, and round even to the Top of the Hill, leaving no Way, not so much as for themselves to come out, but by the Ladder placed up to the Side of the Hill, and then lifted up and placed again from the first Stage up to the Top; which Ladder when it was taken down nothing but what had Wings or Witchcraft to assist it, could come at them.

This was excellently well contriv'd; nor was it less than what they afterwards found Occasion for, which serv'd to convince me, that as human Prudence has the Authority of Providence to justify it, so it has doubtless the Direction of Providence to set it to Work; and would we listen carefully to the Voice of it, I am fully persuaded we might prevent many of the Disasters which our Lives are now, by our own Negligence, subjected to: But this by the Way.

I return to the Story. They liv'd two Years after this in perfect Retirement, and had no more Visits from the Savages: They had, indeed, an Alarm given them one Morning, which put them into a great Consternation; for some of the *Spaniards* being out early one Morning on the West Side, or rather the End of the Island, which by the Way was that End where I never went, for Fear of

---

1 The rafts Crusoe built during his twenty-eight years on the island.

being discover'd, they were surpriz'd with seeing above twenty Canoes of *Indians* just coming on Shore.

They made the best of their Way Home in Hurry enough, and giving the Alarm to their Comrades, they kept close all that Day; and the next, going out only at Night to make Observation: But they had the good Luck to be mistaken; for where-ever the Savages went, they did not land that Time on the Island, but pursued some other Design.

And now they had another Broil with the three *English* Men; one of which, a most turbulent Fellow, being in a Rage at one of the three Slaves, which I mention'd they had taken, because the Fellow had not done some Thing right which he bid him do, and seem'd a little untractable in his showing him, drew a Hatchet out of a Frog-Belt[1] in which he wore it by his Side, and fell upon the poor Savage, not to correct him, but to kill him. One of the *Spaniards*, who was by, seeing him give the Fellow a barbarous Cut with the Hatchet, which he aim'd at his Head, but struck into his Shoulder; so that he thought he had cut the poor Creature's Arm off, run to him, and entreating him not to murther the poor Man, clapt in between him and the Savage, to prevent the Mischief.

The Fellow being enrag'd the more at this, struck at the *Spaniard* with his Hatchet, and swore he would serve him as he intended to serve the Savage; which the *Spaniard* perceiving, avoided the Blow; and with a Shovel which he had in his Hand, for they were all working in the Field about their Corn-Land, knock'd the Brute down: Another of the *English* Men running at the same Time to help his Comrade, knock'd the *Spaniard* down; and then two *Spaniards* more came in to help their Man, and a third *English* Man fell in upon them: They had none of them any Fire Arms, or any other Weapons but Hatchets and other Tools, except this third *English* Man, he had one of my old rusty Cutlashes,* with which he made at the two last *Spaniards*, and wounded them both: This Fray set the whole Family in an Uproar, and more Help coming in, they took the three *English* Men Prisoners. The next Question was, What should be done with them, they had been so often mutinous, and were so furious, so desperate, and so idle withal, that they knew not what Course to take with them; for they were mischievous to the highest Degree, and valued not what Hurt they did to any Man; so that, in short, it was not safe to live with them.

---

1 An attachment to a belt, for carrying a sword, hatchet, or bayonet.

The *Spaniard*, who was Governour, told them in so many Words, That if they had been of his own Country, he would have hang'd them; for all Laws and all Governours was to preserve Society; and those who were dangerous to the Society, ought to be expell'd out of it; but as they were *English* Men, and that it was to the generous Kindness of an *English* Man that they all ow'd their Preservation and Deliverance, he would use them with all possible Lenity,[1] and would leave them to the Judgment of the other two *English* Men, who were their Countrymen.

One of the two honest *English* Men stood up, and said, they desir'd it might not be left to them; for, says he, I am sure we ought to sentence them to the Gallows; and with that gives an Account how *Will. Atkins*, one of the three, had proposed to have all the five *English* Men join together, and murther all the *Spaniards* when they were in their Sleep.

When the *Spanish* Governour heard this, he calls to *William Atkins*, How Seignior *Atkins*, says he, would you murther us all? What have you to say to that? That hardened Villain was so far from denying it, that he said it was true, and G—d d—m him they would do it still before they had done with them. Well, but Seignior *Atkins*, says the *Spaniard*, What have we done to you, that you will kill us? And what would you get by killing us? And what must we do to prevent you killing us? Must we kill you, or you will kill us? Why will you put us to the Necessity of this, Seignior *Atkins*, says the *Spaniard* very calmly and smiling.

Seignior *Atkins* was in such a Rage at the *Spaniard*'s making a Jest of it, that had he not been held by three Men, and withal had no Weapons near him, it was thought he would have attempted to have kill'd the *Spaniard* in the Middle of all the Company.

This hair-brain'd[2] Carriage[3] oblig'd them to consider seriously what was to be done; the two *English* Men and the *Spaniard* who sav'd the poor *Savage* was of the Opinion, they should hang one of the three for an Example to the rest, and that particularly, it should be he that had twice attempted to commit Murther with his Hatchet, and indeed there was some Reason to believe he had done it, for the poor *Savage* was in such a miserable Condition, with the Wound he had receiv'd, that it was thought he could not live.

But the Governor *Spaniard* still said No, it was an *English* Man that had sav'd all their Lives, and he would never consent to put

---

1 Lenience.

2 Variant of hare-brained.

3 Conveyance.

an *English* Man to Death, tho' he had murther'd half of them, nay, he said, if he had been kill'd himself by an *English* Man, and had Time left to speak, it should be, that they should pardon him.

This was so positively insisted on by the Governor *Spaniard*, that there was no gain-saying it; and as merciful Councils are most apt to prevail where they are so earnestly press'd, so they all came into it; but then it was to be consider'd, what should be done to keep them from doing the Mischief they design'd; for all agreed, Governor and all, that Means were to be used for preserving the Society from Danger; after a long Debate it was agreed, First, That they should be disarm'd, and not permitted to have either Gun, or Powder, or Shot, or Sword, or any Weapon, and should be turn'd out of the Society, and left to live where they would, and how they would, by themselves; but that none of the rest, either *Spaniards* or *English* should converse with them, speak with them or have any thing to do with them; that they should be forbid to come within a certain Distance of the Place where the rest dwelt; and that if they offer'd to commit any Disorder, so as to spoil, burn, kill, or destroy any of the Corn, Plantings, Buildings, Fences, or Cattle belonging to the Society, they should dye without Mercy, and they would shoot them wherever they could find them.

The Governor, a Man of great Humanity, musing upon the Sentence, consider'd a little upon it, and turning to the two honest *English* Men said, Hold, you must reflect, that it will be long e'er they can raise Corn and Cattle of their own, and they must not starve: We must therefore allow them Provisions, so he caused to be added, That they should have a Proportion of Corn given them to last them eight Months, and for Seed to sow, by which Time they might be suppos'd to raise some of their own; that they should have six Milch Goats, four He-Goats, and six Kids given them, as well for present Subsistence, as for a Store; and that they should have Tools given them for their Work in the Fields; such as, six Hatchets, an Axe, a Saw, and the like: But they should have none of these Tools, or Provisions, unless they would swear solemnly, that they would not hurt or injure any of the *Spaniards* with them, or of their Fellow *English* Men.

Thus they dismiss'd them the Society, and turn'd them out to shift for themselves. They went away sullen and refractory, as neither contented to go away, or to stay; but, as there was no Remedy, they went, pretending, to go and choose a Place where they would settle themselves to plant and live by themselves, and some Provision were given them, but no Weapons.

About four or five Days after, they came again for some Victuals, and gave the Governor an Account where they had pitch'd their Tents, and mark'd themselves out an Habitation and Plantation; and it was a very convenient Place indeed, on the remotest Part of the Island, N.E. much about the Place where I landed in my first Voyage, when I was driven out to Sea, the Lord knows whether, in my Attempt to surround the Island.

Here they built themselves two handsome Huts, and contriv'd them, in a Manner, like my first Habitation, being close under the Side of a Hill, having some Trees growing already on three Sides of it, so that by planting others it would be very easily cover'd from the Sight, unless narrowly search'd for; they desir'd some dry'd Goats-Skins for Beds and Covering, which were given them, and upon giving their Words, that they would not disturb the rest, or injure any of their Plantations, they gave them Hatchets, and what other Tools they could spare; some Peas, Barley, and Rice, for sowing; and in a Word, any thing they wanted, but Arms and Ammunition.

They liv'd in this separate Condition about six Months, and had gotten in their first Harvest, tho' the Quantity was but small, the Parcel of Land they had planted being but little; for indeed, having all their Plantation to form, they had a great deal of Work upon their Hands; and when they came to make Boards and Pots, and such Things, they were quite out of their Element, and could make nothing of it; and when the rainy Season came on, for want of a Cave in the Earth, they could not keep their Grain dry, and it was in great Danger of spoiling; And this humbled them much; so they came and begg'd the *Spaniards* to help them, which they very readily did, and in four Days work'd a great Hole in the Side of the Hill for them, big enough to secure their Corn, and other Things from the Rain, but it was but a poor Place, at best, compar'd to mine; and especially as mine was then, for the *Spaniards* had greatly enlarg'd it, and made several new Apartments in it.

About three quarters of a Year after this Separation, a new Frolick took these Rogues, which, together with the former Villany they had committed, brought Mischief enough upon them, and had very near been the Ruin of the whole Colony: The three new Sociates[1] began it seems to be weary of the laborious Life they led, and that without Hope of bettering their Circumstances; and a Whim took them, that they would make a Voyage to the Continent from whence the Savages came, and would try if they could not

1 Associates.

seize upon some Prisoners among the Natives there, and bring them Home, so to make them do the laborious Part of their Work for them.

The Project was not so preposterous, if they had gone no further; but they did nothing, and proposed nothing, but had either Mischief in the Design, or Mischief in the Event: And if I may give my Opinion, they seem'd to be under a Blast from Heaven; for if we will not allow a visible Curse to pursue visible Crimes, how shall we reconcile the Events of Things, with the Divine Justice?[1] It was certainly an apparent Vengeance on their Crime of Mutiny and Piracy, that brought them to the State they were in; and as they shew'd not the least Remorse for the Crime, but added new Villanies to it, such as, particularly, the Piece of monstrous Cruelty, of wounding a poor Slave, because he did not, or perhaps could not, understand to do what he was directed; and to wound him in such a Manner, as, no Question, made him a Cripple all his Life; and in a Place where no Surgeon or Medicine could be had for his Cure; and what was still worse, the murtherous Intent, or to do Justice to the Crime, the intentional Murther, for such, to be sure it was, as was afterwards the form'd Design they all laid, to murther the *Spaniards* in cold Blood, and in their Sleep.

But I leave observing, and return to the Story: The three Fellows comes down to the *Spaniards* one Morning and in very humble Terms desir'd to be admitted to speak with them: The *Spaniards* very readily heard what they had to say, which was this, That they were tir'd of living in the Manner they did; that they were not handy enough to make the Necessaries they wanted; and that having no Help, they found they should be starv'd: But if the *Spaniards* would give them Leave to take one of the Canoes which they came over in, and give them Arms and Ammunition, proportion'd for their Defence, they would go over to the Main, and seek their Fortune, and so deliver them from the Trouble of supplying them with any other Provisions.

The *Spaniards* were glad enough to be rid of them, but yet very honestly represented to them the certain Destruction they were running into; told them they had suffer'd such Hardships upon that very Spot, that they could without any Spirit of Prophesy tell

1 Crusoe depicts "visible Crimes," or the "Events of Things," as second causes. On the recurrent theme of the invisible world and on second causes, see *Essay on the History and Reality of Apparitions* (1727) and *Serious Reflections* (1720).

them, that they would be starv'd, or be murther'd, and bad them consider of it.

The Men reply'd audaciously, they should be starv'd if they stay'd here, for they could not work, and would not work; and they could but be starv'd abroad, and if they were murther'd, there was an End of them, they had no Wives or Children to cry after them; and in short, insisted importunately upon their Demand, declaring, that they would go, whether they would give them any Arms or no.

The *Spaniards* told them, with great Kindness, that if they were resolv'd to go, they should not go like naked[1] Men, and be in no Condition to defend themselves; and that tho' they could ill spare their Fire-Arms, having not enough for themselves, yet they would let them have two Muskets, a Pistol, and a Cutlash, and each Man a Hatchet, which they thought was sufficient for them.

In a word, they accepted the Offer, and having baked them Bread enough to serve them a Month, and given them as much Goats Flesh as they could Eat while it was sweet,[2] and a great Basket full of dry'd Grapes, a Pot full of fresh Water, and a young Kid alive to kill, they boldly set out in a Canoe for a Voyage over the Sea, where it was at least 40 Miles[3] broad.

The Boat was indeed a large one, and would have very well carry'd fifteen or twenty Men; and therefore, was rather too big for them to manage: But as they had a fair Breeze, and the Flood-Tide with them, they did well enough: They had made a Mast of a long Pole, and a Sail of four large Goat Skins dry'd, which they had sow'd or lac'd together, and away they went merrily enough; the *Spaniards* call'd after them, *Bon Veyajo*;[4] and no Man ever thought of seeing them any more.

The *Spaniards* were often saying to one another, and to the two honest *English* Men, who remain'd behind, how quietly and comfortably they liv'd now those three turbulent Fellows were gone; as for their ever coming again, that was the remotest thing from their Thoughts that could be imagin'd; when behold, after two and twenty Days Absence, one of the *English* Men being abroad upon his Planting-Work, sees three strange Men coming towards him at a Distance, with Guns upon their Shoulders.

1 Here, unarmed.

2 I.e., not soured by rot.

3 Each nautical mile is one minute of latitude, or 1.1508 statute (land) miles.

4 *Bien viaje*, in modern Spanish, equivalent to the French *bon voyage*.

Away run the *English* Man, as if he was bewitch'd, comes frighted and amaz'd* to the Governour *Spaniard*, and tells him they were all undone, for there were Strangers landed upon the Island, he could not tell who: The *Spaniard*, pausing a while, says to him, How do you mean, you cannot tell who? They are the Savages to be sure. No, no, says the *English* Man, they are Men in Cloaths with Arms: Nay, then, says the *Spaniard*, Why are you concern'd? If they are not Savages, they must be Friends, for there is no Christian Nation upon Earth but will do us good rather than harm.

While they were debating thus, comes the three *English* Men, and standing without* the Wood, which was new planted, hallo'd to them: They presently knew their Voices, and so all the Wonder of that kind ceased. But now the Admiration[1] was turn'd upon another Question, (*viz.*) what could be the matter, and what made them come back again?

It was not long before they brought the Men in, and enquiring where they had been, and what they had been doing; they gave them a full Account of their Voyage in a few Words, (*viz.*) That they reach'd the Land in two Days, or something less, but finding the People alarmed at their coming and preparing with Bows and Arrows to fight them, they durst not go on Shore, but sail'd on to the Northward six or seven Hours, till they came to a great Opening, by which they perceiv'd, that the Land they saw from our Island was not the Main, but an Island; that entering that opening of the Sea, they saw another Island on the Right-Hand North, and several more West, and being resolv'd to land somewhere, they put over to one of the Islands which lay West, and went boldly on Shore; that they found the People very courteous and friendly to them, and that they gave them several Roots and some dried Fish, and appear'd very sociable; and the Women, as well as the Men, were very forward to supply them with any thing they could get for them to eat, and brought it to them a great way upon their Heads.

They continued here four Days, and enquir'd, as well as they could of them by Signs, what Nations were this way and that way; and were told of several fierce and terrible People that lived almost every way, who, as they made Signs to them, us'd to eat Men. But as for themselves they said, that they never eat Men or Women, except only such as they took in the Wars, and then they own'd that they made a great Feast, and eat their Prisoners.

1 Attention.

The *English* Men enquir'd when they had a Feast of that kind, and they told him about two Moons ago,[1] pointing to the Moon, and then to two Fingers; and that their great King had two hundred Prisoners now, which he had taken in his War; and they were feeding them to make them fat for the next Feast. The *English* Men seem'd mighty desirous to see those Prisoners, but the other mistaking them, thought they were desirous to have some of them to carry away for their own eating. So they beckoned to them, pointing to the setting of the Sun, and then to the rising, which was to signify, that the next Morning at Sun rising they would bring some for them; and accordingly the next Morning they brought down five Women and eleven Men, and gave them to the *English* Men, to carry with them on their Voyage, just as we would bring so many Cows and Oxen down to a Sea-Port Town, to victual a Ship.

As brutish and barbarous as these Fellows were at Home, their Stomachs turn'd at this Sight, and they did not know what to do; to refuse the Prisoners, would have been the highest Affront to the Savage Gentry that offer'd them; and what to do with them they knew not; however upon some Debates they resolv'd to accept of them, and in Return they gave the Savages that brought them one of their Hatchets, an old Key, a Knife, and six or seven of their Bullets, which, tho' they did not understand, they seem'd extremely pleas'd with: And then tying the poor Creatures Hands behind them, they (the People) dragg'd the poor Prisoners into the Boat for our Men.

The *English* Men were oblig'd to come away as soon as they had them, or else they that gave them this noble Present, would certainly have expected that they should have gone to work with them, have kill'd two or three of them the next Morning, and perhaps have invited the Donors to Dinner.

But having taken their Leave with all the Respects and Thanks that could well pass between People, where on either Side they understood not one Word they could say, they put off with their Boat and came back towards the first Island, where, when they arrived, they set eight of their Prisoners at Liberty, there being too many of them for their Occasion.

In their Voyage they endeavoured to have some Communication with their Prisoners, but it was impossible to make them understand any thing; nothing they could say to them, or give them, or do for them, but was look'd upon as going about to murder them.

1 Two months ago.

They first of all unbound them, but the poor Creatures skream'd at that, especially the Women, as if they had just felt the Knife at their Throats; for they immediately concluded they were unbound on purpose to be kill'd.

If they gave them any thing to eat, it was the same thing; then they concluded it was for fear they should sink in Flesh, and so not be fat enough to kill. If they look'd at one of them more particularly, the Party presently concluded, it was to see whether he or she was fattest and fittest to kill. Nay, after they had brought them quite over, and began to use them kindly, and treat them well, still they expected every Day to make a Dinner or a Supper for their new Masters.

When the three Wanderers had given this unaccountable History, or Journal of their Voyage, the *Spaniard* ask'd them, Where their new Family was, and being told that they had brought them on Shore, and put them into one of their Huts, and were come up to beg some Victuals for them; they, (the *Spaniards*) and the other two *English* Men, that is to say, the whole Colony, resolv'd to go all down to the Place and see them, and did so, and *Friday*'s Father with them.

When they came into the Hut, *there they sat* all bound; for when they had brought them on Shore, they bound their Hands that they might not take the Boat and make their Escape. There, I say, they sat, all of them stark naked. *First*, there were three Men, lusty comely* Fellows, well shap'd, strait and fair Limbs, about thirty to thirty five Years of Age; and five Women, whereof two might be from thirty to forty, two more not above four or five and twenty, and the fifth, a tall comely Maiden about sixteen or seventeen: The Women were well favour'd agreeable Persons,[1] both in Shape and Features, only tawny,[2] and two of them, had they been perfect white, would have pass'd for very handsome Women even in *London* it self, having pleasant agreeable Countenances, and of a very modest Behaviour, especially when they came afterwards to be cloathed, and dress'd, as they call'd it, tho' the Dress was very indifferent it must be confess'd; of which hereafter.

The Sight, you may be sure, was something uncouth[3] to our *Spaniards*; who were (to give them a just[4] Character) Men of the best Behaviour, of the most calm, sedate Tempers, and per-

---

1 Good-looking.

2 Not Caucasian.

3 Shockingly strange.

4 Fair, accurate.

fect good Humour that ever I met with, and in particular, of the most Modesty, as will presently appear; I say, the Sight was very uncouth, to see two naked Men, and five naked Women, all together bound, and in the most miserable Circumstances that human Nature could be suppos'd to be, (*viz.*) to be expecting every Moment to be dragg'd out, and have their Brains knock'd out, and then to be eaten up like a Calf that is kill'd for a Dainty.*

The first Thing they did, was to cause the old *Indian*, *Friday*'s Father, to go in and see first if he knew any of them, and then if he understood any of their Speech: As soon as the old Man came in, he look'd seriously at them, but knew none of them; neither could any of them understand a Word he said, or a Sign he could make, except one of the Women.

However, this was enough to answer the End, which was to satisfy them, that the Men into whose Hands they were fallen, were Christians; that they abhor'd eating of Men or Women, and that they might be sure they would not be kill'd: As soon as they were assur'd of this, they discover'd such a Joy, and by such aukward, and several Ways, as is hard to describe; for it seems they were of several Nations.

The Woman, who was their Interpreter, was bid in the next Place to ask them, if they were willing to be Servants, and to work for the Men who had brought them away, to save their Lives; at which they all fell a Dancing; and presently one fell to taking up this, and another that, any Thing that lay next, to carry on their Shoulders, to intimate that they were willing to work.

The Governour, who found, that the having Women among them would presently be attended with some Inconvenience, and might occasion some Strife, and perhaps Blood; ask'd the three Men, what they intended to do with these Women, and how they intended to use them; whether as Servants, or as Women? One of the *English* Men answer'd very boldly and readily, That they would use them as both: To which the Governour said, I am not going to restrain you from it, you are your own Masters as to that: But this I think is but just, for avoiding Disorders and Quarrels among you, and I desire it of you, for that Reason only, *viz.* That you will all engage, that if any of you take any of these Women, as a Woman or Wife, that he shall take but one; and that having taken one, none else should touch her; for tho' we cannot marry any of you, yet 'tis but reasonable, that while you stay here, the Woman any of you takes, should be maintain'd by the Man that takes her, and should be his Wife, I mean, says he, while he continues here, and that none else shall have any Thing to do with her: All this appear'd so just, that every one agreed to it without any Difficulty.

Then the *English* Men ask'd the *Spaniards*, if they design'd to take any of them? But every one of them answer'd, NO: Some of them said, they had Wives in *Spain*, and the others did not like Women that were not Christians; and all together declar'd, that they would not touch one of them; which was an Instance of such Virtue, as I have not met with in all my Travels. On the other hand, to be short, the five *English* Men took them every one a Wife, that is to say, a temporary Wife;[1] and so they set up a new Form of Living; for the *Spaniards* and *Friday*'s Father liv'd in my old Habitation, which they had enlarg'd exceedingly within. The three Servants which were taken in the late Battle of the Savages, liv'd with them; and these carry'd on the main Part of the Colony, supplying all the rest with Food, and assisting them in any Thing as they could, or as they found Necessity requir'd.

But the Wonder of this Story was, how five such refractory ill match'd Fellows should agree about these Women, and that two of them should not pitch upon the same Woman, especially seeing two or three of them were without Comparison, more agreeable than the other: But they took a good Way enough to prevent quarrelling among themselves; for they set the five Women by themselves in one of their Huts, and they went all into the other Hut, and drew Lots among them, who should chuse first.

He that drew to chuse first, went away by himself to the Hutt where the poor naked Creatures were, and fetch'd out her he chose; and it was worth observing, that he that chose first took her that was reckon'd the homeliest, and the oldest of the five, which made Mirth enough among the rest; and even the *Spaniards* laught at it: But the Fellow consider'd better than any of them, that it was Application and Business that they were to expect Assistance in, as much as any Thing else; and she prov'd the best Wife of all the Parcel.

When the poor Women saw themselves set in a Row thus, and fetch'd out one by one, the Terrors of their Condition return'd upon them again, and they firmly believ'd that they were now a going to be devour'd; accordingly, when the *English* Sailor came in and fetch'd out one of them; the rest set up a most lamentable Cry, and hung about her, and took their Leave of her with such Agonies and such Affection, as would have griev'd the hardest

1 As wives for their time on the island, which they do not expect to be permanent.

Heart in the World; nor was it possible for the *English* Men to satisfy them, that were not to be immediately murther'd, 'till they fetch'd the old Man, *Friday*'s Father, who immediately let them know that the five Men, who had fetch'd them out one by one, had chosen them for their Wives.

When they had done, and the Fright the Women were in was a little over, the Men went to Work, and the *Spaniards* came and helped them; and in a few Hours they had built them every one a new Hut or Tent for their Lodging apart; for those they had already, were crowded with their Tools, Houshold-Stuff, and Provision. The 3 wicked ones had pitch'd farthest off, and the two honest ones nearer, but both on the North Shore of the Island, so that they continu'd separated as before; And thus my Island was peopled in three Places; and as I might say, three Towns were begun to be planted.

And here 'tis very well worth observing, That as it often happens in the World (what the wise Ends of God's Providence are in such a Disposition of Things, I cannot say;) the two honest Fellows had the 2 worst Wives, and the 3 Reprobates, that were scarce worth hanging, that were fit for nothing, and neither seem'd born to do themselves good, or any one else, had three clever, diligent, careful, and ingenious Wives; not that the two first were ill[1] Wives, as to their Temper or Humour; for all the five were most willing, quiet, passive, and subjected Creatures, rather like Slaves than Wives: But my Meaning is, they were not alike capable, ingenious, or industrious, or alike cleanly and neat.

Another Observation I must make, to the Honour of a dilligent Application on one Hand, and to the Disgrace of a slothful, negligent, idle Temper, on the other, that when I came to the Place and view'd the several Improvements, Plantings, and Management of the several little Colonies; the two Men had so far out-gone the three, that there was no Comparison. They had indeed both of them as much Ground laid out for Corn, as they wanted, and the Reason was, because, according to my Rule, Nature dictated, that it was to no Purpose to sow more Corn than they wanted, but the Difference of the Cultivation, of the Planting, of the Fences, and indeed of every Thing else was easy to be seen at first View.

The two Men had innumerable young Trees planted about their Huts, that when you came to the Place, nothing was to be seen but a Wood, and tho' they had twice had their Plantation demolish'd, once by their own Countrymen, and once by the

1 Bad.

Enemy, as shall be shewn in its Place; yet they had restor'd all again, and every Thing was thriving and flourishing about them; they had Grapes planted in Order, and manag'd like a Vineyard, tho' they had themselves never seen any Thing of that Kind; and by their good ordering their Vines, their Grapes were as good again, as any of the others. They had also found themselves out a Retreat in the thickest Part of the Woods, where, tho' there was not a natural Cave, as I had found, yet they made one with incessant Labour of their Hands, and where when the Mischief which follow'd happen'd, they secur'd their Wives and Children, so as they could never be found; they having by sticking innumerable Stakes and Poles of the Wood, which, as I said, grew so easily, made the Wood unpassable, except in some Places, where they climb'd up to get over the out-side Part, and then went on by Ways of their own leaving.

As to the three Reprobates, as I justly call them, tho' they were much civiliz'd by their new Settlement, compar'd to what they were before, and were not so quarrelsome, having not the same Opportunity; yet one of the certain Companions of a profligate* Mind never left them, and that was their Idleness; it is true, they planted Corn, and made Fences; but *Solomon*'s Words were never better verified than in them, *I went by the Vineyard of the Slothful, and it was all over-grown with Thorns*;[1] for when the *Spaniards* came to view their Crop, they could not see it in some Places for Weeds; the Hedge had several Gaps in it, where the wild Goats had got in, and eaten up the Corn; perhaps, here and there, a dead Bush was cramm'd in to stop them out for the present, but it was only shutting the Stable-door after the Steed was stolen;[2] whereas, when they look'd on the Colony of the other two, there was the very Face of Industry and Success upon all they did; there was not a Weed to be seen in all their Corn, or a Gap in any of their Hedges; and they on the other Hand verified *Solomon*'s Words in another Place, *That the diligent Hand makes rich*,[3] for every Thing grew and thriv'd, and they had Plenty within and without; they had more tame Cattle then the other,

---

1 Proverbs 24:30–31: "I went by the field of the slothful, and by the vineyard of the man void of understanding; And, lo, it was all grown over with thorns" (King James Version [KJV]).

2 Version of old saying that it is too late to shut the stable door after the horse has been stolen.

3 Proverbs 10:4: "He becometh poor that dealeth with a slack hand: but the hand of the diligent maketh rich" (KJV).

more Utensils and Necessaries within Doors, and yet more Pleasure and Diversion too.

It is true, the Wives of the three were very handy and cleanly within Doors, and having learn'd the *English* Ways of Dressing and Cooking from one of the other *English* Men, who, as I said, was Cook's-mate on board the Ship; they dress'd their Husbands Victuals very nicely and well; whereas the other could not be brought to understand it, but then the Husband, who, as I say, had been Cook's-mate, did it himself; but as for the Husbands of the three Wives, they loyter'd about, fetch'd Turtles Eggs, and caught Fish, and Birds; in a word, any thing but Labour, and they fared accordingly. The Diligent liv'd well and comfortably, and the Slothful liv'd hard and beggarly; and so I believe, generally speaking, it is all over the World.

But I now come to a Scene, different from all that had happen'd before, either to them, or to me; and the Original of the Story was this.

Early one Morning there came on Shore five or six Canoes of *Indians*, or *Savages*, call them which you please; and there is no room to doubt, they came upon the old Errand of feeding upon their Slaves: But that Part was now so familiar to the *Spaniards*, and to our Men too, that they did not concern themselves about it, as I did; but having been made sensible by their Experience, that their only Business was to lie concealed, and that if they were not seen by any of the Savages, they would go off again quietly when their Business was done, having as yet, not the least Notion of there being any Inhabitants in the Island; I say, having been made sensible of this, they had nothing to do but to give Notice to all the three Plantations, to keep within Doors, and not shew themselves, only placing a Scout in a proper Place, to give Notice when the Boats went to Sea again.

This was without doubt very right, but a Disaster spoil'd all these measures, and made it known among the Savages, that they were Inhabitants there, which was in the End the Desolation of almost the whole Colony; after the Canoes with the Savages were gone off, the *Spaniards* peep'd abroad again, and some of them had the Curiosity to go to the Place where they had been, to see what they had been doing: Here to their great Surprize they found three Savages left behind, and lying fast asleep upon the Ground; it was suppos'd, they had either been so gorg'd with their inhuman Feast, that like Beasts they were asleep, and would not stir when the others went, or they were wandred into the Woods, and did not come back in time to be taken in.

The *Spaniards* were greatly surpriz'd at this Sight, and perfectly at a Loss what to do; the *Spaniard* Governour, as it happen'd was with them, and his Advice was ask'd but he profess'd he knew not what to do; as for Slaves, they had enough already, and as to killing them, they were none of them inclin'd to that; the *Spaniard* Governour told me, they could not think of shedding innocent Blood, for as to them, the poor Creatures had done them no Wrong, invaded none of their Property, and they thought they had no just Quarrel against them, to take away their Lives.

And here I must in Justice to these *Spaniards*, observe, that let the Accounts of *Spanish* Cruelty in *Mexico* and *Peru*,[1] be what they will, I never met with seventeen Men of any Nation whatsoever, in any foreign Country, who were so universally Modest, Temperate, Virtuous, so very good Humour'd, and so Courteous as these *Spaniards*; and as to Cruelty, they had nothing of it in their very Nature, no Inhumanity, no Barbarity, no out-rageous* Passions, and yet all of them Men of great Courage and Spirit.

Their Temper and Calmness had appear'd in their bearing the unsufferable Usage of the three *English* Men; and their Justice and Humanity appear'd now in the Case of the Savages, as above; after some Consultation, they resolv'd upon this, that they would lie still a while longer, till if possible, these three Men might be gone; but then the Governour *Spaniard* recollected, that the three Savages had no Boat, and that if they were left to rove about the Island, they would certainly discover that there were Inhabitants in it, and so they should be undone that way.

Upon this, they went back again, and there lay the Fellows fast asleep still, so they resolv'd to waken them, and take them Prisoners, and they did so; the poor Fellows were strangely

---

1 Conquistadors like Hernán Cortés (1485–1547) and Francisco Pizarro (c. 1475–1541) were ruthless in conquering Mexico and Peru, virtually wiping out some Indigenous populations (still others fell to germs), and imperial rivals of Spain for the Americas tended to inflate the reputation of Spanish cruelty, invoking "The Black Legend" to accuse the Spaniards of being more vicious than any other Europeans in their dealings with Indigenous populations in the Americas. Defoe, citing inflated numbers, alludes with seeming sympathy to Spanish atrocities in numerous publications; in the *Review* (28 June 1711) he writes that Spanish "Cruelty" was justified, for "I do not see how *Cortez* could do less than he did," faced with "Mountains of Gold and Silver," as he was, "Who can blame him?"; in *Serious Reflections* he asserts that Spanish cruelty was the means by which Providence dealt with pagan practitioners of "human Sacrifice" (206).

frighted when they were seiz'd upon and bound, and afraid like the Women that they should be murther'd and eaten; for it seems those People think all the World does as they do, eating Mens Flesh; but they were soon made easy as to that, and away they carry'd them.

It was very happy to them that they did not carry them Home to their Castle, I mean to my Palace under the Hill; but they carry'd them first to the Bower, where was the chief of their Country-work, such as the keeping the Goats, the planting the Corn, *&c.* and afterwards, they carry'd them to the Habitation of the two *English* Men.

Here they were set to work, tho' it was not much they had for them to do; and whether it was by Negligence in guarding them, or that they thought the Fellows could not mend themselves, I know not, but one of them run away, and taking into the Woods, they could never hear of him more.

They had good reason to believe, he got Home again soon after, in some other Boats or Canoes of Savages who came on Shore three or four Weeks afterwards, and who carrying on their Revels as usual, went off again in two Days time: This Thought terrify'd them exceedingly, for they concluded, and that not without good Cause indeed, that if this Fellow came safe Home among his Comrades, he would certainly give them an Account, that there were People in the Island, as also how few and weak they were; for this Savage, as I observ'd before, had never been told, and it was very happy he had not, how many they were, or where they liv'd; nor had he ever seen or heard the Fire of any of their Guns, much less had they shewn him any of their other retir'd Places: Such as the Cave in the Valley, or the new Retreat, which the two *English* Men had made, *and the like.*

The first Testimony they had, that this Fellow had given Intelligence of them, was, that about two Months after this, six Canoes of Savages, with about seven, or eight, or ten Men in a Canoe, came rowing along the North Side of the Island, where they never used to come before, and landed about an Hour after Sunrise, at a convenient Place, about a Mile from the Habitation of the two *English* Men, where this escap'd Man had been kept: As the *Spaniard* Governour said, had they been all there, the Damage would not have been so much, for not a Man of them would have escaped; but the Case differ'd now very much, for two Men to fifty was too much odds: The two Men had the Happiness to discover them about a League off, so that it was above an Hour before they landed, and as they landed a Mile from their Huts, it was some time before they could come at them: Now having great Reason to believe that they were betray'd, the first Thing they did, was to bind the two Slaves which were left, and cause two of the three Men, who they brought with the Women, who it seems proved very faithful to them, to lead them with their two Wives, and whatever they could carry away with them, to their retir'd Place in the Woods, which I have spoken of above, and there to bind the two Fellows Hand and Foot till they heard farther.

In the next Place, seeing the Savages were all come on Shore, and that they bent their Course directly that Way, they open'd the Fences where their Milch-Goats were kept, and drove them all out, leaving their Goats to straggle into the Woods, whether they pleas'd, that the Savages might think they were all bred wild; but the Rogue who came with them was too cunning for that, and gave them an Account of it all, for they went directly to the Place.

When the two poor frighted Men had secur'd their Wives and Goods, they sent the other Slave they had of the three, who came with the Women, and who was at their Place by accident, away to the *Spaniards*, with all Speed, to give them the Alarm and desire speedy Help, and in the mean time they took their Arms, and what Ammunition they had, and retreated towards the Place in the Wood, where their Wives were sent, keeping at a Distance, yet so that they might see, if possible, which Way the Savages took.

They had not gone far, but that, from a rising Ground they could see the little Army of their Enemies come on directly to their Habitation, and in a Moment more, could see all their Huts and Houshold-Stuff flaming up together, to their great Grief and Mortification, for they had a very great Loss, to them irretrievable, at least for some time. They kept their Station for a while, till they found the Savages, like wild Beasts, spread themselves all over the Place, rumaging[1] every Way, and every Place they could think of, in Search for Prey, and in particular for the People, of whom it now plainly appear'd they had Intelligence.

The two *English* Men seeing this, thinking themselves not secure where they stood, because as it was likely some of the wild People might come that Way, so they might come too many together, thought it proper to make another Retreat about half a Mile farther, believing, as it afterwards happen'd, that the farther they stroul'd, the fewer would be together.

Their next Halt was at the Entrance into a very thick grown Part of the Woods, and where an old Trunk of a Tree stood, which

1 Rummaging, searching.

was hollow and vastly large; and in this Tree they both took their standing,[1] resolving to see there what might offer.

They had not stood there long, but two of the Savages appear'd running directly that Way, as if they had already had Notice where they stood, and were coming up to attack them; and a little way farther, they spy'd three more coming after them, and five more beyond them, all coming the same Way, besides which, they saw seven or eight more at a Distance, running another Way; for in a word, they ran every Way, like Sports-men beating for their Game.

The poor Men were now in great Perplexity, whether they should stand and keep their Posture,[2] or fly: But after a very short Debate with themselves, they consider'd, that if the Savages ranged the Country thus before Help came, they might perhaps find out their Retreat in the Woods, then all would be lost; so they resolv'd to stand them there; and if they were too many to deal with, then they would get up to the Top of the Tree, from whence they doubted not to defend themselves, *Fire excepted*, as long as their Ammunition lasted, tho' all the Savages that were landed, which was near 50, were to attack them.

Having resolv'd upon this, they next consider'd whether they should fire at the first two, or wait for the three, and so take the middle Party, by which the two and the five that follow'd would be separated, and they resolv'd to let the two first pass by, unless they should spy them in the Tree, and come to attack them; the two first Savages also confirm'd them in this Regulation, by turning a little from them towards another Part of the Wood, but the three and the five after them, came forwards directly to the Tree, as if they had known the *English* Men were there.

Seeing them come so strait towards them, they resolv'd to take them in a Line, as they came; and as they resolv'd to fire but one at a time, perhaps the first Shot might hit them all three, to which purpose, the Man who was to fire, put three or four small Bullets into his Peice, and having a fair Loop-hole,[3] as it were from a broken Hole in the Tree, he took a sure aim, without being seen, waiting till they were within about thirty Yards of the Tree, so that he could not miss.

While they were thus waiting, and the Savages came on, they plainly saw, that one of the three was the run-away Savage that had escap'd from them, and they both knew him distinctly, and

---

1 Position.

2 Position.

3 Hole to shoot through.

resolv'd that, if possible, he should not escape, tho' they should both fire; so the other stood ready with his Peice, that if he did not drop at the first Shot, he should be sure to have a second.

But the first was too good a Marks-man to miss his Aim; for as the Savages kept near one another, a little behind in a Line, in a word, he fir'd, and hit two of them directly: The foremost was kill'd outright, being shot in the Head: The second, which was the run-away *Indian*, was shot thro' the Body, and fell, but was not quite dead: And the third had a little Scratch in the Shoulder, perhaps by the same Ball that went thro' the Body of the Second, and being dreadfully frighted, tho' not much hurt, sat down upon the Ground, skreaming and yelling in a hideous manner.

The five that were behind, more frighted with the Noise, than sensible of the Danger, stood still at first; for the Woods made the Sound a thousand Times bigger than it really was; the Echo's rattling from one Side to another, and the Fowls rising from all Parts skreaming, and making every Sort, a several Kind of Noise, according to their Kind, just as it was when I fir'd the first Gun, that perhaps was ever shot off in that Place, since it was an Island.

However, all being silent again, and they not knowing what the Matter was, came on unconcern'd, 'till they came to the Place where their Companions lay in a Condition miserable enough: And here the poor ignorant Creatures, not sensible that they were within Reach of the same Mischief, stood all of a Huddle over the wounded Man, talking and, as may be suppos'd, enquiring of him, how he came to be hurt; and who, 'tis very rational to believe, told them, that a Flash of Fire first, and immediately after that, Thunder from their Gods, had kill'd those two, and wounded him: This, I say, is rational; for nothing is more certain than that, as they saw no Man near them, so they had never heard a Gun in all their Lives, or so much as heard of a Gun; neither knew they any Thing of killing or wounding, at a Distance, with Fire and Bullets; if they had, one might reasonably believe, they would not have stood so unconcern'd, in viewing the Fate of their Fellows, without some Apprehension of their own.

Our two Men, tho' as they confess'd to me, it griev'd them to be oblig'd to kill so many poor Creatures, who at the same Time had no Notion of their Danger; yet having them all thus in their Power, and the first having loaded his Piece again, resolv'd to let fly both together among them; and singling out by Agreement which to aim at, they shot together, and kill'd or very much wounded four of them; the fifth frighted even to Death, tho' not hurt, fell with the rest; so that our Men seeing them all fall together, thought they had kill'd them all.

The Belief that the Savages were all kill'd, made our two Men come boldly out from the Tree before they had charg'd their Guns again, which was a wrong Step; and they were under some Surprize when they came to the Place, and found no less than four of the Men alive, and of them two very little hurt, and one not at all: This oblig'd them to fall upon them with the Stocks of their Muskets; and first they made sure of the run-away Savage, that had been the Cause of all the Mischief, and of another that was hurt in his Knee, and put them out of their Pain; then the Man that was not hurt at all, came and kneel'd down to them, with his two Hands held up, and made piteous Moans to them by Gestures and Signs, for his Life; but could not say one Word to them that they could understand.

However they sign'd to him to sit down at the Foot of a Tree thereby; and one of the *English* Men, with a Piece of Rope-Twine which he had, by great Chance, in his Pocket, ty'd his two Feet fast together, and his two Hands behind him, and there they left him; and, with what Speed they could, made after the other two, which were gone before; fearing they, or any more of them, should find the Way to their cover'd Place in the Woods, where their Wives and the few Goods they had left, lay. They came once in Sight of the two Men, but it was at a great Distance; however, they had the Satisfaction to see them cross over a Valley towards the Sea, the quite contrary Way from that which led to their Retreat, which they were afraid of; and being satisfy'd with that, they went back to the Tree, where they left their Prisoner, who, as they suppos'd, was deliver'd by his Comrades; for he was gone, and the two Pieces of Rope-Yarn, with which they had bound him, lay just at the Foot of the Tree.

They were now in as great Concern as before, not knowing what Course to take, or how near the Enemy might be, or in what Numbers; so they resolv'd to go away to the Place where their Wives were, to see if all was well there, and to make them easy, who were in Fright enough to be sure; for tho' the Savages were their own Country Folk, yet they were most terribly afraid of them, and perhaps the more, for the Knowledge they had of them.

When they came there, they found the Savages had been in the Wood, and very near that Place, but had not found it; for it was indeed inaccessible, by the Trees standing so thick, *as before*, had not the Persons seeking it been directed by those that knew it, which these did not; they found therefore every Thing very safe, only the Women in a terrible Fright: While they were here, they had the Comfort to have seven of the *Spaniards* come to their Assistance; the other ten, with their Servants, and old *Friday*,[1] I mean *Friday*'s Father, were gone in a Body to defend their Bower, and the Corn, and Cattle that was kept there, in Case the Savages should have rov'd over to that Side of the Country; but they did not spread so far. With the seven *Spaniards* came one of the three Savages, who, as I said, were their Prisoners formerly; and with them also came the Savage, who the *English* Men had left bound Hand and Foot at the Tree; for it seems they came that Way, saw the Slaughter of the seven Men, and unbound the eighth, and brought him along with them; where, however, they were oblig'd to bind him again, as they had the two others, who were left when the third run away.

The Prisoners began now to be a Burthen to them; and they were so afraid of their escaping, that they were once resolving to kill them all, believing they were under an absolute Necessity to do so, for their own Preservation: However, the *Spaniard* Governour would not consent to it, but order'd, for the present, that they should be sent out of the Way to my old Cave in the Valley, and be kept there with two *Spaniards* to guard them, and give them Food for their Subsistence, which was done; and they were bound there Hand and Foot for that Night.

When the *Spaniards* came, the two *English* Men were so encourag'd, that they could not satisfy themselves to stay any longer there: But taking five of the *Spaniards* and themselves, with four Muskets and a Pistol among them, and two stout Quarter-Staves;* away they went in Quest of the Savages. And first they came to the Tree where the Men lay that had been kill'd; but it was easy to see, that some more of the Savages had been there; for they had attempted to carry their dead Men away, and had dragg'd two of them a good Way, but had given it over. From thence they advanc'd to the first rising Ground, where they stood, and saw their Camp destroy'd, and where they had the Mortification still to see some of the Smoak; but neither could they here see any of the Savages: They then resolv'd, tho' with all possible Caution, to go forward towards their ruin'd Plantation: But a little before they came thither, coming in Sight of the Sea Shore, they saw plainly the Savages all embarking again in their Canoes, in order to be gone.

1 His name is never given.

They seem'd sorry at first; and there was no Way to come at them, to give them a parting Blow: But upon the whole were very well satisfy'd to be rid of them.

The poor *English* Men being now twice ruin'd, and all their Improvement destroy'd, the rest all agreed to come and help them rebuild, and to assist them with needful Supplies. Their three Country-men, who were not yet noted for having the least Inclination to do any Good; yet as soon as they heard of it (for they living remote Eastward, knew nothing of the Matter 'till all was over) came and offer'd their Help and Assistance, and did very friendly work for several Days, to restore their Habitation, and make Necessaries for them: And thus in a little Time they were set upon their Legs again.

About two Days after this, they had the farther Satisfaction of seeing three of the Savages Canoes come driving on Shore, and at some Distance from them, two drown'd Men; by which they had Reason to believe, that they had met with a Storm at Sea, and had overset some of them, for it had blown very hard the very Night after they went off.

However, as some might miscarry, so on the other hand, enough of them escap'd to inform the rest, as well of what they had done, as of what had happen'd to them; and to whet them on to another Enterprize of the same Nature, which they, it seems, resolv'd to attempt, with sufficient Force to carry all before them; for except what the first Man had told them of Inhabitants, they could say little to it of their own Knowledge; for they never saw one Man, and the Fellow being kill'd that had affirm'd it, they had no other Witness to confirm it to them.

It was five or six Months after this, before they heard any more of the Savages; in which Time, our Men were in Hopes, they had either forgot their former bad Luck, or given over the Hopes of better; when on a sudden they were invaded with a most formidable Fleet, of no less than eight and twenty Canoes full of Savages, arm'd with Bows and Arrows, great Clubs, wooden Swords, and such like Engines of War; and they brought such Numbers with them, that, in short, it put all our People into the utmost Consternation.

As they came on Shore in the Evening, and at the Easter-most Side of the Island, our Men had that Night to consult and consider what to do; and in the first Place, knowing that their being entirely conceal'd, was their only Safety before, and would much more be so now, while the Number of their Enemies was so great, they therefore resolv'd first of all to take down the Huts which were built for the two *English* Men, and drive away their Goats to the old Cave, because they suppos'd the Savages would go directly thither, as soon as it was Day, to play the old Game over again, tho' they did not now land within two Leagues of it.

In the next Place, they drove away all the Flock of Goats they had at the old Bower, as I call'd it, which belong'd to the *Spaniards*; and in short, left as little Appearance of Inhabitants any where as was possible; and the next Morning early they posted themselves with all their Force, at the Plantation of the two Men, and wait for their coming: As they guess'd, so it happen'd; these new Invaders leaving their Canoes at the East End of the Island, came ranging along the Shore directly towards the Place, to the Number of two hundred and fifty, as near as our Men could judge. Our Army was but small indeed; but that which was worse, they had not Arms for all their Number neither. The whole Account, it seems, stood thus; First, as to Men.

17 *Spaniards*.
5 *English* Men.
1 old *Friday*, or *Friday*'s Father.
3 the three Slaves taken with the women, who prov'd very faithful.
3 other Slaves who liv'd with the *Spaniards*.

To arm these, they had,

11 Muskets.
5 Pistols.
3 Fowling-Peices.[1]
5 Muskets or Fowling-Peices, which were taken by me from the mutinous Seamen, who I reduc'd.[2]

To their Slaves, they did not give either Musket, or Fuzee, but they had every one a Halberd,* or a long Staff, like a Quarter-Staff,* with a great Spike of Iron fasten'd into each End of it, and, by his Side a Hatchet, also every one of our Men had Hatchets: Two of the Women could not be prevail'd upon, but they would come into the Fight, and they had Bows and Arrows, which the *Spaniards* had taken from the Savages, when the first Action happen'd, which I have spoken of, where the *Indians* fought with one another, and the Women Hatchets too.

---

1 Gun filled with shot; scattershot firearm used to kill birds and other small animals.

2 In Part I.

The *Spaniard* Governour, who I have describ'd so often, commanded the whole; and *Wm. Atkins*, who tho' a dreadful Fellow for Wickedness, was a most daring bold Fellow, Commanded under him. The Savages came forward like Lyons, and our Men, which was the worst of their Fate, had no Advantage in their Situation; only, that *Will. Atkins*, who now prov'd a most useful Fellow, with six Men, was planted, just behind a small Thicket of Bushes, as an advanc'd Guard, with Orders, to let the first of them pass by, and then fire into the middle of them, and as soon as he had fir'd, to make his Retreat as nimbly as he could round a Part of the Wood, and so come in behind the *Spaniards* where they stood, having a Thicket of Trees also before them.

When the Savages came on, they run straggling about every way in Heaps,[1] out of all manner of Order, and *W. Atkins* let about 50 of them pass by him, then seeing the rest come in a very thick Throng, he orders three of his Men to fire, having loaded their Musquets[2] with six or seven Bullets a piece, about as big as large Pistol Bullets. How many they kill'd or wounded they knew not, but the Consternation and Surprize was inexpressible among the Savages; they were frighted to the last Degree, to hear such a dreadful Noise, and see their Men kill'd, and others hurt, but see no Body that did it; when in the middle of their Fright, *W. Atkins*, and his other three let fly again, among the thickest of them; and in less than a Minute the first three, being loaded again, gave them a third Volley.

Had *W. Atkins*, and his Men retir'd immediately, as soon as they had fir'd, as they were order'd to do; or had the rest of the Body been at Hand to have pour'd in their Shot continually, the Savages had been effectually routed; for the Terror that was among them, came principally from this, (*viz.*) That they were kill'd by the Gods with Thunder and Lightning, and could see no Body that hurt them; but *W. Atkins* staying to load again, discover'd the Cheat;[3] some of the Savages who were at a distance, spying them, came upon them behind, and tho' *Atkins* and his Men fir'd at them also, two or three times, and kill'd above 20, retiring as fast as they could, yet they wounded *Atkins* himself, and kill'd one of his Fellow *English* Men with their Arrows, as they did afterwards one *Spaniard*, and one of the *Indian* Slaves who came with the Women; this Slave was a most gallant Fellow, and fought most

---

1 Disorganized packs.

2 Muskets.

3 I.e., he revealed the trick or strategy.

desperately, killing five of them with his own Hand, having no Weapon, but one of the Arm'd-staves[1] and a Hatchet.

Our Men being thus hard laid at, *Atkins* wounded, and two other Men kill'd, retreated to a rising Ground in the Wood, and the *Spaniards*, after firing three Vollies upon them retreated also, for their Number was so Great, and they were so Desperate, that tho' above 50 of them were kill'd, and more than so many wounded, yet they came on in the Teeth of our Men, fearless of Danger, and shot their Arrows like a Cloud; and it was observ'd, that their wounded Men, who were not quite disabled, were made Out-rageous by their Wounds, and fought like Mad-men.

When our Men retreated, they left the *Spaniard* and the *English* Man that was kill'd, behind them; and the Savages when they came up to them, kill'd them over again in a wretched manner, breaking their Arms, Legs, and Heads, with their Clubs and wooden Swords, like true Savages: But finding our Men were gone, they did not seem to pursue them, but drew themselves up in a kind of a Ring, which is, it seems, their Custom, and shouted twice in token of their Victory: After which, they had the Mortification to see several of their wounded Men fall, dying with the mere Loss of Blood.

The *Spaniard* Governour having drawn his little Body up together upon a rising Ground, *Atkins*, tho' he was wounded, would ha' had him march'd and charg'd them again altogether at once: But the *Spaniards* reply'd, Seignior *Atkins*, you see how their wounded Men fight, let them alone 'till Morning; all these wounded Men will be stiff and sore with their Wounds, and faint with the Loss of Blood; and so we shall have the fewer to engage.

The Advice was good: But *Will. Atkins* reply'd merrily, That's true, Seignior, and so shall I too; and that's the Reason I would go on while I am warm.[2] Well, Seignior *Atkins*, says the *Spaniards*, you have behav'd gallantly, and done your Part, we will fight for you, if you cannot come on, but I think it best to stay 'till Morning; so they waited.

But as it was a clear Moon-light Night, and they found the Savages in great Disorder about their dead and wounded Men, and a great Hurry and Noise among them where they lay, they afterwards resolv'd to fall upon them in the Night, especially if they could come to give them but one Volley before they were discover'd, which they had a fair Opportunity to do; for one of the

1 Quarter-staffs, weapons.

2 Geared up, in the zone.

two *English* Men, in whose Quarter it was where the Fight began, led them round between the Woods, and Sea Side Westward, and then turning short South, they came so near where the thickest of them lay, that before they were seen or heard, eight of them fir'd in among them, and did dreadful Execution upon them; in half a Minute more, eight others fir'd after them, pouring in their small Shot in such a Quantity, that abundance were kill'd and wounded; and all this while they were not able to see who hurt them, or which Way to fly.

The *Spaniards* charg'd again with the utmost Expedition, and then divided themselves into three Bodies, and resolv'd to fall in among them altogether: They had in each Body eight Persons, that is to say, 24, whereof were 22 Men, and the 2 Women, who by the way fought desperately.

They divided the Fire Arms equally in each Party, and so of the Halberds and Staves: They would have had the Women keep back, but they said they were resolv'd to die with their Husbands: Having thus form'd their little Army, they march'd out from among the Trees, and came up to the Teeth of the Enemy, shouting and hallowing as loud as they could; the Savages stood all together, but were in the utmost Confusion, hearing the Noise of our Men Shouting from three Quarters together; they would have fought if they had seen us: And as soon as we came near enough to be seen, some Arrows were shot, and poor old *Friday* was wounded, tho' not dangerously: But our Men gave them no Time; but running up to them, fir'd among them three Ways, and then fell in with the But-ends of their Muskets, their Swords, arm'd Staves, and Hatchets and laid about them so well, that, in a word, they set up a dismal Skreaming and Howling, flying to save their Lives, which Way soever they could.

Our Men were tyr'd with the Execution; and kill'd, or mortally wounded, in the two Fights, about 180 of them; the rest, being frighted out of their Wits, scour'd thro' the Woods, and over the Hills, with all the Speed, Fear, and nimble Feet could help them to do; and as we did not trouble ourselves much to pursue them, they got all together to the Sea Side where they landed, and where their Canoes lay: But their Disaster was not at an End yet; for it blew a terrible Storm of Wind, that Evening, from the Sea-ward; so that it was impossible for them to go off; nay, the Storm continuing all Night, when the Tide came up, their Canoes were most of them driven by the Surge of the Sea, so high upon the Shore, that it requir'd infinite Toil to get them off; and some of them were even dash'd to Pieces against the Beach, or against one another.

Our Men, tho' glad of their Victory, yet got little Rest that Night; but having refresh'd themselves as well as they could, they resolv'd to march to that Part of the Island where the Savages were fled, and see what Posture they were in: This necessarily led them over the Place where the Fight had been, and where they found several of the poor Creatures not quite dead, and yet past recovering Life; a Sight disagreeable enough to generous Minds: For a truly great Man, tho' obliged, by the Law of Battle, to destroy his Enemy, takes no Delight in his Misery.

However, there was no Need to give any Orders in this Case; for their own Savages, who were their Servants, dispatch'd those poor Creatures with their Hatchets.

At length, they came in View of the Place, where the more miserable Remains of the Savages Army lay, where there appear'd about an hundred still; their Posture was generally sitting upon the Ground, with their Knees up towards their Mouth, and the Head put between the two Hands, leaning down upon the Knees.

When our Men came within two Musket-shot of them, the *Spaniard* Governour order'd two Muskets to be fir'd without Ball, to alarm them; this he did, that by their Countenance he might know what to expect, (*viz.*) whether they were still in Heart to fight, or were so heartily beaten, as to be dispirited and discourag'd, and so he might manage accordingly.

This Stratagem took; for as soon as the Savages heard the first Gun, and saw the Flash of the second, they started up upon their Feet, in the greatest Consternation imaginable; and as our Men advanced swiftly towards them, they all run skreaming and yawling[1] away, with a kind of a howling Noise, which our Men did not understand, and had never heard before; and thus they ran up the Hills into the Country.

At first, our Men had much rather the Weather had been calm, and they had all gone away to Sea: But they did not then consider that this might probably have been the Occasion of their coming again in such Multitudes, as not to be resisted, or, at least, to come so many, and so often as would quite desolate the Island, and starve them: *Will. Atkins*, therefore, who, notwithstanding his Wound, kept always with them, prov'd the best Counsellour in this Case: His Advice was to take the Advantage that offer'd, and clap in between them and their Boats, and so deprive them of the Capacity of ever returning any more to plague the Island.

---

1 Howling.

They consulted long about this, and some were against it, for fear of making the Wretches fly to the Woods, and live there desperate, and so they should have them to hunt like wild Beasts, be afraid to stir out about their Business, and have their Plantations continually riffled,[1] all their tame Goats destroy'd, and in short, be reduc'd to a Life of continual Distress.

Will. Atkins told them, They had better have to do with a hundred Men, than with a hundred Nations; that as they must destroy their Boats, so they must destroy the Men, or be all of them destroy'd themselves: In a word, he shew'd them the Necessity of it, so plainly, that they all came in to it; so they went to Work immediately with the Boats; and getting some dry Wood together, from a dead Tree, they try'd to set some of them on Fire; but they were so wet, that they would not burn; however, the Fire so burn'd the upper Part, that it soon made them unfit for swimming in the Sea as Boats. When the *Indians* saw what they were about, some of them came running out of the Woods, and coming as near as they could to our Men, kneel'd down, and cry'd, *Oa, Oa, Waramokoa,* and some other Words of their Language, which none of the others understood any thing of; but as they made pitiful Gestures, and strange Noises, it was easy to understand, they begg'd to have their Boats spar'd, and that they would be gone, and never come there again.

But our Men were now satisfied, that they had no Way to preserve themselves, or to save their Colony, but effectually to prevent any of these People from ever going Home again; depending upon this, that if ever so much as one of them got back into their Country to tell the Story, the Colony was undone; so that letting them know, that they should not have any Mercy, they fell to work with their Canoes, and destroy'd them every one, that the Storm had not destroy'd before; at the Sight of which, the Savages rais'd a hideous Cry in the Woods, which our People heard plain enough; after which, they ran about the Island like distracted Men; so that in a word, our Men did not really know at first what to do with them.

Nor did the *Spaniards,* with all their Prudence, consider, that while they made those People thus desperate, they ought to have kept good Guard at the same Time upon their Plantations; for tho' it is true, they had driven away their Cattle, and the *Indians* did not find out their main Retreat, I mean my old Castle at the Hill, nor the Cave in the Valley, yet they found out my Plantation

1 Rifled, searched through quickly and carelessly.

at the Bower, and pull'd it all to pieces, and all the Fences and Planting about it; trod all the Corn under-foot; tore up the Vines and Grapes, being just then almost ripe, and did to our Men an inestimable Damage, tho' to themselves not one Farthing-worth of Service.

Tho' our Men were able to fight them upon all Occasions, yet they were in no Condition to pursue them, or hunt them up and down; for as they were too nimble of Foot for our Men, when they found them single, so our Men durst not go about single, for fear of being surrounded with their Numbers. The best was, they had no Weapons, for tho' they had Bows they had no Arrows left, nor any Materials to make any, nor had they any edg'd Tool or Weapon among them.

The Extremety and Distress they were reduc'd to was great, and indeed deplorable; but at the same Time, our Men were also brought to very bad Circumstances by them; for tho' their Retreats were preserv'd, yet their Provision was destroy'd, and their Harvest spoil'd, and what to do, or which Way to turn themselves, they knew not: The only Refuge they had now, was the Stock of Cattle they had in the Valley by the Cave, and some little Corn which grew there; and the Plantation of the three *English* Men, *Will. Atkins* and his Comrades, who were now reduced to two, one of them being kill'd by an Arrow which struck him on the Side of his Head, just under the Temples, so that he never spoke more; and it was very remarkable, that this was the same barbarous Fellow who cut the poor Savage Slave with his Hatchet, and who afterwards intended to have murther'd all the *Spaniards*.

I look'd upon their Case to have been worse at this time, than mine was at any time, after I first discover'd the Grains of Barley and Rice, and got into the manner of planting and raising my Corn, and my tame Cattle; for now they had, as I may say, a hundred Wolves upon the Island, which would devour every Thing they could come at, yet could very hardly be come at themselves.

The first Thing they concluded, when they saw what their Circumstances were, was, that they would, if possible, drive them up to the farther Part of the Island, South-West, that if any more Savages came on Shore, they might not find one another. Then, that they would daily hunt and harass them, and kill as many of them as they could come at, till they had reduced their Number; and if they could at last tame them, and bring them to any thing, they would give them Corn, and teach them how to plant and live upon their daily Labour.

In order to this, they so follow'd them, and so terrified them with their Guns, that in a few Days, if any of them fir'd a Gun at an *Indian*, if he did not hit him, yet he would fall down for Fear; and so dreadfully frighted they were, that they kept out of sight farther and farther, till at last our Men following them, and every Day almost killing and wounding some of them, they kept up in the Woods and hollow Places so much, that it reduced them to the utmost Misery for want of Food, and many were afterwards found dead in the Woods, without any Hurt, but meerly starv'd to Death.

When our Men found this, it made their Hearts relent, and Pity mov'd them, especially the *Spaniard* Governour, who was a most gentlemanly generous minded Man, as ever I met with in my Life; and he propos'd, if possible, to take one of them alive, and bring him to understand what they meant, so far as to be able to act as Interpreter, and to go among them and see if they might be brought to some Conditions, that might be depended upon to save their Lives, and do us no Spoil.

It was some while before any of them could be taken, but being weak and half-starv'd, one of them was at last surpriz'd and made a Prisoner; he was sullen at first, and would neither eat or drink, but finding himself kindly used, and Victuals given him, and no Violence offer'd him, he at last grew tractable[1] and came to himself.

They brought old *Friday* to him, who talk'd often with him, and told him how kind the other would be to them all, that they would not only save their Lives, but would give them a Part of the Island to live in, provided they would give Satisfaction that they would keep in their own Bounds, and not come beyond it, to injure or prejudice others, and that they should have Corn given them, to plant and make it grow for their Bread, and some Bread given them for their present Subsistence; and old *Friday* bad the Fellow go and talk with the rest of his Countrymen, and see what they said to it, assuring them, that if they did not agree immediately, they should be all destroy'd.

The poor Wretches thoroughly humbled, and reduc'd in Number to about 37, clos'd with the Proposal at the first offer, and begg'd to have some Food given them; upon which, twelve *Spaniards* and two *English* Men well arm'd, with three *Indian* Slaves, and old *Friday*, march'd to the Place where they were; the three *Indian* Slaves carry'd them a large Quantity of Bread;

1 Easy to manage.

some Rice boil'd up to Cakes, and dry'd in the Sun; and three live Goats; and they were order'd to go to the Side of a Hill, where they sat down, eat the Provisions very thankfully, and were the most faithful Fellows to their Words, that could be thought of; for, except when they came to beg Victuals and Directions, they never came out of their Bounds; and there they liv'd when I came to the Island, and I went to see them.

They had taught them both to plant Corn, make Bread, breed tame Goats and milk them; they wanted nothing but Wives, and they soon would have been a Nation. They were confin'd to a Neck of Land, surrounded with high Rocks behind them, and lying plain towards the Sea before them, on the South-east Corner of the Island: They had Land enough, and it was very good and fruitful; they had a Piece of Land about a Mile and half broad, three or four Mile in Length.

Our Men taught them to make wooden Spades, such as I made for myself, and gave them among them twelve Hatchets, and three or four Knives, and there they liv'd the most subjected innocent Creatures that ever were heard of.

After this, the Colony enjoy'd a perfect Tranquillity with respect to the Savages, till I came to revisit them, which was above two Years:[1] Not, but that now and then some Canoes of Savages came on Shore for their triumphal unnatural Feasts, but as they were of several Nations, and perhaps had never heard of those that came before, or the Reason of it, they did not make any Search or Enquiry after their Countrymen, and if they had, it would have been very hard to have found them out.

Thus, I think, I have given a full Account of all that happen'd to them, to my return, at least that was worth Notice. The *Indians* or Savages were wonderfully civilliz'd by them, and they frequently went among them, but forbid on Pain of Death, any one of the *Indians* coming to them, because they would not have their Settlement betray'd again.

One Thing was very remarkable, (*viz.*) that they taught the Savages to make Wicker-work, or Baskets; but they soon outdid their Masters; for they made abundance of most ingenious Things in Wicker-work; particularly, all Sorts of Baskets, Sieves, Bird-Cages, Cup-boards, *&c.* as also Chairs to sit on, Stools, Beds, Couches, and abundance of other Things, being very ingenious at such Work, when they were once put in the way of it.

1 More than two years later.

My coming was a particular Relief to these People, because we furnish'd them with Knives, Scissers, Spades, Shovels, Pick-axes, and all Things of that kind which they could want.

With the Help of these Tools, they were so very handy, that they came at last to build up their Huts, or Houses, very handsomely; radling[1] or working it up like Basket-work all the way round, which was a very extraordinary Piece of Ingenuity, and look'd very odd, but was an exceeding good Fence, as well against Heat, as against all Sorts of Vermine; and our Men were so taken with it, that they got the wild Savages to come and do the like for them; so that when I came to see the two *English* Mens Colonies, they look'd at a distance, as if they liv'd all, like Bees in a Hive; and as for *W. Atkins*, who was now become a very industrious necessary and sober Fellow, he had made himself such a Tent of Basket-work as I believe was never seen; it was 120 Paces round in the outside, as I measur'd by my Steps; the Walls were as close work'd as a Basket in Pannels, or Squares of 32 in Number, and very strong, standing about seven Foot high; in the middle was another, not above 22 Paces round, but built stronger, being Eight-square in its Form, and in the eight Corners stood eight very strong Posts, round the top of which he laid strong Pieces pinn'd together with wooden Pins, from which he rais'd a Piramid for the Roof of eight Rafters, very handsome I assure you, and join'd together very well, tho' he had no Nails, and only a few Iron Spikes, which he made himself too, out of the old Iron that I had left there; and indeed this Fellow shew'd abundance of Ingenuity in several Things, which he had no Knowledge of; he made him a Forge, with a pair of wooden Bellows to blow the Fire; he made himself Charcoal for his Work, and he form'd out of one of the Iron Crows, a middling good Anvil to hammer upon; in this manner he made many Things, but especially Hooks, Staples and Spikes, Bolts and Hinges; but to return to the House, after he had pitch'd the Roof of his inner-most Tent, he work'd it up between the Rafters with Basket-work, so firm, and thatch'd that over again so ingeniously with Rice-straw, and over that a large Leaf of a Tree, which cover'd the Top, that his House was as dry as if it had been til'd or slated. Indeed he own'd that the Savages made the Basket-work for him.

The outer Circuit was cover'd, as a Lean too,[2] all round this inner Appartment, and long Rafters lay from the two and thirty Angles to the top Posts of the inner House, being about 20 Foot

1 Twisting, interweaving.

2 Lean-to.

distant; so that there was a Space like a Walk within the outer Wicker-wall, and without the inner, near 20 Foot wide.

The inner Place he partition'd off with the same Wicker-work, but much fairer, and divided it into six Appartments, so that he had six Rooms on a Floor; and out of every one of these there was a Door, first into the Entry or Coming into the Main-tent, and another Door into the Space or Walk that was round it; so that Walk was also divided into six equal Parts, which serv'd not only for Retreat, but to store up any Necessaries which the Family had Occasion for. These six Spaces not taking up the whole Circumference, what other Appartments the outer Circle had, were thus order'd: As soon as you were in at the Door of the outer Circle, you had a short Passage strait before you to the Door of the inner House, but on either Side was a wicker Partition, and a Door in it, by which you went, first, into a large Room or Store-house, 20 Foot wide, and about 30 Foot long, and thro' that into another not quite so long; so that in the outer Circle was ten handsome Rooms, six of which were only to be come at thro' the Appartments of the inner Tent, and serv'd as Closets or retiring Rooms to the respective Chambers of the inner Circle, and four large Warehouses or Barns, or what you please to call them, which went in thro' one another, two on either Hand of the Passage, that led thro' the outer Door to the inner Tent.

Such a Piece of Basket-work, I believe, was never seen in the World, nor a House or Tent, so neatly contriv'd, much less, so built. In this great Bee-hive liv'd the three Families, that is to say, *W. Atkins* and his Companion; the third was kill'd, but his Wife remain'd with three Children; for she was it seems big with Child when he dy'd, and the other two were not at all backward* to give the Widow her full Share of every thing,[1] I mean as to their Corn, Milk, Grapes, *&c.* and when they kill'd a Kid, or found a Turtle on the Shore; so that they all liv'd well enough, tho' it was true, they were not so Industrious as the other two, as has been observ'd already.

One Thing, however, cannot be omitted (*viz.*) that as for Religion, I don't know that there was any thing of that kind among them; they pretty often indeed put one another in Mind that there was a God, by the very common Method of Seamen, (*viz.*) Swearing by his Name; nor were their poor ignorant Savage-Wives much the better for having been married to Christians, as we must call them; for as they knew very little of God themselves,

1 I.e., they gave the widow her fair share.

so they were utterly uncapable of entring into any Discourse with their Wives about a God, or to talk any thing to them concerning Religion.

The utmost of all the Improvement, which I can say the Wives had made from them, was, that they had taught them to speak *English* pretty well, and all the Children they had, which was near 20 in all, were taught to speak *English* too, from their first learning to speak, tho' they at first spoke it in a very broken Manner, like their Mothers. There were none of these Children above six Year old when I came thither, for it was not much above seven Year that they had fetch'd these five Savage Ladies over, but they had all been pretty fruitful, for they had all Children, more or less: I think the Cook's-mate's Wife was big of her sixth Child; and the Mothers were all a good sort of well-govern'd, quiet laborious Women, modest and decent, helpful to one another; mighty observant and subject to their Masters, I cannot call them Husbands; and wanted nothing but to be well instructed in the Christian Religion, and to be legally married; both which were happily brought about afterwards by my Means, or at least, in Consequence of my coming among them.

Having thus given an Account of the Colony in general, and pretty much of my five runagate[1] *English* Men, I must say something of the *Spaniards*, who were the main Body of the Family; and in whose Story there are some Incidents also remarkable enough.

I had a great many Discourses with them about their Circumstances when they were among the Savages: They told me readily, that they had no Instances to give of their Application or Ingenuity in that Country; that they were a poor miserable dejected Handful of People, that if Means had been put into their Hands, had yet so abandon'd themselves to despair, and so sunk under the Weight of their Misfortunes, that they thought of nothing but starving: One of them, a grave and very sensible Man, told me, he was convinc'd they were in the Wrong; that it was not the Part of wise Men to give up themselves to their Misery, but always to take Hold of the Helps which Reason offer'd, as well for present Support, as for future Deliverance. He told me that Grief was the most senseless insignificant Passion in the World; for that it regarded only Things past, which were generally impossible to be recall'd, or to be remedy'd, but had no View to Things to come, and had no Share in any Thing that look'd like Deliverance, but

1 Renegade, a deserter.

rather added to the Affliction, than propos'd a Remedy: And upon this, he repeated a *Spanish* Proverb; which tho' I cannot repeat in just the same Words that he spoke it in, yet I remember I made it into an *English* Proverb of my own, thus:

In Trouble to be troubl'd,
Is to have your Trouble doubl'd.

He run on then in Remarks upon all the little Improvements I had made in my Solitude; my unwearied Application, as he call'd it, and how I had made a Condition, which in its Circumstances was at first much worse than their's a thousand Times, more happy than their's was, even now when they were all together. He told me, it was remarkable, that *English* Men had a greater Presence of Mind, in their Distress, than any People that ever he met with, that their unhappy Nation, and the *Portuguese*, were the worst Men in the World to struggle with Misfortunes; for that their first Step in Dangers, after the common Efforts were over, was always to despair, lie down under it, and die, without rousing their Thoughts up to proper Remedies for Escape.

I told him, their Case and mine differ'd exceedingly, that they were cast upon the Shore without Necessaries, without Supply of Food, or of present Sustenance, 'till they could provide: That it is true, I had this Disadvantage and Discomfort, that I was alone; but then the Supplies I had providentially* thrown into my Hands, by the unexpected driving of the Ship on Shore, was such a Help as would have encourag'd any Creature in the World to have apply'd himself as I had done. Seignior, says the *Spaniard*, had we poor *Spaniards* been in your Case, we should never have gotten half those Things out of the Ship as you did: Nay, says he, we should never have found Means to have gotten a Raft to carry them, or to have gotten the Raft on Shore without Boat or Sail; and how much less should we have done, said he, if any of us had been alone? Well, I desir'd him to abate his Compliment, and go on with the History of their coming on Shore, where they landed; He told me, they unhappily landed at a Place where there were People without Provisions; whereas had they had the common Sense to have put off to Sea again, and gone to another Island a little farther, they had found Provisions, tho' without People; there being an Island that Way, as they have been told, where there was Provisions, tho' no People; that is to say, That the *Spaniards* of *Trinidad* had frequently been there, and had fill'd the Island with Goats and Hogs at several Times; where they have bred in such Multitudes, and where Turtle and Sea Fowls were in such Plenty, that they could ha' been in no Want of Flesh, tho' they had found no Bread; whereas here, they were only sustain'd with a few Roots and Herbs, which they understood not, and which had no Substance in them, and which the Inhabitants gave them sparingly enough, and who could treat them no better, unless they would turn Cannibals, and eat Mens Flesh, which was the great Dainty of their Country.

They gave me an Account, how many Ways they strove to civilize the Savages they were with, and to teach them rational Customs in the ordinary Way of living, but in vain; and how they retorted it upon them, as unjust, that they who came there for Assistance and Support, should attempt to set up for Instructors of those that gave them Bread; intimating, it seems, that none should set up for the Instructors of others, but those who could live without them.

They gave me dismal Accounts of the Extremities they were driven to; how sometimes they were many Days without any Food at all; the Island they were upon being inhabited by a Sort of Savages that lived more indolent, and for that Reason were less supplied with the Necessaries of Life, than they had Reason to believe others were in the same Part of the World; and yet they found, that these Savages were less ravenous and voracious, than those who had better Supplies of Food.

Also they added, That they could not but see with what Demonstrations of Wisdom and Goodness the governing Providence of God directs the Events of Things in the World: Which, they said, appear'd in their Circumstances; for if press'd by the Hardships they were under, and the Barrenness of the Country where they were, they had search'd after a better Place to live in; they had then been out of the Way of the Relief that happen'd to them by my Means.

Then they gave me an Account, how the Savages, who they liv'd among, expected them to go out with them into their Wars: And it was true, that, as they had Fire-Arms with them, had they not had the Disaster to lose their Ammunition, they should not have been serviceable only to their Friends, but have made themselves terrible both to Friends and Enemies; but being without Powder and Shot, and yet in a Condition, that they could not in Reason deny to go out with their Landlords to their Wars; so when they came into the Field of Battle, they were in a worse Condition than the Savages themselves; for they neither had Bows or Arrows, nor could they use those the Savages gave them; so that they could do nothing, but stand still, and be wounded with Arrows, 'till they came up to the Teeth of their Enemy; and then indeed the three Halberds they had, were of Use to them; and they would often drive a whole little Army before them with those Halberds and sharpen'd Sticks put into the Muzzles of their Muskets: But that for all this they were some Times surrounded with Multitudes, and in great Danger from their Arrows, 'till at last they found the Way to make themselves large Targets[1] of Wood, which they cover'd with Skins of wild Beasts, whose Names they knew not; and these cover'd them from the Arrows of the Savages; that notwithstanding these, they were some Times in great Danger, and were once five of them knock'd down together with the Clubs of the Savages, which was the Time when one of them was taken Prisoner, that is to say, the *Spaniard* who I had reliev'd: That at first they thought had been kill'd; but when afterwards they heard he was taken Prisoner, they were under the greatest Grief imaginable, and would willingly have all ventur'd their Lives to have rescu'd him.

They told me, That when they were so knock'd down, the rest of their Company rescu'd them, and stood over them, fighting 'till they were come to themselves, all but him who they thought had been dead; and then they made their Way with their Halberds and Pieces, standing close together in a Line, thro' a Body of above a thousand Savages, beating down all that came in their Way, got the Victory over their Enemies, but to their great Sorrow, because it was with the Loss of their Friend; who the other Party, finding him alive, carry'd off with some others, as I gave an Account in my former.[2]

They describ'd most affectionately, how they were surpriz'd with Joy at the Return of their Friend and Companion in Misery, who they thought had been devour'd by wild Beasts of the worst Kind, (*viz.*) by wild Men; and yet how more and more they were surpriz'd with the Account he gave them of this Errand, and that there was a Christian in any Place near, much more one that was able, and had Humanity enough to contribute to their Deliverance.

They describ'd how they were astonish'd at the Sight of the Relief I sent them, and at the Appearance of Loaves of Bread, Things they had not seen since their coming to that miserable

1 Circular shields.

2 In Part I, when Crusoe and Friday rescue the Spaniard and Friday's father, who are about to be killed by the cannibals (184–85).

Place; how often they cross'd it,[1] and bless'd it, as Bread sent from Heaven; and what a reviving Cordial it was to their Spirits to taste it, as also of the other Things I had sent for their Supply: And after all, they would have told me something of the Joy they were in, at the Sight of a Boat and Pilots to carry them away to the Person and Place from whence all these new Comforts came; but they told me, it was impossible to express it by Words, for their excessive Joy, naturally driving them to unbecoming Extravagancies, they had no way to describe them, but by telling me that they border'd upon Lunacy, having no way to give Vent to their Passion, suitable to the Sense that was upon them; that in some it work'd one Way, and in some another; and that some of them thro' a Surprize of Joy would burst out into Tears, others be stark mad, and others immediately faint. This Discourse extreamly affected* me, and call'd to my Mind *Friday*'s Extasy, when he met his Father, and the poor Peoples Extasy, when I took them up at Sea, after their Ship was on Fire; the Mate of the Ship's Joy, when he found himself deliver'd in the Place where he expected to perish; and my own Joy, when after 28 Years Captivity, I found a good Ship ready to carry me to my own Country: All these Things made me more sensible of the Relation of those poor Men, and more affected with it.

Having thus given a View of the State of Things, as I found them, I must relate the Heads of what I did for these People, and the Condition in which I left them: It was their Opinion and mine too, that they would be troubl'd no more with the Savages; or that if they were, they would be able to cut them off, if they were twice as many as before; so they had no Concern about that: Then I entred into a serious Discourse with the *Spaniard*, who I call Governour, about their Stay in the Island; for as I was not come to carry any of them off, so it would not be just to carry off some, and leave others, who perhaps would be unwilling to stay, if their Strength was diminished.

On the other hand, I told them, I came to establish them there, not to remove them; and then I let them know, that I had brought with me Relief of sundry Kinds for them; That I had been at a great Charge to supply them with all Things necessary, as well for their Convenience, as their Defence; and that I had such and such particular Persons with me, as well to encrease and recruit their Number, as by the particular necessary Employments which they were bred to, being Artificers,* to assist them in those Things, in which, at present, they were to seek.

---

1 The Spanish Catholics make the sign of the cross over the bread.

They were all together when I talk'd thus to them; and before I delivered to them the Stores I had brought, I ask'd them one by one, If they had entirely forgot and bury'd the first Animosities that had been among them, and would shake Hands with one another, and engage in a strict Friendship and Union of Interest, that so there might be no more Misunderstanding or Jealousies.

Will. Atkins, with abundance of Frankness and good Humour, said they had met with Afflictions enough to make them all sober, and Enemies enough to make them all Friends; that for his Part he would live and die with them; and was so far from designing any Thing against the *Spaniards*, that he own'd they had done nothing to him, but what his own mad Humour made necessary, and what he would have done, and perhaps much worse in their Case; and that he would ask them Pardon, if I desir'd it, for the foolish and brutish Things he had done to them; and was very willing and desirous of living in Terms of entire Friendship and Union with them; and would do any Thing that lay in his Power to convince them of it; and as for going to *England*, he car'd not if he did not go thither this twenty Years.

The *Spaniards* said, they had indeed at first disarm'd and excluded *Will. Atkins* and his two Country-men for their ill Conduct, as they had let me know; and they appeal'd to me, for the Necessity they were under, to do so: But that *Will. Atkins* had behav'd himself so bravely in the great Fight they had with the Savages, and on several Occasions since; and had shew'd himself so faithful to, and concern'd for, the general Interest of them all, that they had forgotten all that was past, and thought he merited as much to be trusted with Arms, and supply'd with Necessaries, as any of them; and that they had testify'd their Satisfaction in him, by committing the Command to him, next to the Governour himself: And as they had an entire Confidence in him and all his Country-men, so they acknowledg'd they had merited that Confidence by all the Methods that honest Men could merit to be valued, and trusted; and they most heartily embrac'd the Occasion of giving me this Assurance, that they would never have any Interest separate from one another.

Upon these frank and open Declarations of Friendship, we appointed the next Day to dine all together; and indeed we made a splendid Feast: I caused the Ship's Cook and his Mate to come on Shore, and dress our Dinner; and the old Cook's Mate, we had on Shore, assisted. We brought on Shore six Pieces of good Beef, and four Pieces of Pork out of the Ship's Provision, with our Punch Bowl and Materials to fill it; and in particular, I gave them ten Bottles of *French* Claret, and ten Bottles of *English* Beer; Things that neither the *Spaniards*, or the *English* Men, had tasted for many Years; and which, it may be supposed, they were exceeding glad of.

The *Spaniards* added to our Feast five whole Kids, which the Cooks roasted; and three of them were sent cover'd up close on Board the Ship, to the Seamen, that they might feast on fresh Meat from on Shore, as we did with their Salt Meat from on Board.

After this Feast, at which we were very innocently merry, I brought out my Cargoe of Goods, wherein, that there might be no Dispute about dividing, I shew'd them that there was sufficient for them all; and desir'd that they might all take an equal Quantity of the Goods that were for wearing; that is to say, equal when made up, as first, I distributed Linnen sufficient to make every one of them four Shirts, and at the *Spaniards* request afterwards, made them up six; these were exceeding comfortable to them, having been what, as I may say, they had long since forgot the use of, or what it was to wear them.

I allotted the thin *English* Stuffs, which I mention'd before, to make every one a light Coat, like a Frock,[1] which I judged fittest for the Heat of the Season, cool and loose; and order'd, that whenever they decayed, they should make more, as they thought fit. The like for Pumps, Shoes, Stockings and Hats, *&c.*

I cannot express what Pleasure, what Satisfaction, sat upon the Countenances of all these poor Men, when they saw the Care I had taken of them, and how well I had furnish'd them; they told me I was a Father to them, and that having such a Correspondent as I was, in so remote a Part of the World, it would make them forget that they were left in a desolate Place; and they all voluntarily engag'd to me not to leave the Place without my Consent.

Then I presented to them the People I had brought with me, particularly, the Taylor, the Smith, and the two Carpenters, all of them most necessary People; but above all, my general Artificer, than whom, they could not name any Thing that was more useful to them: And the Taylor, to shew his Concern for them, went to work immediately, and with my Leave, made them every one a Shirt the first Thing he did; and which was still more, he taught the Women, not only how to sow and stitch, and use the Needle, but made them assist to make the Shirts for their Husbands, and for all the rest.

---

1 Coat with long skirts.

As to the Carpenters, I scarce need mention, how useful they were, for they took in pieces all my clumsy unhandy Things, and made them clever convenient Tables, Stools, Bed-steads, Cupboards, Lockers, Shelves, and every Thing they wanted of that Kind.

But to let them see how Nature made Artificers at first, I carried the Carpenters to see *Will. Atkins*'s Basket-house, as I call'd it, and they both own'd they never saw an Instance of such natural Ingenuity before; nor any thing so regular, and so handily built, at least of its Kind: And one of them, when he saw it, after musing a good while, turning about to me, I am sure, says he, that Man has no need of us, you need do nothing, but give him Tools.

Then I brought them out all my Store of Tools, and gave every Man a Digging-spade, a Shovel, and a Rake, for we had no Harrows[1] or Plows; and to every separate Place, a Pick-axe, a Crow, a broad Axe, and a Saw; always appointing, that as often as any were broken or worn out, they should be supply'd without grutching,[2] out of the general Stores that I left behind.

Nails, Staples, Hinges, Hammers, Chisels, Knives, Scissars, and all sorts of Tools, and Iron-work, they had without Tale,[3] as they requir'd, for no Man would care to take more than they wanted, and he must be a Fool that would wast or spoil them, on any Account whatever; and for the Use of the Smith, I left two Ton of unwrought Iron for a Supply.

My Magazine of Powder and Arms, which I brought them, was such, even to Profusion, that they could not but rejoice at them, for now they could march as I us'd to do, with a Musket upon each Shoulder, if there was Occasion, and were able to fight a thousand Savages, if they had but some little Advantages of Situation, which also they could not miss of if they had Occasion.

I carry'd on shore with me the young Man, whose Mother was starv'd to Death, and the Maid also; she was a sober well educated religious young Woman, and behav'd so inoffensively, that every one gave her a good Word; she had indeed an unhappy Life with us, there being no Woman in the Ship but her self; but she bore it with Patience; after a while seeing Things so well order'd, and in so fine a way of thriving upon my Island, and considering that they had neither Business or Acquaintance in the *East-Indies*,

---

1 Heavy frame with teeth, dragged over plowed earth to break it up and cover seed.

2 Complaining.

3 Without restriction.

or Reason for taking so long a Voyage: I say, considering all this, both of them came to me, and desir'd I would give them leave to remain on the Island, and be enter'd among my Family, as they call'd it.

I agreed to it readily, and they had a little Plat[1] of Ground allotted to them, where they had three Tents or Houses set up, surrounded with a Basket-work, Pallisado'd like *Atkins's*, adjoyning to his Plantation: Their Tents were contriv'd, so that they had each of them a Room apart to lodge in, and a middle Tent like a great Store-house to lay all their Goods in, and to eat and drink in; and now the other two *English* Men remov'd their Habitation to the same Place, and so the Island was divided into three Colonies, and no more, *viz.* the *Spaniards* with old *Friday*, and the first Servants, at my old Habitation under the Hill; which was, in a word, the capital City; and where they had so enlarg'd and extended their Works, as well under as on the outside of the Hill, that they liv'd, tho' perfectly conceal'd, yet full at large; never was there such a little City in a Wood, and so hid, I believe, in any Part of the World; for I verily believe, a thousand Men might have rang'd the Island a Month, and if they had not known there was such a Thing, and look'd on Purpose for it, they would not have found it; for the Trees stood so thick and so close, and grew so fast, matted into one another, that nothing but cutting them down first could discover the Place; except the only two narrow Entrances, where they went in and out, could be found, which was not very easy; one of them was just down at the Water-Edge of the Creek, and it was afterwards above 200 Yards to the Place; and the other was up the Ladder at twice,[2] as I have already formerly describ'd it; and they had a large Wood thick planted, also, on the Top of the Hill, which contain'd above an Acre, which grew apace, and cover'd the Place from all Discovery there, with only one narrow Place between two Trees, not easy to be discover'd to enter on that Side.

The other Colony was that of *W. Atkins*'s, where there were four Families of *English* Men, I mean those I had left there, with their Wives and Children; three Savages that were Slaves; the

1 Plot.

2 Crusoe is referring to how he protected his lair's entryway in Part I: "it was by setting two ladders; one to a part of the rock which was low, and then broke in, and left room to place another ladder upon that; so when the two ladders were taken down, no man living could come down to me without mischieving himself" (128).

Widow and Children of the *English* Man that was kill'd; the young Man and the Maid; and by the way, we made a Wife of her also, before we went away: There was also the two Carpenters and the Taylor, who I brought with me for them; also the Smith, who was a very necessary Man to them, especially as a Gunsmith, to take Care of their Arms; and my other Man, who I call'd, *Jack of all Trades*; who was in himself as good, almost, as 20 Men, for he was not only a very ingenious Fellow, but a very merry Fellow, and before I went away, we married him to the honest Maid that came with the Youth in the Ship, I mention'd before.

And now I speak of Marrying, it brings me naturally to say something of the *French* Ecclesiastic* that I had brought with me out of the Ship's Crew, who I took up at Sea. It is true, this Man was a *Roman*,* and perhaps it may give Offence to some hereafter, if I leave any Thing extraordinary upon Record, of a Man, who, before I begin, I must, (to set him out in just Colours) represent in Terms very much to his Disadvantage, in the Account of Protestants; as *first*, that he was a Papist;* *secondly*, a popish* Priest; and *thirdly*, a *French* popish Priest.

But Justice demands of me, to give him a due Character; and I must say, he was a grave, sober, pious, and most religious Person; exact in his Life, extensive in his Charity, and exemplar in almost every Thing he did; what then can any one say, against my being very sensible of the Value of such a Man, notwithstanding his Profession? Tho' it may be my Opinion, perhaps, as well as the Opinion of others, who shall read this, that he was mistaken?

The first Hour that I began to converse with him, after he had agreed to go with me to the *East-Indies*, I found Reason to delight exceedingly in his Conversation; and he first began with me about Religion in the most obliging Manner imaginable.

Sir, says he, you have not only, under God, (and at that he cross'd his Breast) sav'd my Life, but you have admitted me to go this Voyage in your Ship, and by your obliging Civility have taken me into your Family, giving me an Opportunity of free Conversation. Now, Sir, says he, you see by my Habit what my Profession is, and I guess by your Nation what yours is: I may think it is my Duty, and doubtless it is so, to use my utmost Endeavours on all Occasions, to bring all the Souls I can to the Knowledge of the Truth, and to Embrace the Catholick Doctrine; but as I am here under your Permission, and in your Family, I am bound in Justice to your Kindness, as well as in Decency and good Manners, to be under your Government; and therefore, I shall not, without your Leave, enter into any Debates on the Point of Religion in which we may not agree, farther then you shall give me Leave.

I told him, his Carriage* was so modest, that I could not but acknowledge it; that it was true, we were such People as they call'd Hereticks;* but that he was not the first Catholick that I had convers'd with, without falling into any Inconveniencies, or carrying the Questions to any height in Debate: That he should not find himself the worse us'd for being of a different Opinion from us, and if we did not converse without any Dislike on either Side upon that Score, it should be his Fault, not ours.

He reply'd, that he thought all our Conversation might be easily separated from Disputes; That it was not his Business to cap[1] Principles with every Man he discours'd with; and that he rather desir'd me to converse with him as a Gentleman, than as a Religieuse;[2] that if I would give him leave at any time to discourse upon religious Subjects, he would readily comply with it; and that then, he did not doubt but I would allow him also to Defend his own Opinions, as well as he could; but that without my Leave, he would not break in upon me with any such thing.

He told me farther, that he would not cease to do all that became him in his Office, as a Priest, as well as a private Christian, to procure the Good of the Ship, and the Safety of all that was in her; and tho' perhaps we would not join with him, and he could not pray *with* us, he hoped he might pray *for* us, which he would do upon all Occasions. In this manner we convers'd, and as he was of a most obliging gentleman-like Behaviour, so he was, if I may be allow'd to say so, a Man of good Sence, and as I believe, of great Learning.

He gave me a most divertingt Account of his Life, and of the many extraordinary Events of it; of many Adventures which had befallen him in the few Years that he had been abroad in the World, and particularly this was very remarkable, (*viz.*) That in the Voyage he was now engag'd in, he had had the Misfortune to be five times ship'd and unship'd, and never to go to the Place whether any of the Ships he was in, were at first design'd: That his first Intent was to have gone to *Martinico*, and that he went on board a Ship bound thither, at St. *Malo*;[3] but being forc'd into *Lisbon* by bad Weather, the Ship receiv'd some Damage,

---

1 To compete.

2 He wants to be spoken to as an individual, not as a member of a religious order.

3 Port in northwestern France, in Brittany.

by running a Ground in the Mouth of the River *Tagus*, and was oblig'd to unload her Cargo there; that finding a *Portuguese* Ship there bound to the *Maderas** and ready to sail, and supposing he should easily meet with a Vessel there bound to *Martinico*, he went on board, in order to sail to the *Maderas*; but the Master of the *Portuguese* Ship being but an indifferent Mariner, had been out in his Reckoning,[1] and they drove to *Fial*;[2] where, however, he happen'd to find a very good Market for his Cargo, which was Corn, and therefore resolv'd not to go to the *Maderas*, but to load Salt at the *Isle of May*,[3] and to go away to *Newfoundland*: He had no Remedy in this Exigence, but to go with the Ship, and had a pretty good Voyage as far as the *Banks*,[4] so they call the Place, where they catch the Fish, where meeting with a *French* Ship, bound from *France* to *Quebeck* in the River of *Canada*, and from thence to *Martinico*, to carry Provisions, he thought he should have an Opportunity to compleat his first Design: But when he came to *Quebeck*, the Master of the Ship dy'd, and the Ship proceeded no farther; so the next Voyage he shipp'd himself for *France*, in the Ship that was burnt, when we took them up at Sea, and then shipp'd with us for the East *Indies*, as I have already said: Thus he had been disappointed in five Voyages, all, *as I may call it*, in one Voyage, besides what I shall have Occasion to mention farther of the same Person.

But, I shall not make Digressions into other Men's Stories, which have no Relation to my own. I return to what concerns our Affair in the Island: He came to me one Morning, for he lodg'd among us all the while we were upon the Island; and it happen'd to be just when I was going to visit the *English* Men's Colony, at the farthest Part of the Island, *I say*, he came to me and told me, with a very grave Countenance, that he had for two or three Days desir'd an Opportunity of some Discourse with me, which he hop'd should not be displeasing to me, because he thought it might in some Measure correspond with my general Design, which was the Prosperity of my new Colony, and perhaps might put it, at least more than he yet thought it was, in the Way of God's Blessing.

---

1 Had been wrong in his calculations.

2 Faial or Fayal, a volcanic island, one of the Azores, in the North Atlantic, 930 miles west of Lisbon.

3 Maio, one of the Cape Verde Islands, an archipelago in the central Atlantic, off the West African coast.

4 The Grand Banks, once known for its cod fisheries, off the Newfoundland coast.

I look'd a little surpriz'd at the last Part of his Discourse, and turning a little short, *How Sir*, said I, *can it be said*, that we are not in the Way of God's Blessing, after such *visible Assistances* and *wonderful Deliverances* as we have seen here, *and of which I have given you a large Account?*

If you had pleas'd, *Sir, said he with a world of Modesty, and yet with great Readiness*, to have heard me, you would have found no room to have been displeas'd, much less to think so hard of me, that I should suggest, that you have not had wonderful Assistances and Deliverances; and I hope, on your Behalf, that you are in the Way of God's Blessing, and your Design is exceeding good, and will prosper: But, Sir, tho' it were more so, than is even possible to you, yet there may be some among you that are not equally right in their Actions: And you know, that in the Story of the Children of *Israel*, one *Achan*[1] in the Camp remov'd God's Blessing from them, and turn'd His Hand so against them, that six and thirty of them, tho' not concern'd in the Crime, were the Object of Divine Vengeance, and bore the Weight of that Punishment.

I was sensibly touch'd with his Discourse, and told him, his Inference was so just, and the whole Design seem'd so sincere, and was really so religious in its own Nature, that I was very sorry I had interrupted him, and beg'd him to go on; and in the mean Time, because it seem'd, that what we had both to say might take up some Time, I told him, I was going to the *English* Mens Plantations, and ask'd him to go with me, and we might discourse of it by the Way: He told me, he would more willingly wait on me thither, because there partly the Thing was acted, which he desir'd to speak to me about, so we walk'd on; and I press'd him to be free and plain with me, in what he had to say.

Why then, Sir, says he, be pleased to give me Leave to lay down a few Propositions, as the Foundation of what I have to say, that we may not differ in the general Principles, tho' we may be of some differing Opinions in the Practice of Particulars. First, Sir, tho' we differ in some of the doctrinal Articles of Religion; and it is very unhappy that it is so, especially in the Case before us, as I shall shew afterwards: Yet there are some general Principles in which we both agree, (*viz.*) first, That there is a God; and that this God having given us some stated general Rules for our

1 In Joshua 7, Achan, during the destruction of Jericho, steals gold and silver for himself. Having caused thirty-six (innocent) Israelites to be killed by a neighboring tribe, Achan and his family are stoned to death as punishment.

Service and Obedience, we ought not willingly and knowingly to offend him; either by neglecting to do what he has commanded, or by doing what he has expresly forbidden: And let our different Religions be what they will, this general Principle is readily own'd by us all, That the Blessing of God does not ordinarily follow a presumptuous sinning against his Command; and every good Christian will be affectionately concern'd to prevent any that are under his Care, living in a total Neglect of God and his Commands. It is not your Men being Protestants, whatever my Opinion may be of such, that discharges me from being concern'd for their Souls, and from endeavouring, if it lies before me, that they should live in as little Distance from and Enmity with their Maker, as possible, especially if you give me Leave to meddle so far in your Circuit.

I could not yet imagine what he aim'd at, and told him, I granted all he had said, and thank'd him, that he would so far concern himself for us; and begg'd he would explain the Particulars of what he had observ'd, that like *Joshua*, to take his own Parable, I might put away the accursed Thing from us.[1]

Why then, Sir, says he, I will take the Liberty you give me; and there are three Things, which, if I am right, must stand in the Way of God's Blessing, upon your Endeavours here, and which I should rejoice for your Sake and their own to see remov'd. And Sir, says he, I promise myself, that you will fully agree with me in them all, as soon as I name them; especially, because I shall convince you, that every one of them may, with great Ease, and very much to your Satisfaction, be remedy'd.

He gave me no Leave to put in any more Civilities, but went on: *First, Sir*, says he, you have here four *English* Men, who have fetch'd Women from among the Savages, and have taken them as their Wives, and have had many Children by them all, and yet are not marry'd to them after any stated legal Manner, as the Laws of God and Man require; and therefore are yet, in the Sence of both, no less than *Adulterers*, and living in Adultery.* To this, Sir, *says he*, I know you will object, That there was no Clergy-man or Priest, of any Kind, or of any Profession, to perform the Ceremony; nor any Pen, and Ink, or Paper, to write down a Contract of Marriage, and have it sign'd between them: And I know also, Sir, what the *Spaniard* Governour has told you, I mean, of the Agreement that he oblig'd them to make, when they took these Women (*viz.*) That

1 In Joshua 13, the Israelites cannot stand strong before enemies until they cast out what is accursed among them.

they should chuse them out by Consent, and keep separately to them; which, by the way, is nothing of a Marriage, no Agreement with the Women, as Wives, but only an Agreement among themselves, to keep them from quarrelling.

But, Sir, the Essence of the Sacrament of Matrimony (so he call'd it, being a *Roman*)[1] consists not only in the mutual Consent of the Parties to take one another, *as Man and Wife*, but in the formal and legal Obligation, that there is in the Contract, to compel the Man and Woman at all Times, to own and acknowledge each other, obliging the Men to abstain from all other Women, to engage in no other Contract while these subsist; and on all Occasions, as Ability allows, to provide honestly for them and their Children, and to oblige the Women to the same or like Conditions, *mutatis mutandis*,[2] on their Side.

Now, Sir, *says he*, These Men may, when they please, or when Occasion presents, abandon these Women, disown their Children, leave them to perish, and take other Women, and marry them whilst these are living; and here he added, with some Warmth, How, Sir, is God honour'd in this unlawful Liberty? And how shall a Blessing succeed your Endeavours in this Place? *However good in themselves*, and *however sincere in your Design*, while these Men, who at present are your Subjects, under your absolute Government and Dominion, are allow'd by you to live in open Adultery?

I confess, I was struck at the Thing itself, but much more with the convincing Arguments he supported it with; for it was certainly true, that tho' they had no Clergy-man upon the Spot, yet a formal Contract on both Sides, made before Witnesses, and confirm'd by any Token,[3] which they had all agreed to be bound by, tho' it had been but breaking a Stick between them, engaging the Men to own these Women for their Wives, upon all Occasions, and never to abandon them or their Children, and the Women to the same with their Husbands; had been an effectual lawful Marriage in the Sight of God; and it was a great Neglect that it was not done.

But I thought to have gotten off with my young Priest, by telling him, that all that Part was done when I was not here, and they

---

1 For Protestants (unlike Roman Catholics), matrimony is not a sacrament.

2 With the necessary changes having been made.

3 Something that serves as a tangible representation, a visible symbol, of the agreement.

had liv'd so many Years with them now, that if it was an Adultery, it was past Remedy, they could do nothing in it now.

Sir, *says he, asking you Pardon for such Freedom*, you are right in this, that it being done in your Absence, you could not be charg'd with that Part of the Crime: But I beseech you, flatter not your self, that you are not therefore under an Obligation to do your utmost now, to put an End to it. How can you think, but that, let the Time past lie on who it will, all the Guilt for the future, will lie entirely upon you? Because it is certainly in your Power now to put an End to it, and in no Body's Power but your's.

I was so dull still, that I did not take him right; but I imagin'd, that by putting an End to it, he meant that I should part them, and not suffer them to live together any longer; *And I said to him*, I could not do that by any Means, for that it would put the whole Island into Confusion: He seem'd surpriz'd, that I should so far mistake him. No, Sir, *says he*, I do not mean, that you should now separate them, but legally and effectually marry them now; and as, Sir, my Way of marrying them, may not be so easy to reconcile them to, tho' it will be as effectual, even by your own Laws, so your Way may be as well before God, and as valid among Men; I mean, by a written Contract, sign'd by both Man and Woman, and by all the Witnesses present, which all the Laws of *Europe* would decree to be valid.

I was amaz'd to see so much true Piety, and so much Sincerity of Zeal, besides the unusual Impartiality in his Discourse, as to his own Party or Church, and such true Warmth for the preserving People that he had no Knowledge of, or Relation to, I say, for preserving them from transgressing the Laws of God; the like of which I had indeed not met with any where: But recollecting what he had said, of marrying them by a written Contract, which I knew would stand, too, I return'd it back upon him, and told him, I granted all that he had said to be just, and on his Part very kind, that I would discourse with the Men upon the Point now, when I came to them: And I knew no Reason why they should scruple to let him marry them all, which I knew well enough would be granted to be as authentick and valid in *England*, as if they were marry'd by one of our own Clergy-men: What was afterwards done in this Matter, I shall speak of by itself.

I then press'd him to tell me what was *the second Complaint* which he had to make, acknowledging, that I was very much his Debtor for *the First*, and thank'd him heartily for it: He told me, he would use the same Freedom and Plainness in the Second, and hop'd I would take it as well; and this was, that notwithstanding these *English* Subjects of mine, *as he call'd them*, had lived with those Women for almost seven Years, had taught them to speak *English*, and even to read it; and that they were, as he perceiv'd, Women of tolerable Understanding, and capable of Instruction; yet they had not to this Hour taught them any thing of the Christian Religion, no not so much as to know that there was a God, or a Worship, or in what Manner God was to be served, or that their own Idolatry, and worshipping they knew not who, was false and absurd.

This he said was an unaccountable Neglect, and what God would certainly call them to Account for, and perhaps at last take the Work out of their Hands: He spoke this very affectionately and warmly. I am persuaded, *says he*, had those Men liv'd in the savage Country, whence their Wives came, the Savages would have taken more Pains to have brought them to be Idolaters, and to worship the Devil, than any of these Men, *so far as he could see*, had taken with them to teach them the Knowledge of the true God: Now, Sir, *said he*, tho' I do not acknowledge your Religion, or you mine, yet we should be glad to see the Devil's Servants, and the Subjects of his Kingdom, taught to know the general Principles of the Christian Religion; that they might, at least, hear of God, and of a Redeemer, and of the Resurrection, and of a future State, Things which we all believe; they had at least been so much nearer coming into the Bosom of the true Church, than they are now in the publick Profession of Idolatry and Devil Worship.

I could hold no longer; I took him in my Arms, and embrac'd him with an Excess of Passion: *How far*, said I to him, have I been from understanding the most essential Part of a Christian! (*viz.*) to love the Interest of the Christian Church, and the good of other Mens Souls? I scarce have known what belongs to being a Christian. O, Sir, do not say so, *reply'd he*, this Thing is not your Fault. No, *says I*, but why did I never lay it to Heart as well as you? 'Tis not too late yet, *said he*, be not too forward to condemn yourself: But what can be done now, *said I*, you see I am going away? Will you give me Leave, *said he*, to talk with those poor Men about it? Yes, with all my Heart, *said I*, and will oblige them to give Heed to what you say too: As to that, *said he*, we must leave them to the Mercy of Christ; but 'tis our Business to assist them, encourage them, and instruct them; and if you will give me Leave, and God his Blessing, I do not doubt but the poor ignorant Souls shall be brought home into the great Circle of Christianity, if not into the particular Faith that we all embrace, and that even while you stay here: Upon this, *I said*, I shall not only give you Leave, but give you a thousand Thanks for it. What follow'd on this Account, I shall mention also again in its Place.

I now press'd him for the *third* Article, in which we were to blame. Why really, *says he*, it is of the same Nature, and I will proceed, *asking your Leave*, with the same Plainness as before; it is about your poor Savages, who are, as I may say, your conquer'd Subjects. It is a Maxim, Sir, that is or ought to be received among all Christians of what Church or pretended Church soever, (*viz.*) *The Christian Knowledge ought to be propogated by all possible Means, and on all possible Occasions*: 'Tis on this Principle that our Church sends Missionaries into *Persia*, *India*, and *China*,[1] and that our Clergy, even of the superior Sort, willingly engage in the most hazardous Voyages, and the most dangerous Residence among Murtherers and Barbarians, to teach them the Knowledge of the true God, and to bring them over to embrace the Christian Faith. Now, Sir, you have such an Opportunity here, to have six or seven and thirty poor Savages brought over from Idolatry to the Knowledge of God their Maker and Redeemer, that I wonder how you can pass such an Occasion of doing Good, which is really worth the Expence of a Man's whole Life.

I was now struck dumb indeed, and had not one Word to say. I had here a Spirit of true Christian Zeal for God and Religion before me, let his particular Principles be of what kind soever; as for me, I had not so much as entertain'd a Thought of this in my Heart before, and I believe should not have thought of it; for I look'd upon these Savages as Slaves, and People, who, had we had any Work for them to do, we would ha' used as such, or would ha' been glad to have transported them to any other Part of the World; for our Business was to get rid of them, and we would all have been satisfy'd, if they had been sent to any Country, so they had never seen their own: *But to the Case*, I say I was confounded at his Discourse, and knew not what Answer to make him. He look'd earnestly at me, seeing me in some Disorder; Sir, *says he*, I shall be very sorry, if what I have said gives you any Offence: No, No, *says I*, I am offended with no Body but myself; but I am perfectly confounded, not only to think that I should never take any Notice of this before, but with reflecting what Notice I am able to take of it now. You know, Sir, *said I*, what Circumstances I am in, I am bound to the *East-Indies* in a Ship freighted by Merchants, and to whom it would be

1 Christian missionary work in Persia, India, and China goes back to the 1300s.

an unsufferable Piece of Injustice to detain their Ship here, the Men lying all this while at Victuals and Wages upon the Owners Account. It is true, I agreed to be allow'd 12 Days here, and if I stay more, I must pay 3 *l. Sterling per Diem* Demorage,[1] nor can I stay upon Demorage above eight Days more, and I have been here 13 Days already, so that I am perfectly unable to engage in this Work, unless I would suffer my self to be left behind here again, in which Case if this single Ship should miscarry in any Part of her Voyage, I should be just in the same Condition that I was left in here at first, and from which I have been so wonderfully delivered.

He own'd the Case was very hard upon me, as to my Voyage; but laid it home upon my Conscience, whether the Blessing of saving seven and thirty Souls, was not worth my venturing all I had in the World for; I was not so sensible of that *as he was*? I return'd upon him thus, why, Sir, it is a valuable Thing indeed to be an Instrument in God's Hand to convert seven and thirty Heathens to the Knowledge of Christ, but as you are an Ecclesiastic, and are given over to the Work, so that it seems so naturally to fall into the Way of your Profession; how is it, that you do not rather offer your self to undertake it, than press me to it?

Upon this he fac'd about, just before me, as we walk'd along, and putting me to a full Stop, made me a very low Bow; I most heartily thank God and you, Sir, *says he*, for giving me so evident a Call to so blessed a Work, and if you think your self discharg'd from it, and desire me to undertake it, I will most readily do it, and think it a happy Reward for all the Hazards and Difficulties of such a broken disappointed Voyage as I have met with, that I may be drop'd at last into so glorious a Work.

I discover'd a kind of Rapture in his Face, while he spoke this to me; his Eyes sparkl'd like Fire, his Face glow'd, and his Colour came and went, as if he had been falling into Fits; in a word, he was fir'd with the Joy of being embark'd in such a Work. I paus'd a considerable while before I could tell what to say to him, for I was really surpriz'd to find a Man of such Sincerity and Zeal, and carry'd out in his Zeal beyond the ordinary Rate of Men, not of his Profession only, but even of any Profession whatsoever. But after I had consider'd it a while, I ask'd him seriously if he was in earnest and that he would venture on the single Consideration of an Attempt on those poor People, to be lock'd up in an unplanted

---

1 Demurrage, the payment due for delaying a vessel past the time it was supposed to sail. In this case, three pounds sterling is due per day.

Island for, perhaps, his Life, and at last might not know whether he should be able to do them any Good, or not?

He turn'd short upon me, and ask'd me what I call'd a Venture? Pray, Sir, *said he*, what do you think I consented to go in your Ship to the *East-Indies* for? Nay, *said I*, that I know not, unless it was to preach to the *Indians*: Doubtless it was, said he; and do you think, if I can convert these seven and thirty Men to the Faith of Christ, it is not worth my time, tho' I should never be fetch'd off the Island again; nay, is it not infinitely of more worth to save so many Souls, than my Life is, or the Life of 20 more of the same Profession? Yes, Sir, *says he*, I would give Christ and the blessed Virgin Thanks all my Days, if I could be made the least happy Instrument of saving the Souls of these poor Men, tho' I was never to set my Foot off of this Island, or see my native Country any more. But since you will honour me, says he, with putting me into this Work, *for which I will pray for you all the Days of my Life*, I have one humble Petition* to you, *said he*, besides; What is that, *said I*? Why, says he, it is, that you will leave your Man *Friday* with me, to be my Interpreter to them, and to assist me, for without some Help, I cannot speak to them, or they to me.

I was sensibly troubled at his requesting *Friday*, because I could not think of parting with him, and that for many Reasons; he had been the Companion of my Travels; he was not only faithful to me, but sincerely affectionate to the last Degree, and I had resolv'd to do something considerable for him,[1] if he out-liv'd me, as it was probable he would; then I knew that, as I had bred *Friday* up to be a Protestant, it would quite confound him to bring him to embrace another Profession; and he would never, while his Eyes were open, believe, that his old Master was a Heretick and would be damn'd, and this might in the End ruin the poor Fellows Principles, and so turn him to his first Idolatry.[2]

However, a suddain Thought reliev'd me in this Strait,[3] and it was this; I told him, I could not say, that I was willing to part with *Friday* on any Account whatever, tho' a Work that to him was of more Value than his Life, ought to be to me of much less Value than the keeping or parting with a Servant: But on the other hand, I was persuaded, that *Friday* would by no Means consent to part with me, and I could not force him to it without his Consent,

1 Upon his death, leave Friday money.

2 I.e., return him to the Pagan beliefs he had before Crusoe converted him to Christianity.

3 Predicament.

without manifest Injustice, because I had promised I would never put him away, and he had promis'd and engag'd to me, that he would never leave me, unless I put him away.

He seem'd very much concern'd at it, for he had no rational Access to these poor People, seeing he did not understand one Word of their Language, nor they one Word of his: To remove this Difficulty, I told him, *Friday*'s Father had learn'd *Spanish*, which I found he also understood, and he should serve him for an Interpreter; so he was much better satisfied, and nothing could persuade him, but he would stay to endeavour to convert them; but Providence gave another and very happy Turn to all this.

I come back now to the first Part of his Objections. When we came to the *English* Men, I sent for them altogether, and after some Account given them of what I had done for them, (*viz.*) what necessary Things I had provided for them, and how they were distributed, which they were very sensible of, and very thankful for. I began to talk to them of the scandalous Life they led, and gave them a full Account of the Notice the Clergy-man had already taken of it, and arguing how unchristian and irreligious a Life it was. I first ask'd them if they were married Men or Batchelors? They soon explain'd their Condition to me, and shew'd me that two of them were Widowers, and the other three were single Men or Batchelors. I ask'd them with what Consciences they could take these Women and lie with them, as they had done, call them their Wives, and have so many Children by them, and not be marry'd lawfully to them.

They all gave me the Answer that I expected, (*viz.*) that there was no Body to marry them; that they agreed before the Governour to keep them as their Wives; and to keep them, and own them[1] as their Wives; and they thought as Things stood with them, they were as legally married, as if they had been married by a Parson, and with all the Formalities in the World.

I told them, that no doubt they were married in the Sight of God, and were bound in Conscience to keep them as their Wives, but that the Laws of Men being otherwise, they might pretend they were not married, and so desert the poor Women and Children hereafter; and that their Wives being poor desolate Women, friendless and moniless, would have no way to help themselves. I therefore told them, that unless I was assur'd of their honest Intent, I could do nothing for them; but would take Care that what I did, should be for the Women and their Children

1 Admit to them being their wives.

without them, and that unless they would give some Assurances, that they would marry the Women, I could not think it was convenient they should continue together as Man and Wife, for that it was both scandalous to Men, and offensive to God, who they could not think would bless them, if they went on thus.

All this went on as I expected, and they told me, especially *Will. Atkins*, who seem'd now to speak for the rest; that they lov'd their Wives as well, as if they had been born in their own Native Country, and would not leave them upon any Account whatever; and they did verily believe their Wives were as virtuous and as modest, and did to the utmost of their Skill, as much for them, and for their Children, as any Women could possibly do, and they would not part with them on any Account: And *Will. Atkins* for his own Particular, added, if any Man would take him away, and offer to carry him Home to *England*, and make him Captain of the best Man of War in the Navy, he would not go with him, if he might not carry his Wife and Children with him, and if there was a Clergy-man in the Ship, he would be married to her now with all his Heart.

This was just as I would have it; the Priest was not with me at that Moment, but was not far off: So to try him farther, I told him I had a Clergy-man with me, and if he was sincere, I would have him married the next Morning, and bid him consider of it, and talk with the rest; he said, as for himself, he need not consider of it at all, for he was very ready to do it, and was glad I had a Minister with me, and he believ'd they would be all willing also. I then told him that my Friend the Minister was a *French* Man, and could not speak *English*, but that I would act the Clerk* between them: He never so much as ask'd me whether he was Papist or Protestant, which was indeed what I was afraid of: But, I say, they never enquir'd about it. So we parted, I went back to my Clergy-man, and *Will. Atkins* went in to talk with his Companions. I desir'd the *French* Gentleman not to say any thing to them, till the Business was thorough ripe, and I told him what Answer the Men had given me.

Before I went from their Quarter, they all came to me, and told me, they had been considering what I had said, that they were very glad to hear I had a Clergy-man in my Company, and they were very willing to give me the Satisfaction I desir'd, and to be formally Married as soon as I pleas'd, for they were far from desiring to part with their Wives, and that they meant nothing but what was very honest when they chose them; so I appointed them to meet me the next Morning, and that in the mean time they should let their Wives know the meaning of the Marriage-Law; and that it was not only to prevent any Scandal, but also to oblige them, that they should not forsake them, whatever might happen.

The Women were easily made sensible of the Meaning of the Thing, and were very well satisfied with it, as, indeed, they had Reason to be; so they fail'd not to attend all together at my Appartment the next Morning, where I brought out my Clergy-man; and tho' he had not on a Ministers Gown, after the Manner of *England*, or the Habit of a Priest, after the Manner of *France*; yet having a black Vest something like a Cassock,[1] with a Sash round it, he did not look very unlike a Minister; and as for his Language, I was his Interpreter.

But the Seriousness of his Behaviour to them, and the Scruples* he made of marrying the Women, because they were not baptiz'd, and profess'd *Christians*, gave them an exceeding Reverence for his Person; and there was no need after that, to enquire whether he was a Clergy-man or no.

Indeed, I was afraid his Scruple would have been carry'd so far, as that he would not have marry'd them at all; nay, notwithstanding all I was able to say to him, he resisted me, though modestly, yet very steadily, and at last refused absolutely to marry them, unless he had first talk'd with the Men, and the Women too; and though at first I was a little backwards to it, yet at last I agreed to it with a good Will, perceiving the Sincerity of his Design.

When he came to them, he let them know, that I had acquainted him with their Circumstances, and with the present Design: That he was very willing to perform that Part of his Function, and marry them as I had desir'd; but that before he could do it, he must take the Liberty to talk with them. He told them, that in the Sight of all indifferent[2] Men, and in the Sense of the Laws of Society, they had liv'd all this while in an open Adultery; and that it was true, that nothing but the Consenting to marry, or effectually separating them from one another now, could put an End to it; but there was a Difficulty in it too, with respect to the Laws of *Christian* Matrimony, which he was not fully satisfy'd about, *viz*. That of marrying one that is a profess'd *Christian*, to a Savage, an Idolater, and a Heathen, one that is not baptiz'd; and yet that he did not see that there was Time left for it to endeavour to perswade the Women to be baptiz'd, or to profess

1 Loose outer robe or gown.

2 Impartial.

the Name of *Christ*, whom they had, he doubted, heard nothing of, and without which they could not be baptiz'd.

He told them, he doubted they were but indifferent Christians themselves; that they had but little Knowledge of God, or of his Ways; and therefore he could not expect that they had said much to their Wives on that Head yet; but that unless they would promise him to use their Endeavour with their Wives, to persuade them to become Christians, and would as well as they could instruct them in the Knowledge and Belief of God that made them, and to worship Jesus Christ that redeem'd them, he could not marry them; for he would have no Hand in joining Christians with Savages; nor was it consistent with the Principles of the Christian Religion; and was indeed expresly forbidden in God's Law.[1]

They heard all this very attentively, and I deliver'd it very faithfully to them, from his Mouth, as near his own Words as I could, only sometimes adding something of my own to convince them how just it was, and how I was of his Mind; and I always very faithfully distinguish'd between what I said from my self, and what were the Clergy-man's Words: They told me it was very true, what the Gentleman had said, that they were but very indifferent *Christians* themselves, and that they had never talk'd to their Wives about Religion: *Lord*! *SIR*, *says Will. Atkins*, How should we teach them Religion? Why we know nothing our selves; and besides, Sir, *said he*, should we go to talk to them of *God*, and *Jesus Christ*, and *Heaven*, and *Hell*, 'twould be to make them laugh at us, and ask us, What we believe ourselves? And if we should tell them we believe all the Things that we speak of to them, such as of good People going to *Heaven*, and wicked People to the *Devil*, they would ask us, Where we intend to go our selves, that believe all this, and are such wicked Fellows, as we indeed are? Why, Sir, 'tis enough to give them a Surfeit of Religion at first Hearing: Folks must have some Religion themselves, before they pretend to teach other People: *Will. Atkins, said I to him*; though I am afraid what you say has too much Truth in it, yet can you not tell your Wife that she is in the Wrong? That there is a God, and a Religion better than her own; that her Gods are Idols, that they can neither hear or speak; that there is a great Being that made all Things, and that can destroy all that he had made; that he rewards the Good, and punishes the Bad, and that we are to be judg'd by him at last for all we do here: You are not so ignorant, but even Nature it self

1 E.g., as in 2 Corinthians 6:14: "Be ye not unequally yoked together with unbelievers" (KJV).

will teach you that all this is true, and I am satisfy'd you know it all to be true, and believe it your self.

That's true, Sir, said *Atkins*; but with What Face can I say any Thing to my Wife of all this, when she will tell me immediately it cannot be true?

Not true, *said I*, What do you mean by that? Why, Sir, *said he*, She will tell me it cannot be true, that this God I shall tell her of can be just, or can punish, or reward, since I am not punish'd, and sent to the Devil, that have been such a wicked Creature as she knows I have been, even to her, and to every Body else; and that I should be suffer'd to live, that have been always acting so contrary to what I must tell her is Good, and to what I ought to have done.

Why, truly *Atkins*, *said I*, I am afraid thou speakest too much Truth; and with that I let the Clergy-man know what *Atkins* had said, for he was impatient to know: *O! said the Priest*; tell him there is one Thing will make him the best Minister in the World to his Wife, and that is, *Repentance*; for none teach Repentance like true Penitents: He wants nothing but to repent, and then he will be so much the better qualify'd to instruct his Wife: He will be then able to tell her, that there is not only a God, and that he is the just Rewarder of Good and Evil, but that he is a merciful Being, and with infinite Goodness and Long-suffering, forbears to punish those that offend, waiting to be gracious, and willing not the Death of a Sinner, but rather that he should return and live; that often-times suffers wicked Men to go on a long Time, and even reserves Damnation to the general Day of Retribution; that it is a clear Evidence of God, and of a future State, that righteous Men receive not their Reward, or wicked Men their Punishment, 'till they come into another World; and this will lead him to teach his Wife the Doctrine of the Resurrection, and of the last Judgment; let him but repent for himself, he will be an excellent Preacher of Repentance to his Wife.

I repeated all this to *Atkins*, who look'd very serious all the while, and who we could easily perceive, was more than ordinarily affected with it: When being eager, and hardly suffering me to make an End, *I know all this*, Master says he, *and a great deal more*; but I ha'nt the Impudence to talk thus to my Wife, when God, and my own Conscience knows, and my Wife will be an undeniable Evidence against me, that I have liv'd, as if I had never heard of a God, or future State, or any Thing about it; and to talk of my repenting, ALAS! *And with that he fetch'd a deep Sigh*; and I could see, that Tears stood in his Eyes; 'Tis past all that with me:

Past it, ATKINS, *said I*, What dost thou mean by that? I know well enough what I mean, says he, *I mean 'tis too late*, and that is too true.

I told my Clergy-man, Word for Word, what he said; the poor zealous Priest (I must call him so; for, be his Opinion what it will, he had certainly a most singular[1] Affection for the Good of other Mens Souls; and it would be hard to think he had not the like for his own) I say, this zealous affectionate Man, could not refrain Tears also: But, recovering himself, he said to me, ask him but one Question, Is he easy that it is too late, or is he troubled, and wishes it were not so? I put the Question fairly to *Atkins*, and he answered with a great deal of Passion, How could any Man be easy in a Condition that certainly must end in eternal Destruction; that he was far from being easy, but that, on the contrary, he believed it would one Time or other ruin him.

What do you mean by that, said I? Why? He said he believ'd he should one Time or other cut his Throat to put an End to the Terror of it.

The Clergy-man shook his Head with a great Concern in his Face, when I told him all this: But turning quick to me upon it, *says he*, If that be his Case, you may assure him it is not too late; Christ will give him Repentance: But pray, *says he*, explain this to him, That as no Man is sav'd but by Christ and the Merit of his Passion,[2] procuring divine Mercy for him, how can it be too late for any Man to receive Mercy? Does he think he is able to sin beyond the Power or Reach of divine Mercy?[3] Pray tell him, there may be a Time when provok'd Mercy will no longer strive, and when God may refuse to hear, but that 'tis never too late for Men to ask Mercy; and we that are Christ's Servants are commanded *to preach* Mercy at all times, *in the Name of Jesus Christ, to all those that sincerely repent*; so that 'tis never too late to repent.

I told *Atkins* all this, and he heard me with great Earnestness; but it seem'd as if he turn'd off the Discourse to the rest; for he said to me he would go and have some Talk with his Wife; so he went out a while, and we talk'd to the rest. I perceiv'd they were all stupidly ignorant as to Matters of Religion; much as I was when I

1 Remarkable.

2 In other words, people are saved only through the sufferings and death (the so-called passions) of Jesus Christ.

3 In Christianity, despair, or the belief that one is beyond salvation, is a form of the cardinal sin of pride and is the one sin that cannot be forgiven.

went rambling away from my Father; and yet that there were none of them backward to hear what had been said; and all of them seriously promis'd, that they would talk with their Wives about it, and do their Endeavour to persuade them to turn Christians.

The Clergy-man smil'd upon me, when I reported what Answer they gave, but said nothing a good while; but, *at last*, shaking his Head, We that are Christ's Servants, *says he*, can go no farther than to exhort and instruct, and when Men comply, submit to the Reproof, and Promise what we ask, 'tis all we can do; we are bound to accept their good Words: But believe me, Sir, *said he*, whatever you may have known of the Life of that Man you call *Will. Atkins*, I believe he is the only sincere Convert among them; I take that Man to be a true Penitent; I wont despair of the rest; but that Man is apparently struck with the Sense of his past Life; and I doubt not, but when he comes to talk Religion to his Wife, he will talk himself effectually into it; for attempting to teach others, is sometimes the best way of teaching our selves. I knew a Man, who having nothing but a summary Notion of Religion himself, and being wicked and profligate to the last Degree in his Life, made a thorough Reformation in himself, by labouring to convert *a Jew*. If that poor *Atkins* begins but once to talk seriously of Jesus Christ to his Wife, my Life for it, he talks himself into a thorough Convert, makes himself a Penitent: And who knows what may follow?

Upon this Discourse however, and their promising, as above, to endeavour to persuade their Wives to embrace Christianity, he marry'd the other three Couple; but *Will. Atkins* and his Wife were not yet come in; after this, my Clergy-man, waiting a while, was curious to know where *Atkins* was gone; and, turning to me, *says he*, I entreat you, Sir, let us walk out of your Labyrinth here, and look; I dare say, we shall find this poor Man somewhere or other talking seriously to his Wife, and teaching her already something of Religion. I began to be of the same Mind; so we went out together, and I carry'd him a Way which none knew but my self, and where the Trees were so thick set, as that it was not easy to see thro' the Thicket of Leaves, and far harder to *see in*, than to *see out*; when, coming to the Edge of the Wood, I saw *Atkins* and his tawny Savage Wife sitting under the Shade of a Bush, very eager in Discourse; I stopp'd short 'till my Clergy-man came up to me; and then having show'd him where they were, we stood and look'd very steadily at them a good while.

We observ'd him very earnest with her, pointing up to the Sun, and to every Quarter of the Heavens, then down to the Earth, then out to the Sea, then to himself, then to her, to the Woods, to the Trees. Now, says my Clergy-man, you see my Words are made good, the Man preaches to her; mark him now, he is telling her, that our God has made him, and her, and the Heavens, the Earth, the Sea, the Woods, the Trees, *&c.* I believe he is, *said I*; immediately we perceiv'd *Will. Atkins* start up upon his Feet, fall down on his Knees, and lift up both his Hands: We supposed he said something, but we could not hear him, it was too far for that; he did not continue kneeling half a Minute, but comes and sits down again by his Wife, and talks to her again; we perceiv'd then the Woman very attentive, but whether she said anything or no we could not tell; while the poor Fellow was upon his Knees I could see the Tears run plentifully down my Clergy-man's Cheeks, and I could hardly forbear my self; but it was a great Affliction to us both that we were not near enough to hear any Thing that pass'd between them.

Well, however, we could come no nearer for fear of disturbing them, so we resolv'd to see an End of this Piece of *still*[1] *Conversation*, and it spoke loud enough to us without the Help of Voice. He sat down again, as I have said, close by her, and talk'd again earnestly to her, and two or three times we could see him embrace her most passionately; another time we saw him take out his Handkerchief and wipe her Eyes, and then kiss her again with a kind of Transport very unusual; and after several of these Things we see him, on a suddain, jump up again and lend her his Hand to help her up, when immediately, leading her by the Hand a Step or two, they both kneel'd down together, and continu'd so about two Minutes.

My Friend could bear it no longer, but cries out aloud, St. PAUL St. PAUL! *behold he prayeth*;[2] I was afraid *Atkins* would hear him, therefore I entreated him to with-hold himself awhile, that we might see an End of the Scene, which to me, I must confess, was the most affecting, and yet the most agreeable that ever I saw in my Life: Well, he strove with himself and contain'd himself for a while, but was in such Raptures of Joy, to think that the poor Heathen Woman was become a Christian, that he was not able to contain himself; he wept several times, then throwing up his Hands and crossing his Breast, said over several Things Ejaculatory[3] and

1 Silent.

2 In Acts 9:11, Saul, soon to be Paul, is visited by a disciple called Ananias, whom God has bidden to "enquire in the house of Judas for one called Saul of Tarsus: for, behold, he prayeth" (KJV).

3 Suddenly and strongly uttered.

by way of giving God Thanks for so miraculous a Testimony of the Success of our Endeavours; some he spoke softly, and I could not well hear, others audibly, some in *Latin*, some in *French*; then two or three times the Tears of Joy would interrupt him, that he could not speak at all: But I begg'd that he would compose himself, and let us more narrowly and fully observe what was before us, which he did for a Time, and the Scene was not ended there yet; for after the poor Man and his Wife were risen again from their Knees, we observ'd he stood talking still eagerly to her; and we observ'd by her Motion, that she was greatly affected with what he said, by her frequent lifting up her Hands, laying her Hand to her Breast, and such other Postures, as usually express the greatest Seriousness and Attention; this continu'd about half a Quarter of an Hour, and then they walk'd away too; so that we could see no more of them in that Situation.

I took this Interval to talk with my Clergy-man: And first I told him, I was glad to see the Particulars we had both been Witnesses to; that tho' I was hard enough of Belief in such Cases, yet that I began to think it was all very sincere here, both in the Man and his Wife, however ignorant they might both be; and I hop'd such a Beginning would have a yet more happy End; and who knows, *said I*, but these two may in Time, by Instruction and Example, work upon some of the other? Some of them! *said he, turning quick upon me*, ay, *upon all of them*; depend upon it, if those two Savages, for he has been but little better, as you relate it, should embrace Jesus Christ, they will never leave 'till they work upon all the rest; for true Religion is naturally communicative, and he that is once made a Christian, will never leave a Pagan behind him, if he can help it. I own'd it was a most Christian Principle to think so, and a Testimony of a true Zeal, as well as a generous Heart in him: But, my Friend, said I, will you give me Leave to start[1] one Difficulty here, I cannot tell how to object the least Thing against that affectionate Concern, which you shew for the turning the poor People from their Paganism to the Christian Religion: But how does this comfort you, while these People are in your Account out of the Pale of the Catholick Church, without which you believe there is no Salvation; so that you esteem these but Hereticks, and for other Reasons as effectually lost, as the Pagans themselves.

To this he answer'd with abundance of Candor and Christian Charity, thus; Sir, I am a Catholick of the *Roman* Church, and a

1 Introduce.

Priest of the Order of St. *Benedict*,[1] and I embrace all the Principles of the *Roman* Faith: But yet if you will believe me, *and that I do not speak in Compliment to you, or in respect to my Circumstances, and your Civilities*; I say, nevertheless, I do not look upon you, who call your selves reform'd,[2] without some Charity: I dare not say, *tho' I know it is our Opinion in general*; I say, I dare not say that you cannot be sav'd: I will by no means limit the Mercy of Christ so far, as to think that he cannot receive you into the Bosom of his Church in a Manner to us unperceivable, and which it is impossible for us to know, and I hope you have the same Charity for us; I pray daily for your being all restor'd to Christ's Church, by whatsoever Methods he, who is *All-wise*, is pleas'd to direct: In the mean time, sure you will allow it to consist with me, as a *Roman*, to distinguish far, between a Protestant and a Pagan; between one that calls on Jesus Christ, tho' in a Way which I do not think is according to the true Faith, and a Savage, a Barbarian, that knows no God, no Christ, no Redeemer; and if you are not within the Pale* of the Catholick Church, we hope you are nearer being restor'd to it than those that know nothing of God or his Church: and I rejoice therefore, when I see this poor Man, who you say has been a Profligate, and almost a Murtherer, kneel down and pray to Jesus Christ, as we suppose he did, tho' not fully inlighten'd; believing that God, from whom every such Work proceeds, will sensibly touch his Heart, and bring him to the further Knowledge of that Truth in his own Time; and if God shall influence this poor Man to convert and instruct the ignorant Savage his Wife, I can never believe that he shall be cast away himself; and have I not Reason then to rejoyce, the nearer any are brought to the Knowledge of Christ, tho' they may not be brought quite home into the Bosom of the Catholick Church, just at the Time when I may desire it; leaving it to the Goodness of Christ to perfect his Work in his own time, and in his own Way. Certainly I would rejoyce if all the Savages in *America* were brought like this poor Woman to pray to God, tho' they were to be all Protestants at first, rather than they should continue Pagans and Heathens; firmly believing, that he that had bestow'd the first Light to them, would further illuminate them with a Beam of his heavenly Grace, and bring them into the Pale of his Church, when he should see good.

---

1 St. Benedict of Nursia (c. 480–543) established numerous monasteries in Italy; the monastic order that followed the Rule of St. Benedict was prosperous in Europe as a whole.

2 Crusoe is a Protestant, a product of the Protestant Reformation.

I was astonish'd at the Sincerity and Temper of this truly pious Papist, as much as I was oppress'd by the Power of his Reasoning; and it presently occur'd to my Thoughts, that if such a Temper was universal, we might be all Catholick Christians, whatever Church or particular Profession we joyn'd to, or joyn'd in; that a Spirit of Charity would soon work us all up into right Principles; and in a word, as he thought that the like Charity would make us all Catholicks, so I told him I believ'd, had all the Members of his Church the like Moderation, they would soon be all Protestants. And there we left that Part, for we never disputed at all.

However, I talk'd to him another way, and *taking him by the Hand*, my Friend, says I, I wish all the Clergy of the *Roman* Church were blest with such Moderation, and had an equal Share of your Charity. I am entirely of your Opinion; but I must tell you, that if you should preach such Doctrine in *Spain* or *Italy*, they would put you into the *Inquisition*.[1]

It may be so, said he, I know not what they might do in *Spain* or *Italy*, but I will not say, they would be the better Christians for that Severity, for I am sure there is no Heresy[2] in too much Charity.

Well, as *Will. Atkins* and his Wife were gone, our Business there was over; so we went back our own Way; and when we came back, we found them waiting to be call'd in; observing this, I ask'd my Clergy-man if we should discover to him that we had seen him under the Bush, or no; and it was his Opinion we should not, but that we should talk to him first, and hear what he would say to us; so we call'd him in alone, no Body being in the Place but our selves; and I began with him thus:

Will. Atkins, said I, prethee what Education had you? What was your Father?

W. A. A better Man than ever I shall be. *Sir, my Father was a Clergy-man.*

R. C. What Education did he give you?

1 In other words, they would subject you to interrogation by the Inquisition. The judicial prosecution of heresy in Christian ecclesiastical courts began at the end of the twelfth century in France. Ultimately, torture was part of the process, and unrepentant heretics could be burned at the stake. In 1478, King Ferdinand (1452–1516) and Queen Isabella (1451–1504) established the Spanish Inquisition, first to ensure the orthodoxy of Muslims and Jews who converted to Catholicism, and later to persecute Protestants.

2 Belief contrary to Christian doctrine.

W. A. He would have taught me well, Sir, but I despis'd all Education, Instruction, or Correction, like a Beast as I was.

R. C. It's true, *Solomon* says, *he that despises Reproof is brutish.*[1]

W. A. Ay, Sir, I was brutish indeed, I murther'd my Father; for God's sake, Sir, talk no more about that, Sir, I murther'd my poor Father.

Pr. Ha! a Murtherer!

Here the Priest started (for I interpreted every Word as he spoke it) and look'd pale. It seems he believ'd that Will. had really kill'd his own Father.

R. C. No, no, Sir, I do not understand him so; *Will. Atkins*, explain your self, you did not kill your Father, did you, with your own Hands?

W. A. No, Sir, I did not cut his Throat, but I cut the Thread of all his Comforts, and shortn'd his Days; I broke his Heart by the most ungrateful unnatural Return, for the most tender affectionate Treatment that ever Father gave, or Child could receive.

R. C. Well, I did not ask you about your Father, to extort this Confession; I pray God give you Repentance for it, and forgive you that, and all your other Sins; but I ask'd you, because I see that, tho' you have not much Learning, yet you are not so Ignorant as some are, in Things that are Good; that you have known more of Religion a great deal than you have practised.

W. A. Tho' you, Sir, did not extort the Confession that I make about my Father, Conscience does; and when ever we come to look back upon our Lives, the Sins against our indulgent Parents are certainly the first that touch us; the Wounds they make lie deepest, and the Weight they leave, will lie heaviest upon the Mind, of all the Sins we can commit.

R. C. You talk too feelingly and sensibly for me *Atkins*; I cannot bear it.

W. A. You bear it, Master! I dare say you know nothing of it.

R. C. Yes, *Atkins*, every Shore, every Hill, nay, I may say, every Tree in this Island, is witness to the Anguish of my Soul, for my Ingratitude and base Usage of a good tender Father; a Father much like yours, by your Description; and I murther'd my Father as well as you, *Will. Atkins*; but I think, for all that, my Repentance is short of yours too by a great deal.

I would have said more, if I could have restrain'd my Passions; but I thought this poor Man's Repentance was so much sincerer than mine, that I was going to leave off

---

1 See Proverbs 12:1.

the Discourse and retire, for I was surpriz'd with what he said; and thought, that instead of my going about to teach and instruct him, the Man was made a Teacher and Instructer to me, in a most surprizing and unexpected manner.

I laid all this before the young Clergy-man, who was greatly affected with it, and said to me; did I not say, Sir, that when this Man was converted, he would Preach to us all? I tell you, Sir, if this one Man be made a true Penitent, here will be no need of me, he will make Christians of all in the Island. But having a little compos'd my self, I renew'd my Discourse with *Will. Atkins.*

But, *WILL, said I,* How comes the Sence of this Matter to touch you just now.

W. A. Sir, you have set me about a Work that has struck a Dart thro' my very Soul; I have been talking about God and Religion to my Wife, in order, as you directed me to make a Christian of her, and she has preach'd such a Sermon to me, as I shall never forget while I live.

R. C. No, no, it is not your Wife has preach'd to you, but when you were moving religious Arguments to her, Conscience has flung them back upon you.

W. A. Ay, Sir, with such a Force as is not to be resisted.

R. C. Pray *Will.* let us know what pass'd between you and your Wife, for I know something of it already.

W. A. Sir, it is impossible to give you a full Account of it; I am too full to hold it, and yet have no Tongue to express; but let her have said what she will, and tho' I cannot give you an Account of it, this I can tell you of it, that I resolve to amend and reform my Life.

R. C. But tell us some of it. How did you begin *Will?* For this has been an extraordinary Case, that's certain. She has preach'd a Sermon indeed, if she has wrought this upon *you.*

W. A. Why, I first told her the Nature of our Laws about Marriage, and what the Reasons were, that Men and Women were oblig'd to enter into such Compacts, as it was neither in the Power of one or other to break; that otherwise, Order and Justice could not be maintain'd, and Men would run from their Wives, and abandon their Children, mix confusedly with one another, and neither Families be kept entire, or Inheritances be settled by legal Descent.

R. C. You talk like a Civilian,[1] *Will.* could you make her understand what you meant by Inheritance, and Families; they know

1 One who studies civil law.

no such Thing among the Savages, but marry any how without regard to Relation, Consanguinity,[1] or Family; Brother and Sister, nay, as I have been told, even the Father and Daughter, and Son and the Mother.

W. A. I believe, Sir, you are misinform'd, and my Wife assures me of the contrary, and that they abhor it; perhaps, for any farther Relations they may not be so exact as we are, but she tells me they never touch one another in the near Relations you speak of.

R. C. Well, what did she say, to what you told her?

W. A. She said, she lik'd it very well, and it was much better than in her Country.

R. C. But did you tell her what Marriage was?

W. A. Ay, ay, there began all our Dialogue. I ask'd her if she would be marry'd to me our Way? She ask'd me what Way that was? I told her Marriage was appointed by God; and here we had a strange Talk together, indeed, as ever Man and Wife had I believe.

N.B. This Dialogue between W. Atkins and his Wife, as I took it down in Writing, just after he told it me, was as follows.

Wife. Appointed by your God! why have you a God in your Country?

W. A. Yes, my Dear, God is in every Country.

Wife. No you God in my Country; my Country have the great old *Benamuckee* God.[2]

W. A. Child, I am very unfit to shew you who God is; God is in Heaven, and made the Heaven and the Earth, the Sea, and all that in them is.

Wife. No makee de Earth; no, you God make all Earth, no make my Country.~

~W. A. laugh'd a little at her Expression of God not making her Country.

Wife. No Laugh, why laugh me? This no Thing to laugh.[3]

~ He was justly reprov'd by his Wife, for she was more serious than he at first.

---

1 Blood relatives.

2 In Part I, Friday tells Crusoe this is his people's God, to whom they go when they die (171).

3 The elocutions of "Mary," "Wife," are reminiscent of Friday's speech patterns and linguistic errors in Part I, after years of life with Crusoe. In Gildon's satirical pamphlet *The Life and Strange Surprizing Adventures of Mr. D— DeF—*, Friday berates (and beats) "Defoe" for making him learn English so quickly and yet never master it.

W.A. That's true indeed, I will not Laugh any more my Dear.

Wife. Why you say, you God make all?

W.A. Yes, Child, our God made the whole World, and you, and I, and all Things; for he is the only true God, there is no God but him, he lives for ever in Heaven.

Wife. Why you not tell me long ago?

W.A. That's true, indeed, but I have been a wicked Wretch, and have not only forgotten to acquaint thee with any Thing before, but have lived without God in the World my self.

Wife. What have you de great God in you Country, you no kno' him? No say O* to him? No do good Thing for him? That no possible!

W.A. It is too true; tho' for all that, we live as if there was no God in Heaven, or that he had no Power on Earth.

Wife. But why, God let you do so? Why he no makee you good live.

W.A. It is all our own Fault.

Wife. But you say me, he is Great, much Great, have much great Power; can makee kill, when he will; why he no makee kill when you no serve him? No say O to him? No be good Mans.

W.A. That is true; he might strike me Dead, and I ought to expect it, for I have been a wicked Wretch, that is true; but God is merciful, and does not deal with us as we deserve.

Wife. But then, do not you tell God Tankee for that too.

W.A. No, indeed, I have not thank'd God for his Mercy, any more than I have fear'd God for his Power.

Wife. Then you God no God; me no think, believe, he be such one, great much Power, Strong; no makee kill you tho' you makee him much Angry.

W.A. What? Will my wicked Life hinder you from believing in God! what a dreadful Creature am I; and what a sad Truth is it, that the horrid Lives of Christians hinders the Conversion of Heathens?

Wife. How me tink you have great much God~ up there, and yet no do well no do good Thing; can he tell? Sure he no tell what you do?

~She points up to Heaven.

W.A. Yes, yes, he knows and sees all Things; he hears us speak, sees what we do, knows what we think, tho' we do not speak.

Wife. What! he no hear you swear, curse, speak the great Damn.

W.A. Yes, yes, he hears it all.

Wife. Where be then the muchee great Power strong?

W.A. He is merciful, that's all we can say for it; and this proves him to be the true God; he is God and not Man; and therefore we are not consum'd.~

> *~Here Will. Atkins told us he was struck with Horror, to think how he could tell his Wife so clearly, that God sees, and hears, and knows the secret Thoughts of the Heart, and all that we do; and yet that he had dar'd to do all the vile Things he had done.*

Wife. Merciful! what you call that?

W.A. He is our Father and Maker, and he pities and spares us.

Wife. So then he never makee kill, never angry when you do wicked; then he no good himself, or no great able.

W.A. Yes, yes, my Dear, he is infinitely good, and infinitely great, and able to punish too, and some Times to shew his Justice and Vengeance, he lets fly his Anger to destroy Sinners, and make Examples; many are cut off in their Sins.

Wife. But no make kill you yet, then he tell you, *may be* that he no make you kill, so you make de Bargain with him, you do bad Thing, he no be angry at you, when he be angry at other Mans.

W. A. No indeed, my Sins are all Presumptions upon his Goodness; and he would be infinitely just if he destroy'd me, as he has done other Men.

Wife. Well, and yet no kill, no makee you dead, what you say to him for that, you no tell him Tankee for all that too.

W.A. I am an unthankful, ungrateful Dog, that's true.

Wife. Why? He no makee you much good better, you say he makee you.

W. A. He made me as he made all the World; 'tis I have deform'd my self, and abus'd his Goodness, and made myself an abominable Wretch.

Wife. I wish you makee God know me, I no makee him angry, I no do bad wicked Thing.

> *Here Will. Atkins said his Heart sunk within him, to hear a poor untaught Creature desire to be taught to know God, and he such a wicked Wretch, that he could not say one Word to her about God, but what the Reproach of his own Carriage would make most irrational to her to believe; nay, that already she had told him, that she could not believe in God, because he that was so wicked was not destroy'd.*

W.A. My Dear, you mean, you wish I could teach you to know God, not God to know you; for he knows you already, and every Thought in your Heart.

Wife. Why then he know what I say to you now? He know me

wish to know him; how shall me know who makee me?

W. A. Poor Creature, he must teach thee, I cannot teach thee; I'll pray to him to teach thee to know him, and to forgive me that I am unworthy to teach thee.

> *The poor Fellow was in such an Agony at her desiring him to make her know God, and her wishing to know him, that, he said, he fell down on his Knees before her, and pray'd to God to enlighten her Mind with the saving Knowledge of Jesus Christ, and to pardon his Sins, and accept of his being the unworthy Instrument of instructing her in the Principles of Religion; after which he sat down by her again, and their Dialogue went on. N.B. This was the Time when we saw him kneel down, and hold up his Hands.*

Wife. What you put down the Knee for? What you hold up the Hand for? What you say? Who you speak to? What is all that?

W. A. My Dear, I bow my Knees in Token of my Submission to him that made me; I said O to him, as you call it, and as you say, your old Men do to their Idol *Benamukee*; that is, I pray'd to him.

Wife. What you say O to him for?

W. A. I pray'd to him to open your Eyes, and your Understanding, that you may know him, and be accepted by him.

Wife. Can he do that too?

W. A. Yes, he can, he can do all Things.

Wife. But now he hear what you say?

W. A. Yes, he has bid us pray to him, and promis'd to hear us.

Wife. Bid you pray? When he bid you? How he bid you? What! you hear him speak?

W. A. No, we do not hear him speak, but he has reveal'd himself many Ways to us.

> *Here he was at a great Loss to make her understand, that God has reveal'd himself to us by his Word, and what his Word was: But at last he told it her thus:*

W. A. God has spoken to some good Men in former Days, even from Heaven, by plain Words; and God has inspir'd good Men by his Spirit; and they have written all his Laws down in a Book.

Wife. Me no understand that, where is Book?

W. A. Alas, my poor Creature, I have not this Book; but I hope I shall one Time or other get it for you, and help you to read it.

> *Here he embrac'd her with great Affection; but with inexpressible Grief, that he had not a Bible.*

Wife. But how you makee me know, that God teachee them to write that Book?

W. A. By the same Rule that we know him to be God.

Wife. What Rule, what Way you know him?

W. A. Because he teaches and commands nothing but what is good, righteous, and holy; and tends to make us perfectly good, as well as perfectly happy; and because he forbids and commands us to avoid all that is wicked, that is evil in itself, or evil in its Consequence.

Wife. That me would understand, that me fain* see; if he teachee all good Thing, forbid all wicked Thing, he reward all good Thing, punish all wicked Thing, he makee all Thing, he give all Thing, he hear me when I say O to him, as you go do just now; he makee me good, if I wish be good, he spare me, no makee kill me, when I no be good; all this you say he do, yet he be great God; me take, think, believe him be great God; me say O to him too with you my Dear.

Here the poor Man could forbear no longer; but raising her up, made her kneel by him, and he pray'd to God aloud to instruct her in the Knowledge of himself by his Spirit, and that by some good Providence, if possible, she might sometime or other come to have a Bible, that she might read the Word of God, and be taught by it to know him.

This was the Time that we saw him lift her up by the Hand, and saw him kneel down by her, as above.

They had several other Discourses it seems after this, too long to set down here; and particularly she made him promise, that since he confest his own Life had been a wicked abominable Course of Provocations against God, that he would reform it, and not make God angry any more, least he should *make him dead*, as she call'd it, and then she should be left alone, and never be taught to know this God better; and least he should be miserable, as he had told her wicked Men should be after Death.

This was a strange Account, and very affecting to us both, but particularly to the young Clergy-man; he was indeed wonderfully surpriz'd with it, but under the greatest Affliction imaginable, that he could not talk to her, that he could not speak *English* to make her understand him; and as she spoke but very broken *English*, he could not understand her; However he turn'd himself to me, and told me, that he believed there must be more to do with this Woman than to marry her: I did not understand him at first, but at length he explain'd himself, (*viz.*) that she ought to be baptiz'd.

I agreed with him in that Part readily, and was for going about it presently: No, no, hold Sir, *said he*, tho' I would have her be baptiz'd by all Means, yet I must observe, that *Will. Atkins*, her Husband, has indeed brought her in a wonderful Manner to be willing to embrace a religious Life, and has given her just Ideas of the Being of a God, of his Power, Justice, Mercy; yet I desire to know of him, if he had said any Thing to her of Jesus Christ, and of the Salvation of Sinners, of the Nature of Faith in him, and Redemption by him, of the holy Spirit, the Resurrection, the last Judgment, and a future State.

I call'd *Will. Atkins* again, and ask'd him; but the poor Fellow fell immediately into Tears, and told us he had said something to her of all those Things, but that he was himself so wicked a Creature, and his own Conscience so reproach'd him with his horrid ungodly Life, that he trembled at the Apprehensions, that her Knowledge of him, should lessen the Attention she should give to those Things, and make her rather contemn Religion than receive it: But he was assur'd, he said, that her Mind was so dispos'd to receive due Impressions of all those Things, that if I would but discourse with her, she would make it appear to my Satisfaction, that my Labour would not be lost upon her.

Accordingly I call'd her in, and placing myself as Interpreter between my religious Priest and the Woman, I entreated him to begin with her; but sure such a Sermon was never preach'd by a popish Priest in these latter Ages of the World; and, *as I told him*, I thought he had all the Zeal, all the Knowledge, all the Sincerity of a Christian, without the Error of a *Roman* Catholick; and that I took him to be such a Clergy-man, as the *Roman* Bishops were before the Church of *Rome** assum'd spiritual Sovereignty over the Consciences of Men.

In a word, he brought the poor Woman to embrace the Knowledge of Christ, and of Redemption by him, not with Wonder and Astonishment only, as she did the first Notions of a God, but with Joy and Faith, with an Affection and a surprising Degree of Understanding, scarce to be imagin'd, much less to be express'd; and at her own Request she was baptiz'd.

When he was preparing to baptize her, I entreated him that he would perform that Office with some Caution, that the Man might not perceive he was of the *Roman* Church, if possible, because of other ill Consequences which might attend a Difference among us in that very Religion, which we were instructing the other in: He told me, that as he had no consecrated Chapel, no proper Things for the Office, I should see he would do it in a Manner that I should not know by it, that he was a *Roman* Catholick my self, if I had not known it before: And so he did; for saying only some Words over to himself in *Latin*, which I could not understand, he pour'd a whole Dish-ful of Water upon the Woman's

Head, pronouncing in *French*, very loud, MARY,[1] *which was the Name, her Husband desir'd me to give her; for I was her Godfather*, I baptize thee in the Name of the Father, and of the Son, and of the Holy Ghost; so that none could know any Thing by it, what Religion he was of: He gave the Benediction afterwards in *Latin*; but either *Will. Atkins* did not know but it was in *French*, or else did not take Notice of it, at that time.

As soon as this was over we married them; and after the Marriage was over he turn'd himself to *Will. Atkins*, and in a very affectionate Manner exhorted him, not only to persevere in that good Disposition he was in, but to support the Convictions that were upon him by a Resolution to reform his Life; told him it was in vain to say he repented, if he did not forsake his Crimes: Represented to him, how God had honoured him with being the Instrument of bringing his Wife to the Knowledge of the Christian Religion, and that he should be careful he did not dishonour the Grace of God, and that if he did, he would see the Heathen a better Christian than himself, the Savage converted, and the Instrument cast away.

He said a great many good Things to them both, and then recommending them in a few Words to God's Goodness, gave them the Benediction again, I repeating every Thing to them in *English*, and thus ended the Ceremony: I think it was the most pleasant, agreeable Day to me that ever I passed in my whole Life.

But my Clergy-man had not done yet; his Thoughts hung continually upon the Conversion of the seven and thirty Savages, and fain he would have stay'd upon the Island to have undertaken it; but I convinc'd him, first, that his Undertaking was impracticable in it self; and secondly, that perhaps I would put it into a Way of being done in his Absence to his Satisfaction; of which, by and by.

Having thus brought the Affair of the Island to a narrow Compass, I was preparing to go on board the Ship, when the young Man who I had taken out of the famish'd Ship's Company came to me, and told me, he understood I had a Clergy-man with me, and that I had caused the *English* Men to be married to the Savages, whom they called Wives; that he had a Match too, which he desir'd might be finish'd before I went, between two Christians, which he hop'd would not be disagreeable to me.

---

1 As with Friday, her original name is not given. Significantly, "Mary" is a homonym for "marry"; the Indigenous woman's marriage (and deference) to Atkins not only serves to (unequally) unite different nationalities but also unites the Protestant Crusoe and the Catholic priest in their Christianizing aims.

I knew this must be the young Woman who was his Mother's Servant, for there was no other Christian Woman on the Island; so I began to persuade him not to do any Thing of that Kind rashly, or because he found himself in this solitary Circumstance: I represented to him that he had some considerable Substance in the World and good Friends as I understood by himself, and by his Maid also; that the Maid was not only poor, and a Servant, but was unequal to him, she being six or seven and twenty Years old, and he not above seventeen or eighteen; that he might very probably with my Assistance, make a remove from this Wilderness, and come into his own Country again, and that then it would be a thousand to one but he would repent his Choice; and the Dislike of that Circumstance might be disadvantagious to both: I was going to say more but he interrupted me, smiling, and told me, with a great Deal of Modesty, that I mistook in my Guesses, that he had nothing of that Kind in his Thoughts, his present Circumstance being melancholly and disconsolate enough; and he was very glad to hear that I had Thoughts of putting them in a Way to see their Country again, and nothing should have put him upon staying there, but that the Voyage I was going was so exceeding long and hazardous, and would carry him quite out of the Reach of all his Friends; that he had nothing to desire of me, but that I would settle him in some little Property in the Island where he was, give him a Servant or two and some few Necessaries, and he would settle himself here like a Planter, waiting the good Time, when if ever I return'd to *England*, I would redeem him, and hop'd I would not be unmindful of him when I came into *England*; that he would give me some Letters to his Friends in *London*, to let them know how good I had been to him, and in what Part of the World, and what Circumstance I had left him in; that he promised me, that whenever I redeem'd him, the Plantation, and all the Improvements he had made upon it, let the Value be what it would, should be wholly mine.

His Discourse was very prettily delivered,[1] considering his Youth, and was the more agreeable to me, because he told me positively the Match was not for himself: I gave him all possible Assurances, that if I liv'd to come safe to *England*, I would deliver his Letters and do his Business effectually, and that he might depend I would never forget the Circumstance I had left him in;[2] but still I was impatient to know who was the Person to be

1 He was very well-spoken.

2 Crusoe breaks these promises.

married, upon which he told me it was my *Jack of all Trades*, and his Maid *Susan*.

I was most agreeably surpriz'd, when he nam'd the Match, for indeed I thought it very suitable; the Character of that Man I have given already; and as for the Maid, she was a very honest, modest, sober and religious young Woman, had a very good Share of Sense, was agreeable enough in her Person, spoke very handsomely and to the Purpose, always with Decency and good Manners, and not backwards to speak when any Thing required it, or impertinently forward to speak when it was not her Business; very Handy and Housewifely in any Thing that was before her; an excellent Manager, and fit indeed to have been Governess to the whole Island; she knew very well how to behave to all Kind of Folks she had about her, and to better, if she had found any there.

The Match being proposed in this Manner, we married them the same Day, and as I was Father at the Altar, as I may say, and gave her away, so I gave her a Portion; for I appointed her and her Husband a handsom large Space of Ground for their Plantation; and indeed this Match and the Proposal the young Gentleman made to give him a small Property in the Island, put me upon parcelling it out amongst them, that they might not quarrel afterwards about their Situation.

This sharing out the Land to them, I left to *Will. Atkins*, who indeed was now grown a most sober grave managing Fellow, perfectly reform'd, exceeding Pious and Religious, and as far as I may be allow'd to speak positively in such a Case, I verily believe, was a true sincere Penitent.

He divided Things so justly and so much to every one's Satisfaction, that they only desired one general Writing under my Hand[1] for the whole, which I caused to be drawn up and sign'd and seal'd to them, setting out the Bounds and Situation of every Man's Plantation, and testifying that I gave them thereby severally[2] a Right to the whole Possession and Inheritance of the respective Plantations or Farms, with their Improvements[3] to them and their Heirs, reserving all the rest of the Island as my own Property, and a certain Rent for every particular Plantation after eleven Years, if I or any one from me or in my Name came to demand it, producing an attested Copy of the same Writing.[4]

---

1 Produced by me.

2 Individually, in turn.

3 Including any improvements made to the lands/estates.

4 I.e., rents will be due starting in the twelfth year, should Crusoe or any factor of his come to claim it from the islanders.

As to the Government and Laws among them, I told them I was not capable of giving them better Rules, than they were able to give themselves, only made them promise me to live in Love and good Neighbourhood with one another; and so I prepared to leave them.

One Thing I must not omit and this is, that being now settled in a Kind of Common-Wealth[1] among themselves, and having much Business in Hand, it was but odd to have seven and thirty *Indians* live in a Nook of the Island, independent, and indeed un-employ'd; for excepting the providing themselves Food, which they had Difficulty enough in too, sometimes, they had no manner of Business or Property to manage: I propos'd therefore to the Governour *Spaniard*, that he should go to them with *Friday*'s Father, and propose to them to remove, and either plant for themselves, or take them into their several Families as Servants to be maintain'd for their Labour, but without being absolute Slaves, for I would not admit them to make them Slaves by Force by any Means, because they had their Liberty given them by Capitulation, and as it were Articles of Surrender, which they ought not to break.

They most willingly embrac'd the Proposal, and came all very chearfully along with him; so we allotted them Land, and Plantations, which three or four accepted of, but all the rest chose to be employ'd as Servants in the several Families we had settled; and thus my Colony was in a Manner settled, as follows: The *Spaniards* possess'd my original Habitation, which was the Capital City, and extended their Plantations all along the side of the Brook, which made the Creek that I have so often describ'd, as far as my Bower; and as they encreas'd their Culture,[2] it went always Eastward; the *English* liv'd in the North-East Part, where *W. Atkins*, and his Comrades began, and came on Southward, and South-West, towards the back Part of the *Spaniards*; and every Plantation had a great Addition of Land to take in, if they found Occasion, so that they need not jostle one another for want of Room.

All the East End of the Island was left uninhabited, that if any of the Savages should come on Shore there only for their usual customary Barbarities they might come and go, if they disturb'd no Body, no Body would disturb them; and no doubt but they were often ashore, and went away again; for I never heard that the Planters were ever attack'd or disturb'd any more.

---

1 An independent community with marks of a democratic republic.

2 Cultivation of the land.

It now came into my Thoughts, that I had hinted to my Friend the Clergy-man, that the Work of converting the Savages, might perhaps be set on foot in his Absence, to his Satisfaction; and I told him, that now I thought it was put in a fair Way; for the Savages being thus divided among the Christians, if they would but every one of them do their Part with those which came under their Hands, I hop'd it might have a very good Effect.

He agreed presently in that, if *said he*, they will do their Part; but how, *says he*, shall we obtain that of them? I told him, we would call them altogether, and leave it in Charge with them, or go to them one by one, which he thought best, so we divided it; he to speak to the *Spaniards*, who were all Papists, and I to the *English*, who were all Protestants; and we recommended it earnestly to them, and made them promise, that they never would make any Distinction of Papist or Protestant, in their exhorting the Savages to turn Christians; but teach them the general Knowledge of the true God; and of their Saviour Jesus Christ; and they likewise promis'd us, that they would never have any Differences or Disputes one with another, about Religion.

When I came to *W. Atkins*'s *House*, I may call it so, for such a House, or such a Piece of Basket-Work, I believe, was not standing in the World again; I say, when I came there, I found the young Woman I have mention'd above, and *W. Atkins*'s Wife, were become Intimates;[1] and this prudent religious young Woman, had perfected the Work *Will. Atkins* had begun; and tho' it was not above four Days after what I have related,[2] yet the new baptiz'd Savage Woman was made such a Christian, as I have seldom heard of any like her in all my Observation, or Conversation, in the World.

It came next into my Mind in the Morning before I went to them, that amongst all the needful Things I had to leave with them, I had not left them a Bible; in which, I shew'd my self less considering for them, than my good Friend the Widow was for me, when she sent me the Cargo of an hundred Pounds

---

1 Friends.

2 Crusoe stays on the island "five and twenty" days; the fact that he leaves the island "not above four Days after" the marriage of the English Protestant Atkins and the (formerly) Pagan Indigenous woman "Mary" seems to indicate that the marriage occurs on 1 May, the anniversary of the 1707 Act of Union of England and Scotland, a detail that in itself supports Defoe's claims to have written a kind of allegorical history (about the forming of Great Britain, then, and about his role in bringing the same about).

from *Lisbon*, where she pack'd up 3 Bibles, and a Prayer-book: However, the good Woman's Charity had a greater Extent than ever she imagin'd; for they were reserv'd for the Comfort and Instruction of those, that made much better Use of them than I had done.

I took one of the Bibles in my Pocket, and when I came to *Will. Atkins*'s Tent or House, and found the young Woman, and *Atkins*'s baptiz'd Wife, had been discoursing of Religion together; for *W. Atkins told it me, with a great deal of Joy*: I ask'd if they were together now, and he said, yes; so I went into the House, and he with me, and we found them together very earnest in Discourse; O Sir, says *Will. Atkins*, when God has Sinners to reconcile to himself, and Aliens[1] to bring Home, He never wants a Messenger; my Wife has got a new Instructor; I knew I was unworthy, as I was uncapable of that Work; that young Woman has been sent hither from Heaven; she is enough to convert a whole Island of Savages; the young Woman blush'd, and rose up to go away, but I desir'd her to sit still; I told her, she had a good Work upon her Hands, and I hop'd God would bless her in it.

We talk'd a little, and I did not perceive they had any Book among them, tho' I did not ask; but I put my Hand in my Pocket, and pull'd out my Bible; here, *says I*, to *Atkins*, I have brought you an Assistant that perhaps you had not before; the Man was so confounded, that he was not able to speak for some Time; but recovering himself, he takes it with both his Hands, and turning to his Wife, here, *my dear*, says he; did not I tell you, our God tho' he lives above, could hear what we said? Here's the Book I pray'd for, when you and I kneel'd down under the Bush; now God has heard us, and sent it; when he had said so, the Man fell into such Transports of a passionate Joy, that between the Joy of having it, and giving God Thanks for it, the Tears run down his Face like a Child that was crying.

The Woman was surprised, and was like to have run into a Mistake, that none of us were aware of; for she firmly believ'd God had sent the Book upon her husband's Petition;[2] It is true, that providentially it was so, and might be taken so in a consequent Sense; but I believe, it would have been no difficult Matter at that Time, to have persuaded the poor Woman to have believ'd, that an express Messenger came from Heaven, on Purpose to bring that individual Book; but it was too serious a Matter, to suffer any

1 Alienated souls.

2 In other words, in answer to his prayer.

Delusion to take Place; so I turn'd to the young Woman and told her, we did not desire to impose upon the new Convert, in her first, and more ignorant understanding of Things; and begg'd her to explain to her, that God may be very properly said to answer our Petitions, when in the Course of his Providence, such Things are in a particular Manner brought to pass, as we petition'd for; but we do not expect Returns from Heaven, in a miraculous and particular Manner, and that it is our Mercy, that it is not so.

This the young Woman did afterwards effectually; so that there was I assure you, no Priestcraft[1] used here; and I should have thought it one of the most unjustifiable Frauds in the World, to have had it so; but the Surprise of Joy upon *Will. Atkins*, is really not to be expressed; and there we may be sure, there was no Delusion: Sure, no Man was ever more thankful in the World for any Thing of its Kind, than he was for this Bible; nor I believe, never any Man was glad of a Bible from a better Principle; and tho' he had been a most profligate Creature, desperate, headstrong, outragious, furious, and wicked to a great Degree; yet this Man is a standing Rule to us all, for the well instructing Children, (*viz.*) that Parents should never give over to teach and instruct, or ever despair of the Success of their Endeavours, let the Children be ever so obstinate, refractory, or to Appearance, insensible* of Instruction; for if ever God in his Providence, touches the Consciences of such, the Force of their Education returns upon them, and the early Instruction of Parents is not lost; tho' it may have been many Years laid asleep; but some Time or other, they may find the Benefit of it.

Thus it was with this poor Man; however ignorant he was, or divested of Religion and Christian Knowledge: He found he had some to do with now, more ignorant than himself; and that the least Part of the Instruction of his good Father that could now come to his Mind, was of Use to him.

Among the rest it occurr'd to him, he said, how his Father us'd to insist much upon the inexpressible Value of the Bible; the Privilege and Blessing of it to Nations, Families, and Persons; but he never entertain'd the least Notion of the Worth of it till now; when being to talk to Heathens, Savages, and Barbarians, he wanted the Help of the written Oracle for his Assistance.

The young Woman was very glad of it also for the present Occasion, tho' she had one, and so had the Youth on board our Ship among their Goods, which were not yet brought on Shore;

---

1 Derogatory term for the knowledge and work of priests.

and now having said so many Things of this young Woman, I cannot omit telling one Story more of her, and my self, which has something in it very informing and remarkable.

I have related, to what Extremity the poor young Woman was reduced; how her Mistress was starv'd to Death, and did die on board that unhappy Ship we met at Sea; and how the whole Ship's Company being reduc'd to the last Extremity; the Gentlewoman, and her Son, and this Maid, were first hardly used[1] as to Provisions; and at last totally neglected and starv'd; that is to say, brought to the last Extremity of Hunger.

One Day being discoursing with her upon the Extremities they suffer'd, I ask'd her, if she could describe by what she had felt, what it was to starve, and how it appear'd; she told me, she believ'd she could; and she told her Tale very distinctly thus.

'First, Sir, said she, we had for some Days far'd exceeding hard, and suffer'd very great Hunger; but now, at last, we were wholly without Food of any Kind, except Sugar, and a little Wine, and a little Water. The first Day, after I had receiv'd no Food at all, I found my self towards Evening, first empty and sickish at my Stomach, and nearer Night mightily enclin'd to yawning and sleepy; I laid down on a Couch in the great Cabin to sleep, and slept about three Hours, and awak'd a little refresh'd; having taken a Glass of Wine when I lay down; after being about three Hours awake, it being about five a-Clock in the Morning, I found my self empty, and my Stomach sickish, and lay'd down again, but could not sleep at all, being very faint, and ill; and thus I continu'd all the second Day, with a strange Variety, first Hungry, then sick again, with reachings[2] to vomit; the second Night being oblig'd to go to Bed again, without any Food, more than a Draught* of fair[3] Water; and being asleep, I dream'd I was at *Barbadoes*, and that the Market was mightily stock'd with Provisions; that I bought some for my Mistress, and went and din'd very heartily.

'I thought my Stomach was as full after this, as any would have been after, or at a good Dinner; but when I wak'd, I was exceedingly sunk in my Spirits, to find my self in the extremity of Famine: The last Glass of Wine we had, I drank, and put Sugar in it, because of its having some Spirit to supply Nourishment; but there being no Substance in the Stomach for the digesting Office[4]

1 Poorly treated.
2 Retchings.
3 Fresh.
4 Facility.

to work upon, I found the only effect of the Wine was, to raise disagreeable Fumes from the Stomach, into the Head; and I lay, as they told me, stupid, and senseless, as one drunk for some Time.

'The third Day in the Morning, after a Night of strange and confus'd inconsistent Dreams; and rather dozing than sleeping, I wak'd, ravenous and furious,[1] with Hunger; and I question, had not my Understanding return'd and conquer'd it; I say, I question, whether if I had been a Mother, and had had a little Child with me, its Life would have been safe or not?[2]

'This lasted about three Hours; during which Time I was twice raging mad as any Creature in *Bedlam*, as my young Master told me, and as he can now inform you.

'In one of these Fits of Lunacy or Distraction, whether by the Motion of the Ship, or some Slip of my Foot, I know not; I fell down, and struck my Face against the Corner of a Palat Bed[3] in which my Mistress lay; and with the Blow the Blood gush'd out of my Nose; and the Cabin Boy bringing me a little Bason, I sat down and bled into it a great deal; and as the Blood run from me, I came to my self; and the Violence of the Flame or Fever, I was in, abated, and so did the ravenous Part of the Hunger.

'Then I grew sick, and reached[4] to vomit, but could not; for I had nothing in my Stomach to bring up: After I had bled some Time, I swoon'd, and they all believ'd I was dead; but I came to my self soon after, and then had a most dreadful Pain in my Stomach, not to be described; not like the Cholick,* but a gnawing eager Pain for Food; and towards Night it went off with a kind of earnest Wishing or Longing for Food; something like, as I suppose, the Longing of a Woman with Child. I took another Draught of Water with Sugar in it; but my Stomach loathed the Sugar, and brought it all up again; then I took a Draught of Water without Sugar, and that stay'd with me;[5] and I laid me down upon the Bed, praying most heartily, that it would please God to take me away; and composing my Mind in Hopes of it, I slumber'd a while, and then waking, thought my self dying, being light with Vapours from an empty Stomach, I

1 Here, not extreme anger but an extreme state of being: furiously hungry.

2 In other words, she wonders if she might have turned cannibal; the first of several such statements she makes before consuming the day-old blood from her own nosebleed.

3 Pallet bed, a small bed with a mattress stuffed with straw.

4 Retched.

5 I kept the water down; I was not ill again.

recommended my Soul then to God, and earnestly wish'd that some Body would throw me into the Sea.

'All this while my Mistress lay by me just as I thought expiring, but bore it with much more Patience than I, and gave the last bit of Bread she had left to her Child, my young Master, who would not have taken it, but she oblig'd him to eat it; and I believe it sav'd his Life.

'Towards the Morning I slept again, and first when I awak'd, I fell into a violent Passion of Crying, and after that had a second Fit of violent Hunger; I got up ravenous, and in a most dreadful Condition; had my Mistress been dead, as much as I lov'd her, I am certain, I should have eaten a Piece of her Flesh, with as much Relish, and as unconcern'd, as ever I did the Flesh of any Creature appointed for Food; and once or twice I was going to bite my own Arm: At last, I saw the Bason in which was the Blood I had bled at my Nose the Day before; I ran to it, and swallow'd it with such Haste, and such a greedy Appetite, as if I had wonder'd no Body had taken it before, and afraid it should be taken from me now.

'Tho' after it was down, the Thoughts of it fill'd me with Horror, yet it check'd the Fit of Hunger, and I drank a Draught of fair Water, and was compos'd and refresh'd for some Hours after it: This was the 4th Day, and thus I held it,[1] 'till towards Night, when within the Compass of three Hours, I had all these several Circumstances over again, one after another, (*viz.*) sick, sleepy, eagerly hungry, Pain in the Stomach, then ravenous again, then sick again, then lunatick, then crying, then ravenous again; and so every quarter of an Hour, and my Strength wasted exceedingly: At Night I laid me down, having no Comfort, but in the Hope that I should die before Morning.

'All this Night I had no Sleep; but the Hunger was now turn'd into a Disease; and I had a terrible Cholick and Griping, by Wind instead of Food, having found its Way into the Bowels; and in this Condition I lay 'till Morning, when I was surpriz'd a little with the Cries and Lamentations of my young Master, who call'd out to me that his Mother was dead: I lifted my self up a little; for I had not Strength to rise, but found she was not dead, tho' she was able to give very little Signs of Life.

'I had then such Convulsions in my Stomach, for want of some Sustenance, that I cannot describe; with such frequent Throws[2] and Pangs of Appetite, that nothing but the Tortures of Death

---

1 Thus I remained.

2 Throes.

can imitate; and in this Condition I was when I heard the Seamen above cry out, *A Sail, a Sail*, and hallow and jump about, as if they were distracted.

'I was not able to get off from the Bed, and my Mistress much less; and my young Master was so sick, that I thought he had been expiring; so we could not open the Cabin Door, or get any Account what it was that occasion'd such a Combustion,[1] nor had we had any Conversation with the Ship's Company for two Days; they having told us, that they had not a Mouthful of any Thing to eat in the Ship; and they told us afterwards, they thought we had been dead.

'It was this dreadful Condition we were in when you were sent to save our Lives; and how you found us, Sir, you know as well as I, and better too.'

This was her own Relation, and is such a distinct Account of starving to Death, as I confess, I never met with, and was exceeding entertaining[2] to me; I am the rather apt to believe it to be a true Account, because the Youth gave me an Account of a good Part of it; tho' I must own, not so distinct and so feelingly as his Maid; and the rather, because it seems his Mother fed him at the Price of her own Life: But the poor Maid, tho' her Constitution being stronger than that of her Mistress, who was in Years, and a weakly Woman too, she might struggle harder with it; I say, the poor Maid might be supposed to feel the Extremity something sooner than her Mistress, who might be allowed to keep the last Bit something longer than she parted with any to relieve the Maid. No Question, as the Case is here related, if our Ship, or some other, had not so providentially met them, a few Days more would have ended all their Lives, unless they had prevented it by eating one another; and even that, as their Case stood, would have serv'd them but a little while, they being 500 Leagues from any Land, or any Possibility of Relief, other than in the miraculous Manner it happen'd: But this is by the Way; I return to my Disposition of Things[3] among the People.

And, *First*, It is to be observ'd here, That for many Reasons I did not think fit to let them know any Thing of the Sloop I had fram'd, and which I thought of setting up among them; for I found, *at least at my first coming*, such Seeds of Divisions among them, that I saw it plainly had I set up the Sloop, and left it among them, they would upon every light Disgust have separated, and

---

1 Uproar.

2 Interesting (archaic usage).

3 In other words, his description of how things were.

gone away from one another, or perhaps have turn'd Pirates, and so made the Island a Den of Thieves, instead of a Plantation of sober and religious People, so as I intended it; nor did I leave the two Pieces of Brass Cannon that I had on Board, or the two Quarter-Deck Guns, that my Nephew took extraordinarily for the same Reason: I thought it was enough to qualify them for a defensive War against any that should invade them; but not to set them up for an offensive War, or to encourage them to go Abroad to attack others, which in the End would only bring Ruin and Destruction upon themselves and all their Undertaking: I reserv'd the Sloop therefore, and the Guns, for their Service another Way, as I shall observe in its Place.[1]

I have now done with the Island:[2] I left them all in good Circumstances, and in a flourishing Condition, and went on board my Ship again the — of —,[3] having been five and twenty Days among them; and as they were all resolv'd to stay upon the Island 'till I came to remove them, I promis'd to send some further Relief from the *Brasils*, if I could possibly find an Opportunity; and particularly I promis'd to send them some Cattel, such as Sheep, Hogs, and Cows:[4] For as to the two Cows and Calves which I brought from *England*, we had been oblig'd by the Length of our Voyage to kill them at Sea, for want of Hay to feed them.

The next Day, giving them a Salute of five Guns at parting, we set sail, and arriv'd at the Bay of *All-Saints** in the *Brasils* in about 22 Days; meeting nothing remarkable in our Passage, but this, That about three Days after we sail'd, being becalm'd, and the Current setting strong to the E.N.E. running, as it were, into a Bay or Gulph on the Land Side, we were driven something out of our Course, and once or twice our Men cry'd Land to the Eastward; but whether it was the Continent or Islands, we could not tell by any Means.

---

1 I.e., its place in the narrative.

2 The first of two such statements; issued in the present tense.

3 The fifth of May. Dates left blank in the 1719 first edition. In the seventh edition (1747), the text reads "fifth Day of May." The math supports that designation: Crusoe tells us he returned to the island on 10 April 1695 and that he was on the island for "five and twenty days," and that he left not more than four days after the 1 May marriage date (recalling the 1 May 1707 passage of the Act of Union of Great Britain) of Mary and Will.

4 Crusoe sends some animals but breaks his promise about eventually returning to take the people off of the island.

But the third Day towards Evening, the Sea smooth, and the Weather calm, we saw the Sea, as it were, cover'd towards the Land with something very black, not being able to discover what it was, 'till after some Time, our chief Mate going up the main Shrowds[1] a little Way, and looking at them with a Perspective, cry'd out it was an Army. I could not imagine what he meant by an Army, and spoke a little hastily, calling the Fellow a Fool, or some such Word: Nay, Sir, *says he*, don't be angry, for 'tis an Army and a Fleet too; for I believe there are a thousand Canoes, and you may see them paddle along, and they are coming towards us too, apace.

I was a little surpriz'd then indeed, and so was my Nephew, the Captain; for he had heard such terrible Stories of them in the Island, and having never been in those Seas before, that he could not tell what to think of it, but said two or three Times, we should all be devour'd. I must confess, considering we were becalm'd, and the Current set strong towards the Shore, I lik'd it the worse: However, I bad him not be afraid, but bring the Ship to an Anchor, as soon as we came so near to know that we must engage them.

The Weather continu'd calm, and they came on apace towards us; so I gave Order to come to an Anchor, and furle all our Sails: As for the Savages, I told them they had nothing to fear but Fire; and therefore they should get their Boats out, and fasten them, one close by the Head,[2] and the other by the Stern, and man them both well, and wait the Issue in that Posture: This I did, that the Men in the Boats might be ready with Skeets[3] and Buckets to put out any Fire these Savages might endeavour to fix to the Out-side of the Ship.

In this Posture we lay by for them, and in a little while they came up with us; but never was such a horrid Sight seen by Christians: My Mate was much mistaken in his Calculation of their Number, I mean of a thousand Canoes; the most we could make of them when they came up, being about a hundred and six and twenty; and a great many of them too; for some of them had sixteen or seventeen Men in them, and some more; and the least six or seven.

When they came nearer to us, they seem'd to be struck with Wonder and Astonishment, as at a Sight which they had doubtless

1 Shrouds, or the ropes and cables that support the mast sideways.
2 Here meaning the front (the bow, the fore) of the ship.
3 Any scoops for throwing water over the sides of the ship.

never seen before; nor could they at first, as we afterwards understood, know what to make of us: They came boldly up however very near to us, and seem'd to go about to row round us; but we call'd to our Men in the Boats, not to let them come too near them.

This very Order brought us to an Engagement with them, without our designing it; for five or six of their large Canoes came so near our Long-Boat, that our Men beckon'd with their Hands to them to keep back, which they understood very well, and went back; but at their Retreat, about 50 Arrows came on board us from those Boats; and one of our Men in the Long-Boat was very much wounded.

However, I call'd to them not to fire by any Means; but we handed down some Deal Boards into the Boat, and the Carpenter presently set up a kind of a Fence like waste Boards[1] to cover them from the Arrows of the Savages, if they should shoot again.

About half an Hour afterwards they came all up in a Body a-stern[2] of us, and pretty near us, so near that we could easily discern what they were, tho' we could not tell their Design: and I easily found they were some of my old Friends, the same Sort of Savages that I had been used to engage with; and in a little Time more they row'd a little farther out to Sea, 'till they came directly Broad-side with us, and then row'd down strait upon us, 'till they came so near, that they could hear us speak: Upon this I order'd all my Men to keep close, lest they should shoot any more Arrows, and made all our Guns ready; but being so near as to be within hearing, I made *Friday* go out upon the Deck, and call out aloud to them in his Language, to know what they meant, which accordingly he did; whether they understood him or not, that I knew not: But as soon as he had call'd to them, six of them, who were in the foremost or nighest Boat to us, turns their Canoes from us; and stooping down, shew'd us their naked Backsides, just as if in *English*, saving your Presence, they had *bid us kiss* —;[3] whether this was a Defiance or Challenge, we know not; or whether it was done in meer Contempt, or as a Signal to the rest; but immediately *Friday* cry'd out they were going to shoot, and unhappily for him poor Fellow; they let fly about 300 of their Arrows, and, to

1 Boards about two feet high, attached to the sides of a ship in order to keep out high water.

2 They approached from the rear; the stern is the back end of the ship.

3 The context makes it clear: "Kiss my arse."

my inexpressible Grief, kill'd poor *Friday*, no other Man being in their Sight. The poor Fellow was shot with no less than three Arrows, and about three more fell very near him; such unlucky Marksmen they were.

I was so enrag'd with the Loss of my old Servant, the Companion of all my Sorrows and Solitudes, that I immediately order'd five Guns to be loaded with small Shot, and four with great, and gave them such a Broad-side,* as they had never heard in their Lives before, to be sure.

They were not above half a Cable Length[1] off when we fir'd; and our Gunners took their Aim so well, that three or four of their Canoes were overset, as we had Reason to believe, by one Shot only.

The ill Manners of turning up their bare Backsides to us, gave us no great Offence; neither did I know for certain, whether that which would pass for the greatest Contempt among us, might be understood so by them, or not; therefore in Return, I had only resolv'd to have fir'd four or five Guns at them with Powder only, which I knew would fright them sufficiently: But when they shot at us directly with all the Fury they were capable of, and especially as they had kill'd my poor *Friday*, who I so entirely lov'd and valu'd, and who indeed so well deserv'd it;[2] I not only had been justify'd before God and Man, but would have been very glad, if I could to have overset every Canoe there, and drown'd every one of them.

I can neither, tell how many we kill'd, or how many we wounded, at this Broad-side; but sure such a Fright and Hurry never was seen among such a Multitude; there were 13 or 14 of their Canoes split and overset in all, and the Men all set a swimming; the rest frighted out of their Wits, scour'd away as fast as they could, taking but little Care to save those whose Boats were split or spoil'd with our Shot: So I suppose, that they were many of them lost: And our Men took up one poor Fellow swimming for his Life, above an Hour after they were all gone.

Our small Shot from our Cannon must needs kill and wound a great many; but, in short, we never knew any Thing how it went with them; for they fled so fast, that in three Hours or thereabouts, we could not see above three or four straggling Canoes; nor did we ever see the rest any more; for a Breeze of Wind springing up the same Evening, we weighed and set Sail for the *Brasils*.

---

1 A cable length is 608 feet, so this is about three hundred feet.

2 That is, deserved to be loved and valued by Crusoe.

We had a Prisoner indeed; but the Creature was so sullen, that he would neither eat or speak; and we all fancy'd he would starve himself to Death: But I took a Way to cure him; for I made them take him and turn him into the Long-boat, and made him believe they would toss him into the Sea again, and so leave him where they found him, if he would not speak: Nor would that do; but they really did throw him into the Sea, and came away from him; and then he follow'd them; for he swam like a Cork, and call'd to them in his Tongue, tho' they knew not one Word of what he said: However, at last they took him in again, and then he began to be more tractable; nor did I ever design they should drown him.

We were now under Sail again; but I was the most disconsolate Creature alive, for want of my Man *Friday*, and would have been very glad to have gone back to the Island, to have taken one of the rest from thence for my Occasion, but it could not be; so we went on. We had one Prisoner, as I have said; and it was a long while before we could make him understand any Thing: But, in time, our Men taught him some *English*, and he began to be a little tractable; afterwards we enquir'd what Country he came from, but could make nothing of what he said; for his Speech was so odd, all Guterals, and spoke in the Throat in such an hollow odd Manner, that we could never form a Word after him;[1] and we were all of Opinion, that they might speak that Language as well, if they were gagg'd, as otherwise:[2] Nor could we perceive that they had any Occasion, either for Teeth, Tongue, Lips, or Palat, but form'd their Words, just as a hunting Horn forms a Tune with an open Throat; he told us however some time after when we had taught him to speak a little *English*, that they were going with their Kings to fight a great Battle. When he said Kings, we ask'd him how many Kings? He said, they were FIVE NATION, we could not make him understand the plural S. and that they all join'd to go against *Two Nation*. We ask'd him, what made them come up to us? He said, *to makee te great Wonder look*: Where it is to be observed, That all those Natives, as also those of *Africa*, when they learn *English*, they always add two E's at the End of the Words where we use one, and place the Accent upon them, as *makèè takèè*,[3] and the

1 We could never pronounce his words.

2 His speech was as unintelligible as if he were gagged.

3 In his edition of *Farther Adventures*, Owens quotes in a footnote an account by Dr. Layfield, chaplain to George Clifford, Earl of Cumberland, who traveled to the Caribbean in the late (*continued*)

like; and we could not break them of it; nay, I could hardly make *Friday* leave it off, tho' at last he did.

And now I name the poor Fellow once more, I must take my last Leave of him; poor honest *Friday*! we bury'd him with all the Decency and Solemnity possible, by putting him into a Coffin, and throwing him into the Sea: And I caused them to fire eleven Guns for him, and so ended the Life of the most grateful, faithful, honest, and most affectionate Servant, that ever Man had.

We went now away with a fair Wind for *Brasil*, and in about twelve Days Time we made Land in the Latitude of five Degrees South of the Line,* being the North-Eastermost Land of all that Part of *America*. We kept on S. by E. in Sight of the Shore four Days, when we made *Cape St. Augustine*,[1] and in three Days came to an Anchor off of *the Bay of all Saints*, the old Place of my Deliverance, from whence came both my good and evil Fate.

Never Ship came to this Part that had less Business than I had; and yet it was with great Difficulty that we were admitted to hold the least Correspondence on Shore, not my Partner himself, who was alive, and made a great Figure[2] among them; not my two Merchants Trustees, not the Fame of my wonderful Preservation in[3] the Island, could obtain me that Favour: But my Partner remembring, that I had given 500 Moidores* to the Prior of the Monastery of the *Augustines*, and 272 to the Poor, went to the Monastery, and oblig'd the Prior that then was, to go to the Governour, and get Leave for me personally, with the Captain and one more besides eight Seamen, to come on Shore, and no more; and this upon Condition absolutely capitulated for, that we should not offer to land any Goods out of the Ship,[4] or to carry any Person away without Licence.

They were so strict with us, as to landing any Goods, that it was with extream Difficulty that I got on Shore three Bales of *English* Goods, such as fine broad Cloaths, Stuffs, and some Linnen which I had brought for a Present to my Partner.

---

sixteenth century and wrote this about native Dominicans' pronunciation of English words: "to all words ending in a consonant they alwayes set the second vowell, as for chinne they say chine-ne, so making most of the monasillables, dissillables" (231n182).

1 Cabo de Santo Agostinho (Cape of Saint Augustine) is thirty-five kilometers south of the city of Recife, Pernambuco, Brazil.

2 Was a prominent man.

3 The story of my survival.

4 Should not try to bring anything on land.

He was a very generous broad hearted Man, tho' like me, he came from little at first; and tho' he knew not that I had the least Design of giving him any Thing, he sent me on Board a Present of fresh Provisions, Wine, and Sweet-meats, worth above 30 Moidores, including some Tobacco, and three or four fine Medals in Gold: But I was even with him in my Present, which, as I have said, consisted of fine broad Cloath, *English* Stuffs, Lace, and fine Hollands:[1] Also I deliver'd him about the Value of 100 *lib. Sterl.*[2] in the same Goods for other Uses; and I oblig'd him to set up the Sloop which I had brought with me from *England*, as I have said, for the Use of my Colony,[3] in order to send the Refreshments[4] I intended to my Plantation.

Accordingly, he got Hands,[5] and finish'd the Sloop in a very few Days, for she was already fram'd, and I gave the Master of her such Instructions, as he could not miss the Place, *nor did he miss them, as I had an Account from my Partner afterwards*. I got him soon loaded with the small Cargo I sent them; and one of our Seamen that had been on shore with me there, offer'd to go with the Sloop, and settle there upon my Letter to the Governour *Spaniard*, to allot him a sufficient Quantity of Land for a Plantation; and giving him some Cloaths, and Tools for his Planting-Work, which he said he understood, having been an old Planter at *Maryland*,[6] and a Buckaneer[7] into the Bargain.

I encourag'd the Fellow, by granting all he desir'd; and as an Addition, I gave him the Savage, which we had taken Prisoner of War, to be his Slave, and order'd the Governour *Spaniard* to give him his Share of every Thing he wanted, with the rest.

When we came to fit this Man out, my old Partner told me, there was a certain very honest Fellow, a *Brasil* Planter of his Acquaintance, who had fallen into the Displeasure of the Church; I know not what the Matter is with him, *says he*; but on my Conscience, I think he is a Heretick in his Heart, and he

---

1 Linens made in Holland, i.e., the Netherlands.

2 One hundred pounds sterling, English currency.

3 Before deciding against leaving it with them, that is.

4 The supplies.

5 He hired workers.

6 Established in 1634, Maryland was the second North American British colony; its tobacco plantations flourished due to the importation of indentured servants and (later) enslaved Africans.

7 A buccaneer, a pirate by any other name, although buccaneers tended not to raid their own nations' ships. From the French *boucanier*, one who cures meat on a barbecue frame.

has been obliged to conceal himself for Fear of the Inquisition;[1] that he wou'd be very glad of such an Opportunity to make his Escape with his Wife and two Daughters; and if I would let them go to my Island, and allot them a Plantation, he would give them a small Stock to begin with; for the Officers of the Inquisition had seiz'd all his Effects and Estate, and he had nothing left but a little Houshold-Stuff and two Slaves. And *adds he*, Tho' I hate his Principles, yet I would not have him fall into their Hands; for he would assuredly be burnt alive, if he does.

I granted this presently, and join'd my *English* Man with them, and we conceal'd the Man, and his Wife, and Daughters on Board our Ship, 'till the Sloop put out to go to Sea; and then (having put all their Goods on board the Sloop, some Time before) we put them on Board the Sloop, after he was got out of the Bay.

Our Seaman was mightily pleas'd with this new Partner; and their Stock indeed was much alike rich in Tools, in Preparations, and a Farm, but nothing to begin with, but as above: However, they carry'd over with them, which was worth all the rest, some Materials for planting Sugar Canes, with some Plants of Canes; which he, I mean, the *Portugal* Man, understood very well.

Among the rest of the Supplies sent my Tenants in the Island, I sent them by their Sloop, three Milch Cows, and five Calves, about 22 Hogs among them, three Sows big with Pig,[2] two Mares, and a Stone-Horse.[3]

For my *Spaniards*, according to my Promise, I engag'd three *Portugal* Women to go, and recommended it to them to marry them, and use them kindly. I could have procur'd more Women, but I remember'd, that the poor persecuted Man had two Daughters, and there was but five of the *Spaniards* that wanted;[4] the rest had Wives of their own, tho' in another Country.

All this Cargoe arriv'd safe, and as you may easily suppose, very welcome to my old Inhabitants, who were now with this Addition between sixty and seventy People, besides little Children; of which, there was a great many: I found Letters at *London* from them all by the Way of *Lisbon*, when I came back to *England*; of which I shall also take some Notice immediately.[5]

I have now done with my Island, and all Manner of Discourse

---

1 The Spanish Inquisition.

2 Piglets.

3 A stallion, not castrated.

4 Crusoe maintains a steady ratio of women to men.

5 The first of two mentions of letters from the island.

about it;[1] and who ever reads the rest of my Memorandum's, would do well to turn his Thoughts entirely from it, and expect to read of the Follies of an old Man, not warn'd by his own Harms, much less by those of other Men, to beware of the like; not cool'd by almost fourty Years Misery and Disappointments, not satisfy'd with Prosperity beyond Expectation, not made cautious by Affliction and Distress beyond Imitation.

I had no more Business to go to the *East-Indies*, than a Man at full Liberty, and having committed no Crime, has to go to the Turn-key at *Newgate*,[2] and desire him to lock him up among the Prisoners there, and starve him. Had I taken a small Vessel from *England*, and went directly to the Island; had I loaded her, as I did the other Vessel, with all the Necessaries for the Plantation, and for my People, took a Patent from the Government here,[3] to have secur'd my Property, in Subjection only to that of *England*; had I carry'd over Cannon and Ammunition, Servants and People, to plant, and taking Possession of the Place, fortify'd and strength-en'd it in the Name of *England*, and encreas'd it with People, as I might easily have done; had I then settled myself there, and sent the Ship back, loaden with good Rice, as I might also have done in six Months Time, and order'd my Friends to have fitted her out again for our Supply; had I done this, and stay'd there myself, I had, at least, acted like a Man of common Sense; but I was possessed with a wandering Spirit, scorn'd all Advantages, I pleas'd myself with being the Patron[4] of those People I plac'd there, and doing for them in a kind of haughty majestick Way, like an old Patriarchal Monarch; providing for them, as if I had been Father of the whole Family, as well as of the Plantation: But I never so much as pretended to plant in the Name of any Government or Nation, or to acknowledge any Prince, or to call my People Subjects to any one Nation more than another; nay, I never so much as gave the Place a Name; but left it as I found it belonging to no Body; and the People under no Discipline or Government

1 Having returned to the island in his mind and in the story, if not in reality, Crusoe now issues a second statement of leave-taking, more emphatic than the first.

2 London prison on Newgate Street; it burned down in the Great Fire of 1666 and was rebuilt in 1672.

3 Got a patent from the government that allowed him to take possession of land in the "New World."

4 From the Latin *patronus*, protector of clients, from *pater*, father. Source of support, or, alternatively, lord of the manor, even master (slave-owners were called "patrons" or "patroon").

but my own; who, tho' I had influence over them as Father and Benefactor, had no Authority or Power, to Act or Command one Way or other, farther than voluntarily Consent mov'd them to comply; yet even this, had I stay'd there, would have done well enough; but as I rambl'd from them, and came there no more, the last Letters I had from any of them,[1] was by my Partners means; who afterwards sent another Sloop to the Place, and who sent me Word, tho' I had not the Letter till five Years after it was written; that they went on but poorly, were Male-content with their long Stay there: That *Will. Atkins* was dead; that five of the *Spaniards* were come away, and that tho' they had not been much molested by the Savages, yet they had had some Skirmishes with them; and that they begg'd of him to write to me, to think of the Promise I had made, to fetch them away, that they might see their own Country again before they dy'd.

But I was gone *a Wild Goose Chase* indeed; and they that will have any more of me, must be content to follow me thro' a new Variety of Follies, Hardships, and wild Adventures; wherein the Justice of Providence may be duly observ'd, and we may see how easily Heaven can gorge us with our own Desires; make the strongest of our Wishes, be our Affliction, and punish us most severely with those very Things, which we think, it would be our utmost Happiness to be allow'd in.

Let no wise Man flatter himself, with the Strength of his own Judgment, as if he was able to chuse any particular Station of Life for himself: Man is a short-sighted Creature, sees but a very little Way before him; and as his Passions, are none of his best Friends, so his particular Affections, are generally his worst Counsellors.

I say this, with Respect to the impetuous Desire I had from a Youth, to wander into the World; and how evident it now was, that this Principle was preserv'd in me for my Punishment: How it came on, the Manner, the Circumstance, and the Conclusion of it, it is easy to give you historically, and with its utmost Variety of Particulars: But the secret Ends of Divine Power, in thus permitting us, to be hurry'd down the Stream of our own Desires, is only to be understood by those who can listen to the Voice of Providence, and draw religious Consequences from God's Justice, and their own Mistakes.

Be it, I had Business, or no Business, away I went; 'tis no Time now to enlarge any farther upon the Reason, or Absurdity of my

---

1 The second and last mention of the unheeded (and apparently unanswered) letters from the island.

own Conduct; but to come to the History, I was embark'd for the Voyage, and the Voyage I went.

I should only add here, that my honest and truly pious Clergyman left me here; a Ship being ready to go to *Lisbon*, he ask'd me leave to go thither, being still as he observ'd, bound never to finish any Voyage he began: How happy had it been for me, if I had gone with him!

But it was too late now; all Things Heaven appoints are best; had I gone with him, I had never had so many Things to be thankful for, and you had never heard of the second Part of the Travels and Adventures of *Robin. Crusoe*; so I must leave here the fruitless exclaiming at my self, and go on with my Voyage.[1]

From the *Brasils*, we made directly away over the *Atlantick Sea*, to the *Cape de bon Esperance*, or as we call it, the *Cape of Good Hope*; and had a tollerable good Voyage, our Course generally South-East; now and then a Storm, and some contrary Winds, but my Disasters at Sea were at an end; my future Rubs and cross Events[2] were to befal me on Shore; that it might appear the Land was as well prepar'd to be our Scourge, as the Sea; when Heaven, who directs the Circumstances of Things, pleases to appoint it to be so.

Our Ship was on a trading Voyage, and had a Supra Cargo on board, who was to direct all her Motions after she arrived at the *Cape*; only being limited to certain Numbers of Days, for Stay, by Charter party, at the several Ports she was to go to: This was none of my Business, neither did I meddle with it at all; my Nephew the Captain, and the Supra-Cargo, adjusting all those Things between them, as they thought fit.

We made no Stay at the *Cape* longer than was needful, to take in fresh Water, but made the best of our Way for the Coast of *Coremandel*; we were indeed inform'd, that a *French* Man of War of fifty Guns, and two large Merchant Ships, were gone for the *Indies*, and as I knew we were at War with *France*, I had some Apprehensions of them; but they went their own Way, and we heard no more of them.

I shall not pester my Account, or the Reader, with Descriptions of Places, Journals of our Voyages, Variations of the Compass, Latitudes, Meridian-Distances, Trade-Winds, Situation of Ports, and the like; such as almost all the Histories of long Navigation are full of, and makes the reading tiresome enough, and are

1 And go on with his narrative, that is.

2 Difficulties (rubs) and unfortunate events.

perfectly unprofitable to all that read it, except only to those who are to go to those Places themselves.

It is enough to name the Ports and Places, which we touch'd at, and what occurr'd to us upon our passing from one to another; we touch'd first at the Island of *Madagascar*; where, tho' the People are fierce and treacherous, and in particular, very well arm'd with Launces, and Bows, which they use with inconceivable Dexterity; yet we fared very well with them a while, they treated us very civilly; and for some Trifles which we gave them, such as Knives, Scissars, *&c.* they brought us eleven good fat Bullocks, middling in Size, but very good in Flesh;[1] which we took in, partly for fresh Provisions for our present spending,[2] and the rest, to salt for the Ship's Use.

We were obliged to stay here some Time after we had furnish'd our selves with Provisions; and I, that was always too curious, to look into every Nook of the World where ever I came, was for going on Shore as often as I could; it was on the East Side of the Island that we went on Shore, one Evening, and the People, who by the Way are very numerous, came thronging about us, and stood gazing at us at a Distance; but as we had traded freely with them, and had been kindly used, we thought our selves in no Danger; but when we saw the People, we cut three Boughs out of a Tree, and stuck them up at a Distance from us, which it seems, is a Mark in the Country, not only of Truce and Friendship, but when it is accepted, the other Side set up three Poles or Boughs, which is a Signal, that they accept the Truce too; but then, this is a known Condition of the Truce, that you are not to pass beyond their three Poles towards them, nor they to come past your three Poles or Boughs, towards you; so that you are perfectly secure within the three Poles, and all the Space between your Poles and theirs, is allow'd like a Market, for free Converse, Traffick, and Commerce: When you go there, you must not carry your Weapons with you; and if they come into that Space they stick up their Javelines and Launces, all at the first Poles, and come on unarm'd; but if any Violence is offer'd them, and the Truce thereby broken; away they run to the Poles, and lay hold of their Weapons, and then the Truce is at an End.

It happen'd one Evening when we went on Shore, that a greater Number of their People came down than usual, but all was very

1 Clearly, an unequal, even exploitative, trade, as the word "Trifles" indicates.

2 Rate of consumption.

friendly and civil, and they brought in several Kinds of Provisions, for which we satisfy'd them, with such Toys[1] as we had; their Women also brought us Milk, and Roots, and several Things very acceptable to us, and all was quiet; and we made us a little Tent or Hut, of some Boughs of Trees, and lay on Shore all Night.

I knew not what was the Occasion, but I was not so well satisfy'd to lye on Shore as the rest, and the Boat riding at an Anchor, about a Stone cast from the Land, with two Men in her to take care of her; I made one of them come on Shore, and getting some Boughs of Trees to cover us also in the Boat, I spread the Sail on the Bottom of the Boat, and lay under the Cover of the Branches of Trees all Night in the Boat.

About two a-Clock in the Morning, we heard one of our Men make a terrible Noise on the Shore, calling out for God's sake, to bring the Boat in, and come and help them, for they were all like to be murther'd; at the same Time, I heard the Fire of 5 Muskets, which was the Number of the Guns they had, and that, three Times over; for it seems, the Natives here, were not so easily frighted with Guns, as the Savages were in *America*, where I had to do with them.

All this while, I knew not what was the matter; but rouzing immediately from Sleep with the Noise, I caus'd the Boat to be thrust in, and resolvd, with three Fusils[2] we had on board, to land, and assist our Men.

We got the Boat soon to the Shore, but our Men were in too much Haste; for being come to the Shore, they plung'd into the Water to get to the Boat with all the Expedition they could, being pursu'd by between three and four hundred Men: Our Men were but nine in all, and only five of them had Fuzees with them; the rest had indeed Pistols and Swords, but they were of small Use to them.

We took up seven of our Men, and with Difficulty enough too, three of them being very ill wounded; and that which was still worse, was, that while we stood in the Boat to take our Men in, we were in as much Danger as they were in on Shore; for they pour'd their Arrows in upon us so thick, that we were fain to barricade the Side of the Boat up with the Benches, and two or three loose Boards, which to our great Satisfaction we had by meer Accident or Providence in the Boat.

And yet, had it been Day-light, they are it seems each exact

---

1 Trinkets, gewgaws (usually of little significance).

2 Light flintlock muskets.

Marks-men, that if they could have seen but the least Part of any of us, they would have been sure of us; we had by the Light of the Moon a little Sight of them, as they stood pelting us from the Shore with Darts and Arrows; and having got ready our Fire-arms, we gave them a Volley, that we could hear by the Cries of some of them, that we had wounded several; however, they stood thus in Battle Array on the Shore till break of Day, which we supposed was, that they might see the better to take their Aim at us.

In this Condition we lay, and could not tell how to weigh our Anchor or set up our Sail, because we must needs stand up in the Boat, and they were as sure to hit us, as we were to hit a Bird in a Tree with small Shot; we made Signals of Distress to the Ship, which, tho' we rode a League off, yet my Nephew the Captain hearing our firing, and by Glasses, perceiving the Posture we lay in,[1] and that we fir'd towards the Shore, pretty well understood us; and weighing Anchor, with all speed, he stood as near the Shore as he durst with the Ship, and then sent another Boat with ten Hands in her to assist us; but we call'd to them not to come too near, telling them what Condition we were in; however, they stood in nearer to us; and one of the Men taking the End of a Tow-Line in his Hand, and keeping our Boat between him and the Enemy, so that they could not perfectly see him, swam on board us and made fast the Line to the Boat; upon which, we slipp'd our little Cable, and leaving our Anchor behind, they tow'd us out of Reach of the Arrows, we all the while lying close behind the Barricado we had made.

As soon as we were got from between the Ship and the Shore, that she could lay her Side to the Shore, she run along just by them, and pour'd in a Broad-side among them loaden with Pieces of Iron and Lead, small Bullets, and such Stuff, besides the great Shot which made a terrible Havock amongst them.

When we were got on board and out of Danger, we had Time to examine into the Occasion of this Fray; and indeed our Supra-Cargo who had been often in those Parts, put me upon it; for he said, he was sure the Inhabitants would not have touch'd us after we had made a Truce, if we had not done something to provoke them to it; at length it came out, (*viz.*) that an old Woman who had come to sell us some Milk, had brought it within our Poles, with a young Woman with her, who also brought some Roots or Herbs; and while the old Woman, whether she was Mother to the young Woman or no, they could not tell, was selling us the Milk,

1 The position we were in.

one of our Men offer'd some Rudeness to the Wench* that was with her, at which the old Woman made a great Noise: However, the Seaman would not quit his Prize, but carried her out of the old Woman's Sight among the Trees, it being almost dark; the old Woman went away without her, and as we suppose, made an Outcry among the People she came from; who upon Notice, rais'd this great Army upon us in three or four Hours; and it was great odds, but we had been all destroy'd.

One of our Men was killed with a Launce thrown at him just at the beginning of the Attack, as he sally'd out of the Tent they had made; the rest came off free, all but the Fellow who was the Occasion of all the Mischief, who paid dear enough for his black Mistress;[1] for we could not hear what became of him, a great while; we lay upon the Shore two Days after, tho' the Wind presented, and made Signals for him; made our Boat sail up Shore and down Shore, several Leagues, but in vain; so we were oblig'd to give him over, and if he alone had suffer'd for it, the Loss had been the less.

I could not satisfie my self, however, without venturing on Shore once more, to try if I could learn any Thing of him or them; it was the third Night after the Action, that I had a great Mind to learn if I could by any Means what Mischief we had done and how the Game stood on the *Indians* Side: I was careful to do it in the dark least we should be attack'd again; but I ought indeed to have been sure, that the Men I went with had been under my Command, before I engag'd in a Thing so hazardous and mischievous as I was brought into by it, without my Knowledge or Design.

We took twenty stout Fellows with us as any in the Ship, besides the Supra-Cargo and my self, and we landed two Hours before Midnight, at the same Place where the *Indians* stood drawn up the Evening before; I landed here, because, my Design as I have said, was chiefly to see if they had quitted the Field, and if they had left any Marks behind them of the Mischief we had done them; and I thought, if we could surprize one or two of them, perhaps we might get our Man again by Way of Exchange.

We landed without any Noise, and divided our Men into two Bodies, whereof, the Boatswain commanded one, and I the other; we neither saw or heard any Body stir when we landed, and we march'd up one Body at a Distance from the other, to the Place,

1 Defoe's euphemism for the apparent rape victim, who is not mentioned again. Note: "black" does not here denote being of African descent.

but at first could see nothing it being very dark; till by and by, our Boatswain that led the first Party, stumbled and fell over a Dead Body; this made them halt a while, for knowing by the Circumstances that they were at the Place, where the *Indians* had stood, they waited for my coming up here; we concluded to halt till the Moon began to rise, which we knew would be in less than an Hour, when we could easily discern the Havock we had made among them; we told[1] two and thirty Bodies upon the Ground, whereof two were not quite dead: Some had an Arm, and some a Leg shot off, and one his Head; those that were wounded we supposed, they had carried away.

When we had made, as I thought, a full Discovery of all we could come at the Knowledge of, I was resolv'd for going on board; but the Boatswain and his Party sent me Word, that they were resolv'd to make a Visit to the *Indian* Town, where these Dogs, as they call'd them dwelt, and ask'd me to go along with them; and if they could find them, as still they fancy'd they should, they did not doubt getting a good Booty, and it might be, they might find *Tho. Jeffry* there,[2] *that was the Man's Name we had lost.*

Had they sent to ask my Leave to go, I knew well enough what Answer to have given them; for I would have commanded them instantly on board, knowing it was not a Hazard fit for us to run, who had a Ship, and Ship-loading in our Charge, and a Voyage to make, which depended very much upon the Lives of the Men; but as they sent me Word they were resolved to go, and only ask'd me and my Company to go along with them; I positively refus'd it, and rose up, *for I was sitting on the Ground* in Order to go to the Boat; one or two of the Men began to importune me to go, and when I refus'd positively, began to grumble, and say they were not under my Command and they would go: Come *Jack*, says one of the Men, will go with me? I'll go for one, *Jack* said he would, and another followed, and then another; and in a Word, they all left me but one, who I persuaded to stay, and a Boy left in the Boat; so the Supra-Cargo and I, with the third Man, went back to the Boat, where we told them we would stay for them, and take Care to take in as many of them as should be left; for I told them it was a mad Thing they were going about, and suppos'd most of them would run the Fate[3] of *Thom. Jeffry*.

---

1 Counted.

2 Thomas Jeffry, the apparent rapist.

3 Meet the same fate as.

They told me, like Seamen, they would warrant it they would come off again, and they would take Care, *&c.* So away they went; I entreated them to consider the Ship and the Voyage; that their Lives were not their own, and that they were entrusted with the Voyage in some Measure; that if they miscarried, the Ship might be lost for want of their Help, and that they could not answer it to God or Man; I said a great deal more to them on that Head, but I might as well have talk'd to the Main-mast of the Ship; they were mad upon their Journey, only they gave me good Words, and begg'd I would not be angry; that they would be very cautious, and they did not doubt but they would be back again in an about an Hour at farthest; for the *Indian* Town, they said, was not above half a Mile off, tho' they found it above two Miles before they got to it.

Well, they all went away, as above; and tho' the Attempt was desperate, and such, as none but mad Men would have gone about, yet to give them their due, they went about it as warily, as boldly; they were gallantly arm'd that's true, for they had every Man a Fuzee or Musquet, a Bayonet, every Man a Pistol, some of them had broad fuses, some of them Hangers,* and the Boatswain and two more, had Pole-Axes; besides all which, they had among them thirteen Hand-Grenadoes; bolder Fellows, and better provided, never went about any wicked Work in the World.

When they went out, their chief Design was Plunder, and they were in mighty Hopes of finding Gold there; but a Circumstance which none of them were aware of, set them on Fire with Revenge, and made Devils of them all. When they came to the few *Indian* Houses which they thought had been the Town, which was not above Half a Mile off; they were under a great Disappointment, for there was not above twelve or thirteen Houses, and where the Town was, or how big, they knew not; they consulted therefore what to do, and was some Time before they could resolve: for if they fell upon these, they must cut all their Throats, and it was ten to one but some of them might escape, it being in the Night, tho' the Moon was up; and if one escap'd, he would run away and raise all the Town, so they should have a whole Army upon them; again, on the other Hand, if they went away and left those untouch'd, for the People were all asleep, they could not tell which Way to look for the Town.

However, the last was the best Advice, so they resolv'd to leave them, and look for the Town as well as they could; they went on a little way, and found a Cow ty'd to a Tree; this they presently concluded would be a good Guide to them; for they said, the Cow certainly belong'd to the Town before them, or the Town behind them; and if they unty'd her they should see which Way she went; if she went back, they had nothing to say to her; but if she went forward, they had nothing to do but to follow her; so they cut the Cord which was made of twisted Flags,* and the Cow went on before them; in a Word, the Cow led them directly to the Town, which as they report, consisted of above 200 Houses, or Huts; and in some of these, they found several Families living together.

Here they found all in Silence, as profoundly secure, as Sleep, and a Country that had never seen an Enemy of that Kind could make them; and first, they call'd another Council, to consider what they had to do; and in a Word, they resolv'd to divide themselves into three Bodies, and to set three Houses on Fire in three Parts of the Town; and as the Men came out, to seize them and bind them; if any resisted, they need not be ask'd what to do then, and so to search the rest of the Houses for Plunder; but they resolv'd to march silently first, thro' the Town, and see what Dimensions it was of, and if they might venture upon it or no.

They did so, and desperately resolv'd that they would venture upon them; but while they were animating one another to the Work, three of them that were a little before the rest, call'd out aloud to them, and told them they had found *Thom. Jeffry*; they all run up to the Place, and so it was indeed; for there they found the poor Fellow hang'd up naked by one Arm, and his Throat cut; there was an *Indian* House just by the Tree, where they found sixteen or seventeen of the principal *Indians* who had been concern'd[1] in the Fray with us before; and two or three of them wounded with our Shot; and our Men found they were awake, and talking one to another in that House, but knew not their Number.

The Sight of their poor mangled Comrade so enrag'd them, as before, that they swore to one another they would be reveng'd, and that not an *Indian* that came into their Hands should have any Quarter, and to Work they went immediately, and yet not so madly as by the Rage and Fury they were in might be expected: Their first Care was to get something that would soon take Fire; but after a little search, they found that would be to no Purpose; but the most of the Houses were low, and thatch'd with Flags or Rushes, of which the Country is full; so they presently made some wild Fire, as we call it, by wetting a little Powder in the Palms of their hands, and in a quarter of an Hour, they set the Town on fire in four or five Places; and particularly that House where the

1 Involved.

Indians were not gone to Bed. As soon as the Fire began to blaze, the poor frighted Creatures began to rush out to save their Lives, but met with their Fate in the Attempt, and especially at the Door, where they drove them back, the Boatswain himself killing one or two with his Pole-Ax; The House being large, and many in it, he did not care to go in, but call'd for a Hand-Grenado, and threw it among them, which at first frighted them, but when it burst, made such Havock among them, that they cry'd out in a hideous Manner.

In short, most of the *Indians* who were in the open Part of the House, were kill'd or hurt with the Grenado, except two or three more who press'd to the Door, which the Boatswain and two more kept with their Bayonets in the Muzzles of their Pieces, and dispatch'd all that came that Way: But there was another Apartment in the House where the Prince or King, or whatever he was and several others were, and these they kept in till the House, which was by this Time all of a light Flame, fell in upon them, and they were smother'd or burnt together.

All this while they fir'd not a Gun, because they would not waken the People faster than they could master them; but the Fire began to waken them fast enough, and our Fellows were glad to keep a little together in Bodies; for the Fire grew so raging, all the Houses being made of light combustible Stuff, that they could hardly bear the Street between them, and their Business was to follow the Fire for the surer Execution: As fast as the Fire either forc'd the People out of those Houses which were burning, or frighted them out of others, our People were ready at their Doors to knock them on the Head, still calling and hallowing to one another to remember *Thom. Jeffries*.

While this was doing, I must confess I was very uneasy, and especially when I saw the Flames of the Town, which, it being Night, seem'd to be just by me.

My Nephew, the Captain, who was rous'd by his Men too, seeing such a Fire, was very uneasy, not knowing what the Matter was, or what Danger I was in; especially hearing the Guns too; for by this Time they began to use their Fire-Arms; a thousand Thoughts oppress'd his Mind concerning me and the Supra-Cargo, what should become of us: And at last, tho' he could ill spare any more Men, yet not knowing what Exigence we might be in, he takes another Boat, and with 13 Men and himself, comes on Shore to me.

He was surpriz'd to see me and the Supra-Cargo in the Boat with no more than two Men; and tho' he was glad that we were well, yet he was in the same Impatience with us to know what was doing; for the Noise continu'd and the Flame encreas'd: In short, it was next to an Impossibility for any Men in the World, to restrain their Curiosity, to know what had happen'd, or the Concern for the Safety of the Men: In a word, the Captain told me, he would go and help his Men, let what would come. I argu'd with him, as I did before, with the Men, the Safety of the Ship, the Danger of the Voyage, the Interests of the Owners and Merchants, *&c*, and told him, I would go and the two Men, and only see if we could at a Distance learn what was like to be the Event, and come back and tell him.

It was all one, to talk to my Nephew, as it was to talk to the rest before; he would go he said, and he only wish'd he had left but Ten Men in the Ship; for he could not think of having his Men lost for want of Help, he had rather lose the Ship, the Voyage, and his Life and all; and away went he.

In a Word, I was no more able to stay behind now, than I was to persuade them not to go; so in short, the Captain order'd two Men to row back the Pinnace, and fetch twelve Men more, leaving the Long-Boat at an Anchor, and that when they came back, six Men should keep the two Boats, and six more come after us; so that he left only 16 Men in the Ship; for the whole Ship's Company consisted of 65 Men, whereof two were lost in the late Quarrel, which brought this Mischief on.

Being now on the March, you may be sure we felt little of the Ground we trode on; and being guided by the Fire, we kept no Path, but went directly to the Place of the Flame: If the Noise of the Guns was surprising to us before, the Cries of the poor People were now of quite another Nature, and fill'd us with Horror. I must confess, I never was at the sacking a City, or at the taking a Town by storm. I had heard of *Oliver Cromwell* taking *Drogheda* in *Ireland*, and killing Man, Woman and Child:[1] And I had read of Count *Tilly*, sacking of the City of *Magdeburgh*, and cutting the Throats of 22000 of all Sexes:[2] But I never had

1 In September 1649, Oliver Cromwell (1599–1658), the English general of the Parliamentary army and later Lord Protector of England, pursued his campaign to conquer Ireland by besieging the town of Drogheda, north of Dublin. The town refused to surrender, and Cromwell's men breached the walls. Almost the entire town, including civilians, was massacred; exact numbers are unknown, but several thousand were killed.

2 The Flemish soldier Jan (or Johann) Tserclaes, Count of Tilly (1559–1632), commanded the Catholic army in the Thirty Years' War; storming the Protestant German city of Magdeburg in eastern Germany,

an Idea[1] of the Thing itself before, nor is it possible to describe it, or the Horror that was upon our Minds at hearing it.

However, we went on, and at length came to the Town, tho' there was no entring the Streets of it for the Fire: The first Object we met with was the Ruins of a Hut or House, or rather the Ashes of it, for the House was consum'd; and just before it, plain now to be seen by the Light of the Fire, lay four Men and three Women kill'd; and as we thought, one or two more lay in the Heap among the Fire: In short there were such Instances of a Rage altogether barbarous, and of a Fury, something beyond what was human, that we thought it impossible our Men could be guilty of it, or if they were the Authors of it, we thought they ought to be every one of them put to the worst of Deaths: But this was not all, we saw the Fire encreas'd foreward, and the Cry went on just as the Fire went on; so that we were in the utmost Confusion. We advanc'd a little Way farther, and behold, to our Astonishment, three Women naked, and crying in a most dreadful Manner, come flying, as if they had indeed had Wings, and after them sixteen or seventeen Men, Natives, in the same Terror and Consternation, with three of our *English* Butchers, for I can call them no better, in their Rear, who, when they could not overtake them, fir'd in among them, and one that was kill'd by their Shot fell down in our Sight; when the rest saw us, believing us to be their Enemies, and that we would murther them as well as those that pursu'd them, they set up a most dreadful Shreik, especially the Women; and two of them fell down as if already dead with the Fright.

My very Soul shrunk within me, and my Blood run chil in my Veins, when I saw this; and I believe, had the three *English* Sailors that pursu'd them come on, I had made our Men kill them all: However we took some Ways to let the poor flying Creatures know, that we would not hurt them, and immediately they came up to us, and kneeling down, with their Hands lifted up, made piteous Lamentation to us to save them, which we let them know we would; whereupon they crept altogether in a Huddle close behind us, as for Protection. I left my Men drawn up together, and charg'd them to hurt no Body, but if possible to get at some of our People, and see what Devil it was possess'd them, and what

---

his troops pillaged the city, committing rape and robbery in addition to killing more than twenty thousand. Defoe's protagonist in *Memoirs of a Cavalier* gives an account of the sacking (60–61).

1 An image, a picture.

they intended to do; and in a word, to command them off; assuring them, that if they stay'd 'till Day-light, they would have an hundred thousand Men about their Ears: I say, I left them, and went among those flying People, taking only two of our Men with me; and there was indeed a piteous Spectacle among them: Some of them had their Feet terribly burnt with trampling and running thro' the Fire, others their Hands burnt; one of the Women had fallen down in the Fire, and was very much burnt before she could get out again, and two or three of the Men had Cuts in their Backs and Thighs from our Men pursuing; and another was shot thro' the Body, and dy'd while I was there.

I would fain have learn'd what the Occasion of all this was, but I could not understand one Word they said; tho' by Signs[1] I perceiv'd that some of them knew not what was the Occasion themselves. I was so terrify'd in my Thoughts at this outrageous Attempt, that I could not stay there, but went back to my own Men, and resolv'd to go into the Middle of the Town thro' the Fire, or whatever might be in the Way, and put an End to it, cost what it would: Accordingly, as soon as I came back to my Men, I told them my Resolution, and commanded them to follow me, when in the very Moment came four of our Men with the Boatswain at their Head, roving over the Heaps of Bodies they had kill'd, all cover'd with Blood and Dust, as if they wanted more People to massacre, when our Men hallow'd to them as loud as they could hallow, and with much ado one of them made them hear; so that they knew who we were, and came up to us.

As soon as the Boatswain saw us, he set up a Hallow like a Shout of Triumph; for having, as he thought, more Help come, and without bearing to hear me, Captain, says he, noble Captain, I am glad you are come; we have not half done yet, villanous Hell-hound Dogs, I'll kill as many of them as poor *Tom.* has Hairs upon his Head. We have sworn to spare none of them, we'll root out the very Nation of them from the Earth, and thus he run on out of Breath too with Action, and would not give us Leave to speak a Word.

At last, raising my Voice, that I might silence him a little; barbarous Dog, said I, what are you doing? I won't have one Creature touch'd more, upon pain of Death; I charge you upon your Life, to stop your Hands, and stand still here, or you are a dead Man this Minute.

Why, Sir, says he, Do you know what you do, or what they have

---

1 I.e., by the people's gestures and postures.

done? If you want a Reason for what we have done, come hither; and with that he shew'd me the poor Fellow hanging with his Throat cut.

I confess, I was urg'd then myself, and at another Time should have been foreward enough; but I thought they had carry'd their Rage too far, and thought of *Jacob*'s Words to his Sons *Simeon* and *Levi*; *Cursed be their Anger for it was fierce, and their Wrath for it was cruel*:[1] But I had now a new Task upon my Hands; for when the Men I carry'd with me saw the Sight as I had done, I had as much to do to restrain them, as I should have had with the other; nay, my Nephew himself fell in with them, and told me in their Hearing, that he was only concern'd for fear of the Men being overpowr'd; for as to the People, he thought not one of them ought to live; for they had all glutted themselves with the Murther of the poor Man, and that they ought to be used like Murtherers: Upon these Words, away run eight of my Men with the Boatswain and his Crew, to compleat their bloody Work; and I seeing it quite out of my Power to restrain them, came away pensive and sad; for I could not bear the Sight, much less the horrible Noise and Cries of the poor Wretches that fell into their Hands.

I got no Body to come back with me but the Supra-Cargo and two Men; and with these I walk'd back to the Boats. It was a very great Piece of Folly in me, I confess, to venture back, as it were alone; for as it began now to be almost Day, and the Alarm had run over the Country, there stood about 40 Men arm'd with Launces and Bows at the little Place where the 12 or 13 Houses stood mention'd before; but by Accident I miss'd the Place, and came directly to the Sea-side, and by the Time I got to the Sea-side, it was broad Day; immediately I took the Pinnace, and went aboard, and sent her back to assist the Men in what might happen.

I observ'd about the Time that I came to the Boat-side, that the Fire was pretty well out, and the Noise abated; but in about half an Hour after I got on Board, I heard a Volley of our Mens Fire-arms, and saw a great Smoak; this, as I understood afterwards, was our Men falling upon the Men, who as I said stood at the few Houses on the Way, of whom they kill'd sixteen or seventeen, and set all those Houses on Fire, but did not meddle with the Women or Children.

By that Time the Men got to the Shore again with the Pinnace, our Men began to appear; they came dropping in, some and some, not in two Bodies and in Form as they went, but all in Heaps,

---

1 See Genesis 49:5–7.

straggling here, and there, in such a Manner, that a small Force of resolute Men might have cut them all off.

But the Dread of them was upon the whole Country; and the Men were amaz'd, and surpriz'd, and so frighted, that I believe a hundred of them would have fled at the Sight of but five of our Men; nor in all this terrible Action was there a Man who made any considerable Defence, they were so surpriz'd between the Terror of the Fire and the sudden Attack of our Men in the Dark, that they knew not which Way to turn themselves; for if they fled one Way, they were met by one Party, if back again, by another; so that they were every where knock'd down: Nor did any of our Men receive the least Hurt, except one that strain'd his Foot, and another had one of his Hands very much burnt.

I was very angry with my Nephew the Captain, and indeed with all the Men in my Mind, but with him in particular; as well for his acting so out of his Duty as Commander of the Ship, and having the Charge of the Voyage upon him, as in his prompting rather than cooling the Rage of his Men in so bloody and cruel an Enterprize. My Nephew answer'd me very respectfully, but told me, that when he saw the Body of the poor Seaman, who they had murther'd in such a cruel and barbarous Manner, he was not Master of himself, neither could he govern his Passion: He own'd he should not have done so, as he was Commander of the Ship, but as he was a Man, and Nature mov'd him,[1] he could not bear it: As for the rest of the Men, they were not subject to me at all, and they knew it well enough; so they took no Notice of my Dislike.

The next Day we set sail, so we never heard any more of it: Our Men differ'd in the Account of the Number they kill'd: Some said one Thing, some another; but according to the best of their Accounts put altogether, they kill'd or destroy'd about 150 People, Men, Women, and Children, and left not a House standing in the Town.

As for the poor Fellow *Tho. Jeffreys*, as he was quite dead, for his Throat was so cut, that his Head was half off, it would do him no Service to bring him away, so they left him where they found him, only took him down from the Tree, where he was hang'd by one Hand.

However just our Men thought this Action, I was against them in it; and I always, after that Time, told them, God would blast the Voyage; for I look'd upon all the Blood they shed that Night to be Murther in them: For tho' it is true, that they had kill'd

1 His response was natural.

Tho. Jeffreys, yet it was as true, that *Jeffreys* was the Aggressor, had broken the Truce, and had violated, or debauch'd[1] a young Woman of theirs who came down to them innocently, and on the Faith of their publick Capitulation.[2]

The Boatswain defended this Quarrel when we were afterwards on board: He said, It is true that we seem'd to break the Truce, but really had not, and that the War was begun the Night before by the Natives themselves, who had shot at us, and kill'd one of our Men without any just Provocation; so that as we were in a Capacity to fight them now, we might be also in a Capacity to do our selves Justice upon them in an extraordinary Manner, that tho' the poor Man had taken a little Liberty with a Wench, he ought not to have been murther'd, and that in such a villanous Manner; and that they did nothing but what was just, and what the Laws of God allow'd to be done to Murtherers.

One would think this should have been enough to have warn'd us against going on Shore among Heathens and Barbarians: But it is impossible to make Mankind wise, but at their own Expence and their Experience seems to be always of most Use to them, when it is dearest bought.

We are now bound to the Gulph of *Persia*, and from thence to the Coast of *Coremandel*,* only to touch at *Surrat*: But the chief of the Supra-Cargo's Design lay at the Bay of *Bengale*, where if he miss'd of his Business outward bound, he was to go up to *China*, and return to the Coast as he came Home.

The first Disaster that befel us, was in the Gulph of *Persia*, where five of our Men venturing on Shore on the *Arabian* side of the Gulph, were surrounded by the *Arabians*, and either all kill'd or carry'd away into Slavery; the rest of the Boat's Crew were not able to rescue them, and had but just Time to get off their Boat. I began to upbraid them with the just Retribution of Heaven in this Case: But the Boatswain very warmly told me, he thought I went farther in my Censures than I could shew any Warrant[3] for in Scripture, and referr'd to the 13 St. *Luke*, Vers. 4th. where our Saviour intimates, that those Men, on whom the Tower of *Siloam* fell, were not Sinners above all the *Galileans*: But that which indeed put me to Silence in the Case, was, That not one of these five Men, who were now lost, were of the Number of those who went on Shore to the Massacre of *Madagascar*; (*so I always call'd it, tho' our Men could*

1 He had either raped or seduced; the implication suggests rape.

2 Submission.

3 License.

not bear the Word Massacre *with any Patience*:) And indeed, this last Circumstance, as I have said, put me to Silence for the present.

But my frequent preaching to them on this Subject had worse Consequences than I expected; and the Boatswain, who had been the Head of the Attempt, came up boldly to me one Time, and told me, he found, that I continually brought that Affair upon the Stage,[1] that I made unjust Reflections upon it, and had used the Men very ill on that Account, and himself in particular; that as I was but a Passenger, and had no Command in the Ship, or Concern in the Voyage, they were not oblig'd to bear it; that they did not know, but I might have some ill Design in my Head, and perhaps to call them to Account for it, when they came to *England*; and that therefore, unless I would resolve to have done with it, and also, not to concern my self any farther with him, or any of his Affairs, he would leave the Ship; for he did not think it was safe to sail with me among them.

I heard him patiently enough 'till he had done, and then told him, that I did confess I had all along oppos'd the *Massacre of Madagascar*, for such I would always call it; and that I had on all Occasions spoken my Mind freely about it, tho' not more upon him than any of the rest: That as to my having no Command in the Ship, that was true; nor did I exercise any Authority, only took my Liberty of speaking my Mind in Things which publickly concern'd us all; and what Concern I had in the Voyage was none of his Business; that I was a considerable Owner of the Ship; and in that Claim I conceived I had a Right to speak even farther than I had yet done, and would not be accountable to him or any one else, and begun to be a little warm with him: He made but little Reply to me at that Time, and I thought that Affair had been over. We were at this Time in the Road at *Bengale*,[2] and being willing to see the Place, I went on Shore with the Supra-Cargo in the Ship's Boat, to divert myself, and towards Evening was preparing to go on Board, when one of the Men came to me, and told me, he would not have me trouble myself to come down to the Boat, for they had Orders not to carry me on Board any more. Any one may guess what a Surprize I was in at so insolent a Message; and I ask'd the Man, Who bad him deliver that Errand to me? He told me, the Cockswain.* I said no more to the Fellow, but bad him let them know he had deliver'd his Message, and that I had given him no Answer to it.

---

1 In other words, that he kept bringing up the massacre.

2 Coastal waters of the Bay of Bengal.

I immediately went and found out the Supra-Cargo, and told him the Story, adding what I presently foresaw, (*viz.*) That there would certainly be a Mutiny in the Ship, and entreated him to go immediately on Board the Ship in an *Indian* Boat, and acquaint the Captain of it: But I might ha' spar'd this Intelligence; for before I had spoken to him on Shore, the Matter was effected on Board. The Boatswain, the Gunner, the Carpenter; and in a Word, all the Inferiour Officers, as soon as I was gone off in the Boat, came up to the Quarter-Deck, and desir'd to speak with the Captain, and there the Boatswain making a long Harangue for the Fellow talk'd very well, and repeating all he had said to me, told the Captain in few Words, That as I was now gone peaceably on Shore, they were loth to use any Violence with me; which, if I had not gone on Shore, they would otherwise have done, to oblige me to have gone: They therefore thought fit to tell him, That as they shipp'd themselves to serve in the Ship under his Command, they would perform it well and faithfully: But if I would not quit the Ship, or the Captain oblige me to quit it, they would all leave the Ship, and sail no farther with him; and at that Word, ALL, he turn'd his Face about towards the Main-mast, which was it seems the Signal agreed on between them; at which, all the Seamen being got together, they cry'd out, *One* and ALL, *One* and ALL.

My Nephew, the Captain, was a Man of Spirit, and of great Presence of Mind; and tho' he was surpriz'd, you may be sure, at the Thing, yet he told them calmly, that he would consider of the Thing, but that he could do nothing in it 'till he had spoken to me about it. He us'd some Arguments with them, to shew them the Unreasonableness and Injustice of the Thing: But it was all in vain, they swore and shook Hands round before his Face, that they would go all on Shore, unless he would engage[1] to them, not to suffer me to come any more on Board the Ship.

This was a hard Article upon him, who knew his Obligation to me, and did not know how I might take it; so he began to talk cavalierly to them, told them that I was a very considerable Owner of the Ship, and that in Justice he could not put me out of my own House; that this was next Door to serving me, as the famous Pirate *Kid*[2] had done, who made the Mutiny in a Ship, set the Captain on Shore in an uninhabited Island, and run away with

---

1 Promise.

2 Captain William Kid(d) (1654–1701), a Scottish captain, hired by the English government as a privateer in pursuit of pirates; he turned pirate and was hanged in London in 1701.

the Ship; that let them go into what Ship they would, if ever they came to *England* again, it would cost them dear; that the Ship was mine, and that he could not put me out of it; and that he would rather lose the Ship and the Voyage too, than disoblige me so much; so they might do as they pleas'd: However, he would go on Shore, and talk with me on Shore, and invited the Boatswain to go with him, and perhaps they might accommodate the Matter with me.

But they all rejected the Proposal, and said, they would have nothing to do with me any more, neither on Board, or on Shore; and if I came on Board, they would all go on Shore. Well, said the Captain, if you are all of this Mind, let me go on Shore and talk with him; so away he came to me with this Account, a little after the Message had been brought to me from the Cockswain.

I was very glad to see my Nephew, I must confess; for I was not without Apprehensions, that they would confine him by Violence, set sail, and run away with the Ship, and then I had been stripp'd naked[1] in a remote Country, and nothing to help myself: In short, I had been in a worse Case, than when I was all alone in the Island.

But they had not come that length, it seems, to my great Satisfaction; and when my Nephew told me what they had said to him, and how they had sworn, and shook Hands, that they would *one* and *all* leave the Ship, if I was suffer'd to come on Board, I told him, he should not be concern'd at it at all, for I would stay on Shore. I only desir'd he would take Care and send me all my necessary Things on Shore, and leave me a sufficient Sum of Money, and I would find my Way to *England*, as well as I could.

This was a heavy Piece of News to my Nephew; but there was no Way to help it, but to comply with it: So, in short, he went on Board the Ship again, and satisfy'd the Men, that his Uncle had yielded to their Importunity, and had sent for his Goods from on Board the Ship; so that Matter was over in a very few Hours, the Men return'd to their Duty, and I began to consider what Course I should steer.

I was now alone in the remotest Part of the World, *as I think I may call it*; for I was near three thousand Leagues by Sea farther off from *England*, than I was at my Island; only it is true, I might travel here by Land over the Great Mogul's Country[2] to *Surratte*,

1 Not of the clothes on his body, but of his belongings and ship.

2 The Mughal Empire was established over almost all of the Indian sub-continent in the sixteenth century. Aurangzeb (1618–1707) was the

might go from thence to *Basora*[1] by Sea, up the Gulph of *Persia*, and from thence might take the Way of the Caravans over the Desert of *Arabia* to *Aleppo* and *Scanderoon*;[2] from thence by Sea again to *Italy*, and so over Land into *France*, and this put together might be, at least, a full Diameter of the Globe; but if it were to be measur'd, I suppose it would appear to be a great deal more.

I had another Way before me, which was to wait for some *English* Ships, which were coming to *Bengale* from *Achin* on the Island of *Sumatra*,[3] and get passage on Board them for *England*: But as I came hither without any Concern with the *English East-India* Company,* so it would be difficult to go from hence without their License, unless with great Favour of the Captains of the Ships, or of the Companies Factors, and to both, I was an utter Stranger.

Here I had the particular Pleasure, speaking by Contraries, to see the Ship set sail without me, a Treatment I think a Man in my Circumstances scarce ever met with, except from Pirates running away with a Ship, and setting those that would not agree with their Villany, on Shore: indeed this was next Door to it, both Ways; however, my Nephew left me two Servants, or rather one Companion, and one Servant, the first was Clerk to the Purser, who he engag'd to go with me, and the other was his own Servant; I took me also a good Lodging in the House of an *English* Woman, where several Merchants lodg'd; some *French*, two *Italians*, or rather Jews, and one *English* Man: Here I was handsomely enough entertain'd; and that I might not be said to run rashly upon any Thing, I stay'd here above nine Months, considering what Course to take, and how to manage myself; I had some *English* Goods with me of Value, and a considerable Sum of Money, my Nephew furnishing me with a thousand Pieces of Eight, and a Letter of Credit for more, if I had Occasion, that I might not be straiten'd[4] whatever might happen.

I quickly dispos'd of my Goods, and to Advantage too; and, as I originally intended, I bought here some very good Diamonds,

---

last of the Mughal emperors and expanded the empire to its greatest extent.

1 Basra, in southeastern Iraq.

2 Aleppo is the largest city in northern Syria. Scanderoon (Iskenderun) is its port.

3 Achin, Banda Aceh, is the capital of the province of Aceh, on the north-west coast of Sumatra (the second-largest island of the Indonesian archipelago).

4 In dire straits financially.

which, of all other Things, was the most proper for me in my present Circumstances, because I might always carry my whole Estate about me.[1]

After a long Stay here, and many Proposals made for my Return to *England*, but none falling out to my Mind, the *English* Merchant who lodged with me, and with whom I had contracted an intimate[2] Acquaintance, came to me one Morning: Country-man, says he, I have a Project to communicate to you, which, as it suits with my Thoughts, may for ought I know, suit with your's also, when you shall have thoroughly consider'd it.

Here we are posted, *says he*, you by Accident, and I by my own Choice, in a Part of the World very remote from our own Country; but it is in a Country, where, by us who understand Trade and Business, a great deal of Money is to be got: If you will put a thousand Pound to my thousand Pound, we will hire a Ship here, the first we can get to our Minds; you shall be Captain, I'll be Merchant, and we will go a trading Voyage to *China*; for what should we stand still for? The whole World is in Motion, rouling round and round; all the Creatures of God, heavenly Bodies and earthly are busy and diligent, Why should we be idle? There are no Drones[3] in the World but Men, Why should we be of that Number?

I lik'd his Proposal very well, and the more, because it seem'd to be express'd with so much good Will, and in so friendly a Manner: I will not say, but that I might by my loose and unhing'd[4] Circumstances be the fitter to embrace a Proposal for Trade, or indeed for any Thing else; whereas, otherwise, Trade was none of my Element: However, I might perhaps say with some Truth, that if Trade was not my Element, Rambling was, and no Proposal for seeing any Part of the World which I had never seen before, could possibly come amiss to me.

It was however, some Time before we could get a Ship to our Minds; and when we had got a Vessel, it was not easy to get *English* Sailors; that is to say, so many as were necessary to govern the Voyage, and manage the Sailors which we should pick up there: After some Time we got a Mate, a Boatswain, and a Gunner

1 In other words, sinking his money into diamonds makes it easy to carry his wealth with him.

2 Friendly.

3 Male bees in a social bee colony whose only task is to impregnate their queen; Crusoe uses the word here to suggest idleness, laziness.

4 Unstable, disordered.

English; a *Dutch* Carpenter, and three *Portugueze* Fore-mast Men;[1] with these we found, we could do well enough, having *Indian* Seamen, such as they are, to make up.

There are so many Travellers, who have wrote the History of their Voyages and Travels this Way, that it would be very little Diversion[2] to any Body, to give a long Account of the Places we went to, and the People who inhabit there; those Things I leave to others, and refer the Reader to those Journals and Travels of *English* Men, of which, many I find are publish'd, and more promis'd every Day; 'tis enough to me to tell you, That I made this Voyage to *Achin*, in the Island of *Sumatra*, and from thence to *Siam*,[3] where we exchang'd some of our Wares for Opium, and some Arrack,[4] the first, a Commodity which bears a great Price among the *Chinese*, and which at that Time, was very much wanted there; In a Word, we went up to *Suskan*,[5] made a very great Voyage; was eight Months out, and return'd to *Bengale*, and I was very well satisfied with my Adventure: I observe that our People in *England*, often admire how the Officers which the Company send into *India*, and the Merchants which generally stay there, get such very great Estates as they do, and sometimes come Home worth 60, to 70 100 thousand Pound at a Time.[6]

But it is no Wonder, or at least we shall see so much farther into it,[7] when we consider the innumerable Ports and Places where they have a free Commerce; that it will then be no Wonder; and much less will it be so, when we consider, that at all those Places and Ports where the *English* Ships come, there is so much, and such constant Demand for the Growth of all other Countries, that there is a certain Vent for the Returns, as well as a Market abroad, for the Goods carried out.

In short, we made a very good Voyage, and I got so much Money by the first Adventure, and such an Insight into the Method of getting more, that had I been twenty Year younger, I

1 Common sailors, ones who sail "before the mast."

2 Entertainment.

3 Present-day Thailand.

4 Distilled alcoholic drink typically produced in south and southeast Asia, made from the fermented sap of coconut flowers, sugarcane, grain, or fruit, depending upon the country of origin.

5 Zhoushan, a large island off the northeastern coast of China.

6 These are enormous sums (in modern purchasing power approximately ten to thirty million pounds); Britons who returned with wealth gained in India were called "Nabobs."

7 In other words, they will gain a greater understanding of it.

should have been tempted to have staid here and sought no farther, for making my Fortune; but what was all this, to a Man on the wrong Side of threescore, that was rich enough, and came abroad, more in Obedience to a restless Desire of seeing the World, than a covetuous Desire of getting it; and indeed I think, 'tis with great Justice, that I now call it a restless Desire for it was so; when I was at Home, I was restless to go abroad; and now I was abroad, I was restless to be at Home: I say, what was this Gain to me? I was rich enough, nor had I any uneasie Desires about getting more Money and therefore, the Profit of the Voyage to me, were Things of no great Force, for the prompting me forward to farther Undertakings; and I thought that by this Voyage, I had made no Progress at all, because I was come back as I might call it, to the Place from whence I came as to a Home; whereas, my Eye, which like that, which *Solomon* speaks of, *was never satisfy'd with Seeing*,[1] was still more desirous of Wand'ring and Seeing; I was come into a Part of the World, which I was never in before; and that Part in particular, which I had heard much of; and was resolv'd to see as much of as I could, and then I thought, I might say, I had seen all the World, that was worth seeing.

But my Fellow Traveller and I, had different Notions; I do not name[2] this, to insist upon my own, for I acknowledge his were the most just and the most suited to the end of a Merchant's Life; who, when he is abroad upon Adventures,[3] 'tis his Wisdom to stick to that as the best Thing for him, which he is like to get the most Money by: My new Friend kept himself to the Nature of the Thing, and would have been content to have gone like a Carrier's[4] Horse, always to the same Inn, backward and forward, provided he could, as he call'd it, *find his Account in it*; on the other Hand, mine was the Notion of a mad rambling Boy, that never cares to see a Thing twice over.

But this was not all; I had a Kind of Impatience upon me to be nearer Home, and yet, the most unsettled Resolution imaginable which Way to go; In the Interval of these Consultations, my Friend, who was always upon the Search for Business, propos'd another Voyage to me among the Spice Islands,[5] and to

1 Ecclesiastes 1:8: "the eye is not satisfied with seeing, nor the ear filled with hearing" (KJV). In other words, the eye wants to see still more.

2 Mention.

3 Here used in the sense of commercial projects, trading ventures, in contrast to Crusoe's own twice-titular "*Adventures*."

4 A mail-carrier's.

5 The Maluka Islands, or the Moluccas, an Indonesian archipelago.

bring Home a Loading of Cloves from the *Manillas*,[1] or there abouts; Places where indeed the *Dutch* do trade, but Islands, belonging partly to the *Spaniards*; tho' we went not so far, but to some other, where they have not the whole Power as they have at *Batavia*, *Ceylon*, &c.[2] we were not long in preparing for this Voyage; the chief Difficulty was in bringing me to come into it; however, at last nothing else offering, and finding that really stirring about and trading, the Profit being so great, and as I may say certain, had more Pleasure in it, and more Satisfaction to the Mind than sitting still, which to me especially, was the unhappiest Part of Life: I resolv'd on his Voyage too, which we made very successfully, touching at *Borneo*, and several Islands, whose Names I do not remember, and came Home in about five Months; we sold our Spice, which was chiefly Cloves, and some Nutmegs, to the *Persian* Merchants, who carried them away for the Gulph; and making near five of one,[3] we really got a great deal of Money.

My Friend, when we made up this Account[4] smil'd at me; well now, said he, with a Sort of agreeable insulting my indolent Temper; is not this better than walking about here, like a Man *of nothing to do*, and spending our Time in staring at the Nonsense and Ignorance of the Pagans? Why truly, says I, my Friend, I think it is; and I begin to be a Convert to the Principles of Merchandizing; but I must tell you, said I, by the Way, you do not know what I am a doing, for if once I conquer my backwardness, and embark heartily; as old as I am, I shall harrass you up and down the World, till I tire you; for I shall pursue it so eagerly, I shall never let you lye still.

But to be short with my Speculations, a little while after this, there came in a *Dutch* Ship from *Batavia*, she was a Coaster,[5] not an *European* Trader, and of about two hundred Ton Burthen: The Men, as they pretended having been so sickly, that the Captain had not Men enough to go to Sea with; he lay by at *Bengal*, and

1 I.e., the Philippines. The capital, Manila, is on the island of Luzon.

2 Batavia is the Dutch name for Jakarta, Indonesia's capital; after the Dutch took Jakarta and razed it in 1619, they renamed the new city Batavia, the capital of the colony in the Dutch East Indies. The large island of Ceylon, just off the east coast of India, is now called Sri Lanka. It was part of the Dutch East Indies, seized from the Portuguese in the 1650s.

3 In other words, making near five times what they paid for it.

4 In other words, when they saw how much they had made.

5 Small ship that trades in coastal waters.

having it seems got Money enough, or being willing for other Reasons, to go for *Europe*, he gave publick Notice, that he would sell his Ship: This came to my Ears before my new Partner heard of it; and I had a great Mind to buy it, so I goes Home to him, and told him of it; he considered a while, for he was no rash Man neither; but musing some Time, he reply'd, she is a little too big; but however, we will have her; accordingly we bought the Ship, and agreeing with the Master, we paid for her, and took Possession; when we had done so, we resolved to entertain[1] the Men if we could, to join them with those we had, for the pursuing our Business; but on a sudden, they having receiv'd not their Wages, but their Share of the Money, not one of them was to be found; we enquir'd much about them, and at length were told, that they were all gone together by Land to *Agra*,[2] the great City of the *Mogul*'s Residence; and from thence were to travel to *Suratte*,* and so by Sea, to the Gulph of *Persia*.

Nothing had so heartily troubled me a good while; as that I miss'd the Opportunity of going with them; for such a Ramble I thought, and in such Company, as would both have guarded me and diverted me,[3] would have suited mightily with my great Design; and I should both have seen the World, and gone homewards too; but I was much better satisfy'd a few Days after, when I came to know what sort of Fellows they were; for in short, their History was, that this Man they call'd Captain was the Gunner only, not the Commander; that they had been a trading Voyage, in which, they were attack'd on Shore, by some of the *Mallayans*, who had kill'd the Captain, and three of his Men; and that after the Captain was kill'd, these Men Eleven in Number, had resolv'd to run away with the Ship, which they did; and brought her in at the Bay of *Bengale*, leaving the Mate and five Men more on Shore, of whom, we shall hear farther.

Well, let them come by the Ship how they would, we came honestly by her, *as we thought*, tho' we did not I confess, examine into Things so exactly as we ought, for we never enquir'd any Thing of the Seamen; who, if we had examin'd, would certainly have

---

1 Entreat, convince the men to entertain the possibility of joining.

2 Indian city, in the province of Uttar Pradesh, on the banks of the river Yamuna in north-central India. Mughal emperors lived there at various times.

3 I.e., would have kept me both safe and entertained (diverted); at the same time, the word "diverted" suggests a correlation between travel (i.e., being diverted out of his way) and entertainment.

falter'd in their Account, contradicted one another, and perhaps contradicted themselves, or one how or other, we should have seen Reason to have suspected them; but the Man shew'd us a Bill of Sale for the Ship, to one *Emanuel Clostershoven*, or some such Name; for I suppose it was all a Forgery, and call'd himself by that Name, and we could not contradict him; and being withal, a little too unwary, or at least, having no Suspicion of the Thing, we went thro' with our Bargain.

We pick'd up some more *English* Seamen here after this, and some *Dutch*; and now we resolved for a second Voyage, to the South East for Cloves, *&c.* that is to say, among the *Philippine* and *Mollucco* Isles; and in short, not to fill this Part of my Story with Trifles, when what is yet to come, is so remarkable; I spent from first to last six Years[1] in this Country, trading from Port to Port, backward and forward, and with very good Success; and was now the last Year with my new Partner, going in the Ship above-mention'd, on a Voyage to *China*; but designing first to *Siam*, to buy Rice.

In this Voyage, being by contrary Winds oblig'd to beat up and down a great while in the Straits of *Mallacca*,[2] and among the Islands; we were no sooner got clear of those difficult Seas, but we found our Ship had sprung a Leak, and we were not able by all our Industry to find it out where it was: This forc'd us to make for some Port, and my Partner who knew the Country better than I did, directed the Captain to put into the River of *Cambodia*,[3] *for I had made the* English *Mate, one Mr.* Thomson, *Captain, not being willing to take the Charge of the Ship upon my self*: This River lies on the North Side of the great Bay or Gulph, which goes up to *Siam*.

While we were here, and going often on Shore for Refreshment, there comes to me one Day an *English* Man, and he was it seems a Gunner's Mate, on board an *English East-India* Ship, which rode in the same River, up at, or near the City of *Cambodia*; what brought him hither we know not; but he comes up to me, and speaking *English*: Sir, says he, you are a Stranger to me, and I to you; but I have something to tell you, that very nearly concerns you.

I look'd steadily at him a good while, and thought at first I had known him, but I did not; if it very nearly concerns me, said I, and

1 In other words, six consecutive years.

2 The Strait of Malacca is between peninsular Malaysia and Sumatra, connecting the Indian Ocean and the South China Sea.

3 The Mekong River, in present-day Vietnam and Cambodia.

not your self, what moves you to tell it me? I am moved says he, by the eminent Danger you are in, and for ought I see, you have no Knowledge of it; I know no Danger I am in, said I, but that my Ship is leaky, and I cannot find it out; but I purpose to lay her a-Ground to Morrow, to see if I can find it; but Sir, says he, leaky, or not leaky, find it, or not find it, you will be wiser than to lay your Ship on Shore to Morrow, when you hear what I have to say to you; do you know Sir, said he, the Town of *Cambodia*, lyes about fifteen Leagues up this River? and there are two large *English* Ships about five Leagues on this Side, and three *Dutch*; well *said I*, and what is that to me? Why Sir, *said he*, is it for a Man that is upon such Adventures as you are upon, to come into a Port, and not examine first what Ships there are there, and whether he is able to deal with them? I suppose you don't think you are a Match for them: I was amused[1] very much at his Discourse, but not amaz'd at it, for I could not conceive what he meant; and I turn'd short upon him and said, Sir, I wish you would explain your self; I cannot imagine what Reason I have to be afraid of any Company Ships, or *Dutch* Ships; I am no Interloper,[2] what can they have to say to me?

He look'd like a Man half angry, half pleas'd, and pausing a while, but smiling; well Sir, *says he*, if you think your self secure, you must take your Chance; I am sorry your Fate should blind you against good Advice; but assure your self, if you do not put to Sea immediately, you will the very next Tide be attack'd by five Long-Boats full of Men, and perhaps if you are taken, you'll be hang'd for a Pirate, and the Particulars be examin'd afterwards: I thought Sir, added he, I should have met with a better Reception than this, for doing you a Piece of Service of such Importance: I can never be ungrateful, *said I*, for any Service, or to any Man that offers me any Kindness, but it is past my Comprehension said I, what they should have such a Design upon me for; however, *since you say*, there is no Time to be lost, and that there is some villainous Design in Hand against me, I'll go on board this Minute, and put to Sea immediately, if my Men can stop the leak, or if we can swim without stopping it. But, Sir, said I, shall I go away ignorant of the Reason of all this? Can you give me no farther Light into it?

I can tell you but Part of the Story, Sir, says he, but I have a *Dutch* Seaman here with me, and I believe I could persuade him to tell you the rest; but there is scarce time for it. But the short

---

1 Puzzled.

2 Trader who encroaches on the territory of a trading monopoly.

of the Story is this, the first Part of which, I suppose, you know well enough, (*viz.*) that you was with this Ship at *Sumatra*, that there your Captain was murther'd by the *Mallayans*, with three of his Men, and that you or some of those who were on board with you, ran away with the Ship, and are since turn'd *PIRATES*; this is the Sum of the Story, and you will be all seiz'd as Pirates I can assure you, and executed, with very little Ceremony; for you know, Merchants Ships shew but little Law to *Pirates*, if they get them into their Power.

Now you speak plain *English*, said I, and I thank you; and tho' I know nothing, that we have done, like what you talk of, but am sure we came honestly and fairly by the Ship, yet seeing such Work is a doing as you say, and that you seem to mean honestly, I'll be upon my guard; nay, Sir, says he, do not talk of being upon your guard; the best Defence, is to be out of the Danger, if you have any Regard to your Life, and the Life of all your Men; put out to Sea without fail at High Water, and as you have a whole Tide before you, you will be gone too far out before they can come down, for they came away at High Water; and as they have twenty Miles to come, you get near two Hours of them, by the Difference of the Tide, not reckoning the length of the Way; besides, as they are only Boats, and not Ships, they will not venture to follow you far out to Sea, especially if it blows.

Well, *says I*, you have been very kind in this, what shall I do for you, to make you amends? Sir, says he, you may not be so willing to make me any amends, because you may not be convinc'd of the Truth of it: I'll make an offer to you; I have nineteen Months Pay due to me, on board the Ship —— which I came out of *England* in, and the *Dutch* Man that is with me, has seven Months Pay due to him; if you will make good our Pay to us, we will go along with you; if you find nothing more in it, we will desire no more; but if we do convince you, that we have sav'd your Lives, and the Ship, and the Lives of all the Men in her, we will leave the rest to you.[1]

I consented to this readily, and went immediately on board, and the two Men with me; as soon as I came to the Ship Side, my Partner who was on board, came out on the Quarter-Deck, and call'd to me with a great deal of Joy, *O ho! O ho! we have stop'd the leak! we have stop'd the leak!* Say you so, *said I*, thank God; but weigh the Anchor then immediately; weigh! *says he*: What do you

1 In other words, if you find that our story was wrong, you need not pay us further, but if you find that we were right, we will leave it up to you to decide if you might wish to pay us more.

mean by that? What is the Matter, *says he*? Ask no Questions, *says I*, but all Hands to work, and *weigh*, without loosing a Minute; he was surpriz'd, but however, he call'd the Captain, and he immediately order'd the Anchor to be got up; and tho' the Tide was not quite done, yet a little Land Breeze blowing, we stood out to Sea; then I call'd him into the Cabin and told him the Story at large, and we call'd in the Men, and they told us the rest of it; but as it took us up a great deal of Time, so before we had done, a Seaman comes to the Cabin Door, and calls out to us, that the Captain bad him tell us, we were chas'd; chas'd, *says I*! by who, and by what? By five Sloops or Boats, says the Fellow, full of Men; very well said I, then it is apparent there is something in it; in the next Place I order'd all our Men to be call'd up, and told them, that there was a Design to seize the Ship, and to take us for Pirates, and ask'd them, if they would stand by us, and by one another; the Men answer'd chearfully, that one and all, they would live and die with us; then I asked the Captain, what Way he thought best for us to manage a Fight with them; for resist them I was resolv'd we would, and that, to the last Drop; he said readily, that the Way was to keep them off with our great Shot, as long as we could, and then to fire at them with our small Arms, as long as we could; but when neither of these would do any longer, we should retire to our close Quarters; perhaps they had not Materials to break open our Bulk-Heads,[1] or get in upon us.

The Gunner had in the mean Time, Order to bring two Guns to bear fore[2] and aft[3] out of the Steerage, to clear the Deck, and loaded them with Musquet-Bullets and small Pieces of old Iron, and what next came to Hand, and thus we made ready for Fight; but all this while we kept out to Sea, with Wind enough; and could see the Boats at a Distance, being five large *Long-Boats*, following us with all the sail they could make.

Two of those Boats, which by our Glasses we could see were *English*, out sail'd the rest, were near two Leagues a-Head of them, and gain'd upon us considerably; so that we found they would come up with us; upon which, we fir'd Gun without Ball,[4] to intimate, that they should bring to,[5] and we put out a Flag of Truce, as a Signal for Parley,[6] but they kept crowding after us, till they

1 Ship cabins or water-tight compartments, created by walls.
2 The bow, the front of the ship.
3 The stern, the back of the ship.
4 They fired a harmless warning shot.
5 Bring a sailing ship to a stop without lowering its sails.
6 Conference, negotiation.

came within Shot; when we took in our white Flag, they having made no Answer to it, we hung out a red Flag,[1] and fir'd at them with a Shot: Notwithstanding this, they came on, till they were near enough to call to them with a speaking Trumpet,[2] which we had on board; so we call'd to them, and bid them keep off at their Peril.

It was all one, they crowded after us, and endeavoured to come under our Stern, so to board us on our Quarter; upon which, seeing they were resolute for Mischief, and depended upon the Strength that followed them, I ordered to bring the Ship to, so that they lay upon our Broad-Side, when immediately we fir'd five Guns at them; one of which, had been levelled so true, as to carry away the Stern of the hindermost Boat, and bring them to the Necessity of taking down their Sail, and running all to the Head of the Boat to keep her from sinking; so she lay by, and had enough of it; but seeing the foremost Boat crowd on after us, we made ready to fire at her in particular.

While this was doing, one of the three Boats that was behind, being forwarder than the other two, made up to the Boat which we had disabl'd, to relieve her, and we could afterwards see her take out the Men; we call'd again to the foremost Boat, and offer'd a Truce to parley again, and to know what was her Business with us; but had no Answer, only she crowded close under our Stern; upon this our Gunner, who was a very dexterous Fellow, run out his two Chase-Guns[3] and fired again at her; but the Shot missing, the Men in the Boat shouted, wav'd their Caps, and came on; but the Gunner getting quickly ready again, fir'd among them the second Time; one Shot of which, tho' it miss'd the Boat it self, yet fell in among the Men, and we could easily see, had done a great deal of Mischief among them; but we taking no Notice of that, war'd[4] the Ship again, and brought our Quarter to bear upon them; and firing three Guns more, we found the Boat was split almost to Pieces; in particular, her Rudder, and a Piece of her Stern was shot quite away, so they handed their Sail immediately, and were in great Disorder; but to compleat their Misfortune, our Gunner let fly two Guns at them again; where he hit them we could not

---

1 White flags signify peace, true; red flags signify war with no quarter, no mercy.

2 A trumpet-shaped bull-horn.

3 Guns moved from the broadside positions in a ship, fired from ports cut in the bow of the ship.

4 Continued the war.

tell, but we found the Boat was sinking, and some of the Men already in the Water; upon this, I immediately man'd out[1] our Pinnace, which we had kept close by our Side, with Orders to pick up some of the Men if they could, and save them from drowning, and immediately to come on board with them, because we saw the rest of the Boats began to come up; our Men in the Pinnace followed their Orders, and took up three Men; one of which, was just drowning, and it was a good while before we could recover him; as soon as they were on board, we crowded all the Sail we could make, and stood farther out to Sea, and we found that when the other three Boats came up to the first two, they gave over[2] their Chace.

Being thus deliver'd from a Danger, which tho' I knew not the Reason of it, yet seem'd to be much greater than I apprehended; I took Care that we would change our Course, and not let any one imagine whether we were going; so we stood out to Sea Eastward, quite out of the Course of all *European* Ships, whether they were bound to *China*, or any where else, within the Commerce of the *European* Nations.

When we were now at Sea, we began to consult with the two Seamen, and enquire first what the meaning of all this should be, and the *Dutch* Man let us into the secret of it at once; telling us that the Fellow that sold us the Ship, *as we said*, was no more than a Thief, that had run away with her: Then he told us, how the Captain, whose Name too he told us, tho' I do not remember, was treacherously murthered by the Natives on the Coast of *Mallaca*,[3] with three of his Men, and that he, this *Dutch* Man, and four more, got into the Woods, where they wandered about a great while; till at length, he in particular, in a miraculous Manner made his Escape, and swam off to a *Dutch* Ship, which sailing near the Shore, in its Way from *China*, had sent their Boat on Shore for fresh Water; that he durst not come to that Part of the Shore where the Boat was, but shift in the Night, to take the Water farther off,[4] and the Ship's Boat took him up.

He then told us, that he went to *Battavia*, where two of the Seamen belonging to the Ship arriv'd, having deserted the rest in

1 Put in a crew.

2 Gave up.

3 Melaka, a Dutch-ruled seaport on the west coast of the Malaysian peninsula, on the Strait of Malacca.

4 In other words, he swam out to the ship at a different place from where it was that night.

their Travels, and gave an Account that the Fellow who had run away with the Ship, sold her at *Bengale*, to a Set of Pirates, which were gone a Cruising in her; and that they had already taken an *English* Ship and two *Dutch* Ships very richly laden.

This later Part we found to concern us directly, and tho' we knew it to be false; yet as my Partner said very well, if we had fallen into their Hands, and they had had such a Prepossession against us beforehand, it had been in vain for us to have defended our selves, or to hope for any good Quarter at their Hands, and especially considering that our Accusers had been our Judges, and that we could have expected nothing from them, but what Rage would have dictated, and an ungoverned passion have executed; and therefore it was his Opinion, we should go directly back to *Bengale*, from whence we came, without putting in at any Port whatever; because there, we could give a good Account of our selves, could prove where we were when the Ship put in, who we bought her of, and the like; and which was more then all the rest, if we were put to the Necessity of bringing it before the proper Judges, we should be sure to have some Justice, and not be hang'd first, and judg'd afterward.

I was sometime of my Partner's Opinion; but after a little more serious thinking, I told him, I thought it was a very great Hazard for us to attempt returning to *Bengale*, for that we were on the wrong Side of the Straits of *Malacca*; and that if the Alarm was given, we should be sure to be Way-laid on every side, as well by the *Dutch* of *Battavia*, as the *English* else-where; that if we should be taken, as it were, running away, we should even condemn our selves, and there would want no more Evidence to destroy us; I also asked the *English* Sailor's Opinion, who, said he, was of my Mind, and that we should certainly be taken.

This Danger, a little startled my Partner and all the Ship's Company; and we immediately resolv'd to go away to the Coast of *Tonquin*,* and so on to the Coast of *China*, and pursuing the first Design as to Trade, find some Way or other to dispose of the Ship, and come back in some of the Vessels of the Country, such as we could get: This was approved of as the best Method for our Security; and accordingly we steered away N.N.E. keeping above fifty Leagues off from the usual Course to the Eastward.

This however put us to some Inconveniences; for first the Winds, when we came to the Distance from the Shore, seem'd to be more steadily against us, blowing almost Trade,[1] *as we call it*,

1 Trade winds are so called because they blow regularly in one direction.

from the East, and E.N.E. so that we were a long while upon our Voyage, and we were but ill provided with Victuals for so long a Voyage; and which was still worse, there was some Danger that those *English* and *Dutch* Ships, whose Boats pursued us, whereof some were bound that Way, might be got in before us, and if not, some other Ship, bound to *China*, might have Information of us from them, and pursue us with the same Vigour.

I must confess, I was now very uneasy, and thought myself, including the late Escape from the Long-Boats, to have been in the most dangerous Condition that ever I was in thro' all my past Life; for whatever ill Circumstances I had been in, I was never pursu'd for a Thief before; nor had I ever done any Thing that merited the Name of Dishonest or Fraudulent, much less, Thievish. I had chiefly been my own Enemy, or as I may rightly say, I had been no Body's Enemy but my own: But now I was embarrass'd[1] in the worst Condition imaginable; for tho' I was perfectly innocent, I was in no Condition to make that Innocence appear: and if I had been taken, it had been under a supposed Guilt of the worst Kind; at least, a Crime esteem'd so among the People I had to do with.

This made me very anxious to make an Escape, tho', which Way to do it, I knew not, or what Port or Place we should go to; my Partner seeing me thus dejected, tho' he was the most concern'd at first, began to encourage me; and describing to me the several Ports of that Coast, told me he would put in on the Coast of *Chochinchina*,[2] or the Bay of *Tonquin*, intending to go afterwards to *Macao*,* a Town once in the Possession of the *Portuguese*, and where still a great many *European* Families resided, and particularly the missionary Priests usually went thither, in order to their going forward to *China*.[3]

Hither then we resolv'd to go; and accordingly, tho' after a tedious and irregular Course, and very much straitned[4] for Provisions, we came within Sight of the Coast very early in the Morning; and upon Reflection upon the past Circumstances we were in, and the Danger if we had not escaped, we resolv'd to put into a small River, which however had a Depth enough of Water for us, and to see if we could, either over Land, or by the Ship's Pinnace, come to know what Ships were in any Port thereabouts.

---

1 Perplexed, bewildered.

2 Cochin-China, the old name of what is now Nam-Ky, southern Vietnam.

3 Macao was a base for Jesuit missionaries in China.

4 Straitened, restricted.

This happy Step, was indeed our Deliverance; for tho' we did not immediately see any *European* Ships in the Bay of *Tonquin*, yet the next Morning there came into the Bay two *Dutch Ships*, and a third without any Colours[1] spread out, but which we believ'd to be a *Dutch* Man pass'd by at about two Leagues Distance, steering for the Coast of *China*; and in the Afternoon went by two *English* Ships steering the same Course; and thus, we thought, we saw our selves beset with Enemies, both one Way or other. The Place we were in was wild and barbarous, the People Thieves, even by Occupation or Profession; and tho' it is true we had not much to seek of them, and except getting a few Provisions, car'd not how little we had to do with them, yet it was with much Difficulty that we kept our selves from being insulted by them several Ways.

We were in a small River of this Country, within a few Leagues of its utmost Limits Northward; and by our Boat we coasted North-East to the Point of Land, which opens the great Bay of *Tonquin*; and it was in this beating up[2] along the Shore, that we discover'd, as above, that in a word, we were surrounded with Enemies. The People we were among, were the most barbarous of all the Inhabitants of the Coast; having no Correspondence with any other Nation, and dealing only in Fish, and Oil, and such gross[3] Commodities; and it may be particularly seen, that they are, *as I said*, the most barbarous of any of the Inhabitants, (*viz.*) that among other Customs they have this as one, (*viz.*) That if any Vessel have the Misfortune to be shipwreck'd upon their Coast, they presently make their Men all Prisoners or Slaves; and it was not long before we found a Spice[4] of their Kindness this Way, on the Occasion following.

I have observ'd above, that our Ship sprung a Leak at Sea, and that we could not find it out; and however, it happen'd, that as I have said it was stopp'd unexpectedly in the happy Minute of our being to be seiz'd by the *Dutch* and *English* Ships in the Bay of *Siam*; yet as we did not find the Ship so perfectly fit and sound as we desir'd, we resolv'd, while we were in this Place, to lay her on Shore, take out what heavy Things we had on Board, which were not many, and to wash and clean her Bottom, and, if possible, to find out where the Leaks were.

Accordingly, having lighten'd the Ship, and brought all our

1 Identifying flags.

2 Sailing against the wind.

3 Common and/or inferior.

4 Taste.

Guns and other moveable Things to one side, we try'd to bring her down, that we might come at her Bottom; but on second Thoughts we did not care to lay her dry on Ground, neither could we find out a proper Place for it.

The Inhabitants, who had never been acquainted with such a Sight, came wondring[1] down to the Shore, to look at us; and seeing the Ship lie down on one Side in such a manner, and heeling[2] in towards the Shore; and not seeing our Men, who were at Work on her Bottom, with Stages[3] and with their Boats on the off-Side, they presently concluded, that the Ship was cast away, and lay so fast on the Ground.

On this Supposition they came all about us in two or three Hours Time, with ten or twelve large Boats, having some of them eight, some ten Men in a Boat, intending, no doubt, to have come on Board, and plunder'd the Ship; and if they had found us there, to have carry'd us away for Slaves to their King, or whatever they call him; for we knew nothing who was their Governour.

When they came up to the Ship, and began to row round her, they discover'd us all hard at Work on the Out-side of the Ships Bottom and Side, washing, and graving,[4] and stopping,[5] as every seafaring Man knows how.

They stood for a while gazing at us, and we, who were a little surpriz'd, could not imagine what their Design was; but, being *willing to be sure*,[6] we took this Opportunity to get some of us into the Ship, and others to hand down Arms and Ammunition to those that were at Work, to defend themselves with, if there should be Occasion; and it was no more than Need; for in less than a quarter of an Hour's Consultation, they agreed, it seems, that the Ship was really a Wreck, that we were all at Work endeavouring to save her, or to save our Lives by the Help of our Boats, and when we handed our Arms into the Boats, they concluded, by that Motion, that we were endeavouring to save some of our Goods; upon this they took it for granted we all belong'd to them; and away they came down upon our Men, as if it had been in a Line of Battle.

Our Men, seeing so many of them, began to be frighted; for we lay but in an ill Posture to fight, and cry'd out to us to know what

---

1 Wandering, but also includes the sense of "wondering" about the ship.

2 Leaning, on its side.

3 Scaffolding.

4 Cleaning the ship's bottom, and sealing it with tar or other materials.

5 Plugging the seams of the ship.

6 To be on the safe side.

they should do: I immediately call'd to the Men who work'd upon the Stages, to slip them down, and get up the Side into the ship; and bad those in the Boat to row round and come on Board; and those few of us, who were on Board, work'd with all the strength and hands we had, to bring the Ship to Rights; but however, neither the Men upon the Stages or those in the Boats, could do as they were order'd, before the *Cochinchinesses* were upon them; and two of their Boats boarded our Long-Boat, and began to lay hold of the Men as their Prisoners.

The first Man they laid hold of was an *English* Seaman, a stout strong Fellow, who having a Musket in his Hand, never offer'd to fire it, but laid it down in the Boat, *like a Fool, as I thought*: But he understood his Business better than I could teach him; for he grappled the Pagan, and dragg'd him by main Force, out of their own Boat into ours; where, taking him by the two Ears, he beat his Head, so against the Boat's Gunnel,[1] that the Fellow dy'd instantly in his Hands; and in the mean time, a *Dutch* Man, who stood next, took up the Musket, and with the But-end of it, so laid about him, that he knock'd down five of them, who attempted to enter the Boat: But this was doing little towards resisting thirty or fourty Men, who fearless, because ignorant of their Danger, began to throw themselves into the Long-Boat, where we had but five Men in all to defend it: But one Accident gave our Men a compleat Victory, which deserv'd our Laughter rather than any Thing else, and that was this:

Our Carpenter being preparing to grave[2] the Out-side of the Ship, as well as to pay[3] the Seams, where he had caulk'd[4] her to stop the Leakes, had got two Kettles just let down into the Boat; one fill'd with boiling Pitch,* and the other with Rosin,[5] Tallow,* and Oil, and such Stuff, as the Ship-Wrights[6] use for that Work; and the Man that tended the Carpenter, had a great Iron Laddle in his Hand, with which he supply'd the Men that were at Work with that hot Stuff; two of the Enemies men entred the Boat just where this Fellow stood, being in the Fore-sheets; he immediately saluted them with a Laddle full of the Stuff, boiling hot, which

1 Gunwale, the top edge of the side of a ship.
2 Clean the ship's bottom, and seal it with tar or other materials.
3 Plug or seal with tar or pitch.
4 Caulk is any waterproof sealant or filler.
5 Hard, sticky, highly adhesive amber resin, distilled from crude turpentine or extracted from pine.
6 Ship-builders.

so burnt and scalded them, being half naked, that they roar'd out like two Bulls, and, enrag'd with the Fire, leap'd both into the Sea: The Carpenter saw it, and cry'd out, Well done, *Jack*, give them some more of it; and stepping forward himself, takes one of their Mops,[1] and dipping it in the Pitch-Pot, he and his Man threw it among them so plentifully that, in short, of all the Men in three Boats, there was not one that was not scalded, and burnt with it in a most frightful pitiful Manner, and made such a Howling and Crying, that I never heard a worse Noise, and indeed nothing like it; for it is worth observing, That tho' Pain naturally makes all People cry out, yet every Nation has a particular Way of Exclamation, and make Noises as different from one another, as their Speech; I cannot give the Noise, these Creatures made, a better Name than Howling, nor a Name more proper to the Tone of it; for I never heard any Thing more like the Noise of the Wolves, which as I have said, I heard howl in the Forest on the Frontiers of *Languedoc*.[2]

I was never pleas'd with a Victory better in my Life, not only as it was a perfect Surprize to me, and that our Danger was imminent before: But as we got this Victory without any Blood shed, except of that Man the Fellow kill'd with his naked Hands, and which I was very much concern'd at; for I was sick of killing such poor Savage Wretches, even tho' it was in my own Defence, knowing they came on Errands which they thought just, and knew no better; and that tho' it may be a just Thing, because necessary, for there is no necessary Wickedness in Nature, yet I thought it was a sad Life, which we must be always oblig'd to be killing our Fellow-Creatures to preserve, and indeed I think so still; and I would even now suffer a great deal, rather than I would take away the Life, even of that Person injuring me: And I believe, all considering People, who know the Value of Life, would be of my Opinion, at least, they would, if they entred seriously into the Consideration of it.

But to return to my Story, all the while this was doing, my Partner and I, who manag'd the rest of the Men on Board, had with great Dexterity brought the Ship almost to Rights; and having gotten the Guns into their Places again, the Gunner call'd to me to bid our Boat get out of the Way, for he would let fly among them. I call'd back again to him, and bid him not offer to fire, for the Carpenter would do the Work without him, but bad him heat another Pitch-Kettle, which our Cook, who was on Board, took

1 Sticks with cloth or yarn on the end, for applying tar or pitch.

2 An incident in the Pyrenees in southern France at the end of Part I.

Care of: But the Enemy were so terrify'd with what they had met with in their first Attack, that they would not come on again; and some of them that were farthest off, seeing the Ship swim, as it were upright, begun, as we supposed, to see their Mistake, and give over the Enterprize, finding it was not as they expected: Thus we got clear of this merry Fight; and having gotten some Rice, and some Roots, and Bread, with about sixteen good big Hogs on Board, two Days before, we resolv'd to stay here no longer, but go forward whatever came of it; for we made no Doubt but we should be surrounded the next Day with Rogues enough, perhaps more than our Pitch-Kettle would dispose of for us.

We therefore got all our Things on Board the same Evening, and the next Morning was ready to sail; in the mean time, lying at an Anchor at some Distance, we were not so much concern'd, being now in a fighting Posture, as well as in a sailing Posture, if any Enemy had presented: The next Day having finish'd our Work within Board, and finding our Ship was perfectly heal'd of all her Leaks, we set sail; we would have gone into the Bay of *Tonquin*; for we wanted to inform our selves of what was to be known concerning the *Dutch* Ships that had been there; but we durst not stand in[1] there, because we had seen several Ships go in, as we suppos'd, but a little before; so we kept on N.E. towards the Isle of *Formosa*,* as much afraid of being seen by a *Dutch* or *English* Merchant Ship, as a *Dutch* or *English* Merchant Ship in the *Mediteranean* is of an *Algerine* Man of War.[2]

When we were thus got to Sea, we kept out N.E. as if we would go to the *Munillas* or the *Phillippine* Islands; and this we did, that we might not fall into the Way of any of our *European* Ships; and then we steer'd North 'till we came to the Latitude of 22 Degrees, 30 Min.;[3] by which Means we made the Island *Formosa* directly, where we came to an Anchor, in order to get Water and fresh Provisions, which the People there, who are very courteous and civil in their Manners, supply'd us with willingly, and dealt very fairly and punctually with us in all their Agreements and Bargains; which is what we did not find among other People; and may be owing to the Remains of Christianity, which was once planted here by a *Dutch* Missionary of Protestants,[4] and is a Testimony

---

1 Sail toward shore.

2 A pirate or corsair ship from north Africa, modern-day Algeria.

3 A minute, which is the sixtieth part of a degree.

4 The Dutch took Formosa from Spain in 1624. The Dutch established a Christian church but in 1661 were expelled by Chinese (*continued*)

of what I have often observ'd, *viz.* That the Christian Religion always civilizes the People, and reforms their Manners, where it is receiv'd, whether it works saving Effects upon them or no.

From hence we sail'd still North, keeping the Coast of *China* at an equal Distance, till we knew we were beyond all the Ports of *China*, where our *European* Ships usually come; being resolv'd, if possible, not to fall into any of their Hands, especially in this Country, where, as our Circumstances were, we could not fail of being entirely ruin'd; nay, so great was my Fear in particular, as to my being taken by them, that I believe firmly, I would much rather have chosen to fall into the Hands of the *Spanish Inquisition.*[1]

Being now come to the Latitude of 30 Degrees, we resolv'd to put into the first trading Port we should come at; and standing in for the Shore, a Boat came off two Leagues to us, with an old *Portuguese* Pilot on Board, who knowing us to be an *European* Ship, came to offer his Service, which indeed we were very glad of, and took him on Board; upon which, without asking us whether we would go, he dismiss'd the Boat he came in, and sent them back.

I thought it was now so much in our Choice, to make the old Man carry us whither we would; that I began to talk with him about carrying us to the Gulph of *Nanquin,*[2] which is the most Northern Part of the Coast of *China*: The old Man said he knew the Gulph of *Nanquin* very well; but smiling, ask'd us what we would do there.

I told him, we would sell our Cargo, and purchase *China* Wares,* Callicoes,[3]* raw Silks, Tea, wrought Silks, *&c.* and so would return by the same Course we came: He told us our best Port had been to have put in at *Macao*, where we could not have fail'd of a Market for our Opium, to our Satisfaction, and might

---

pirates who founded an independent state. In 1676, the English East India Company opened a trading center there, but the Chinese recaptured Formosa (now called Taiwan) in 1681 and it became part of the Manchu Empire.

1 An extreme statement, considering the infamy of the Spanish Inquisition in torturing to death Protestants.

2 In the Yangtze delta, the port of Nanjing.

3 In the same year that both *Crusoe* Parts I and II were published, Defoe wrote against the importation of callicoes as detrimental to the cloth industry in Great Britain in the pamphlet *A Brief State of the Question Between the Printed and Painted Callicoes: And the Woollen and Silk Manufacture, as far as it Relates to the Wearing and Using of Printed and Painted Callicoes in Great-Britain* (London, 1719).

for our Money have purchas'd all Sorts of *China* Goods, as cheap as we could at *Nanquin*.

Not being able to put the old Man out of his Talk, of which he was very opiniated or conceited, I told him, we were Gentlemen, as well as Merchants, and that we had a Mind to go and see the great City of *Pecking*,* and the famous Court of the Monarch of *China*. Why then, says the old Man, you should go to *Ningpo*, where, by the River which runs into the Sea there, you may go up within five Leagues of the *Great Canal*.[1] This Canal is a navigable River, which goes thorow the Heart of that vast Empire of *China*, crosses all the Rivers, passes some considerable Hills by the Help of Sluices and Gates, and goes up to the City of *Pecking*, being in Length near 270 Leagues.

Well, said I, *Seignior Portuguese*, but that is not our Business now: The great Question is, If you can carry us up to the City of *Nanquin*, from whence we can travel to *Pecking* afterwards? Yes, he said, he could do so very well, and that there was a great *Dutch* Ship gone up that Way just before. This gave me a little Shock; and a *Dutch* Ship was now our Terror, and we had much rather have met the Devil, at least, if he had not come in too frightful a Figure; and we depended upon it, that a *Dutch* Ship would be our Destruction, for we were in no Condition to fight them; all the Ships they trade with into those Parts being of great Burthen, and of much greater Force than we were.

The old Man found me a little confus'd, and under some Concern, when he nam'd a *Dutch* Ship, and said to me, Sir you need be under no Apprehensions of the *Dutch*, I suppose they are not now at War with your Nation: No, says I, that's true; but I know not what Liberties Men may take when they are out of the Reach of the Law: Why, says he, *you are no Pirates*, what need you fear? They will not meddle with peaceable Merchants sure.

If I had any Blood in my Body that did not fly up into my Face at that Word, it was hinder'd by some Stop in the Vessels, appointed by Nature to prevent it; for it put me into the greatest Disorder and Confusion imaginable: Nor was it possible for me to conceal it so; but that the old Man easily perceiv'd it.

Sir, says he, I find you are in some Disorder in your Thoughts

---

1 The Grand Canal of China links the Yangtze and Yellow Rivers with a chain of human-made waterways; it was started in the fourth century BCE and completed in the 1400s CE. The canal begins in Beijing and runs to Hangzhou, about eleven hundred miles, the longest human-made waterway ever built.

at my Talk, pray be pleas'd to go which Way you think fit, and depend upon it, I'll do you all the Service I can. Why, Seignior, said I, it is true I am a little unsettled in my Resolution at this Time whither to go in particular; and I am something more so, for what you said about *Pirates*, I hope there are no Pirates in these Seas; we are but in an ill Condition to meet with them, for you see we have but a small Force, and but very weakly mann'd.

O Sir, *says he*, do not be concern'd, I do not know that there has been any Pirates in these Seas these fifteen Years, except one which was seen, as I hear, in the Bay of *Siam*, about a Month since; but you may be assured she is gone to the South-ward; nor was she a Ship of any great Force, or fit for the Work; she was not built for a Privateer,[1] but was run away with by a reprobate Crew that were on Board, after the Captain and some of his Men had been murther'd by the *Malayans*, at or near the Island of *Sumatra*.

What! SAID I, *seeming to know nothing of the Matter*, Did they murther the Captain? No, *said he*, I do not understand that they murther'd him; but as they afterwards run away with the Ship, it is generally believ'd they betray'd him into the Hands of the *Malayans*, who did murther him, and perhaps they procur'd them to do it: Why then, *said* I, they deserve Death as much as if they had done it themselves: Nay, *says the old Man*, they do deserve it, and they will certainly have it, if they light upon any *English* or *Dutch* Ship; for they have all agreed together, that if they meet that Rogue, they will give him no Quarter.

But, *said I to him*, you say the Pirate is gone out of those Seas, how can they meet with him? Why, that is true, says he, they do say so; but he was, as I tell you, in the Bay of *Siam*, in the River *Cambodia*, and was discover'd there by some *Dutch* Men who belonged to the Ship, and who were left on Shore when they run away with her; and some *English* and *Dutch* Traders being in the River, they were within a little of taking him: Nay, *said he*, if the foremost Boats had been well seconded by the rest, they had certainly taken him; but he finding only two Boats within Reach of him, tack'd[2] about, and fir'd at these two, and disabled them before the other came up, and then standing off to Sea, the other were not able to follow him, and so he got away: But they have all so exact a Description of the Ship, that they will be sure to know

1 The ship was not built for sturdy use like a privateer ship, i.e., it was not an armed ship like those owned by private individuals who had a government commission to engage in war against enemy merchant ships.

2 Turned.

him; and where-ever they find him, they have vow'd to give no Quarter* to either the Captain, or the Seamen, but to hang them all up at the Yard-Arm.*

What! says I, will they execute them right or wrong, hang them first, and judge them afterwards? O Sir! says the old Pilot, there's no Need to make a formal Business of it with such Rogues as those, let them tye them Back to Back, and set them a diving; 'tis no more than they richly deserve.

I knew I had my old Man fast aboard, and that he could do me no Harm, so that I turn'd short upon him: Well now, Seignior, said I, and this is the very Reason, why I would have you carry us up to *Nanquin*, and not to put back to *Macao*, or to any other part of the Country, where the *English* or *Dutch* Ships come; for be it known to you, Seignior, those Captains of the *English* and *Dutch* Ships, are a Parcel of rash, proud, insolent Fellows, that neither know what belongs to Justice, nor how to behave themselves, as the Laws of God and Nature direct; but being proud of their Offices, and not understanding their Power, they would act the Murtherers to punish Robbers; would take upon them to insult Men falsely accused, and determine them guilty without due Enquiry; and perhaps I may live to call some of them to an Account for it, where they may be taught how Justice is to be executed, and that no Man ought to be treated as a Criminal, 'till some Evidence may be had of the Crime, and that he is the Man.

With this I told him, that this was the very Ship they attack'd, and gave him a full Account of the Skirmish we had with their Boats, and how foolishly and coward-like they behav'd. I told him all the Story of our buying the Ship, and how the *Dutch* Men served us. I told him the Reasons I had to believe that this Story of killing the Master by the *Malayans* was true; as also the running away with the Ship; but that it was all a Fiction of their own, to suggest that the Men were turn'd *Pirates*; and they ought to have been sure it was so, before they had ventur'd to attack us by Surprize, and oblige us to resist them; adding that they would have the Blood of those Men, who we kill'd there in our just Defence, to answer for.

The old Man was amaz'd at this Relation, and told us, we were very much in the Right to go away to the *North*, and that if he might advise us, it should be to sell the Ship in *China*, which we might very well do, and buy or build another in the Country; and, said he, though you will not get so good a Ship, yet you may get one able enough to cary you and all your Goods back again to *Bengale*, or any where else.

I told him, I would take his Advice, when I came to any Port where I could find a Ship for my Turn, or get any Customer to buy this: He reply'd, I should meet with Customers enough for the Ship at *Nanquin*, and that a *Chinese* Jonk* would serve me very well to go back again; and that he would procure me People, both to buy one and sell the other.

Well, but *Seignior*, says I, as you say they know the Ship so well, I may perhaps, if I follow your Measures, be instrumental to bring some honest innocent Men into a terrible Broil,[1] and perhaps to be murther'd in cold Blood; for wherever they find the Ship, they will prove the Guilt upon the Men, by proving this was the Ship, and so innocent Men may probably be overpower'd and murther'd: Why, says the old Man, I'll find out a Way to prevent that also; for as I know all those Commanders you speak of very well, and shall see them all as they pass by, I will be sure to set them to Rights in the Thing, and let them know that they had been so much in the Wrong; that tho' the People, who were on Board at first, might run away with the Ship, yet it was not true that they had turned Pirates; and that in particular, these were not the Men that first went off with the Ship, but innocently bought her for their Trade; and I am persuaded they will so far believe me, as at least to act more cautiously for the Time to come. Well, *says I*, And will you deliver one Message to them from me? Yes, I will, *says he*, if you will give it under your Hand[2] in Writing, that I may be able to prove, that it came from you, and not out of my own Head. I answered, That I would readily give it him under my Hand; so I took a Pen, and Ink, and Paper, and wrote at large[3] the Story of assaulting me with the Long-Boats, *&c.* the pretended Reason of it, and the unjust cruel Design of it; and concluded to the Commanders, that they had done what they not only should ha' been asham'd of, but also, that if ever they came to *England*, and I liv'd to see them there, they should all pay dearly for it, if the Laws of my Country were not grown out of Use before I arrived there.

My old Pilot read this over and over again, and ask'd me several Times if I would stand to it?[4] I answer'd, I would stand to it as long as I had any Thing left in the World, being sensible that I should one Time or other find an Opportunity to put it

---

1 Quarrel, commotion.

2 In your handwriting.

3 At length.

4 Defend or maintain it, insist upon it.

home to them: But we had no Occasion ever to let the Pilot carry this Letter; for he never went back again: While those Things were passing between us, by Way of Discourse, we went forward, directly for *Nanquin*, and in about thirteen Days Sail came to an Anchor at the South West Point of the great Gulph of *Nanquin*, where, by the Way, I came by Accident to understand, that two *Dutch* Ships were gone the length before me, and that I should certainly fall into their Hands; I consulted my Partner again in this Exigency, and he was as much at a Loss as I was, and would very gladly have been safe on Shore almost any where; however, I was not in such Perplexity neither, but I ask'd the old Pilot, if there was no Creek or Harbour, which I might put into, and pursue my Business with the *Chinese* privately, and be in no Danger of the Enemy: he told me, if I would sail to the Southward about two and forty Leagues, there was a little Port call'd *Quinchang*,[1] where the Fathers of the Mission usually landed from *Macao*, on their Progress, to teach the Christian Religion to the *Chinese*, and where no *European* Ships ever put in; and if I thought to put in there, I might consider what farther Course to take when I was on Shore: He confess'd he said, it was not a Place for Merchants, except that at some certain Times, they had a kind of a Fair there, when the Merchants from *Japan* came over thither to buy the *Chinese* Merchandizes.

We all agreed to go back to this Place; the Name of the Port, as he call'd it, I may perhaps spell wrong; for I do not particularly remember it, having lost this, together with the Names of many other Places, set down in a little Pocket-Book,* which was spoil'd by the Water, on an Accident, which I shall relate in its Order; but this I remember, that the *Chinese*, or *Japanese* Merchants we corresponded with, call'd it by a differing Name from that which our *Portuguese* Pilot gave it, and pronounc'd it as above, *Quinchang*.

As we were unanimous in our Resolutions to go to this Place, we weigh'd the next Day, having only gone twice on Shore, where we were to get fresh Water; on both which Occasions, the People of the Country were very civil to us, and brought us abundance of Things *to sell to us*; *I mean, of Provisions*, Plants, Roots, Tea, Rice, and some Fowls; but nothing without Money.

We came to the other Port, (the Wind being contrary) not till five Days, but it was very much to our Satisfaction; and I was joyful, and I may say, thankful, when I set my Foot safe on Shore;

---

1 May refer to the small port of Jinjiang, near the port of Quanzhou in Fujian province in eastern China.

resolving, and my Partner too, that if it was possible to dispose of our selves and Effects, any other Way, tho' not every Way to our Satisfaction, we would never set one Foot on board that unhappy Vessel more; and indeed I must acknowledge, that of all the Circumstances of Life, that ever I had any Experience of, nothing makes Mankind so compleatly miserable, as that, of being in constant Fear: Well does the Scripture say, *the Fear of Man brings a Snare*;[1] it is a Life of Death, and the Mind is so entirely suppress'd by it, that it is capable of no Relief; the animal Spirits[2] sink, and all the Vigour of Nature, which usually supports Men under other Afflictions, and is present to them in the greatest Exigencies, fails them here.

Nor did it fail of its usual Operations upon the Fancy, by heightening every Danger, representing the *English* and *Dutch* Captains, to be Men uncapable of hearing Reason, or of distinguishing between honest Men and Rogues; or between a Story calculated for our own Turn, made out of nothing, on Purpose to deceive; and a true genuine Account of our whole Voyage, Progress, and Design; for we might many Ways have convinc'd any reasonable Creature, that we were not Pirates; the Goods we had on board, the Course we steer'd, our frankly shewing our selves, and entering into such and such Ports; and even our very Manner, the Force we had, the Number of Men, the few Arms, little Ammunition, short Provisions; all these would have serv'd to convince any Men, that we were no Pirates; the Opium, and other Goods we had on board, would make it appear, the Ship had been at *Bengale*; the *Dutch* Men, who it was said, had the Names of all the Men that was in the Ship, might easily see that we were a Mixture of *English*, *Portugueze*, and *Indians*, and but two *Dutch* Men on board: These, and many other particular Circumstances, might have made it evident to the Understanding of any Commander, whose Hands we might fall into, that we were no Pirates.

But Fear, that blind useless Passion, work'd another Way, and threw us into the Vapours; it bewildred[3] our Understandings, and set the Imagination at Work, to form a thousand terrible Things, that perhaps might never happen; we first suppos'd, as indeed every Body had related to us, that the Seamen on board the *English* and *Dutch* Ships, but especially the *Dutch*, were so enraged at the Name of a Pirate, and especially at our beating of their

1 See Proverbs 29:25.
2 Archaic term for physical or animal courage.
3 Traditionally, the sense of being lost in a wilderness.

Boats, and escaping, that they would not give themselves leave to enquire, whether we were Pirates or no; but would execute us off Hand,[1] as we call it, without giving us any Room for a Defence; we reflected that there was really so much apparent Evidence before them, that they would scarce enquire after any more; as first, That the Ship was certainly the same, and that some of the Seamen among them knew her, and had been on board her; and secondly, That when we had Intelligence at the River of *Cambodia*, that they were coming down to examine us, we fought their Boat and fled; so that we made no doubt but they were fully satisfy'd of our being Pirates, as we were satisfy'd of the contrary; and as I often said, I know not but I should have been apt to have taken those Circumstances for Evidence, if the Tables were turn'd, and my Case was theirs, and have made no Scruple of cutting all the Crew to Pieces, without believing, or perhaps considering, what they might have to offer in their Defence.

But let that be how it will, those were our Apprehensions; and both my Partner and I too, scarce slept a Night, without dreaming of Halters, and Yard-Arms; that is to say, Gibbets,[2] of fighting, and being taken; of killing and being kill'd; and one Night I was in such a Fury in my Dream, fancying the *Dutch* Men had boarded us, and I was knocking one of their Seamen down, that I struck my double Fist against the Side of the Cabin I lay in, with such a Force, as wounded my Hand most grievously, broke my Knuckles, and cut and bruised the Flesh; so that it not only wak'd me out of my Sleep, but I was once afraid I should have lost two of my Fingers.

Another Apprehension I had, was of the cruel Usage we might meet with from them, if we fell into their Hands; then the Story of *Amboyna*[3] came into my Head, and how the *Dutch*, might perhaps torture us, as they did our Country Men there; and make some of our Men, by Extremity of Torture, confess those Crimes they never were guilty of; own themselves, and all of us to be Pirates, and so they would put us to death, with a formal Appearance of Justice; and that they might be tempted to do this, for the Gain

---

1 Without hesitation, at once.

2 A gallows, where people were hanged.

3 In 1623, the Dutch attacked the English East India Company's trading factory (i.e., their base for trading) in Amboyna, an island in the Moluccas, in eastern Indonesia. Eighteen English merchants were tortured to death, and the "Amboyna incident" became synonymous, in England, with brutality.

of our Ship and Cargo, which was worth four or five thousand Pound, put altogether.

These Things tormented me and my Partner too, Night and Day; nor did we consider that the Captains of Ships have no Authority to act thus; and if we had surrender'd Prisoners to them, they could not answer the destroying us, or torturing us, but would be accountable for it, when they came into their own Country; this I say, gave me no Satisfaction; for if they will act thus with us, what Advantage would it be to us, that they would be call'd to an Account for it; or if we were first to be murthered, what Satisfaction would it be to us to have them punish'd when they came Home?

I cannot refrain taking Notice here, what Reflections I now had upon the past Variety of my particular Circumstances; how hard I thought it was, that I who had spent forty Years in a Life of continued Difficulties, and was at last come as it were to the Port or Haven, which all Men drive at, (*viz.*) to have Rest and Plenty, should be a Voluntier in new Sorrows, by my own unhappy Choice; and that I, who had escaped so many Dangers in my Youth, should now come to be hang'd in my old Age, and in so remote a Place, for a Crime I was not in the least inclin'd to, much less really guilty of; and in a Place and Circumstance, where Innocence was not like to be any Protection at all to me.

After these Thoughts, something of Religion would come in; and I should be considering, that this seem'd to me to be a Disposition of immediate Providence, and I ought to look upon it, and submit to it as such; that although I was innocent as to Men, I was far from being innocent as to my Maker; and I ought to look in and examine, what other Crimes in my Life, were most obvious to me; and for which, Providence might justly inflict this Punishment, as a Retribution; and that I ought to submit to this, just as I would to a Shipwreck, if it had pleased God, to have brought such a Disaster upon me.

In its Turn, Natural Courage would some Times take its Place; and then I would be talking my self up to vigorous Resolutions, that I would not be taken, to be barbarously used by a Parcel of merciless Wretches, in cold Blood; that it were much better to have fallen into the Hands of the Savages, who were Man-Eaters, and who, I was sure, would feast upon me, when they had taken me; than by those, who would perhaps glut their Rage upon me, by inhuman Tortures and Barbarities; that in the Case of the Savages, I always resolv'd to die fighting, to the last Gasp; and why should I not do so, seeing it was much more dreadful *to me at least*, to think of falling into these Mens Hands, than ever it was to think of being eaten by Men; for the Savages, give them their due, would not eat a Man till he was dead, and kill'd them first, as we do a Bullock; but that these Men had many Arts beyond the Cruelty of Death: When ever these Thoughts prevail'd, I was sure to put my self in a Kind of Fever, with the Agitations of a supposed Fight; my Blood would boil, and my Eyes sparkle, as if I was engag'd;[1] and I always resolv'd that I would take no Quarter at their Hands; but even at last, if I could resist no longer, I would blow up the Ship and all that was in her, and leave them but little Booty to boast of.

By how much the greater Weight, the Anxieties and Perplexities of these Things were to our Thoughts while we were at Sea, by so much the greater was our Satisfaction, when we saw our selves on Shore; and my Partner told me he dream'd, that he had a very heavy Load upon his Back, which he was to carry up a Hill, and found that he was not able to stand long under it; but that the *Portugueze* Pilot came and took it off his Back, and the Hill disappear'd, the Ground before him shewing all smooth and plain, and truly it was so, we were all like Men, who had a Load taken off of their Backs.

For my Part, I had a Weight taken off from my Heart, that it was not able any longer to bear; and as I said above, we resolv'd to go no more to Sea in that Ship; when we came on Shore, the old Pilot who was now our Friend, got us a Lodging and a Warehouse for our Goods, which by the Way, was much the same; it was a little House or Hut, with a large House joining to it, all built with Canes, and pallisadoed round with large Canes, to keep out pilfering Thieves, of which, it seems there were not a few in that Country; however, the Magistrates allowed us also a little Guard, and we had a Sentinel with a kind of Halberd, or Half-pike, who stood Sentinel at our Door; to whom we allow'd a Pint of Rice, and a little Piece of Money, about the Value of three Pence *per* Day, so that our Goods were kept very safe.

The Fair or Mart, usually kept in this Place, had been over some Time; however, we found that there were three or four Jonks in the River, and two *Jappanners*, I mean, Ships from *Japan*, with Goods which they had bought in *China*, and were not gone away, having some *Japonese* Merchants on Shore.

The first Thing our old *Portugueze* Pilot did for us, was to bring us acquainted with[2] three missionary *Romish* Priests, who were in

1 I.e., as if he were in a battle.

2 Introduce us to.

Town, and who had been there some Time, converting the People to Christianity; but we thought, they made but poor Work of it, and made them but sorry Christians when they had done; however, that was none of our Business: One of these was a *French* Man, who they call'd Father *Simon*; he was a jolly well condition'd[1] Man, very free in his Conversation, not seeming so serious and grave, as the other two did; one of whom was a *Portugueze*, and the other a *Genoese*; but Father *Simon* was courteous, easy in his Manner, and very agreeable Company; the other two were more reserv'd, seem'd rigid and austere, and apply'd seriously to the Work they came about, (*viz.*) to talk with, and insinuate them selves among the Inhabitants, wherever they had Opportunity; we often eat and drank with those Men, and tho' I must confess, the Conversion *as they call it*, of the *Chineses*, to Christianity, is so far from the true Conversion requir'd, to bring Heathen People to the Faith of Christ, that it seems to amount to little more, than letting them know the Name of Christ, and say some Prayers to the Virgin *Mary*, and her Son, in a Tongue which they understand not, and to cross themselves and the like; yet it must be confessed that these Religious, who we call Missionaries, have a firm Belief that these People shall be sav'd, and that they are the Instruments of it; and on this Account, they undergo not the Fatigue of the Voyage, and the hazards of living in such Places, but often Times Death it self; with the most violent Tortures, for the Sake of this Work; and it would be a great Want of Charity in us, what ever Opinion we have of the Work it self, and the Manner of their doing it, if we should not have a good Opinion of their Zeal, who undertook it with so many Hazards, and who have no Prospect of the least Temporal Advantage to themselves.

But to return to my Story; this *French* Priest, Father *Simon*, was appointed it seems, by Order of the Chief of the Mission, to go up to *Peking*, the Royal Seat of the *Chinese* Emperor, and waited only for another Priest, who was order'd to come to him from *Macao*, to go along with him; and we scarce ever met together, but he was inviting me to go that Journey telling me, how he would shew me all the glorious Things of that mighty Empire; and among the rest, the greatest City in the World; a City, said he, that your *London*, and our *Paris* put together, cannot be equal to: This was the City of *Peking*, which I confess is very great, and infinitely full of People; but as I look'd on those Things with different Eyes from other Men, so I shall give my Opinion of them in few Words, when

1 Good tempered, cheerful.

I come in the Course of my Travels, to speak more particularly of them.

But first, I come to my Fryar or Missionary; dining with him one Day, and being very merry together, I shew'd some little Inclination to go with him, and he press'd me and my Partner very hard, and with a great many Persuasions to consent; why Father *Simon*, says my Partner, why should you desire our Company so much: You know we are Hereticks, and you do not love us, nor can not keep us Company with any Pleasure? O says he! You may perhaps be good Catholicks in Time; my Business here, is to convert Heathens, and who knows, but I may convert you too; very well Father, said I, so you will preach to us all the Way; I won't be troublesome to you, says he; our Religion does not divest us of good Manners; besides, says he, we are here like Countrymen, and so we are, compared to the Place we are in; and if you are Hugonots[1] and I a Catholick, we may be all Christians at last; at least said he, we are all Gentlemen, and we may converse so, without being uneasy to one another; I lik'd that Part of his Discourse very well, and it began to put me in Mind of my Priest, that I had left in the *Brasils*; but this Father *Simon*, did not come up to his Character,[2] by a great deal; for tho' Father *Simon*, had no Appearance of a Criminal Levity in him neither, yet he had not that Fund of Christian Zeal, strict Piety, and sincere Affection to Religion, that my other good Ecclesiastick had, of whom I have said so much.

But to leave him a little, tho' he never left us, nor solliciting us to go with him; but we had something else before us at first; for we had all this while our Ship, and our Merchandize to dispose of, and we began to be very doubtful what we should do, for we were now in a Place of very little Business; and once I was about to venture to sail for the River of *Kilam*,[3] and the City of *Nanquin*; but Providence seem'd now more visibly as I thought, than ever, to concern it self in our Affair; and I was encouraged from this very Time, to think, I should one Way or other get out of this tangl'd Circumstance, and be brought Home to my own Country again, tho' I had not the least View of the Manner: and when I began sometimes to think of it, could not imagine by what Method it was to be done: Providence, *I say*, began here to clear up our Way a little; and the first Thing that offer'd was, that our old *Portugueze* Pilot, brought a *Japan* Merchant to us, who began

1 Huguenots were French Calvinist Protestants.

2 Father Simon was of a lesser or less impressive character.

3 This river has not been identified with any certainty.

to enquire what Goods we had; and in the first Place, he bought all our Opium, and gave us a very good Price for it, paying us in Gold by Weight, some in small Peices[1] of their own Coin, and some in small Wedges, of about ten or eleven Ounces each; while we were dealing with him for our Opium, it came into my Head, that he might perhaps deal with us for the Ship too, and I order'd the Interpreter to propose it to him; he shrunk up his Shoulders at it, when it was first propos'd to him; but in a few Days after, he came to me with one of the missionary Priests for his Interpreter, and told me, he had a Proposal to make to me, and that was this; he had bought a great Quantity of Goods of us, when he had no Thoughts (or Proposals made to him) of buying the Ship; and that therefore, he had not Money enough to pay for the Ship; but if I would let the same Men who were in the Ship navigate her, he would hire the Ship to go to *Japan*, and would send them from thence to the *Philippine* Islands with another Loading, which he would pay the Freight of, before they went from *Japan*; and that at their Return, he would buy the Ship: I began to listen to his Proposal, and so eager did my Head still run upon Rambling, that I could not but begin to entertain a Notion of going my self with him, and so to sail from the *Philippine* Islands, away to the South Seas; and accordingly I ask'd the *Japonese* Merchant, if he would not hire us to the *Philippine* Islands, and discharge us there; he said, no he could not do that, for then he could not have the Return of his Cargo; but he would discharge us in *Japan* he said, at the Ship's Return; well, still I was for taking him at that Proposal, and going my self; but my Partner, wiser than my self, persuaded me from it, representing the Dangers as well of the Seas, as of the *Japoneses*, who are a false, cruel, and treacherous People; and then of the *Spaniards*, at the *Philippines*, more false, more cruel, and more treacherous than they.

But to bring this long Turn of our Affairs to a Conclusion; the first Thing we had to do, was to consult with the Captain of the Ship, and with his Men, and know if they were willing to go to *Japan*; and while I was doing this, the young Man, who, as I said, my Nephew had left with me as my Companion for my Travels, came to me, and told me, that he thought that Voyage promised very fair, and that there was a great Prospect of Advantage, and he would be very glad if I undertook it; but that if I would not, and would give him leave, he would go as a Merchant, or how I pleas'd to order him; that if ever he came to *England*, and I was there and

1 I.e., pieces of coin currency, fractured into quarters or halves.

alive, he would render me a faithful Account of his Success, and it should be as much mine as I pleas'd.

I was really loth to part with him, but considering the Prospect of Advantage which was really considerable, and that he was a young Fellow, as likely to do well in it, as any I knew, I enclin'd to let him go; but first I told him, I would consult my Partner, and give him an Answer the next Day; my Partner and I discours'd about it, and my Partner made a most generous Offer; he told me, you know it has been an unlucky Ship, and we both resolve not to go to Sea in it again; if your Steward, *so he call'd my Man*, will venture the Voyage, I'll leave my Share of the Vessel to him, and let him make his best of it; and if we live to meet in *England*, and he meets with Success abroad, he shall account for one Half of the Profits of the Ship's Freight to us, the other, shall be his own.

If my Partner, who was no Way concern'd with my young Man, made him such an Offer, I could do no less than offer him the same; and all the Ship's Company being willing to go with him, we made over Half the Ship to him in Property, and took a Writing from him, obliging him to account for the other, and away he went to *Japan*: The *Japan* Merchant prov'd a very punctual honest Man to him, protected him at *Japan*, and got him License to come on Shore, which the *Europeans* in general, have not lately obtain'd; pay'd him his Freight very punctually, sent him to the *Philippines*, loaded with *Japan*, and *China* Wares, and a Supra-Cargo of their own, who trafficking with the *Spaniards*, brought back *European* Goods again, and a great Quantity of Cloves, and other Spice; and there he was not only pay'd his Freight very well, and at a very good Price, but being not willing to sell the Ship then, the Merchant furnish'd him with Goods, on his own Account; that for some Money, and some Spices of his own, which he brought with him, he went back to the *Manillas* to the *Spaniards*, where he sold his Cargo very well: Here having gotten a good Acquaintance at *Manilla*, he got his Ship made a free Ship; and the Governor of *Manilla* hired him, to go to *Accapulco*, in *America*, on the Coast of *Mexico*, and gave him a License to Land there, and travel to *Mexico*, and to pass in any *Spanish* Ship to *Europe*, with all his Men.

He made the Voyage to *Accapulco*, very happily, and there he sold his Ship; and having there also obtained Allowance to travel by Land, to *Porto Belo*,[1] he found Means some how or other, to get

1 Portobelo, then a prominent port in northern Panama on the Caribbean coast.

to *Jamaica*, with all his Treasure; and about eight Years after, came to *England* exceeding Rich; of the which, I shall take Notice in its Place; in the mean Time, I return to our particular Affairs.

Being now to part with the Ship, and Ship's Company; it came before us of Course, to consider what Recompence we should give to the two Men, that gave us such timely Notice of the Design against us in the River of *Cambodia*: The Truth was, they had done us a considerable Service, and deserv'd well at our Hands; tho' *by the Way*, they were a Couple of Rogues too; for as they believ'd the Story of our being Pirates, and that we had really run away with the Ship they came down to us, not only to betray the Design that was form'd against us, but to go to Sea with us as Pirates; and one of them confess'd afterwards, that nothing else but the Hopes of going a Roguing,[1] brought him to do it; however, the Service they did us, was not the less; and therefore, as I had promis'd to be grateful to them, I first order'd the Money to be pay'd them, which they said was due to them on board their respective Ships; that is to say, the *English* Man, nineteen Months Pay, and to the *Dutch* Man seven; and over and above that, I gave them, each of them, a small Sum of Money in Gold, and which contented them very well; then I made the *English* Man Gunner in the Ship, the Gunner being now made Second Mate, and Purser; the *Dutch* Man, I made Boatswain; so they were both very well pleas'd, and prov'd very serviceable, being both able Seamen, and very stout Fellows.

We were now on Shore in *China*; if I thought my self banish'd, and remote from my own Country at *Bengale*, where I had many Ways to get Home for my Money; what could I think of my self now? When I was gotten about a thousand Leagues farther off from Home, and perfectly destitute of all Manner of Prospect of Return.

All we had for it was this, that in about four Months Time, there was to be another Fair at the Place where we were; and then we might be able to purchase all Sorts of the Manufactures of the Country, and withal, might possibly find some *Chinese* Jonks or Vessels, from *Tonquin*, that would be to be sold, and would carry us and our Goods, whether we pleas'd; this I lik'd very well, and resolv'd to wait; besides, as our particular Persons were not obnoxious,[2] so if any *English* or *Dutch* Ships came thither, perhaps we might have an Opportunity to load our Goods, and get Passage to some other Place in *India*, nearer Home.

---

1 Doing dishonest or unprincipled things.

2 Objectionable.

Upon these Hopes we resolv'd to continue here; but to divert our selves, we took two or three Journeys into the Country; first we went ten Days Journey to see the City of *Nanquin*, and a City well worth seeing indeed; they say it has a Million of People in it; which however, I do not believe; it is regularly built, the Streets all exactly strait, and cross one another in direct Lines, which gives the Figure of it great Advantage.

But when I come to compare the miserable People of these Countries with ours, their Fabricks,[1] their Manner of Living, their Government, their Religion, their Wealth, and their Glory as some call it, I must confess, I do not so much as think it is worth naming, or worth my while to write of, or any that shall come after me to read.

It is very observable that we wonder at the Grandeur, the Riches, the Pomp, the Ceremonies, the Government, the Manufactures, the Commerce, and the Conduct of these People; not that it is to be wonder'd at, or indeed in the least to be regarded; but because, having first a true Notion of the Barbarity of those Countries, the Rudeness and the Ignorance that prevails there, we do not expect to find any such things so far off.

Otherwise, what are their Buildings to the Pallaces and Royal Buildings of *Europe*? What their Trade, to the universal Commerce of *England*, *Holland*, *France* and *Spain*? What are their Cities to ours, for Wealth, Strength, Gaiety of Apparel, rich Furniture, and an infinite Variety? What are their Ports, supply'd with a few Jonks and Barks, to our Navigation, our Merchant Fleets, our large and powerful Navys? Our City of *London* has more Trade than all their mighty Empire: One *English*, or *Dutch*, or *French* Man of War, of 80 Guns, would fight and destroy all the Shipping of *China*: But the Greatness of their Wealth, their Trade, the Power of their Government, and Strength of their Armies, is surprising to us, because, as I have said, considering them as a barbarous Nation of Pagans, little better than Savages, we did not expect such Things among them; and this indeed is the Advantage with which all their Greatness and Power is represented to us; otherwise it is in itself nothing at all; for as I have said of their Ships, so may be said of their Armies and Troops; all the Forces of their Empire, tho' they were to bring two Millions of Men into the Field together, would be able to do nothing but ruin the Country, and starve themselves: If they were to besiege a strong Town in *Flanders*, or to fight a disciplin'd Army; one

1 Buildings.

Line of *German* Curiassiers,[1] or of *French* Cavalry, would overthrow all the Horse of *China*; A Million of their Foot could not stand before one embattled[2] Body of our Infantry, posted so as not to be surrounded, tho' they were to be not One to Twenty in Number; nay, I do not boast if I say that 30000 *German* or *English* Foot,[3] and 10000 *French* Horse, would fairly beat all the Forces of *China*; and so of our fortified Towns, and of the Art of our Engineers in assaulting and defending Towns; there's not a fortified Town in *China* could hold out one Month against the Batteries and Attacks of an *European* Army, and at the same time, all the Armies of *China* could never take such a Town as *Dunkirk*,[4] provided it was not starv'd, no, not in a ten Years Siege: They have Fire-Arms, 'tis true, but they are awkward, clumsy, and uncertain in going off; They have Powder, but it is of no Strength; They have neither Discipline in the Field, Exercise to their Arms, Skill to Attack, or Temper to Retreat; and therefore, I must confess, it seem'd strange to me, when I came home, and heard our People say such fine Things of the Power, Riches, Glory, Magnificence, and Trade of the *Chinese*; because I saw and knew that they were a contemptible Hoord or Crowd of ignorant sordid Slaves; subjected to a Government qualified only to rule such a People; and in a word, for I am now launch'd quite beside my Design,[5] I say, in a word, were not its Distance inconceiveably great from *Muscovy*, and was not the *Muscovite* Empire almost as rude, impotent, and ill-govern'd a Crowd of Slaves as they, the Czar of *Muscovy* might with much Ease drive them all out of their Country, and conquer them in one Campaign; and had the Czar, who I since hear is a growing Prince, and begins to appear formidable in the World, fallen this Way, instead of attacking the Warlike *Swedes*, in which Attempt none of the Powers of *Europe* would have envy'd or interrupted him; he might by this time have been Emperor of *China*, instead of being beaten by the King of *Sweden*, at *Narva*, when the Latter was not One to Six in Number.[6] As their Strength and their

1 Armored cavalry, from *cuirass*, a piece of armor that protects the breast and back.

2 Drawn up for battle.

3 Foot soldiers, infantry.

4 Heavily fortified seaport in northern France, unsuccessfully besieged by the English several times in the late seventeenth century. Its destruction was included in the terms of the Treaty of Utrecht (1713), but the French never saw it through.

5 Crusoe's language points to both his travels and his narrative design.

6 Peter (I) the Great (r. 1682–1725) of Russia declared war against Sweden

Grandeur, so their Navigation, Commerce, and Husbandry* is imperfect and impotent, compar'd to the same Things in *Europe*; also in their Knowledge, their Learning, their Skill in the Sciences; they have Globes and Spheres, and a Smatch[1] of the Knowledge of the Mathematicks; but when you come to enquire into their Knowledge, how short-sighted are the wisest of their Students! they know nothing of the Motion of the Heavenly Bodies; and so grosly absurdly ignorant, that when the Sun is eclips'd, they think 'tis a great Dragon has assaulted it, and run away with it, and they fall a clattering with all the Drums and Kettles in the Country, to fright the Monster away, just as we do to hive a Swarm of Bees.

As this is the only Excursion[2] of this kind which I have made in all the Account I have given of my Travels, so I shall make no more Descriptions of Countrys and People, 'tis none of my Business or any part of my Design; but giving an Account of my own Adventures, through a Life of inimitable Wandrings, and a long Variety of Changes, which perhaps few that come after me will have heard the like of; I shall therefore say very little of all the mighty Places, desart Countrys, and numerous People, I have yet to pass thro' more than relates to my own Story, and which my Concern among them will make necessary. I was now, as near as I can compute, in the heart of *China*, about the Latitude of thirty Degrees North of the Line, for we was return'd from *Nanquin*; I had indeed a mind to see the City of *Peking* which I had heard so much of, and Father *Simon* importun'd me daily to do it; at length his Time of going away being set, and the other Missionary, who was to go with him, being arriv'd from *Macao*, it was necessary that we should resolve, either to go, or not to go; so I referr'd him to my Partner, and left it wholly to his Choice, who at length resolv'd it in the Affirmative, and we prepar'd for our Journey. We set out with very good Advantage, as to finding the Way, for we got leave to travel in the Retinue of one of their Mandarins,* a kind of Viceroy[3] or principal Magistrate in the Province where they reside, and who take great State upon

---

in 1700. The Great Northern War ended at Narva in Estonia that same year, with the outnumbered army of Charles XII of Sweden (r. 1697–1718) defeating the Russians.

1 Smattering.

2 Crusoe's language again points to both his travels and the shape of his narrative design.

3 Colony ruler who exercises authority on a sovereign's behalf. A magistrate is a lay judge or a civil law officer.

them, travelling with great Attendance, and with great Homage from the People, who are sometimes greatly impoverish'd by them, because all the Countrys they pass thro' are oblig'd to furnish Provisions for them and all their Attendance: That which I particularly observ'd, as to our travelling with his Baggage, was this, that tho' we receiv'd sufficient Provisions, both for our selves and our Horses, from the Country, as belonging to the Mandarin, yet were oblig'd to pay for every Thing we had, after the Market Price of the Country, and the Mandarin's Steward or Commissary[1] of the Provisions, collected it duly from us; so that our travelling in the Retinue of the Mandarin, tho' it was a very great Kindness to us, was not such a mighty Favour in him, but was indeed a great Advantage to him, considering there were above thirty other People travell'd in the same Manner besides us, under the Protection of his Retinue, or as we may call it, under his Convoy: This, I say, was a great Advantage to him, for the Country furnish'd all the Provisions for nothing, and he took all our Money for them.

We were five and twenty Days travelling to *Peking*, through a Country infinitely populous, but miserably cultivated; the Husbandry, the Oeconomy, and the Way of living, miserable; tho' they boast so much of the Industry of the People; I say, miserable, and so it is, if we who understand how to live were to endure it, or to compare it with our own, but not so to these poor Wretches who know no other: The Pride of these People is infinitely great, and exceeded by nothing, but their Poverty, which adds to that which I call their Misery; and I must needs think the naked Savages of *America* live much more happy, because, as they have nothing, so they desire nothing; whereas these are proud and insolent, and in the main are meer Beggars and Drudges; their Ostentation is inexpressible, and is chiefly shew'd in their Cloths and Building, and in the keeping Multitudes of Servants or Slaves, and, which is to the last Degree ridiculous, their Contempt of all the World but themselves.

I must confess, I travell'd more pleasantly afterwards in the Desarts and vast Wildernesses of Grand *Tartary*,* than here; and yet the Roads here are well pav'd, and well kept, and very convenient for Travellers; but nothing was more awkward[2] to me, than to see such a haughty, imperious, insolent People, in the midst of the grossest Simplicity and Ignorance, for all their fam'd

---

1 Deputy.

2 Incongruous.

Ingenuity is no more: And my Friend Father *Simon* and I, us'd to be very merry upon these Occasions, to see the beggarly Pride of these People; for Example. Coming by the House of a Country Gentleman, as Father *Simon* call'd him, about ten Leagues off of the City of *Nanquin*, we had first of all the Honour to ride with the Master of the House about two Miles: The State he rode in was a perfect Don *Quixotism*,[1] being a Mixture of Pomp and Poverty.

The Habit of this greasy Don was very proper for a Scaramouch or Merry-Andrew,[2] being a dirty Callico, with all the tawdry and Trapping of a Fool's Coat,[3] such as Hanging-sleeves, Tossels, and Cuts and Slashes almost on every Side; it cover'd a Taffaty* Vest, as greasy as a Butcher, and which testify'd that his Honour must needs be a most exquisite Sloven.

His Horse was a poor, lean, starv'd, hobbling Creature, such as in *England* might sell for about 30 or 40 Shillings,* and he had two Slaves follow'd him, on Foot, to drive the poor Creature along; he had a Whip in his Hand, and he belabour'd the Beast as fast about the Head, as his Slaves did about the Tail, and thus he rode by us with about ten or twelve Servants, and we were told he was going from the City to his Country Seat, about half a League before us: We travell'd on gently,[4] but this Figure of a Gentleman rode away before us, and as we stop'd at a Village about an Hour to refresh us, when we came by the Country-Seat of this great Man, we saw him in a little Place, before his Door, eating his Repast; it was a kind of a Garden, but he was easy to be seen, and we were given to understand that the more we look'd on him, the better he would be pleas'd.

He sat under a Tree, something like the Palmetto Tree,[5] which effectually shaded him over the Head, and on the South-side, but under the Tree, also, was plac'd a large Umbrello, which made that Part look well enough; he sat lolling back in a great Elbo Chair, being a heavy corpulent Man, and his Meat being brought him by two Women Slaves; he had two more, whose Office, I think, few

---

1 I.e., with signal qualities of the hero of Miguel de Cervantes's novel *Don Quixote* (1605, 1615); the deluded eponymous hero seeks out chivalric exploits such as those he has read of in popular romances.

2 The boastful fool Scaramouch or Scaramuccia is a stock character in the Italian popular farce tradition of *commedia dell'arte*, where he is often beaten by Harlequin. Merry-Andrew is a clownish buffoon.

3 Motley, incongruous coat.

4 Slowly.

5 Miniature palm.

Gentlemen in *Europe* would accept of their Service in, (*viz.*) One fed the Squire with a Spoon, and the other held the Dish with one Hand, and scrap'd off what he let fall upon his Worship's Beard and Taffaty Vest, while the great fat Brute thought it below him to employ his own Hands in any of those familiar Offices, which Kings and Monarchs would rather do, than be troubled with the clumsy Fingers of their Servants.

I took this time to think what Pain Mens Pride puts them to; and how troublesome a haughty Temper, thus ill manag'd, must be to a Man of common Sense; and leaving the poor Wretch to please himself with our looking at him, as if we admir'd his Pomp, whereas we really pitty'd and contemn'd him, we persu'd our Journey; only Father *Simon* had the Curiosity to stay to inform himself what Dainties the Country Justice had to feed on, in all his State, which he said he had the Honour to taste of, and which was, I think, a Dose that an *English* Hound would scarce have eaten, if it had been offer'd him, (*viz.*) a Mess of boil'd Rice, with a great Piece of Garlick in it, and a little Bag fill'd with Green Pepper, and another Plant which they have there, something like our Ginger, but smelling like Musk, and tasting like Mustard; all this was put together, and a small Lump or Piece of lean Mutton boil'd in it; and this was his Worship's Repast, four or five Servants more attending at a Distance. If he fed them meaner than he was fed himself, the Spice excepted, they must fare very coursly indeed.

As for our Mandarin, with whom we travell'd, he was respected like a King; surrounded always with his Gentlemen, and attended in all his Appearances with such Pomp, that I saw little of him but at a Distance; but this I observ'd, that there was not a Horse in his Retinue, but that our Carriers[1] Pack-Horses in *England* seem to me to look much better, but they were so cover'd with Equipage, Mantles, Trappings[2] and such like Trumpery,[3] that you cannot see whether they are fat or lean; in a word, we could see scarce any thing but their Feet and their Heads.

I was now light hearted, and all my Trouble and Perplexity that I have given an Account of being over, I had no anxious Thoughts about me; which made this Journey the pleasanter to me, nor had I any ill Accident attended me, only in the passing or fording a small River, my Horse fell, and made me free of the Country, as

1 Mail carriers.

2 Accessories, trimmings.

3 Showy but worthless things.

they call it, that is to say, threw me in; the Place was not deep, but it wetted me all over; I mention it because it spoil'd my Pocket-Book, wherein I had set down the Names of several People and Places which I had Occasion to remember, and which, not taking due Care of, the Leaves rotted, and the Words were never after to be read, to my great Loss, as to the Names of some Places I touch'd at in this Voyage.

At length we arriv'd at *Pecking*; I had no Body with me but the Youth who my Nephew, the Captain, had given me to attend me as a Servant, and who prov'd very trusty and diligent, and my Partner had no body with him but one Servant, who was a Kinsman; as for the *Portuguese* Pilot he being desirous to see the Court, we gave him his Passage, that is to say, bore his Charges for his Company; and to use him as an Interpreter, for he understood the Language of the Country, and spoke good *French*, and a little *English*, and indeed, this old Man was a most useful Impliment to us every where, for we had not been above a Week at *Pecking*, when he came laughing, *Ah, Seignior* Inglese, says he, *I have something to tell you will make your Heart glad. My Heart glad*, says I, *What can that be? I don't know any thing in this Country can either give me Joy or Grief to any great Degree. Yes, yes*, said the old Man in broken *English*, *make you glad, me sorrow*; *sorry* he would have said. This made me more inquisitive. *Why*, said I, *will it make you sorry*? *Because*, said he, *you have brought me here 25 days Journey, and will leave me to go back alone, and which way shall I get to my Port afterwards without a Ship, without a Horse, without* Peccune*? So he called Money, being his broken *Latin*, of which he had abundance to make us merry with.

In short, he told us there was a great Caravan of *Muscovite* and *Polish* Merchants in the City, and they were preparing to set out on their Journey by Land to *Muscovy* within four or five Weeks, and he was sure we would take the Opportunity to go with them, and leave him behind to go back all alone. I confess, I was surpris'd with his News, a secret Joy spread it self over my whole Soul, which I cannot describe, and never felt before or since, and I had no power for a good while to speak a Word to the old Man; but at last I turn'd to him; How do you know this, said I, are you sure it is true? Yes, says he, I met this Morning in the Street an old Acquaintance of mine, an *Armenian*, or one you call a *Grecian*, who is among them; he came last from *Astracan*,[1] and was designing to go to *Tonquin*, where I formerly knew him, but has alter'd

1 Astrakhan, a city in southwestern Russia and a port on the Volga River.

his Mind, and is now resolv'd to go with the Caravan to *Muscow*, and so down the River *Wolga*[1] to *Astracan*. Well, Segnior, says I, do not be uneasy about being left to go back alone, if this be a Method for my return to *England*, it shall be your Fault if you go back to *Macao* at all. We then went to consulting together what was to be done, and I ask'd my Partner what he thought of the Pilot's News, and whether it would suit with his Affairs? He told me he would do just as I would, for he had settled all his Affairs so well at *Bengale*, and left his Effects in such good Hands; that as we had made a good Voyage here, if he could vest it in *China* Silks, wrought and raw, such as might be worth the Carriage, he would be content to go *England*, and then make his Voyage back to *Bengale*, by the Company's Ships.

Having resolv'd upon this, we agreed, that if our *Portugal* Pilot would go with us, we would bear his Charges to *Muscow*, or to *England* if he pleas'd; nor indeed were we to be esteem'd over generous in that Part neither, if we had not rewarded him farther, for the Service he had done us was really worth all that, and more; for he had not only been a Pilot to us at Sea, but he had been like a Broker for us on Shore; and his procuring for us the *Japan* Merchant, was some hundreds of Pounds in our Pocket: So we consulted together about it, and being willing to gratify him, which was indeed but doing him Justice, and very willing also to have him with us besides, for he was a most necessary Man on all Occasions, we agreed to give him a Quantity of coin'd Gold, which, as I compute it, came to about 175 Pounds Sterling between us, and to bear all his Charges both for himself and Horse, except only a Horse to carry his Goods.

Having settled this among our selves, we call'd him to let him know what we had resolv'd; I told him, he had complain'd of our being to let him go back alone, and I was now to tell him we was resolv'd he should not go back at all: that as we had resolv'd to go to *Europe* with the Caravan, we resolv'd also he should go with us, and that we call'd him to know his Mind. He shook his Head, and said, it was a long Journey, and he had no *Pecune* to carry him thither, or to subsist himself when he came there. We told him, we believ'd it was so, and therefore we had resolv'd to do something for him, that should let him see how sensible we were of the Service he had done us, and also how agreeable he was to us; and then I told him what we had resolv'd to give him here, which he might lay out as we would do our own; and that as for his

1 The Volga River in central Russia, the longest river in Europe.

Charges, if he would go with us, we would set him safe a-shore, (Life and Casualties excepted) either in *Muscovy* or *England*, which he would, at our own Charge, except only the Carriage of his Goods.[1]

He receiv'd the Proposal like a Man transported and told us he would go with us over the whole World; and so, in short, we all prepar'd our selves for the Journey: However, as it was with us, so it was with the other Merchants, they had many things to do, and instead of being ready in five Weeks, it was four Months and some odd Days, before all Things were got together.

It was the Beginning of *February*, our Stile,[2] when we set out from *Peking*; my Partner and the old Pilot had gone express back to the Port where we had first put in, to dispose of some Goods which we had left there; and I with a *Chinese* Merchant, who I had some Knowledge of at *Nanquin*, and who came to *Pecking* on his own Affairs, went to *Nanquin*, where I bought ninety Pieces of fine Damasks,* with about two hundred Pieces of other very fine Silks, of several Sorts, some mix'd with Gold, and had all these brought to *Peking* against my Partner's Return; besides this, we bought a very large Quantity of raw Silk, and some other Goods, our Cargo amounting in these Goods only to about three thousand five hundred Pounds Sterling, which, together with Tea and some fine Callicoes, and three Camels Loads of Nutmegs and Cloves, loaded in all eighteen Camels for our Share, besides those we rode upon; which with two or three spare Horses, and two Horses loaded with Provisions, made us in short 26 Camels and Horses in our Retinue.

The Company was very great,[3] and, as near as I can remember, made between three and four hundred Horse, and upwards of a hundred and twenty Men, very well armed and provided for all Events; for as the Eastern Caravans are subject to be attack'd by the *Arabs*, so are these by the *Tartars*, but they are not altogether so dangerous as the *Arabs*, nor so barbarous when they prevail.

The Company consisted of People of several Nations, such as *Muscovites* chiefly, for there were above Sixty of them who

---

1 He was not charged for the passage, only for the carriage of his goods.

2 Crusoe refers to the Julian Calendar ("Old Style"), which was twelve days behind the "New Style" Calendar introduced by Pope Gregory XIII in 1582. Under the Old Style, the new year began on 25 March. Britain officially followed the Old Style until 1752, but both usages were common, as indicated by Crusoe's need to distinguish which system he uses.

3 Large.

were Merchants or Inhabitants of *Moscow*, tho' of them, some were *Livonians*,[1] and to our particular Satisfaction, Five of them were *Scots*, who appeared also to be Men of great Experience in Business, and Men of very good Substance.

When we had travell'd one Days Journey, the Guides, who were Five in Number, call'd all the Gentlemen and Merchants, that is to say, all the Passengers,[2] except the Servants, to a great Council, as they call'd it; at this great Council every one deposited a certain Quantity of Money to a common Stock, for the necessary Expence of buying Forrage* on the Way, where it was not otherwise to be had, and for satisfying the Guides, getting Horses, and the like: And here they constituted the Journey, as they call it, (*viz.*) They nam'd Captains and Officers, to draw us all up, and give the Command in case of an Attack, and gave every one their turn of Command; nor was this forming us into Order any more than what we found needful upon the Way, as shall be observ'd in its Place.

The Road all on this Side of the Country is very populous, and is full of Potters and Earthmakers, that is to say, People that tamper'd[3] the Earth for the *China* Ware; and as I was coming along, our *Portugal* Pilot, who had always something or other to say to make us merry, came sneering to me, and told me he would show me the greatest Rarity in all the Country, and that I should have this to say of *China*, after all the ill-humour'd things I had said of it, That I had seen one Thing which was not to be seen in all the World beside. I was very importunate to know what it was: At last he told me it was a Gentleman's House built all with *China* Ware. Well, says I, are not the Materials of their Building, the Product of their own Country, and so it is all *China* Ware, is not it? No no, says he, I mean, it is a House all made of *China* Ware, such as you call it in *England*; or as it is call'd in our Country, *Porcellain*. Well, says I, such a thing may be; how big is it? Can we carry it in a Box upon a Camel? If we can we will buy it. *Upon a Camel!* says the old Pilot, holding up both his Hands, *why there is a Family of Thirty People lives in it.*

I was then curious indeed to see it, and when I came to it, it was nothing but this; It was a Timber House, or a House built, as

1 People from Livonia, part of present-day Latvia, conquered by Russia and taken from Sweden and Poland in 1710.

2 Travelers.

3 The clay for porcelain is tempered by being mixed with water for proper consistency.

we call it in *England*, with Lath and Plaister, but all the Plaistering was really *China* Ware, that is to say, it was plaister'd with the Earth that makes *China* Ware.

The Outside, which the Sun shone hot upon, was glazed, and look'd very well, perfect white, and painted with blue Figures, as the large *China* Ware in *England* is painted,[1] and hard as if it had been burnt:* As to the Inside, all the Walls, instead of Wainscot, were lin'd up with harden'd and painted Tiles, like the little square Tiles, we call Galley Tiles[2] in *England*, all made of the finest China, and the Figures exceeding fine indeed, with extraordinary Variety of Colours mix'd with Gold, many Tiles making but one Figure, but joyn'd so fially,[3] the Mortar being made of the same Earth, that it was very hard to see where the Tiles met: The Floors of the Rooms were of the same Composition, and as hard as the earthen Floors we have in use in several Parts of *England*, especially *Lincolnshire*, *Nottinghamshire*, *Leicestershire*, &c. as hard as Stone, and smooth, but not burnt and painted, except some smaller Rooms like Closets, which were all as it were pav'd with the same Tile; the Ceilings, and in a word, all the plaistering Work in the whole House were of the same Earth;[4] and after all, the Roof was cover'd with Tiles of the same, but of a deep shining black.

This was a *China*-Ware-house indeed, truly and litterally to be call'd so; and had I not been upon the Journey, I could have staid some Days to see and examine the Particulars of it; they told me there were Fountains and Fish-ponds in the Garden, all pav'd at the Bottom and Sides with the same, and fine Statues set up in Rows on the Walks, entirely form'd of the *Porcellain* Earth, and burnt whole.[5]

As this is one of the singularities[6] of *China*, so they may be allow'd to excel in it; but I am very sure they excel in their Accounts of it; for they told me such incredible Things of their Performance in *Crockery*[7] *Ware*, for such it is, that I care not to relate, as knowing it could not be true; they told me in particular, of one Workman that made a Ship with all its Tackle, and Masts,

1 People in England could paint imported porcelain, but England did not manufacture porcelain.
2 Glazed tiles hung on the wall as decorations.
3 Artfully.
4 Clay.
5 Fired in a kiln as a whole object, not fired and then assembled.
6 Remarkable aspects.
7 Cooking.

and Sails, in earthen Ware, big enough to carry fifty Men; if he had told me, he launched it, and made a Voyage to *Japan* in it, I might have said something to it indeed; but as it was, I knew the whole of the Story, which was in short, asking Pardon for the Word, that the Fellow ly'd;[1] so I smil'd, and said nothing to it.

This odd Sight kept me two Hours behind the Caravan, for which, the Leader of it for the Day, fin'd me about the Value of three Shillings, and told me, if it had been three Days Journey without the Wall,[2] as it was three Days within, he must have fin'd me four Times as much, and made me ask Pardon the next Council Day; so I promised to be more orderly; for indeed I found afterward the Orders made for keeping all together, were absolutely necessary for our common Safety.

In two Days more, we pass'd the Great *China* Wall, made for a Fortification against the Tartars; and a very great Work it is; going over Hills and Mountains in a needless Track, where the Rocks are impassible, and the Precipices such, as no Enemy could possibly enter, or indeed climb up, or where if they did, no Wall could hinder them; they tell us, its Length, is near a thousand *English* Miles, but that the Country is five hundred in a strait measur'd Line, which the Wall bounds, without measuring the Windings and Turnings it takes; 'tis about four Fathom high, and as many thick in some Places.

I stood still an Hour or thereabout, without trespassing our Orders, *for so long the Caravan was in passing the Gate*; I say, I stood still an Hour to look at it on every Side, near, and far off, I mean, that was within my View; and the Guide of our Caravan, who had been extolling it for the Wonder of the World, was mighty eager to hear my Opinion of it; I told him it was a most excellent thing to keep off the *Tartars*, which he happen'd not to understand as I meant it, and so took it for a Compliment; but the old Pilot laugh'd: O Seignior *Inglese*, says he, you speak in Colours; in Colours, *said I*, what do you mean by that? Why, you speak what looks white *this Way*, and black *that Way*; gay *one Way*, and dull *another Way*; you tell him it is a good Wall to keep out *Tartars*; you tell me *by that*, it is good for nothing but to keep out *Tartars*, or it will keep out none but *Tartars*; I understand you, Seignior *Inglese*, I understand you, says he, but Seignior *Chinese*, understood you his own way.

1 In Part I, Crusoe claims to have accidentally carved a canoe large enough for thirty men.

2 The Great Wall of China.

Well, says I, Seignior, do you think it would stand out an Army of our Country People, with a good Train of Artillery; or our Engineers, with two Companies of Miners; would not they batter it down in ten Days, that an Army might enter in Battallia,[1] or blow it up in the Air, Foundation and all, that there should be no Sign of it left? Ay, ay, says he, I know that. The *Chinese* wanted mightily to know what I said, and I gave him leave to tell him a few Days after, for we was then almost out of their Country, and he was to leave us in a little Time afterward; but when he knew what I had said, he was dumb all the rest of the Way, and we heard no more of his fine Story of the *Chinese* Power and Greatness, while he stay'd.

After we had pass'd this mighty *Nothing* call'd a Wall, something like the *Picts* Wall,[2] and so Famous in *Northumberland*, and built by the *Romans*; we began to find the Country thinly inhabited, and the People rather confin'd to live in fortify'd Towns and Cities, as being subject to the Inroades and Depredations of the *Tartars*, who rob in great Armies, and therefore, are not to be resisted by the naked Inhabitants of an open Country.

And here I began to find the Necessity of keeping together in a Caravan as we travell'd; for we saw several Troops of *Tartars* roving about; but when I came to see them distinctly, I wonder'd more that the *Chinese* Empire could be conquer'd by such contemptible Fellows; for they are a meer Hoord[3] or Crowd of wild Fellows, keeping no Order, and understanding no Discipline, or manner of Fight.

Their Horses are poor lean starv'd Creatures, taught nothing, and fit for nothing, and this we said, the first Day we saw them, which was after we enter'd the wilder Part of the Country; our Leader for the Day, gave Leave for about sixteen of us to go a Hunting, as they call it; and what was this, but hunting of Sheep; however, it may be call'd Hunting too; for the Creatures are the wildest and swiftest of Foot, that ever I saw of their Kind; only they will not run a great Way, and you are sure of Sport when you begin the Chace; for they appear generally thirty or forty in a Flock, and like true Sheep, always keep together when they fly.

In Pursuit of this odd sort of Game, it was our Hap to meet

---

1 In battle formation.

2 Hadrian's Wall, built by Roman emperor Hadrian (r. 117–138 CE) when he came to Britain in 122, about 140 kilometers (87 miles) long, in northern England. Large sections can still be seen today.

3 Horde.

with about forty *Tartars*; whether they were hunting Mutton as we were, or whether they look'd for another Kind of Prey, I know not; but as soon as they saw us, one of them blew a Kind of a Horn very loud, but with a barbarous Sound, that I had never heard before, and by the way, never care to hear again; we all suppos'd this was to call their Friends about them, and so it was; for in less than Half a Quarter of an Hour, a Troop of forty or fifty more appear'd, at about a Mile Distance, but our Work was over first, as it happen'd.

One of the *Scots* Merchants of *Muscow*, happen'd to be amongst us, and as soon as he heard the Horn, he told us in short, that we had nothing to do, but to charge them immediately without loss of Time; and drawing us up in a Line, he ask'd if we were resolv'd, we told him we were ready to follow him; so he rode directly up to them; they stood gazing at us like a meer Crowd, drawn up in no Order, nor shewing the Face of any Order at all; but as soon as they saw us advance, they let fly their Arrows, which however miss'd us very happily; it seems they mistook not their Aim, but their Distance; for their Arrows all fell a little short of us, but with so true an Aim, that had we been about twenty Yards nearer, we must have had several Men wounded, if not kill'd.

Immediately we halted, and tho' it was at a great Distance, we fir'd, and sent them Leaden Bullets, for Wooden Arrows, following our Shot full Gallop, to fall in among them Sword in Hand, for so our Bold *Scot* that led us directed; he was indeed but a Merchant, but he behav'd with that Vigour and Bravery on this Occasion, and yet, with such a cool Courage too, that I never saw any Man in Action, fitter for Command: As soon as we came up to them, we fir'd our Pistols in their Faces, and then drew, but they fled in the greatest Confusion imaginable; the only Stand any of them made, was on our Right, where three of them stood, and by Signs, call'd the rest to come back to them, having a kind of Scymitar* in their Hands, and their Bows hanging at their Backs: Our brave Commander, without asking any body to follow him, gallops up close to them, and with his Fuzee, knocks one of them off his Horse, kill'd the second with his Pistol, and the third ran away, and thus ended our Fight; but we had this Misfortune attending it, (*viz.*) that all our Mutton that we had in Chace, got away: We had not a Man kill'd or hurt; but as for the *Tartars*, there was about five of them kill'd; who were wounded, we knew not; but this we knew, that the other Party was so frighted with the Noise of our Guns, that they made off, and never made any attempt upon us.

We were all this while in the *Chinese* Dominion, and therefore, the *Tartars* were not so bold as afterwards; but in about five Days we enter'd a vast great wild Desart, which held us three Days and Nights March; and we were oblig'd to carry our Water with us, in great Leather Bottles, and to encamp all Night, just as I have heard they do in the Desart of *Arabia*.

I ask'd whose Dominion this was in, and they told me, this was a kind of Border, that might be call'd *no Man's Land*; being a Part of the Great *Karakathaie*, or Grand *Tartary*,[1] but that however it was all reckon'd to *China*; but that there was no Care taken here, to preserve it from the Inroads of Thieves, and therefore it was reckon'd the worst Desart in the whole World; tho' we were to go over some much larger.

In passing this Wilderness, which I confess was at the first very frightful to me, we saew two or three Times little Parties of the *Tartars*, but they seem'd to be upon their own Affairs, and to have no Design upon us; and so like the Man who met the Devil, if they had nothing to say to us, we had nothing to say to them; we let them go.

Once however, a Party of them came so near, as to stand and gaze at us; whether it was to consider what they should do, whether attack us, or not attack us, that we knew not; but when we were pass'd at some Distance by them, we made a Rear-Guard of forty Men, and stood ready for them, letting the Caravan pass Half a Mile or thereabouts before us; but after a while they march'd off, only we found they saluted us with five Arrows at their parting; one of which, wounded a Horse, so that it disabled him; and we left him the next Day, poor Creature, in great need of a good Farrier;[2] we supposed they might shoot more Arrows, which might fall short of us, but we saw no more Arrows or *Tartars*, that time.

We travell'd near a Month after this, the Ways being not so good as at first, tho' still in the Dominions of the Emperor of *China*, but lay for the most part in Villages, some of which were fortified, because of the Incursions of the *Tartars*. When we came to one of these Towns, (it was about two Days and a Half Journey before we were to come to the City *Naum*) I wanted to buy a Camel, of which there are plenty to be sold all the way upon that Road, and of Horses also, such as they are, because so many Caravans

1 Great Karakathaie, or Grand Tartary: Kara-Khitai, which means "Black China," was thought to be in the Middle Ages in Europe the kingdom of Prester John, the legendary Christian king of Asia.

2 Farriers shoe horses and treat them medically.

coming that way, they are often wanted: The Person that I spoke to to get me a Camel, would have gone and fetch'd it for me, but I like a Fool must be officious, and go my self along with him: The Place was about two Miles out of the Village, where, it seems, they kept the Camels and Horses feeding under a Guard.

I walk'd it on Foot with my old Pilot, being very desirous, forsooth, of a little Variety: When we came to the Place, it was a low marshy Ground, wall'd round with a Stone Wall, piled up dry, without Mortar or Earth among it, like a Park, with a little Guard of *Chinese* Soldiers at the Door. Having bought a Camel, and agreed for the Price, I came away, and the *Chinese* Man that went with me, led the Camel; when on a sudden came up five *Tartars* on Horse-back; two of them seized the Fellow, and took the Camel from him, while other three step'd up to me, and my old Pilot, seeing us as it were unarm'd, for I had no Weapon about me but my Sword, which could but ill defend me against three Horse-men; the first that came up stop'd short upon my drawing my Sword; (for they are errant[1] Cowards) but a Second coming upon my Left, gave me a Blow on the Head, which I never felt till afterward, and wonder'd when I came to my self, what was the matter with me, and where I was, for he laid me flat on the Ground; but my never failing old Pilot, the *Portuguese* (so Providence unlook'd for directs Deliverances from Dangers, which to us are unforeseen) had a Pistol in his Pocket, which I knew nothing of, nor the *Tartars*; neither if they had, I suppose they would not have attack'd us: But Cowards are always boldest when there is no Danger.

The old Man seeing me down, with a bold Heart step'd up to the Fellow that had struck me, and laying hold of his Arm with one Hand, and pulling him down by main Force a little towards him with the other, shot him into the Head, and laid him dead upon the Spot; he then immediately step'd up to him who had stop'd us, as I said, and before he could come forward again, (for it was all done as it were in a Moment) made a Blow at him with a Scymetar* which he always wore, but missing the Man, cut his Horse into the Side of his Head, cut one of his Ears off by the Root, and a great Slice down the Side of his Face; the poor Beast enrag'd with the Wound, was no more to be govern'd by his Rider, tho' the Fellow sat well enough too; but away he flew, and carried him quite out of the Pilot's Reach, and at some Distance rising up upon his hind Legs, threw down the *Tartar*, and fell upon him.

---

1 Variation on "arrant," or notorious.

In this Interval the poor *Chinese* came in, who had lost the Camel, but he had no Weapon; however, seeing the *Tartar* down, and his Horse fallen upon him, away he runs to him, and seizing upon an ugly ill-favour'd Weapon he had by his Side, something like a Pole-ax, but not a Pole-ax neither, he wrench'd it from him, and made shift to knock his *Tartarian* Brains out with it. But my old Man had the Third *Tartar* to deal with still, and seeing he did not fly, as he expected, nor come on to fight him, as he apprehended, but stand stock still, the old Man stood still too, and falls to work with his Tackle to charge his Pistol again; but as soon as the *Tartar* saw the Pistol, whether he supposed it to be the same, or another, I know not, but away he scower'd,[1] and left my Pilot, my Champion I call'd him afterward, a compleat Victory.

By this time I was a little awake, for I thought when first I began to wake, that I had been in a sweet Sleep; but as I said above, I wonder'd where I was, how I came upon the Ground, and what was the matter: In a word, a few Moments after, as Sense return'd, I felt Pain, tho' I did not know where; I clap'd my Hand to my Head, and took it away bloody; then I felt my Head ach, and then in another Moment Memory return'd, and every thing was present to me again.

I jump'd up upon my Feet instantly, and got hold of my Sword, but no Enemies in View: I found a *Tartar* lie dead and his Horse standing very quietly by him; and looking farther, I saw my Champion and Deliverer, who had been to see what the *Chinese* had done, coming back with his Hanger in his Hand; the old Man seeing me on my Feet, came running to me and embrac'd me with a great deal of Joy, being afraid before that I had been kill'd, and seeing me bloody, would see how I was hurt, but it was not much, only what we call a broken Head; neither did I afterwards find any great Inconvenience from the Blow, other than the Place which was hurt, and which was well again in two or three Days.

We made no great Gain however by this Victory, for we lost a Camel, and gain'd a Horse; but that which was remarkable, when we came back to the Village, the Man demanded to be paid for the Camel; I disputed it, and it was brought to a Hearing before the *Chinese* Judge of the Place; that is to say, in *English*, we went before a Justice of the Peace: Give him his due, he acted with a great deal of Prudence and Impartiality; and having heard both Sides he gravely ask'd the *Chinese* Man, that went with me to buy

1 Scoured, ran away quickly.

the Camel, whose Servant he was; I am no Servant, says he, but went with the Stranger; at whose Request says the Justice? At the Stranger's Request, says he: Why then, says the Justice, you were the Stranger's Servant for the Time, and the Camel being deliver'd to his Servant, it was deliver'd to him, and he must pay for it.

I confess the Thing was so clear, that I had not a Word to say; but admiring to see such just Reasoning upon the Consequence, and so accurate stating the Cause, I pay'd willingly for the Camel, and sent for another; but you may observe, I sent for it, I did not go to fetch it my self any more, I had enough of that.

The City of *Naum*, is a Frontier of the *Chinese* Empire; they call it fortify'd, and so it is, as Fortifications go there; for this I will venture to affirm, that all the *Tartars* in *Karakathaie*, which I believe, are some Millions, could not batter down the Walls with their Bows and Arrows; but to call it strong, if it were attack'd with Cannon, would be to make those who understand it, laugh at you.

We wanted,[1] as I have said, above two Days Journey of this City, when Messengers were sent Express to every Part of the Road, to tell all Travellers and Caravans, to halt till they had a Guard sent for them; for that an unusual Body of *Tartars*, making ten thousand in all, had appear'd in the Way, about thirty Miles beyond the City.

This was very bad News to Travellers; however, it was carefully done of the Governour, and we were very glad to hear we should have a Guard; accordingly, two Days after, we had two hundred Soldiers sent us from a Garrison of the *Chineses*, on our left, and three hundred more from the City of *Naum*, and with those we advanc'd boldly; the three hundred Soldiers from *Naum*, march'd in our Front, the two hundred in our Rear, and our Men on each Side of our Camels with our Baggage, and the whole Caravan in the Center; in this Order, and well prepar'd for Battle, we thought our selves a Match for the whole ten thousand *Mongul Tartars*,* if they had appear'd; but the next Day when they did appear, it was quite another Thing.

It was early in the Morning, when marching from a little well situated Town call'd *Changhu*, we had a River to pass, where we were oblig'd to Ferry; and had the *Tartars* had any Intelligence, then had been the Time to have attack'd us, when the Caravan being over, the Rear-Guard, was behind; but they did not appear.

About three Hours after, when we were enter'd upon a Desart of about fifteen or sixteen Miles over, behold, by a Cloud of Dust

---

1 Lacked, were short of.

they rais'd, we saw an Enemy was at Hand, and they were at Hand indeed, for they came on upon the Spur.[1]

The *Chineses*, our Guard on the Front, who had talk'd so big the Day before, began to stagger,[2] and the Soldiers frequently look'd behind them, which is a certain Sign in a Soldier, that he is just ready to run away; my old Pilot was of my mind, and being near me, he call'd out, Seignior *Inglese*, *says he*, those Fellows must be encourag'd, or they will ruin us all; for if the *Tartars* come on, they will never stand it:[3] I am of your Mind *said I*, but what Course must be done; done! *says he*, let fifty of our Men advance, and flank them on each Wing, and encourage them, and they will fight like brave Fellows in brave Company; but without, they will every Man turn his Back; immediately I rode up to our Leader, and told him, who was exactly of our Mind; and accordingly, fifty of us march'd to the right Wing, and fifty to the left, and the rest made a Line of Rescue; and so we march'd, leaving the last two hundred Men to make another Body by themselves, and to guard the Camels; only that if Need were, they should send a hundred Men, to assist the last fifty.

In a Word, the *Tartars* came on, and an innumerable Company they were; how many, we could not tell, but ten thousand we thought was the least: A Party of them came on first and view'd our Posture, traversing the Ground in the Front of our Line; and as we found them within Gun-shot, our Leader ordered the two Wings to advance swiftly, and give them a Salvo on each Wing with their Shot, which was done, but they went off, and I suppose back to give an Account of the Reception they were like to meet with: and indeed that Salute clog'd their Stomach,[4] for they immediately halted, stood a while to consider of it, and wheeling off to the left, they gave over the Design and said no more to us for that Time; which was very agreeable to our Circumstances, which were but very indifferent for a Battle with such a Number.

Two Days after this, we came to the City *Naun*, or *Naum*; we thank'd the Governour for his Care for us, and collected to the Value of a hundred Crowns, or thereabouts, which we gave to the Soldiers sent to guard us; and here we rested one Day: This is a Garrison indeed, and there were nine hundred Soldiers kept here; but the Reason of it was, that formerly, the *Muscovite* Frontiers

1 At full gallop, spurring horses along.

2 Hesitate, waver.

3 Stand and fight.

4 Idiomatic, cooled them off.

lay nearer to them than they do now, the *Muscovites* having abandon'd that Part of the Country, (which lies from this City, West, for about two hundred Miles) as desolate and unfit for Use; and more especially, being so very remote, and so difficult to send Troops thither for its Defence; for we had yet above two thousand Miles to *Muscovy*, properly so call'd.

After this, we pass'd several great Rivers, and two dreadful Desarts, one of which, we were sixteen Days passing over, and which as I said, was to be call'd no Man's Land; and on the 13th of *April*, we came to the Frontiers of the *Muscovite* Dominions: I think the first City, or Town, or Fortress, what ever it might be call'd, that belong'd to the Czar of *Muscovy*, was call'd *Argun*, being on the West Side of the River *Argun*.[1]

I could not but discover an infinite Satisfaction, that I was so soon arriv'd in, as I call'd it, a Christian Country, or at least in a Country, govern'd by Christians; for tho' the *Muscovites* do, *in my Opinion* but just deserve the Name of Christians, yet such they pretend to be, and are very devout in their Way: It would certainly occur to any Man who travels the World as I have done, and who had any Power of Reflection; I say, it would occur to him, to reflect what a Blessing it is to be brought into the World, where the Name of God, and of a Redeemer is known, worship'd and ador'd; and not where the People given up by Heaven to strong Delusions, worship the Devil, and prostrate themselves to Stocks and Stones, worship Monsters, Elements, horrible shap'd Animals, and Statues, or Images of Monsters: Not a Town or City we pass'd thro', but had their Pagods,[2] their Idols, and their Temples, and ignorant People worshipping, even the Works of their own Hands.[3]

Now we came where at least a Face of the Christian Worship appear'd, where the Knee was bow'd to Jesus; and whether ignorantly or not, yet the Christian Religion was own'd, and the Name of the True God was call'd upon, and ador'd; and it made the very Recesses of my Soul rejoice to see it: I saluted the brave *Scots* Merchant I mention'd above, with my first acknowledgment of this; and taking him by the Hand, I said to him, blessed be God, we are once again come among Christians; he smil'd, and answered, do not rejoice too soon Countryman, these *Muscovites*, are but an odd

1 A city in what is now the Chechen Republic, Russia, on the river Argun.

2 Idols of deities.

3 Jeremiah 1:16: "And I will utter my judgments against them touching all their wickedness, who have forsaken me, and have burned incense unto other gods, and worshipped the works of their own hands" (KJV).

Sort of Christians; and but for the Name of it, you may see very little of the Substance, for some Months farther of our Journey.

Well, says I, but still 'tis better than Paganism, and worshipping of Devils: Why, I'll tell you, says he, except the *Russian* Soldiers in Garrisons, and a few of the Inhabitants of the Cities upon the Road, all the rest of this Country, for above a thousand Miles farther, is inhabited by the worst, and most ignorant of Pagans; and so indeed we found it.

We were now launch'd into the greatest Piece of solid Earth, if I understand any thing of the Surface of the Globe, that is to be found in any Part of the Earth; we had at least twelve hundred Miles to the Sea, Eastward; we had at least two thousand to the Bottom of the Baltick Sea, Westward; and above three thousand Miles, if we left that Sea, and went on West to the *British* and *French* Channels: We had full five thousand Miles to the *Indian*, or *Persian* Sea, South; and about eight hundred Miles to the Frozen Sea, North; nay, if some People may be believed, there might be no Sea North-East, till we came round the Pole, and consequently into the North-West, and so had a Continent of Land into *America*, the Lord knows where, tho' I could give some Reasons, why I believe that to be a Mistake.[1]

As we enter'd into the *Muscovite* Dominions, a good while before we came to any considerable Towns, we had nothing to observe there but this; first, that all the Rivers that run to the East, as I understood by the Charts, which some in our Caravan had with them; it was plain, all those Rivers, ran into the Great River *Yamour*, or *Gammour*:[2] This River, by the natural Course of it must run into the East Sea, or *Chinese* Ocean; the Story they tell us, that the Mouth of this River, is choak'd up with Bullrushes, of a monstruous Growth, (*viz.*) three Foot about, and twenty or thirty Foot high, I must be allow'd to say, I believe nothing of; but as its Navigation is of no Use, because there is no Trade that way, the *Tartars*, to whom alone it belongs, dealing in nothing but Cattle, so no Body that ever I heard of, has been curious enough, either to go down to the Mouth of it in Boats, or come up from the Mouth of it in Ships; but this is certain, that this River running due East, in the Latitude of [3] carries a vast Concourse of

1 Numerous attempts were made during the 1700s to find a northeast sea passage to Asia from Europe. None was found until the late 1800s.

2 The Amur river, a boundary between northeastern China and Far Eastern Russia.

3 In the fourth edition of *Farther Adventures* (1722), the blank is filled in: "60 Degrees."

Rivers along with it, and finds an Ocean to empty it self in that Latitude; so we are sure of Sea there.

Some Leagues to the North of this River, there are several considerable Rivers, whose Streams run as due North as the *Yamour* runs East, and these are all found to join their Waters with the Great River *Tartarus*,[1] nam'd so, from the northernmost Nations of the *Mongul Tartars*, who the *Chinese* say, were the first *Tartars* in the World; and who, as our Geographers alledge, are the *Gog*, and *Magog*, mention'd in sacred Story.[2]

These Rivers running all Northward, as well as all the other Rivers, I am yet to speak of, make it evident, that the Northern Ocean bounds the Land also on that side; so that it does not seem rational in the least to think, that the Land can extend itself to join with *America* on that side, or that there is not a Communication between the Northern and the Eastern Ocean; but of this I shall say no more, it was my Observation at that time, and therefore I take Notice of it in this Place. We now advanc'd from the River *Arguna*[3] by easy and moderate Journeys, and were very visibly oblig'd to the Care the Czar of *Muscovy* has taken to have Cities and Town built in as many Places as are possible to place them, where his Soldiers keep Garrison something like the Stationary Soldiers plac'd by the *Romans* in the remotest Countries of their Empire, some of which I had read particularly were plac'd in *Britain* for the Security of Commerce, and for the lodging Travellers; and thus it was here; for where-ever we came, tho' at these Towns and Stations, the Garrisons and Governor were *Russians*, and profess'd Christians, yet the Inhabitants of the Country were meer *Pagans*, sacrificing to Idols, and worshipping the Sun, Moon, and Stars, or all the Host of Heaven, and not only so, but were of all the *Heathens* and *Pagans* that ever I met with, the most barbarous, except only that they did not eat Man's Flesh, as our Savages of *America* did.

Some Instances of this we met with in the Country between *Arguna*, where we enter the *Muscovite* Dominions, and a City of *Tartars* and *Russians* together, call'd *Nortzinskoy*,[4] in which is a continu'd Desart or Forrest, which cost us twenty Days to travel

1 Likely the Lena, easternmost of the three great Siberian rivers that flow into the Arctic Ocean.

2 In Revelation 20:8, Gog and Magog are described as powers under the command of Satan.

3 The Argun River.

4 Nerchinsk, about 140 miles west of the Chinese border.

over it; in a Village near the last of those Places I had the Curiosity to go and see their Way of Living, which is most brutish and unsufferable; they had I suppose a great Sacrifice that Day, for there stood out upon an old Stump of a Tree, an Idol made of Wood, frightful as the Devil, at least as any Thing we can think of to represent the Devil can be made; it had a Head certainly not so much as resembling any Creature that the World ever saw; Ears as big as Goats Horns, and as high; Eyes as big as a Crown-Piece, a Nose like a crooked Ram's Horn, and a Mouth extended four Corner'd like that of a Lion, with horrible Teeth, hooked like a Parrot's under Bill; it was dressed up in the filthiest manner that you could suppose; its upper Garment was of Sheep-Skins, with the Wool outward, a great *Tartar* Bonnet on the Head, with two Horns growing through it, it was about eight Foot high, yet had no Feet or Legs, or any other Proportion of Parts.

This Scare-crow was set up at the outer Side of the Village, and when I came near to it, there was sixteen or seventeen Creatures, whether Men or Women, I could not tell, for they make no Distinction by their Habits, either of Body or Head: These lay all flat on the Ground, round this formidable Block of shapeless Wood: I saw no Motion among them any more, than if they had been all Logs of Wood like the Idol, and at first, really thought they had been so; but when I came a little nearer, they started up upon their Feet, and rais'd a howling Cry, as if it had been so many deep mouth'd[1] Hounds, and walk'd away as if they were displeas'd at our disturbing them: A little way off from the Island, and at the Door of that Tent or Hut, made all of Sheep-Skins and Cow-Skins, dry'd, stood three Butchers, I thought they were such; when I came nearer to them, I found they had long Knives in their Hands, and in the middle of the Tent appear'd three Sheep kill'd, and one young Bullock or Steer: These it seems, were Sacrifices to that sensless Log of an Idol, and these three Men, Priests belonging to it; and the seventeen prostrated Wretches, were the People who brought the Offering, and were making their Prayers to that Stock.

I confess I was more mov'd at their Stupidity and brutish Worship of a Hobgoblin,[2] than ever I was at any Thing in my Life; to see God's most glorious and best Creature, to whom he had granted so many Advantages, *even by Creation*, above the rest of the Works of his Hands, vested with a reasonable Soul, and that

1 Deep-voiced.

2 Something that inspires superstitious fear.

Soul adorn'd with Faculties and Capacities, adapted both to honour his Maker, and be honoured by him, sunk and degenerated to a Degree, so more than stupid, as to prostrate it self to a frightful Nothing, a meer imaginary Object dress'd up by themselves, and made terrible to themselves by their own Contrivance; adorn'd only with Clouts[1] and Rags; and that this should be the Effect of meer Ignorance, wrought up into hellish Devotion by the Devil himself; who envying (to his Maker) the Homage and Adoration of his Creatures, had deluded them into such gross, surfeiting, sordid and brutish Things, as one would think should shock Nature it self.

But what signify'd all the Astonishment and Reflection of Thoughts; thus it was, and I saw it before my Eyes, and there was no room to wonder at it, or think it impossible; all my Admiration turn'd to Rage, and I rid up to the Image, or Monster, call it what you will, and with my Sword cut the Bonnet that was on its Head in two in the middle, so that it hung down by one of the Horns; and one of our Men that was with me took hold of the Sheep-Skin that cover'd it, and pull'd at it, when behold a most hideous Outcry and Howling run thro' the Village, and two or three hundred People came about my Ears, so that I was glad to scour[2] for it; for we saw some had Bows and Arrows; but I resolved from that moment to visit them again.

Our Caravan rested three Nights at the Town, which was about four Miles off, in order to provide some Horses which they wanted; several of the Horses having been lam'd and jaded[3] with the badness of the Way and long March over the last Desart; so we had some Leisure here to put my Design in Execution; I communicated my Project to the *Scots* Merchant of *Muscow*, of whose Courage I had had sufficient Testimony, as above; I told him what I had seen, and with what Indignation I had since thought that human Nature could be so degenerate: I told him, I was resolv'd if I could get but four or five Men well arm'd to go with me, I was resolv'd to go and destroy that vile abominable Idol, and let them see that it had no Power to help itself, and consequently could not be an Object of Worship, or to be pray'd to, much less, help them that offer'd Sacrifices to it.

He laugh'd at me; *says he*, Your Zeal may be good, but what do you propose to your self by it? Propose, *said I*, to vindicate the

---

1 Crude clothes.

2 Run away quickly.

3 Exhausted.

Honour of God, which is insulted by this Devil Worship. But how will it vindicate the Honour of God, *said he*? While the People will not be able to know what you mean by it, unless you could speak to them and tell them so, and then they will fight you and beat you too, I'll assure you, for they are desperate Fellows, and that especially in Defence of their Idolatry. Can we not, said I, do it in the Night and then leave them the Reasons and Causes in Writing in their own Language? Writing! said he, why there is not a Man in five Nations of them that know any thing of a Letter, or how to read a Word in any Language, or in their own. Wretched Ignorance! said I to him, however I have a great Mind to do it, perhaps Nature may draw Inferences from it to them, to let them see how brutish they are, to worship such horrid Things. Look you, Sir, said he, if your Zeal prompts you to it so warmly, you must do it; but in the next Place I would have you consider these wild Nations of People are subjected by Force to the *Czar* of *Muscovy*'s Dominions, and if you do this, 'tis ten to one, but they will come by Thousands to the Governour of *Nertsinskay*, and complain and demand Satisfaction, and if he cannot give them Satisfaction, 'tis ten to one but they revolt, and it will occasion a new War with all the *Tartars* in the Country.

This, I confess, put new Thoughts into my Head for awhile, but I harp'd upon the same String still, and all that Day I was uneasy to put my Project in Execution; towards the Evening the *Scots* Merchant met me by Accident in our Walk about the Town, and desir'd to speak with me; I believe, said he, I have put you off of your good Design, I have been a little concern'd about it since, for I abhor the Idol and the Idolatry as much as you can do: Truly, *says I*, you have put it off a little as to the Execution of it, but you have not put it at all out of my Thoughts, and I believe I shall do it still before I quit this Place, tho' I were to be deliver'd up to them for Satisfaction. No, no, *says he*, God forbid they should deliver you up to such a Crew of Monsters, they shall not do that neither, that would be murdering you indeed. Why, says I, how would they use me? Use you, says he, I'll tell you how they serv'd a poor *Russian*, who affronted them in their Worship just as you did, and who they took Prisoner; after they had lam'd him with an Arrow that he could not run away, they took him and stripp'd him stark naked, and set him up on the top of the Idol Monster, and stood all round him, and shot as many Arrows into him as would stick over his whole Body, and then they burnt him and all the Arrows sticking in him as a Sacrifice to the Idol: And was this the same Idol? Yes, says he, the very same. Well, *says I*, I'll tell you a Story; so I related the Story of our Men at *Madagascar*, and how they burnt and sack'd the Village there, and kill'd Man, Woman and Child, for their murdering one of our Men, just as it is related before; and when I had done, I added, that I thought we ought to do so to this Village.

He listen'd very attentively to the Story, but when I talk'd of doing so to that Village, *says he*, You mistake very much, it was not this Village, it was almost a hundred Mile from this place, but it was the same Idol, for they carry him about in Procession all over the Country: Well, then, says I, then that Idol ought to be punish'd for it, and it shall, says I, if I live this Night out.

In a word, finding me resolute, he lik'd the Design, and told me I should not go alone, but he would go with me, and bring a stout Fellow, one of his Countrymen to go also with us; and one, says he, as famous for his Zeal as you can desire any one to be, against such devilish Things as these. In a word, he brought me his Comrade, a *Scots* Man, who he call'd Captain *Richardson*, and I gave him a full Account of what I had seen; and in a word, of what I intended; and he told me readily, he would go with me if it cost him his Life; so we agreed to go only us three. I had indeed propos'd it to my Partner, but he declin'd it; he said, he was ready to assist me to the utmost, and upon all Occasions for my Defence; but that this was an Adventure quite out of his Way; so, I say, we resolv'd upon our Work only us three and my Man-Servant, and to put it in Execution that Night about Midnight, with all the Secrecy imaginable.

However, upon second Thoughts, we were willing to delay it till the next Night, because the Caravan being to set forward in the Morning, we suppos'd the Governour could not pretend to give them any Satisfaction upon us when we were out of his Power. The *Scots* Merchant, as steady in his Resolution for the Enterprize, as bold in executing, brought me a *Tartar*'s Robe or Gown of the Sheep-Skins, and a Bonnet, with a Bow and Arrows, and had provided the same for himself and his Countryman, that the People, if they saw us, should not be able to determine who we were.

All the first Night we spent in mixing up some combustible Matter with Aqua-vitæ,* Gun-powder, and such other Materials as we could get, and having a good Quantity of Tar in a little Pot, about an Hour after Night we set out upon our Expedition.

We came to the Place about eleven a Clock at Night, and found that the People had not the least Jealousy[1] of Danger

1 Suspicion.

attending their Idol; the Night was cloudy, yet the Moon gave us Light enough to see that the Idol stood just in the same Posture and Place that it did before: The People seemed to be all at their Rest, only, that in the great Hut, or Tent, as we call'd it, where we saw the three Priests, who we mistook for Butchers, we saw a Light, and going up close to the Door, we heard People talking as if there were five or six of them; we concluded therefore, that if we set the Wild-fire* to the Idol, these Men would come out immediately, and run up to the Place to rescue it from the Destruction that we intended for it, and what to do with them we knew not; once we thought of carrying it away and setting Fire to it at a Distance; but when we came to handle it, we found it too bulky for our Carriage, so we were at a Loss again: The second *Scots* Man was for setting Fire to the Tent or Hut, and knocking the Creatures that were there on the Head when they came out; but I could not joyn with that, I was against killing them, if it was possible to be avoided: Well then, said the *Scots* Merchant, I'll tell you what we will do, we will try to take them Prisoners, tye their Hands behind them, and make them stand still, and see their Idol destroy'd.

As it happen'd, we had Twine or Packthread enough about us, which was used to tye our Fire-Works together with; so we resolved to attack these People first, and with as little Noise as we could; the first Thing we did, we knock'd at the Door, which issued just as we desir'd it; for one of their Idol Priests came to the Door: we immediately seiz'd upon him, stop'd his Mouth, and ty'd his Hands behind him, and led him to the Idol, where we gag'd him that he might not make a Noise; ty'd his Feet also together, and left him on the Ground.

Two of us then waited at the Door, expecting that another would come out to see what the Matter was; but we waited so long 'till the third Man came back to us; and then no Body coming out, we knock'd again gently, and immediately out came two more, and we serv'd them just in the same Manner, but was oblig'd to go all with them, and lay them down by the Idol some Distance from one another; when going back, we found two more were come out to the Door, and a third stood behind them within the Door: We seiz'd the two, and immediately ty'd them, when the third stepping back, and crying out, my *Scots* Merchant went in after him, and taking out a Composition we had made, that would only smoke and stink, he set Fire to it, and threw it in among them; by that Time the other *Scots* Man and my Man taking Charge of the two Men who were already bound, and ty'd together also by the Arm, led them away to the Idol; and left them there, to see if their Idol would relieve them, making Haste back to us.

When the Fuze[1] we had thrown in had fill'd the Hut with so much Smoak, that they were almost suffocated, we then threw in a small Leather Bag of another kind, which flam'd like a Candle, and following it in, we found there was but four People left, who, it seems, were two Men and two Women; and, as we suppos'd, had been about some of their Diabolick Sacrifices: They appear'd, in short, frighted to Death, at least so as to sit trembling and stupid,[2] and not able to speak neither for the Smoak.

In a word, we took them, bound them as we had the other, and all without any Noise: I should have said, we brought them out of the House or Hut first; for indeed we were not able to bear the Smoak any more than they were. When we had done this, we carry'd them all together to the Idol; when we came there, we fell to Work with him: And first we daub'd him all over, and his Robes also, with Tar and such other Stuff as we had, which was Tallow mix'd with Brimstone; then we stopp'd his Eyes, and Ears, and Mouth full of Gun-Powder, and then we wrapp'd up a great Piece of Wild-fire in his Bonnet, and then sticking all the Combustibles we had brought with us upon him, we look'd about to see if we could find any Thing else to help to burn him, when my Man remembred, that by the Tent or Hut where the Men were, there lay a Heap of dry Forrage, whether Straw or Rushes I do not remember; away he and one of the *Scots* Men run, and fetch'd their Arms full of that: When we had done this, we took all our Prisoners, and brought them, having unty'd their Feet, and ungagg'd their Mouths, and made them stand up, and set them just before their monstrous Idol, and then set Fire to the whole.

We stay'd by it a quarter of an Hour or there-abouts, 'till the Powder in the Eyes, and Mouth, and Ears of the Idol blew up; and we could perceive had split and deformed the Shape; and in a word, 'till we saw it burn into a meer Block or Log of Wood, and then setting the dry Forrage to it, we found it would be quite consum'd, when we began to think of going away; but the *Scots* Man said no, we must not go, for these poor deluded Wretches will all throw themselves into the Fire and burn themselves with the Idol, so we resolv'd to stay 'till the Forrage was burnt down too, and then we came away, and left them.

---

1 Container saturated with flammable material.

2 Stupified.

In the Morning, we appear'd among our Fellow Travellers exceeding busy, in getting ready for our Journey; nor could any Man suggest that we had been any where but in our Beds, as Travellers might be suppos'd to be, to fit themselves for the Fatigues of that Day's Journey.

But it did not end so; the next Day came a great Multitude of the Country People, not only of this Village, but of a hundred more, for ought I know, to the Town-Gates, and in a most outragious Manner, demanded Satisfaction of the *Russian* Governour, for the insulting their Priest, and burning their Great *Cham-Chi-Thaungu*, such a hard Name they gave the monstrous Creature they worship'd; the People of *Nertsinskay*, were at first in a great Consternation, for they said, the *Tartars* were no less than thirty thousand, and that in a few Days more, would be one hundred thousand strong.

The *Russian* Governour sent out Messengers to appease them, and gave them all the good Words imaginable; he assured them, he knew nothing of it, and that there had not a Soul of his Garrison been abroad; that it could not be from any Body there; and if they would let him know who it was, they should be examplarly punish'd.[1] They return'd haughtily, that all the Country reverenced the great *Cham-Chi-Thaungu*, who dwelt in the Sun, and no Mortal would have decreed to offer Violence to his Image, but some Christian Miscreant, so they call'd them it seems; and they therefore denounc'd[2] War against him, and all the *Russians*, who, they said, were Miscreants and Christians.

The Governor still Patient, and unwilling to make a Breach, or to have any Cause of War alledg'd to be given by him, the Czar having straitly charged them to treat the conquer'd Country with Gentleness and Civility, gave them still all the good Words he could; at last he told them, there was a *Caravan* gone towards *Russia* that Morning, and perhaps it was some of them, who had done them this Injury; and that if they would be satisfy'd with that, he would send after them, to enquire into it; this seem'd to appease them a little, and accordingly the Governour sent after us, and gave us a particular Account how the Thing was; intimating withal, that if any in our Caravan had done it, they should make their Escape; but that whether they had done it or no, we should make all the Haste forward that was possible; and that in the mean Time, he would keep them in Play as long as he could.

---

1 Made an example of in their punishment.

2 Declared.

This was very friendly in the Governour; however, when it came to the Caravan, there was no Body knew any Thing of the Matter; and as for us that were guilty, we were the least of all suspected; none so much as ask'd us the Question; however, the Captain of the Caravan for the Time, took the Hint that the Governour gave us, and we march'd or travell'd, two Days and two Nights, without any considerable Stop; and then we lay at a Village call'd *Plothus*; nor did make any long Stop here, but hasten'd on towards *Jarawena*, another of the Czar of *Muscovy*'s Colonies, and where we expected we should be safe; but it is to be observ'd, that here we began for two or three Days March, to enter upon the vast nameless Desart, of which I shall say more in its Place; and which, if we had now been upon it, 'tis more than probable, we had been all destroy'd: It was the second Day's march from *Plothus*, that by the Clouds of Dust behind us at a great Distance, some of our People began to be sensible we were pursued; we had enter'd the Desart, and had pass'd by a great Lake call'd *Schaks Oser* when we perceiv'd a very great Body of Horse appear on the other Side of the Lake to the North, we travelling West: We observ'd they went away West as we did, but had supposed we would have taken that Side of the Lake, whereas, we very happily took the South Side; and in two Days more, we saw them not, for they believing we were still before them, push'd on till they came to the River *Udda*;[1] this is a very great River when it passes farther North; but where we came to it, we found it narrow and fordable.

The third Day, they either found their Mistake, or had Intelligence of us, and came pouring in upon us, towards the Dusk of the Evening: We had to our great Satisfaction, just pitch'd upon a Place for our Camp, which was very convenient for the Night; for as we were upon a Desart, tho' but at the beginning of it, that was above five hundred Miles over, we had no Towns to lodge at, and indeed expected none but the City *Jarawena*, which we had yet two Days march to; the Desart however, had some few Woods in it on this Side, and little Rivers which ran all into the great River *Udda*; it was in a narrow Strait between two little but very thick Woods, that we pitch'd our little Camp for that Night, expecting to be attack'd in the Night.

No Body knew but ourselves, what we were pursued for; but as it was usual for the *Mongul Tartars* to go about in Troops in that Desart, so the Caravans always fortify themselves every Night

1 The Uda River, Siberia.

against them, as against Armies of Robbers; and it was therefore no new Thing to be pursu'd.

But we had this Night, of all the Nights of our Travels, a most advantageous Camp; for we lay between two Woods, with a little Rivulet running just before our Front, so that we could not be surrounded or attack'd any Way, but in our Front or Rear; we took Care also to make our Front as strong as we could, by placing our Packs, with our Camels and Horses, all in a Line on the Inside of the River, and felling some Trees in our Rear.

In this Posture we encamp'd for the Night, but the Enemy was upon us, before we had finish'd our Situation: They did not come on us like Thieves as we expected, but sent three Messengers to us, to demand the Men to be delivered to them, that had abus'd their Priests, and burn'd their God, *Cham-Chi-Thaungu* with Fire, that they might burn them with Fire; and upon this, they said they would go away, and do us no farther harm, otherwise, they would burn us all with Fire; our Men look'd very blank at this Message, and began to stare at one another, to see who look'd with most Guilt in their Faces; but *no Body* was the Word, no Body did it; the Leader of the Caravan sent Word he was well assur'd, it was not done by any of our Camp; that we were peaceable Merchants, travelling on our Business; that we had done no harm to them, or to any one else; and that therefore, they must look farther for their Enemies who had injur'd them, for we were not the People; so desir'd them not to disturb us, for if they did, we should defend our selves.

They were far from being satisfy'd with this for an Answer, but a great Crowd of them came down in the Morning by break of Day to our Camp, but seeing us in such an unaccountable Situation, they durst come no farther than the Brook in our Front, where they stood and shew'd us such a Number, that indeed terrify'd us very much; for those that spoke least of them, spoke of ten thousand; here they stood and look'd at us a while, and then setting up a great Howl, they let fly a Cloud of Arrows among us, but we were well enough fortify'd for that; for we shelter'd under our Baggage, and I do not remember, that one Man of us was hurt.

Some Time after this, we see them move a little to our Right, and expected them on the Rear, when a cunning Fellow, a *Cossack*, as they call them, of *Jarawena*, in the Pay of the *Muscovites*, calling to the leader of the Caravan, said to him, I'll go send all these People away to *Siheilka*;* this was a City, four or five Days Journey at least to the South, and rather behind us: so he takes his

Bow and Arrows, and getting on Horse-back, he rides away from our Rear directly, as it were back to *Nertsinskoy*; after this, he takes a great Circuit about, and comes to the Army of the *Tartars*, as if he had been sent Express to tell them a long Story; that the People who had burnt the *Cham Chi Thaungu*, were gone to *Siheilka*, with a Caravan of Miscreants, as he call'd them, that is to say, Christians; and that they had resolv'd to burn the God *Schal Isar*, belonging to the *Tongueses*.

As this Fellow was himself a meer *Tartar*, and perfectly spoke their Language, he counterfeited so well, that they all took it from him, and away they drove in a most violent Hurry to *Siheilka*, which it seems was five Days Journey to the North, and in less than three Hours, they were entirely out of our Sight, and we never heard any more of them; and we never knew whether they went to that other Place call'd *Siheilka*, or no.

So we pass'd safely on to the City of *Jarawena*, where there was a Garrison of *Muscovites*, and there we rested five Days, the Caravan being exceedingly fatigued with the last Day's hard march, and with want of Rest in the Night.

From this City we had a frightful Desart, which held us three and twenty Days march: We furnish'd our selves with some Tents here, for the better accommodating our selves in the Night; and the Leader of the Caravan, procured sixteen Carriages or Waggons of the Country, for carrying our Water and Provisions, and these Carriages were our Defence every Night round our little Camp; so that had the *Tartars* appear'd, unless they had been very numerous indeed, they would not have been able to hurt us.

We may well be suppos'd to want Rest again after this long Journey; for in this Desart we saw neither House or Tree, or scarce a Bush; we saw abundance of the Sable-*Hunters, as they call'd them: These are all *Tartars* of the *Mongul Tartary*, of which this County is a Part, and they frequently attack small Caravans, but we saw no Numbers of them together; I was curious to see the Sable Skins they catch'd, but could never speak with any of them, for they durst not come near us, neither durst we straggle from our Company, to go near them.

After we had pass'd this Desart, we came into a Country pretty well inhabited; that is to say, we found Towns and Castles, settled by the Czar of *Muscovy*, with Garrisons of Stationary Soldiers to protect the Caravans, and defend the Country against the *Tartars*, who would otherwise make it very dangerous travelling; and his Czarish Majesty has given such strict Orders for the well guarding the Caravans and Merchants, that if there are any *Tartars* heard of in the Country, Detachments of the Garrisons are always sent to see the Travellers safe from Station to Station.

And thus the Governour of *Adinskoy*,[1] who I had Opportunity to make a Visit to, by means of the *Scots* Merchant who was acquainted with him, offer'd us a Guard of fifty Men, if we thought there was any Danger to the next Station.

I thought long before this, that as we came nearer to *Europe* we should find the Country better peopled, and the People more civiliz'd, but I found my self mistaken in both, for we had yet the Nation of the *Tongueses* to pass through; where we saw the same Tokens of Paganism and Barbarity, or worse, than before, only as they were conquer'd by the *Muscovites*, and entirely reduc'd, they were not so dangerous; but for Rudeness of Manners, Idolatry, and Multi-theism no People in the World ever went beyond them: They are cloth'd all in Skins of Beasts, and their Houses are built of the same: You know not a Man from a Woman, neither by the Ruggedness of their Countenances or their Cloths; and in the Winter, when the Ground is cover'd with Snow, they live under Ground in Houses like Vaults, which have Cavities going from one to another.

If the *Tartars* had their *Cham-Chi-Thaungu* for a whole Village or Country, these had Idols in every Hut and in every Cave; besides, they worship the Stars, the Sun, the Water, the Snow, and in a word, every thing that they do not understand, and they understand but very little; so that almost every Element, every uncommon thing, sets them a sacrificing.

But I am no more to describe People than Countries, any farther than my own Story comes to be concern'd in them: I met with nothing peculiar to my self in all this Country, which I reckon was from the Desart which I spoke of last, at least 400 Miles, Half of it being another Desart, which took us up twelve Days severe travelling, without House, or Tree, or Bush, but were oblig'd again to carry our own Provisions, as well Water as Bread. After we were out of this Desart, and had travell'd two Days, we came to *Janezay*,[2] a *Muscovite* City or Station, on the great River *Janezay*: this River they told us parted *Europe* from *Asia*, tho' our Mapmakers, as I am told, do not agree to it; however, it is certainly the Eastern Boundary of the ancient *Siberia*, which now makes up a Province only of the vast *Muscovite* Empire, but is itself equal in Bigness to the whole Empire of *Germany*.

---

1 Udimskij, city in Siberia.

2 Yeniseysk, a small Russian city.

And yet here I observ'd Ignorance and Paganism still prevail'd, except in the *Muscovite* Garrisons; all the Country between the River *Oby*[1] and the River *Janezay* is as entirely Pagan and the People as barbarous as the remotest of the *Tartars*, nay, as any Nation for ought I know in *Asia* or *America*; I also found, which I observ'd to the *Muscovite* Governours who I had Opportunity to converse with, that the poor Pagans are not much the wiser or the nearer Christianity for being under the *Muscovite* Government; which they acknowledg'd was true enough, but, as they said, was none of their Business: That if the Czar expected to convert his *Siberian*, or *Tonguese*, or *Tartar* Subjects, it should be done by sending Clergy-men among them, not Soldiers; and they added, with more Sincerity than I expected, that they found it was not so much the Concern of their Monarch to make the People Christians, as it was to make them Subjects.

From this River to the great River *Oby*, we cross'd a wild uncultivated Country, I cannot say 'tis a barren Soil; 'tis only barren of People, and good Management, otherwise it is in it self a most pleasant, fruitful and agreeable Country; what Inhabitants we found in it are all Pagans, except such as are sent among them from *Russia*; for this is the Country I mean on both Sides the River *Oby*, whither the *Muscovite* Criminals that are not put to Death, are banish'd, and from whence it is next to impossible they should ever come away.

I have nothing material to say of my particular Affairs till I came to *Tobolski*,[2] the capital City of *Siberia*, where I continu'd some time on the following Occasion.

We had been now almost seven Months on our Journey, and Winter began to come on apace, whereupon my Partner and I call'd a Council about our particular Affairs, in which we found it proper, considering that we were bound for *England*, and not for *Muscow*, to consider how to dispose of our selves; they told us of Sledges and Rane Deer[3] to carry us over the Snow in the Winter time; and indeed they have such Things that it would be incredible to relate the Particulars of, by which Means the *Russians* travel more in the Winter than they can in Summer, because in these Sleds they are able to run Night and Day; the Snow being frozen is one universal Covering to Nature, by

1 The Ob.

2 Tobolsk, the capital of Siberia.

3 Reindeer.

which the Hills, the Vales, the Rivers, the Lakes, all are smooth and hard as a Stone, and they run upon the Surface without any regard to what is underneath.

But I had no occasion to push at a Winter Journey of this kind: I was bound to *England*, not to *Muscow*, and my Rout[1] lay two Ways, either I must go on as the Caravan went till I came to *Jeroslaw*,[2] and then go off West for *Narva*,[3] and the Gulph of *Finland*; and so either by Sea or Land to *Dantzick*,[4] where I might possibly sell my *China* Cargo to good Advantage, or I must leave the Caravan at a little Town on the *Dwina*,[5] from whence I had but six Days by Water to *Arch-Angel*,[6] and from thence might be sure of Shipping, either to *England*, *Holland*, or *Hamburgh*.

Now to go any of these Journeys in the Winter, would ha' been preposterous; for as to *Dantzick*, the *Baltick* would be frozen up, and I could not get Passage, and to go by Land in those Countrys was far less safe than among the *Mongul Tartars*; likewise to go to *Arch-Angel* in *October*, all the Ships would be gone from thence, and even the Merchants who dwell there in Summer, retire South to *Muscow* in the Winter when the Ships are gone; so that I should have nothing but Extremity of Cold to encounter, with a Scarcity of Provisions, and must lye there in an empty Town all the Winter: so that upon the whole I thought it much my better Way to let the Caravan go, and to make Provision to Winter where I was, (*viz.*) at *Tobolski* in *Siberia*, in the Latitude of   Degrees,[7] where I was sure of three Things to wear out a cold Winter with, (*viz.*) Plenty of Provision such as the Country afforded; a warm House, with Fuel enough, and excellent Company; of all which I shall give a full Account in its Place.

I was now in a quite different Climate from my belov'd Island, where I never felt Cold except when I had my Ague; on the Contrary, I had much to do to bear any Cloths on my Back, and never made any Fire but without Doors,[8] and for my Necessity in dressing my Food, *&c.* Now I made me three good Vests, with large Robes or Gowns over them to hang down to the Feet, and

---

1 Route.

2 Town in southeastern Poland.

3 City in present-day Estonia.

4 Gdansk, Poland, on the Baltic coast.

5 The River Daugavaf, which flows through Russia, Belarus, and Latvia, draining into the Gulf of Riga in Latvia (an arm of the Baltic Sea).

6 Archangel'sk, in northern Russia.

7 In the fourth edition of *Farther Adventures*, the blank is filled in as 60.

8 Only made fires outdoors.

button close to the Wrists, and all these lin'd with Furs to make them sufficiently warm.

As to a warm House, I must confess I greatly dislik'd our way in *England* of making Fires in every Room in the House, in open Chimneys, which when the Fire was out, always kept the Air in the Room cold as the Climate: But taking an Appartment in a good House in the Town, I order'd a Chimney to be built like a Furnace, in the Center of six several Rooms, like a Stove, the Funnel to carry the Smoak went up one Way, the Door to come at the Fire went in another, and all the Rooms were kept equally warm, but no Fire seen; just as they heat the Bagnios[1] in *England*.

By this means we had always the same Climate in all the Rooms, and an equal Heat was preserv'd; and how cold soever it was without, it was always warm within, and yet we saw no Fire, nor was ever incommoded with any Smoke.

The most wonderful Thing of all, was, that it should be possible to meet with good Company here, in a Country so barbarous as that of the most northerly Parts of *Europe*, near the frozen Ocean, and within but a very few Degrees of *Nova Zembla*.[2]

But this being the Country where the State Criminals of *Muscovy*, as I observ'd before, are all banish'd, this City was full of Noblemen, Princes, Gentlemen, Colonels, and in short all Degrees of the Nobility, Gentry, Soldiery and Courtiers of *Muscovy*: Here was the famous Prince *Galliozen*,[3] the old General *Robostiski*, and several other Persons of note, and some Ladies.

By means of my *Scots* Merchant, who nevertheless I parted with here, I made an Acquaintance here with several of these Gentlemen, and some of them of the first Rank, and from these in the long Winter Nights in which I stay'd here, I receiv'd several very agreeable Visits: It was talking one Night with Prince ——[4] one of the banish'd Ministers of State belonging to the Czar of *Muscovy*, that my Talk of my particular Case began; he had been telling me abundance of fine Things of the Greatness,

---

1 In this context, bathing houses, but here including sauna facilities for sweating.

2 Novaya Zemlya, an Arctic archipelago of two large islands and some smaller ones, off the northern Russian coast.

3 Prince Vasily Vasilievich Golitsyn (1643–1714), chief minister of Sophia (1657–1704), half sister of Peter the Great and regent of Russia from 1682 until her overthrow by Peter in 1689. Golitsyn was exiled to an Arctic village, where he remained until his death.

4 Unidentified, but in 1718 some high-ranking Russian officials were accused of plotting against Czar Peter. Some were executed, some exiled.

the Magnificence, the Dominions, and the absolute Power of the Emperor of the *Russians*. I interrupted him, and told him I was a greater and more powerful Prince than ever the Czar of *Muscovy* was, tho' my Dominions were not so large, or my People so many. The *Russian Grandee* look'd a little surpriz'd, and fixing his Eyes steddily upon me, began to wonder what I meant.

I told him, his Wonder would cease when I had explain'd myself: First, *I told him*, I had the absolute Disposal of the Lives and Fortunes of all my Subjects: That notwithstanding my absolute Power, I had not one Person disaffected to my Government, or to my Person, in all my Dominions. He shook his Head at that, and said, there indeed I out-did the Czar of *Muscovy*. *I told him*, That all the Lands in my Kingdom were my own, and all my Subjects were not only my Tenants, but Tenants at Will: That they would all fight for me to the last Drop; and that never Tyrant, *for such I acknowledg'd my self to be*, was ever so universally belov'd, and yet so horribly fear'd, by his Subjects.

After amusing them with these Riddles in Government for a while, I open'd the Case, and told them the Story at large of my living in the Island, and how I manag'd both my self and the People there that were under me, just as I have since minuted it down. They were exceedingly taken with the Story, and especially the Prince who told me, with a Sigh, that the true Greatness of Life was to be Master of our selves; That he would not have exchang'd such a State of Life as mine, to have been Czar of *Muscovy*; and that he found more Felicity in the Retirement he seem'd to be banish'd to there, than ever he found in the highest Authority he enjoy'd in the Court of his Master the Czar; That the Heighth of human Wisdom was to bring our Tempers down to our Circumstances, and to make a Calm within, under the Weight of the greatest Scorns without. When he came first hither, he said he us'd to tear the Hair from his Head, and the Cloths from his Back, as others had done before him; but a little Time and Consideration had made him look into himself, as well as round him to Things without; That he found the Mind of Man, if it was but once brought to reflect upon the State of universal Life, and how little this World was concern'd in its true Felicity, was perfectly capable of making a Felicity for it self, fully satisfying to it self, and suitable to its own best Ends and Desires, with but very little Assistance from the World; That Air to breath in, Food to sustain Life, Cloths for Warmth, and Liberty for Exercise in order to Health, compleated, in his Opinion, all that the World could do for us; and tho' the Greatness, the Authority, the Riches, and the Pleasures which some enjoy'd in the World, and which he had enjoy'd his Share of, had much in them that was agreeable to us; yet he observ'd that all those Things chiefly gratify'd the coarsest of our Affections, such as our Ambition, our particular Pride, our Avarice, our Vanity, and our Sensuality; all which were indeed the meer Product of the worst Part of Man, were in themselves Crimes, and had in them the Seeds of all manner of Crime, but neither were related to or concern'd with any of those Virtues that constituted us wise Men, or of those Graces which distinguish'd us as Christians: That being now depriv'd of all the fancy'd Felicity which he enjoy'd, in the full Exercise of all those Vices, he said, he was at leisure to look upon the dark Side of them, where he found all manner of Deformity, and was now convinc'd, that Virtue only makes a Man truly wise, rich, and great, and preserves him in the Way to a superior Happiness in a future State. And in this, he said, they were more happy in their Banishment, than all their Enemies were, who had the full Possession of all the Wealth and Power that they (the Banish'd) had left behind them.

Nor, Sir, says he, do I bring my Mind to this politically,[1] by the Necessity of my Circumstances, which some call miserable; but if I know any thing of my self, I would not now go back, tho' the Czar, my Master, should call me and re-instate me in all my former Grandeur, I say, I would no more go back to it, than I believe my Soul, when it shall be deliver'd from this Prison of the Body, and has had a Taste of the glorious State beyond Life, would come back to the Jail of Flesh and Blood it is now enclos'd in, and leave Heaven to deal in the Dirt and Crime of human Affairs.

He spoke this with so much Warmth in his Temper, so much Earnestness and Motion of his Spirits, which were apparent in his Countenance, that it was evident it was the true Sense of his Soul: There was no room to doubt his Sincerity.

I told him, I once thought my self a kind of a Monarch in my old Station, of which I had given him an Account, but that I thought he was not a Monarch only, but a great Conqueror; for that he that has got a Victory over his own exorbitant Desires, and has the absolute Dominion over himself, whose Reason entirely governs his Will, is certainly greater than he that conquers a City. But, my Lord, *said I*, shall I take the Liberty to ask you a Question? With all my Heart, says he. If the Door of your Liberty was open'd, *said I*, would you not take hold of it to deliver your self from this Exile.

1 From a political point of view.

Hold, said he, your Question is subtil, and requires some serious just Distinctions, to give it a sincere Answer; and I'll give it you from the Bottom of my Heart. Nothing that I know of in this World would move me to deliver my self from this State of Banishment, except these two, First, the Enjoyment of my Relations, and Secondly, a little warmer Climate; but I protest to you, that to go back to the Pomp of the Court, the Glory, the Power, the Hurry of a Minister of State, the Wealth, the Gaiety, and the Pleasures, that is to say, Follies of a Courtier; if my Master should send me Word this Moment, that he restores me to all he banish'd me from; I protest, *If I know my self at all*, I would not leave this Wilderness, these Desarts, and these frozen Lakes, for the Pallace at *Muscow*.

But, my Lord, said I, perhaps you not only are banish'd from the Pleasures of the Court, and from the Power, and Authority, and Wealth you enjoy'd before, but you may be absent too from some of the Conveniences of Life, your Estate perhaps confiscated, and your Effects plunder'd, and the Supplies left you here may not be suitable to the ordinary Demands of Life.

Ay, says he, that is as you suppose me to be a Lord, or a Prince, *&c.* So indeed I am; but you are now to consider me only as a Man, a human Creature, not at all distinguish'd from another, and so I can suffer no Want, unless I should be visited with Sickness and Distempers. However, to put the Question out of Dispute; you see our Manner; we are in this Place five Persons of Rank, we live perfectly retir'd, as suited to a State of Banishment; we have something rescu'd from the Shipwreck of our Fortunes, which keeps us from the meer Necessity of hunting for our Food; but the poor Soldiers who are here, without that Help, live in as much Plenty as we, who go into the Woods and catch Sables and Foxes, the Labour of a Month will maintain them a Year; and as the Way of living is not expensive, so it is not hard to get sufficient to our selves. So that Objection is out of Doors.

I have not room to give a full Account of the most agreeable Conversation I had with this truly great Man; in all which he shew'd, that his Mind was so inspir'd with a superior Knowledge of Things, so supported by Religion, as well as by a vast Share of Wisdom; that his Contempt of the World was really as much as he had express'd, and that he was always the same to the last, as will appear in the Story I am going to tell.

I had been here 8 Months, and a dark dreadful Winter I thought it to be, the Cold so intense, that I could not so much as look abroad without being wrap'd in Furs, and a Mask of Fur before my Face, or rather a Hood with only a Hole for Breath, and two for Sight: The little Day-light we had, was as we reckon'd for three Months, not above five Hours a day, and six at most; only that the Snow lying on the Ground continually, and the Weather clear, it was never quite dark: Our Horses were kept (or rather starv'd) under Ground, and as for our Servants, for we hir'd three Servants here to look after our Horses and selves, we had every now and then their Fingers and Toes to thaw and take care of, lest they should mortify and fall off.

It is true, within Doors we were warm, the Houses being close, the Walls thick, the Lights small, and the Glass all double; our Food was chiefly the Flesh of Deer dry'd and cur'd in the Season; good Bread enough, but bak'd as Biskets; dry'd Fish of several Sorts, and some Flesh of Mutton, and of the Buffeloes, which is pretty good Beef: All the Stores of Provision for the Winter are laid up in the Summer, and well cur'd; our Drink was Water mix'd with Aqua-vitæ instead of Brandy, and for a Treat, Mead[1] instead of Wine, which, however, they have excellent good: The Hunters, who venture abroad all Weathers, frequently brought us in fresh Venison, very fat and good, and sometimes Bear's Flesh, but we did not much care for the last: We had a good Stock of Tea, with which we treated our Friends, as above; and in a word, we liv'd very chearfully and well, all things consider'd.

It was now *March*, and the Days grown considerably longer, and the Weather, at least, tollerable, so the other Travellers began to prepare Sleds to carry them over the Snow, and to get things ready to be going; but my Measures being fix'd, as I have said, for *Arch-Angel*, and not for *Muscovy* or the *Baltick*, I made no Motion; knowing very well that the Ships from the South do not set out for that Part of the World till *May* or *June*, and that if I was there by the beginning of *August*, it would be as soon as any Ships would be ready to go away; and therefore, I say, I made no haste to be gone, as others did; in a word, I saw a great many Peoples nay, all the Travellers go away before me: It seems every Year they go from thence to *Muscow* for Trade, (*viz.*) to carry Furs, and buy Necessaries with them, which they bring back to furnish their Shops; also others went of the same Errand to *Arch-Angel*, but then they also being to come back again above 800 Miles, went all out before me.

In short, about the latter End of *May* I began to make all ready to pack up; and as I was doing this, it occurr'd to me, that

1 Alcoholic beverage, made from fermented honey and water.

seeing all these People were banish'd by the Czar of *Muscovy* to *Siberia*, and yet when they came there, were left at Liberty to go whither they would; why did they not then go away to any Part of the World wherever they thought fit, and I began to examine what should hinder them from making such an Attempt.

But my Wonder was over, when I enter'd upon that Subject with the Person I have mention'd, who answer'd me thus: Consider, First, Sir, said he, the Place where we are; and Secondly, the Condition we are in; especially, said he, the Generality of the People who are banish'd hither; we are surrounded, said he, with stronger Things than Bars and Bolts; on the North Side an unnavigable Ocean, where Ship never sail'd, and Boat never swam; neither, if we had both, could we know where to go with them: Every other Way, said he, we have above a Thousand Miles to pass through the Czar's own Dominions, and By-Ways[1] utterly unpassable, except by the Roads made by the Governour, and by the Towns garrison'd by his Troops; so that we could neither pass undiscover'd by the Road, or subsist any other Way, so that it is in vain to attempt it.

I was silenc'd indeed at once, and found that they were in a Prison, every Jot as secure as if they had been lock'd up in the Castle at *Muscow*; however, it came into my Thought, that I might certainly be made an Instrument to procure the Escape of this excellent Person, and that whatever Hazard I run, I would certainly try if I could carry him off. Upon this I took an Occasion one Evening to tell him my Thoughts: I represented to him, that it was very easy for me to carry him away, there being no Guard over him in the Country, and as I was not going to *Muscow*, but to *Arch-Angel*, and that I went in the nature of a Caravan, by which I was not oblig'd to lye in the stationary Towns in the Desart, but could encamp every Night where I would, we might easily pass uninterrupted to *Arch-Angel*, where I would immediately secure him on board an *English* or *Dutch* Ship, and carry him off safe along with me; and as to his Subsistence, and other Particulars, it should be my Care till he could better supply himself.

He heard me very attentively, and look'd earnestly on me all the while I spoke, nay, I could see in his very Face, that what I said put his Spirits into an exceeding Ferment; his Colour frequently chang'd, his Eyes look'd red, and his Heart flutter'd, that it might be even perceiv'd in his Countenance; nor could he immediately answer me, when I had done, and as it were expected what he

1 Minor roadways.

would say to it; but after he had paus'd a little he embrac'd me, and said, how unhappy are we unguarded Creatures as we are, that even our greatest Acts of Friendship are made Snares to us, and we are made Tempters of one another! My dear Friend, said he, your Offer is so sincere, has such Kindness in it, is so disinterested in it self, and is so calculated for my Advantage, that I must have very little Knowledge of the World, if I did not both wonder at it, and acknowledge the Obligation I have upon me to you for it. But did you believe I was sincere in what I have so often said to you of my Contempt of the World? Did you believe I spoke my very Soul to you, and that I had really obtain'd that Degree of Felicity here, that had plac'd me above all that the World could give me, or do for me? Did you believe I was sincere, when I told you I would not go back, if I was re-call'd even to be all, that once I was in the Court with the Favour of the Czar my Master? Did you believe me, my Friend, to be an honest Man, or did you think me to be a boasting Hypocrite? Here he stop'd, as if he would hear what I would say, but indeed, I soon after perceiv'd, that he stop'd because his Spirits were in Motion, his great Heart was full of Struggles, and he could not go on. I was, I confess, astonish'd at the thing as well as at the Man, and I us'd some Arguments with him to urge him to set himself free: That he ought to look upon this as a Door open'd by Heaven for his Deliverance, and a Summons by Providence, who has the Care and Disposition of all Events, to do himself good, and to render himself useful in the World.

He had by this time recover'd himself: How do you know Sir, says he warmly, that instead of a Summons from Heaven, it may not be a Feint of another Instrument? Representing in all the alluring Colours to me the Shew of Felicity as a Deliverance, which may in itself be my Snare, and tends directly to my Ruin: Here I am free from the Temptation of returning to my former miserable Greatness; there I am not sure but that all the Seeds of Pride, Ambition, Avarice and Luxury, which I know remain in Nature, may revive and take Root, and in a Word, again overwhelm me, and then the happy Prisoner, who you see now Master of his Soul's Liberty, shall be the miserable Slave of his own Senses, in the Full of[1] all personal Liberty: Dear Sir, let me remain in this blessed Confinement, banish'd from the Crimes of Life, rather than purchase a Shew of Freedom, at the Expence of the Liberty

1 Something seems to be missing here; perhaps it should read "in the Full enjoyment of."

of my Reason, and at the Expence of the future Happiness which now I have in my View, but shall then, I fear, quickly loose Sight of; for I am but Flesh, a Man, a meer Man, have Passions and Affections as likely to possess and overthrow me as any Man: O be not my Friend and my Tempter both together.

If I was surpriz'd before, I was quite dumb now, and stood silent, looking at him, and indeed admir'd at what I saw; the Struggle in his Soul was so great, that tho' the Weather was extreamly cold, it put him into a most violent Sweat, and I found he wanted to give Vent to his Mind; so I said a Word or two, that I would leave him to consider of it, and wait on him again, and then I withdrew to my own Appartment.

About two Hours after I heard some Body at, or near, the Door of my Room, and I was going to open the Door, but he had open'd it, and came in: My dear Friend, says he, you had almost overset me, but I am recover'd; do not take it ill that I do not close with your Offer, I assure you, 'tis not for want of a Sense of the Kindness of it in you, and I came to make the most sincere Acknowledgment of it to you; but I hope I have got the Victory over my self.

My Lord, *said I*, I hope you are fully satisfy'd that you do not resist the Call of Heaven. Sir, said he, if it had been from Heaven, the same Power would have influenc'd me to accept it; but I hope, and am fully satisfy'd, that it is from Heaven that I decline it, and I have infinite Satisfaction in the Parting, that you shall leave me an honest Man still, tho' not a free Man.

I had nothing to do but to acquiesce, and make Professions to him of my having no End in it, but a sincere Desire to serve him: He embrac'd me very passionately,[1] and assur'd me, he was sensible of that, and should always acknowledge it, and with that he offer'd me a very fine Present of Sables, too much indeed for me to accept from a Man in his Circumstances, and I would have avoided them, but he would not be refus'd.

The next Morning I sent my Servant to his Lordship, with a small Present of Tea, and two Pieces of *China* Damask, and four little Wedges of *Japan* Gold, which did not all weigh above six Ounces, or thereabout, but were far short of the Value of his Sables, which, indeed, when I came to *England*, I found worth near 200*l.* He accepted the Tea, and one Piece of the Damask, and one of the Pieces of Gold, which had a fine Stamp upon it, of the *Japan* Coinage, which I found he took for the Rariety of it, but

1 I.e., with strong emotion.

would not take any more, and he sent word by my Servant that he desir'd to speak with me.

When I came to him, he told me, I knew what had pass'd between us, and hop'd I would not move him any more in that Affair; but that since I had made such a generous Offer to him, he ask'd me, if I had Kindness enough to offer the same to another Person that he would name to me, in whom he had a great Share of Concern; I told him, that I could not say I enclin'd to do so much for any one but himself, for whom I had a particular Value, and should have been glad to have been the Instrument of his Deliverance; however, if he would please to name the Person to me, I would give him my Answer, and hop'd he would not be displeased with me, if he was with my Answer; he told me, it was only his Son, who, tho' I had not seen, yet was in the same Condition with himself, and above two hundred Miles from him, on the other Side the *Oby*; but that if I consented, he would send for him.

I made no Hesitation, but told him I would do it; I made some Ceremony in letting him understand that it was wholly on his Account, and that seeing I could not prevail on him, I would shew my Respect to him, by my Concern for his Son; but these Things are too tedious to repeat here: He sent away the next Day for his Son, and in about twenty Days he came back with the Messenger, bringing six or seven Horses, loaded with very rich Furs, and which in the whole, amounted to a very great Value.

His Servants brought the Horses into the Town, but left the young Lord at a Distance, till Night, when he came *incognito* into our Appartment, and his Father presented him to me; and in short, we concerted there the manner of our travelling, and every Thing proper for the Journey.

I had bought a considerable Quantity of Sables, black Fox Skins, fine Ermines, and such other Furs as are very rich; I say, I had bought them in that City in Exchange for some of the Goods I brought from *China*; in particular for the Cloves and Nutmegs, of which, I sold the greatest Part here, and the rest afterwards at *Arch-Angel*, for a much better Price than I could have done at *London*; and my Partner who was sensible of the Profit, and whose Business more particularly than mine was Merchandize, was mightily pleas'd with our Stay, on Account of the Traffick[1] we made here.

It was the beginning of *June*, when I left this remote Place, a City, I believe, little heard of in the World; and indeed it is so far

---

1 Trade.

out of the Road of Commerce, that I know not how it should be much talk'd of; we were now come to a very small Caravan, being only thirty two Horses and Camels in all, and all of them pass'd for mine, tho' my new Guest was Proprietor of eleven of them; it was most natural also that I should take more Servants with me than I had before, and the young Lord pass'd for my Steward; what great Man I pass'd for my self, I know not, neither did it concern me to enquire; we had here, the worst and the largest Desart to pass over that we met with in all the Journey; indeed I call it the worst, because the Way was very deep[1] in some Places, and very uneven in others; the best we had to say for it, was, that we thought we had no Troops of *Tartars* and Robbers to fear, and that they never came on this Side the River *Oby*, or at least, but very seldom, but we found it otherwise.

My young Lord had with him, a faithful *Muscovite* Servant, or rather a *Siberian* Servant, who was perfectly acquainted with the Country, and led us by private Roads, that we avoided coming in to the principal Towns and Cities, upon the great Road, such as *Tumen*, *Soly-Kamskoi*,[2] and several others; because the *Muscovite* Garrisons which are kept there, are very curious and strict in their Observation upon Travellers; and searching least any of the banish'd Persons of Note should make their Escape that Way into *Muscovy*; but by this Means, as we were kept out of the Cities, so our whole Journey was a Desart, and we were oblig'd to encamp and lye in our Tents, when we might have had very good Accommodation in the Cities on the Way: This the young Lord was so sensible of, that he would not allow us to lye abroad, when we came to several Cities, on the Way, but lay abroad himself with his Servant in the Woods, and met us always at the appointed Places.

We were just enter'd *Europe*, having pass'd the River *Kama*, which in these Parts, is the Boundary between *Europe* and *Asia*, and the first City on the *European* Side was call'd *Soloy-Kamaskoy*, which is as much as to say, the great City, on the River *Kama*; and here we thought to have seen some evident Alteration in the People, their Manner, their Habit, their Religion, and their Business; but we were mistaken, for as we had a vast Desart to pass, which by Relation, is near seven hundred Miles long in some Places, but not above two hundred Miles over where we

---

1 Muddy.

2 Tyumen is a city sixteen hundred miles east of Moscow; the first Russian settlement in Siberia. Solikamsk is a city in northwestern Russia.

pass'd it; so till we came past that horrible Place, we found very little Difference between that Country and the *Mongul Tartary*; the People, mostly Pagans, and little better than the Savages of *America*, their Houses and Towns full of Idols, and their Way of Living, wholly barbarous, except in the Cities as above, and the Villages near them; where they are Christians as they call themselves, of the *Greek* Church, but have their Religion mingled with so many Reliques of Superstition, that it is scarce to be known in some Places from meer Sorcery and Witchcraft.[1]

In passing this Forrest, I thought indeed we must after all our Dangers were in our Imagination escap'd, as before, have been plunder'd and robb'd, and perhaps murther'd by a Troop of Thieves; of what Country they were, whether the roving Bands of the *Ostiachi*, a Kind of *Tartars* or wild People on the Bank of the *Obi*, had rang'd thus far, or whether they were the Sable-Hunters of *Syberia*, I am yet at a Loss to know; but they were all on Horseback, carry'd Bows and Arrows, and were at first about five and forty in Number; they came so near to us, as within about two Musquet-Shot, and asking no Questions, they surrounded us with their Horse, and look'd very earnestly upon us twice; at length they plac'd themselves just in our Way, upon which, we drew up in a little Line before our Camels, being not above sixteen Men in all; and being drawn up thus, we halted and sent out the *Siberian* Servant, who attended his Lord, to see who they were; his Master was the more willing to let him go, because he was not a little apprehensive, that they were a *Syberian* Troop sent out after him: The Man came up near them with a Flag of Truce, and call'd them, but tho' he spoke several of their Languages or Dialects of Languages rather, he could not understand a Word they said; however, after some Signs to him, not to come nearer to them at his Peril; so he said, he understood them to mean offering to shoot at him if he advanc'd; the Fellow came back no wiser than he went, only that by their Dress, he said, he believ'd them to be some *Tartars* of *Kalmuck*, or of the *Circassian* Hoords; and that there must be more of them upon the great Desart, tho' he never heard that any of them ever were seen so far North before.

1 Compare to the third volume of Defoe's travel narrative (and major work of political and social commentary) on the state of Great Britain, *A Tour Thro' the Whole Island of Great Britain* (1724), where he likens the Scots to North American "savages" and bemoans "this surprizing darkness among the people," worrying "that in a Christian island, as this is said to be, there should be people who know so little of religion, or of the custom of Christians" (215).

This was small Comfort to us; however, we had no Remedy; there was on our left Hand at about a Quarter of a Mile's Distance, a little Grove or Clump of Trees which stood close together, and very near the Road; I immediately resolv'd we would advance to those Trees, and fortify our selves as well as we could there; for first I considered, that the Trees would in a great Measure cover us from their Arrows, and in the next Place, they could not come to charge us in a Body; it was indeed my old *Portugueze* Pilot who proposed it, and who had this excellency attending him, namely, that he was always readiest and most apt to direct and encourage us in Cases of the most Danger; we advanc'd immediately with what Speed we could, and gain'd that little Wood, the *Tartars* or Thieves, for we know not what to call them, keeping their Stand, and not attempting to hinder us; when we came thither, we found to our great Satisfaction, that it was a swampy springy Piece of Ground, and on the one Side, a very great Spring of Water, which running out in a little Rill or Brook, was a little farther, joyn'd by another of the like Bigness, and was in short, the Head or Source of a considerable River, call'd afterwards the *Wirtska*; the Trees which grew about this Spring, were not all above two hundred, but were very large, and stood pretty thick; so that as soon as we got in, we saw our selves perfectly safe from the Enemy, unless they alighted and attack'd us on Foot.

But to make this more difficult, our *Portugueze*, with indefatigable Application, cut down great Arms of the Trees, and laid them hanging *not quite cut off* from one Tree to another, so that he made a continued Fence almost round us.

We stay'd here waiting the Motion of the Enemy some Hours, without perceiving they made any Motion; when about two Hours before Night, they came down directly upon us, and tho' we had not perceiv'd it, we found they had been join'd by some more of the same, so that they were near fourscore Horse, whereof however, we fancy'd some were Women: They came on till they were within half Shot of our little Wood, when we fir'd one Musquet without Ball, and call'd to them in the *Russian* Tongue, to know what they wanted, and bid them keep off; but as if they knew nothing of what we said, they came on with a double Fury directly up to the Wood-side, not imagining we were so barricado'd that they could not break in; our old Pilot was our Captain, as well as he had been our Engineer, and desir'd of us not to fire upon them till they came within Pistol-Shot, and that we might be sure to kill, and that when we did fire, we should be sure to take good Aim; we bad him give the Word of Command, which he delay'd so long, that they were some of them within two Pikes length of us when we fir'd.

We aim'd so true, (or Providence directed our Shot so sure) that we kill'd fourteen of them, and wounded several others, as also several of their Horses; for we had all of us loaded our Pieces with two or three Bullets at least.

They were terribly surpriz'd[1] with our Fire and retreated immediately about one Hundred Rods[2] from us; in which Time, we loaded our Pieces again, and seeing them keep that Distance, we sally'd out and catch'd four or five of their Horses, whose Riders we suppose were kill'd, and coming up to the dead, we could easily perceive they were *Tartars*, but knew not from what Country, or how they came to make an Excursion such an unusual Length.

About an Hour after they made a Motion to attack us again, and rode round our little Wood, to see where else they might break in; but finding us always ready to Face them, they went off again, and we resolv'd not to stir from the Place for that Night.

We slept little you may be sure, but spent the most Part of the Night in strengthing our Situation, and barricadoing the Entrances into the Wood, and keeping a strict Watch, we waited for Day-Light, and when it came, it gave us a very unwelcome Discovery indeed; for the Enemy, who we thought were discourag'd with the Reception they had met with, were now encreas'd to no less than three hundred, and had set up eleven or twelve Huts and Tents, as if they were resolv'd to besiege us; and this little Camp they had pitch'd upon the open Plain, at about three Quarters of a Mile from us. We were indeed surpriz'd at this Discovery; and now I confess, I gave my self over for lost, and all that I had: The Loss of my Effects did not lye so near me, (*tho' they were very considerable*) as the Thoughts of falling into the Hands of such *Barbarians*, at the latter End of my Journey, after so many Difficulties and Hazards as I had gone thro'; and even in Sight of our Port, where we expected Safety and Deliverance; as for my Partner, he was raging; he declar'd, that to lose his Goods would be his Ruin; and he would rather die than be starv'd; and he was for fighting to the last Drop.

The young Lord, as gallant as ever Flesh shew'd it self, was for fighting to the last also; and my old Pilot was of the Opinion we were able to resist them all, in the Situation we were then in; and thus we spent the Day in Debates of what we should do; but

1 Terrified.

2 Measure of length, five and a half yards.

towards Evening, we found that the Number of our Enemies still encreas'd; perhaps as they were abroad in several Parties for Prey, the first had sent out Scouts to call for Help, and to acquaint them of the Booty, and we did not know, but by the Morning they might still be a greater Number; so I began to enquire of those People we had brought from *Tobolski*, if there was no other, or more private Ways by which we might avoid them in the Night, and perhaps either retreat to some Town, or get Help to guard us over the Desart.

The *Syberian*, who was Servant to the young Lord, told us, if we design'd to avoid them and not fight, he would engage to carry us off in the Night, to a Way that went North towards the *Petrou*, by which he made no Question, but we might get away, and the *Tartars* never the wiser; but he said, his Lord had told him, he would not retreat, but would rather chuse to fight. I told him, he mistook his Lord, for that he was too wise a Man to love Fighting for the sake of it; that I knew his Lord was brave enough by what he had shew'd already; but that his Lord knew better, than to desire to have seventeen or eighteen Men fight five hundred, unless an unavoidable Necessity forc'd them to it; and that if he thought it possible for us to escape in the Night, we had nothing else to do but to attempt it. He answer'd, if his Lord gave him such Orders, he would lose his Life if he did not perform it; we soon brought his Lord to give that Order, tho' privately, and we immediately prepar'd for the putting it in Practice.

And first, as soon as it began to be dark, we kindled a Fire in our little Camp, which we kept burning, and prepar'd so as to make it burn all Night, that the *Tartars* might conclude we were still there; but as soon as it was dark, (that is to say, so as we could see the Stars, for our Guide would not stir before) having all our Horses and Camels ready loaden, we followed our new Guide, who I soon found steer'd himself by the Pole, or North Star, all the Country being level for a long Way.

After we had travell'd two Hours very hard, it began to be lighter still, not that it was quite dark all Night, but the Moon began to rise, so that in short, it was rather lighter than we wish'd it to be; but by six a Clock the next Morning we were gotten near forty Miles, tho' the Truth is, we almost spoil'd our Horses. Here we found a *Russian* Village named *Kermazinskoy*, where we rested, and heard nothing of the *Calmuck Tartars* that Day; about two Hours before Night we set out again, and travell'd till eight the next Morning, tho' not quite so quick as before, and about seven a-Clock we pass'd a little River call'd *Kirtza*, and came to a good large Town inhabited by *Russians*, and very populous, call'd *Ozomoys*; there we heard that several Troops or Hoords of *Calmucks* had been abroad upon the Desart, but that we were now compleatly out of Danger of them, which was to our great Satisfaction you may be sure. Here we were oblig'd to get some fresh Horses, and having need enough of Rest, we stay'd five Days; and my Partner and I agreed to give the honest *Syberian*, who brought us thither, the Value of ten Pistoles,[1] for his conducting us.

In five Days more we came to *Veuslima*, upon the River *Witzogda*, and running into the *Dwina*, we were there very happily near the end of our Travels by Land, that River being navigable in seven Days Passage to *Arch-Angel*: From hence we came to *Lawrenskoy* the 3d of *July*, and providing our selves with two Luggage Boats, and a Barge for our own Convenience, we embark'd the 7th, and arriv'd all safe at *Arch-Angel* the 18th, having been a Year and five Months and three Days on the Journey, including our Stay of eight Months and odd Days at *Tobolski*.

We were oblig'd to stay at this Place six Weeks for the Arrival of the Ships, and must have tarry'd longer, had not a *Hamburgher* come in above a Month sooner than any of the *English* Ships; when after some Consideration, that the City of *Hamburgh* might happen to be as good a Market for our Goods as *London*, we all took Freight with him, and having put my Goods on board, it was most natural for me to put my Steward on board to take care of them, by which means my young Lord had a sufficient Opportunity to conceal himself, never coming on Shore in all the time we stay'd there; and this he did, that he might not be seen in the City, where some of the *Muscow* Merchants would certainly have seen and discover'd him.

We sail'd from *Arch-Angel* the 20th of *August* the same Year, and after no extraordinary bad Voyage, arriv'd in the *Elbe* the 13th of *September*. Here my Partner and I found a very good Sale for our Goods, as well those of *China*, as the Sables, *&c.* of *Syberia*; and dividing the Produce of our Effects, my Share amounted to 3475 – 17 – 3 *d.*[2] notwithstanding so many Losses we had sustain'd, and Charges we had been at; only remembring that I had included in this, about six hundred Pounds worth of Diamonds which I had purchas'd at *Bengal*.

Here the young Lord took his leave of us, and went up the

1 Spanish gold coins worth between sixteen and eighteen shillings.

2 In our terms, nearly a million pounds.

Elbe in order to go to the Court of *Vienna*, where he resolv'd to seek Protection, and where he could correspond with those of his Father's Friends who were left alive: He did not part without all the Testimonies he could give me of Gratitude for the Service I had done him, and his Sense of my Kindness to the Prince his Father.

To conclude, having stay'd near four Months in *Hamburgh*, I came from thence over Land to the *Hague*, where I embark'd in the Pacquet,[1] and arriv'd in *London* the 10th of *January*, 1705, having been gone from *England* ten Years and nine Months.

And here, resolving to harrass my self no more, I am preparing for a longer Journey than all these, having liv'd 72 Years a Life of infinite Variety, and learn'd sufficiently to know the Value of Retirement, and the Blessing of ending our Days in Peace.

1 Old form of packet, a packet or mail boat.

Appendix A: Defoe on National Unity—Personal Correspondence[1]

[As a paid agent of the English government, Defoe wrote copiously in explicit support of the Act of Union (1 May 1707) that incorporated England, Scotland, and Wales into Great Britain. Much of Defoe's published writing in 1705–06 (*The History of the Union*, the *Review*, and many separate pamphlets, essays, and poems) has been examined with respect to the rhetorical strategies he used to try to convince both the English and the Scots that a national unity would be in their best interests—using language that resonates with much of the verbiage about societal formation in the first half of *Father Adventures*, wherein Crusoe and his proxies (e.g., the excellent Will Atkins) rhetorically strategize to achieve two things at once: on the one hand, to subtly convince people of different nations, ethnicities, and cultures (e.g., Spanish and Indigenous) to become one by following Crusoe's "English" lead; on the other hand, to convince the motley crew to privilege a Protestant religiosity (rather than holding fast to their Catholic or Pagan roots).[2]

During the time Defoe was writing the letters below, the Scots, like Catholic/Jacobites north and south alike, were characteristically resistant to the idea of Union, due historically to England's historical attempts to forcibly subdue the Scots and due contemporaneously to the perceived favoring of the English priorities in the actual Articles of Union as they emerged. In publication, Defoe worked to ameliorate English Scotophobic depictions of the Scots as at once parasitic, "contagious," godless, and immune to English influence, while insisting to the Scots themselves that they would be treated as equals rather than as junior partners. But Defoe's private letters to English prime minister Robert Harley (1661–1724) and to colleague Robert Fransham offer a unique

---

1 The examples included are drawn from Seager's excellent *Cambridge Edition of the Correspondence of Daniel Defoe*. For critical commentary on Defoe's involvement with national formation, see especially Leith Davis's and Paula Backscheider's extensive discussions in, respectively, *Acts of Union* and *Daniel Defoe: His Life*.

2 In his later opus *A Tour thro' the Whole Island of Great Britain* (1724–26), Defoe often accuses (with what might be called high hysterical flavor) the Scots of being Pagan. See Swenson, *Essential Scots* 60.

window onto Defoe's notion of how diverse societies could come together, not through a balanced incorporation of all elements but through a colonialist fantasy of willing subjection on the part of some elements. Defoe's idealized Great Britain, like Crusoe's idealized island society, gains strength not just by uniting against an external Other but by achieving the voluntary diminution of Otherness within, whether non-English or non-Protestant, as in the first half of *Farther Adventures*.]

1. Letter to Robert Harley, 13 September 1706

[Defoe departed for Edinburgh on 13 September 1706, to try to drum up support for the as-yet-unachieved Union. He was instructed to keep secret his employment by the English government and to pose as an autonomous person. Below, resonant with the priorities of Crusoe and his proxies on the island in *Farther Adventures*, Defoe describes to Harley what he understands his journey's goals to be.]

I beg leav, tho' it be beginning at ye wrong End, to Set Down how I Understand my present business—as foll.

1 To Inform My Self of ye Measures Takeing or Partys forming Against ye Union and Apply my Self to prevent y^m^.

2 In Conversation and by all Reasonable Methods to Dispose peoples minds to ye Union.

3 By writeing or Discourse, to Answer any Objeccons, Libells or Refleccons on ye Union, ye English or ye Court Relateing to the Union.

4 To Remove ye Jealousies and Uneasyness of people about Secret Designs here against ye Kirk &c.

2. Letter to Robert Harley, 24 October 1706

[Arriving in Edinburgh, Defoe reports back to his employer on the extent of ongoing Scottish resistance to the progress that had been made toward unification; like Crusoe and his island proxies in the first half of *Farther Adventures*, Defoe expresses surprise at the difficulties in bringing different groups into voluntary solidarity with one another.]

I am Sorry to Tell you here is a Most Confused scene of affaires, and The Ministry have a Very Difficult Course to steer. You allow me Freedome of speaking Allegories; in such a Case it Seems to me The Presbyterians are hard at work to Restore Episcopacy, and The Rabble to bring to pass y[e] Union.

We have had Two Mobbs Since my last and Expect a Third and of these y[e] Following is a short acco[t].

[...]

Certainly a Scots Rabble is y[e] worst of its kind.

The first night they Onely Threatned hard [...]—they Came up Hallowing in y[e] Dark, Threw some stones at y[e] Guard, broke a few windows and y[e] like and so it Ended.

I was warn'd that night that I should Take Care of my Self and not Appear in y[e] street w[ch] Indeed for y[e] last five days I have done Very Little, haveing been Confin'd by a Violent Cold. However I went up y[e] street in a Friends Coach in y[e] Evening and some of y[e] Mob Not then Gott together were heard to say when I went into a house There was One of ye English Dogs &c.

[...]

I had not been Long There but I heard a Great Noise and looking Out Saw a Terrible Multitude Come up y[e] High street wth A Drum at the head of Them shouting and swearing and Cryeing Out all Scotland would stand together, No Union, No Union, English Dogs and the like.

3. Letter to Robert Harley, 26 November 1706

[As Harley's proxy in Scotland, Defoe assures his employer (not unlike Will Atkins assuring Crusoe) that he takes great care in modifying his rhetorical approaches when addressing different elements of the populace.]

Tho I will Not Answer for Success yet I Trust in Mannagem[t] you shall not be Uneasy at yo[r]. Trusting me here. I have Compass't my First and Main step happily Enough, in That I am Perfectly Unuspect[d] as Corresponding wth anybody in England. I Converse wth Presbyterian, Episcopall-Dissenter, papist and Non-Juror, and I hope wth Equall Circumspeccon. I flatter my Self you will have no Complaints of my Conduct. I have faithfull Emissaries in Every Comp[a] And I Talk to Every body in Their Own way; to y[e] Merchants I am about to Settle here in Trade, Building ships &c.; with y[e] Lawyers I want to purchase a House and Land to bring my family & live Upon it (God knows where ye Money is to pay for it); to day I am Goeing into Partnership with a Memb^{r} of parliam^{t} in a Glass house, to morrow wth Another in a Salt work; wth ye Glasgow Mutineers I am to be a fish Merchant, wth ye Aberdeen Men a woollen, and with ye Perth and Western men a Linen Manufacturer, and still at the End of all Discourse the Union is the Essentiall and I am all to Every one that I may Gain some.

4. Letter to John Fransham, 28 December 1706

[Summarizing recent events, Defoe both refers to his periodical publication *The Review* and admits that his true priorities (contrary to his many protestations otherwise in *The Review*, in other publications, and verbally while in Scotland), and by allusive extension his understanding of the English government's priorities, are not for an equal Union after all but for something more like what Crusoe and his proxies (e.g., Will Atkins, but also the helpful Catholic priest who provides a contrast to the Catholic Jacobites described below) engineer for Crusoe's island community.]

I have been here three months in a most difficult time. The Treaty of an Union has been receiv'd here with a different gust from what we in England expected, and indeed from what any rational people might expect.

The Kirk at first seem'd very ready to comply wth it, and Mr Roswell and Mr Taylor, two dissenting Ministers from London who were here before me, did their endeavour to answer all scruples, and indeed I was in hopes they had effectually answer'd the end of their coming.

But we soon found an alteration, and I must acknowledge chiefly from some hot men in the Assembly who when they came to Town set all in a Flame.

The Jacobite Interest had done their best before, and possest the people with their Trade and a multitude of wild chimera's, and one Mr. Hodges wrote a Book full of Invectives against the Union and the English National, which being sent from England was industriously spread over the whole Kingdom.

[...]

I endeavour in the Review, as I suppose you will see, to put the best Face on the proceedings.

[...]

I cannot enlarge. I dare not prophecy the Event but tis pity the two Nations should be divided any longer; this people are a Sober, Religious and Gallant Nation, the country good, the Soil in most places capable of vast improvements and nothing wanting but English Stocks, English Art and English Trade to make us all one great people.

Appendix B: Defoe on Global Trade—Essays

[Defoe's publications on trade with foreign nations give a window onto his beliefs about the proper mode of relations between England and other parts of the globe. The essays have corollaries to Crusoe's attitudes about the forming of communal solidarity in the first half of *Farther Adventures* and the various exchange-based relationships he enters into in the second half. There are parallels as well to sentiments expressed in Defoe's earlier personal correspondence about the Act of Union of Great Britain (see Appendix A): the difficulty in convincing people to act against their own perceived best interests; the merits of uniting parties against a common external (or internal) foe; the notion of trade and other partnerships not merely as an agreement between two parties but as a competitive arrangement that excludes other parties; the idea of the nation (or other contrived communities) as a personified human body; the necessity of inculcating the sense of "trade" as a voluntary rather than forced relationship; and the implicit but necessary existential thread of engaging with extra-national entities under the auspices of exchange.]

1. From *An Essay upon the Trade to Africa* (1711)

[Defoe here acknowledges the effort it takes to convince people to act against their best interests or best wishes, describes the rhetorical command that is required to make two parties' interests appear to overlap, and asserts the utility in establishing solidarity against shared foes (hence the idea of trade as an exclusionary relationship). Like his protagonist, Defoe is comfortable assuming an equality of commodities from ivory to bullion to human lives. Lastly, he repeats a metaphor common to his political writing, namely the personification of the nation as a body.]

In order to set the Merits of that Cause in a true Light

And

Bring the Disputes between the *African Company*[1] and the *Traders* into a narrower Compass.

It is, no Question, the hardest Thing in the World, to Convince Mens Judgments against their Interest, and persuade Men to Believe, what they desire should not be true.

This I conceive has been one Cause, why the African Company and the Separate Traders have Argued so long against one another to so little purpose: til at last, they seem to give over Disputing for Conviction of one another, and labour to possess other Men, with the Reasonableness of their respective Pretensions; that the World being Judges of their Arguments, that they have the Strength of Reason on their Side may have most Voices, and make their Cause most Popular.

But in this they have not been without their Difficulties, and the Ground they have gotten on either Side, seems hardly worth the Noise it has made: This seems owing Principally to the backwardness of People's making themselves Masters of the Cause, either on one Side or other, and perhaps a little to the unhappy Custom of the Age, viz., Of appearing for or against, as Parties, Prejudices, Friendships, Examples, or Interests guide us, rather than by the true Method of Enquiring into the Bottom of Things, and Impartially Judging, according to the Weight of their proper Merit.

[...]

Unbyass'd Men may see by a clear Light, and make a Judgment of Truth upon the Matter.

In order to this, we shall briefly, and with all possible plainness,

1 The Royal African Company was an English mercantile company, established in 1660 and dissolved in 1750 (first incorporated as the Company of Royal Adventurers Trading to Africa; reconstituted in 1672 as the Royal African Trading Company of England). The Company's original pursuit was gold (and secondary exports such as ivory), but by the late 1690s the traffic in enslaved people was the Company's chief purpose. As such, the Company dominated the Atlantic slave trade during the period. For critical and historical commentary, see, for general information, Wheeler 90–136; and, on Defoe, Knox-Shaw.

enter a little into Merits of the Cause, and search to the Bottom the Transaction it self, between the Company and the Separate Traders: We shall enquire into their Management of the Trade, as it respects themselves, the Trade itself, and the Nation: Their Behavior to one another, how, and upon what Foundation they have begun the present War between them; how they become, as no doubt they now are, Inconsistent with one another; and how their present contending Circumstances are Inconsistent with the Trade itself, and with the Publick Good of Britain.

[...]

Notwithstanding the Authority of their New Foundation, and the Favour of their Prince, which they had then to so great a degree as above; yet such was the Respect had to the Necessity of Possessing the Coast of *Africa*, by Forts and Castles, and the Settlement of Factories, for the Management and Security of the Trade; so evidently it did appear, that without these Forts, Castles, and Settlements, it was impossible to carry on the Trade, or to preserve and enlarge it.

[...]

But to return to the Case in Hand. The Company having obtain'd a Charter from the Crown, and their Trade secur'd with exclusive Privileges, suited to its Preservation at Home, and with Forts, Castles, and Settlements, for its Defence Abroad, went on prosperously for many Years.

If any Persons yet remain'd doubtful of the Necessity and Advantage of this Trade, or of the Magnitude it rose to under the Protection of the several Princes aforesaid, it might not be amiss to enlarge here, by telling them, What in the Space of Twenty Year, or thereabout, they Exported in *English* Manufactures; How many *Negroes* they sent to the *English* Colonies in the *West Indies*; and how many Thousand Ounces of Gold they brought into *England*, beside the Export of Foreign Goods by Debentures, and the Import of many Thousand Pounds *Sterl.* in Wax, Elephants Teeth, Drugs, and valuable Commodities, the Growth of the Country there, and necessary to ours here.

We might tell you how, had this Trade been neglected and left languishing, as it has been since, under the Depredations of Interlopers and Separate Traders, the Hazards of the War, and Losses at Sea; had they been worryed, and kept in constant Alarm by the Attacks and Barking of their Rivals in the Trade, not a third Part of the Poor had been employ'd, whom their Trade kept Alive; not a third Part of the Negroes had been carried to *America*, tho' at double Price; and not a Tenth part of the Gold had been brought in to help our declining Cash to circulate, in a Time when a long War had stopt the Channels of Bullion from Mexico and Peru.

[...]

It could not but be, but that such an Open Invasion of their Trade must be a great Discouragement, as well as a great Loss to the Company: Especially considering two great Things that attended it, 1. The Subtle but unfair and dishonourable Methods which these Interlopers took, to carry on their trade to *Africa*. Such as Bribing the Company's Officers and Factors Abroad; confederating and corresponding with the Company's Enemies in *Africa*, whether Natives or Europeans; running down the price of their Goods to the Negroes, teaching them the craft and knowledge of the Trade, and how to Buy and Sell to their Advantage; raising the rates of the Slaves they buy; and thus in every Article rendering the Company's Trade more difficult to manage, and less profitable.

[...]

We shall not fail, in order to let indifferent People judge of the Pretences on both sides, to examine the Dimensions of the Trade, the Export and Import from and to England, the Number of Negroes sent to the Colonies in the West Indies, and the Price which is given there now for them; and comparing these with the like Article of the Trade during the Company's free Enjoyment of their exclusive Privileges, draw a state of the Difference; that is may be plain to every Man's Eye.

[...]

The Company, as it may well be imagin'd, under the Torture of this growing Evil, like a Body under the Weight of a cruel and incurable Disease, has sensibly wasted and decay'd, suffer'd innumerable Inconveniences and Discouragements.

[...]

Weakness has happened [at] a time when their Strength was most needful; having not only the Natives on Shore to resist but the Enemies of *England* to contend with, viz. the *French*. And here it is humbly noted, in behalf of the Company, That their Forts and Castles indeed were built for the Defence and Protection of their Commerce, either against the Insults of the African Natives, or the Encroachments of the Trading Force of other Nations; such as the Dutch, French, Danes, Prussians, and Portuguese.

[...]

The Rock which as is said Shipwreckt the whole Project, and in the midst of their Triumph split all their Cause, was this: the Want of being able to propose a real and substantial Security for the Preservation of the Trade to the Nation.

2. From *An Essay on the South-Sea Trade* (1712)

[Defoe carries forward the idea of trade partnership not simply as a contract between two entities but rather as a competitive relationship of exclusion. The essay also describes the need to rhetorically lead reluctant parties to a sense of voluntary rather than forced exchange. Lastly, with the example of the toxic grapes (an example also offered by Crusoe in Part I), Defoe betrays his sense that engaging with foreign bodies can be hazardous to the self.]

WITH An Enquiry into the Grounds and Reasons of the present Dislike and Complaint against the Settlement of a *South-Sea* Company.[1]

By the Author of the *REVIEW*.

A NEW Trade being now to be set on Foot, and in a New Manner, with a Capital Stock, and by the Encouragement of the

1 The South Sea Company was a British public-private joint-stock venture that was founded in 1711 to consolidate and decrease the national debt cost. The Company was granted a monopoly (the "Asiento") in the traffic of enslaved Africans to the South Sea islands and South America. Since Spain and Portugal controlled the latter at the time the Company was established, there was no substantial "trade" or profit to be expected for investors, and, in 1720, the bursting of the so-called South Sea Bubble was the source of widespread ruin. For an introduction to both the South Sea Company and Defoe's involvement, see Rogers 155–75.

Government, it has been long expected when some Able Pen would have undertaken to guide the People of this unsettled Age how to think about it.

There has not been in our Memory an Undertaking of such Consequence, and so generally to be engaged in; nor has there been an Undertaking, about which the People, even those who are to be concern'd have been so uneasie, their Opinions of it so confused, and their Knowledge of the Manner and Circumstances of it so small.

There has not been an Undertaking in this Age introduced in such a Method, against which so many People, upon so differing Foundations, are pleased (perhaps some of them hardly knowing why) to oppose themselves: Before it was formed it had the general Suffrage of all Mankind, every Man talk'd of it as a Thing fit to be undertaken, worthy of the Encouragement of Parliament, Government, Queen and Nation: The omitting it was tax'd in Print as a Token of National Blindness, and a Want of Judgment in the Ministry or Managers of all the past Years of this War. The Advantages the *French* made of it were look't upon as the great Supports of the War to them, and what encouraged them to carry it on; and we were reckon'd unaccountably Negligent, in that we either did not make those Advantages ourselves, or prevent the Enemy from making use of them against us.

Several Publick Printed Pamphlets disposed to ridicule the carrying on a War in *Spain*, have laid down this as the main Point, which the first Contrivers of that War should have attempted in the stead of it, and have made a Jest of their Politicks for the Defect; and when the great Quantities of Silver which the *French* Squadrons, and Private Merchant Ships, have brought Home from the *South-Seas* have been spoken of, it has been frequently accompanied with Reflections, and a general Regret, that those happy Advantages should pass by us alledging, that the *English* Nation, who are so much better qualified [in] every Way, both by their Manufactures to Trade *with*, Islands to Trade *from*, and Naval Strength to manage and protect that Trade, should so long lye still, and leave unattempted, a Trade, which in the Enemies Hand is so fatal to us, and which in our Hands might be so fatal to them.

Yet notwithstanding all this, such is the evil Genius of our Times, that now such an Undertaking is set on Foot, either it is so ill digested, or the Persons ushering it into the World are thought so Disagreeable, or Unskilful, or the Thing itself so ill placed in our View, that no Undertaking of the Kind has met with such a Fate as this; and if it must go on, it seems throng'd with Difficulties, calculated to destroy it in its Infancy.

It is needful therefore with the utmost Impartiality to enquire into the Case, and see where the Objections lye; for against the Trade itself, *quasi a Trade to the South-Seas*, no Body will, or can, raise any Objection; the Objection must be founded either on

- The Manner.
- The Method.
- The Persons.
- The Time of its Introduction.
- Or against some Part of the proposed Scheme of carrying on this Trade.

To enquire about this, to weigh duly the Substance of the Objections, and set the whole in a true Light, that we may determine whether this Trade is to be carried on, or no, is the Design of this Essay.

The Act of Parliament, which gives the Power and Limits the Extent of this New Trade, has given it Birth, and a Name, but has not in the least directed in what Posture the Persons to be concern'd shall put themselves, in what Manner they shall carry it on, how they shall proceed, or where they shall begin; nor was it necessary that this should be made any Part of the Foundation, which principally belongs to the Superstructer: The Power of an Act of Parliament was necessary to establish a Company, to give them Exclusive Priviledges, to limit and restrain these Priviledges, and settle Bounds between them and other Trades; but how this Trade is to be begun, how carried on, where they shall fix their Footing, from whence to go on progressively to the End design'd, this is left entirely to the dispose of the Body, to whom the Power and Priviledge of such Trade is deputed.

Now, tho' in the Order of Things we see nothing can be objected against the Regularity of this Proceeding, yet this seeming on one Hand to leave the World in the Dark, as to the Manner of carrying on this Trade, has on the other Hand filled us with the Crude and Indigested, or Ill-digested Notions, and Guesses of the Town; every Man giving his own Opinion in such a Manner, that from the Variety of Proposals, which every one makes, from the Difficulties raised, and from the Objections brought up against the Manner of carrying on this Trade, we are now brought, by Unhappy Degrees, to all Manner of Confusion of Thoughts about it, and from every Body laying down a Way how to carry it on, to every Body crowding in their Suspicions, their Suggestions of *this* and *that* being Impracticable, and the *other* too Hazardous; one Way *not* Safe, another *not* Just, a Third *not* Feasible *and the like*, as if because ye are not at a Certainty which Way it shall be done, or which is the best Way to do it, that therefore it cannot be done at all.

Whether it be the real Opinion of these Objectors that the Thing is impracticable in itself, or whether some Men, for Reasons worse grounded, think it convenient, if possible to have it appear so, is not the present Debate; if the Mist may be taken off by cool Reasoning, and People brought to see by a clear Light, they will be the less influenced by the Design of any, who may find it convenient for other Purposes, that this Case should be as much perplex'd as possible.

To this End this short Tract is made Publick, in which, if the Case may be stated clearly, the false Glosses, Mists and Shadows, with which this Age is amused, taken away, and the Prejudices of People on either Hand removed, perhaps we may come to a right Understanding of the Case: Having premised this by Way of Introduction, it seems naturally to lead the Reader to a View of the Doubts, now started among us about this Trade.

1. Whether this Trade to the *South-Seas* can be carried on, or no?
2. Whether the Manner of proposing this Trade be Rational and Just?

It seems indispensably necessary to enquire into these Things first, before we meddle with the Manner how it is to be carried on, since the Objections that seem most to perplex the Town now, *whether by Design or no*, are laid against the Thing in general, that it will come to Nothing that it is a Chimera, a Sham, has Nothing, in it, is Impracticable, will be Dropt again, was taken up to serve a Turn, *and the like.*

The Allegations to sustain this are such as these.

1. They say the Scheme is Impracticable; that you propose a Thing not to be done; impossible in the general Notions of Trade; that this was not a Season for it; that the Countries you propose to Trade with are in the Possession of the *French* and *Spaniards*, our declar'd Enemies; that 'tis Time enough to talk of Trading thither when you have some of the Country in Possession; that Conquering Nations is a Work which do's not belong to Merchants and Companies, whose Stock will be exhausted by any Attempt of that Kind; that to talk of Trade before Conquest, and

Conquest before any Attempt made, are equally ridiculous.

2. That when any Part of this Country may be taken from the Enemy and possess'd, it ought to be proved that the Enemy shall not be in any Manner able to dispossess you again, to attack or molest you; in which Case Commerce and Trade will not only be interrupted, but entirely disappointed.

3. That neither of the Nations who possess *South America, viz.* The *French* or *Spaniards,* will ever Capitulate with you, or upon any Terms, whether in Peace or War, consent to a Free Trade, and therefore it cannot be expected that the Scheme as it is proposed can answer the Ends of Trade.

4. That it's evident the Affair of Trade was not the main End of the Proposal, but other Aims are couch'd under this Pretence, which other Aims are not pleasing to the Parties concern'd, and therefore were glossed over with this pretended Advantage, to make them pass the more easily and undiscovered with the People; but that the Pretence being equally liable to Objection, as the Thing design'd, so both together render the Minds of the People more uneasie than they were before.

The Second Question lies against the Manner of proposing this Trade, which they say is violent and unusual, a *Force* upon the People against their Will, inconsistent with their Liberty, and that therefore it is entred upon with a general Dissatisfaction, curs'd by them that are to go into it, hated by those that refuse it, and ridicul'd by all; that it is a meer Project of a Party, a Contrivance to serve the Turn they are carrying on by it, and to put a Face of Payment upon a Debt which they know not what to do with, and which made them uneasie; and all this without a Reality, that they might stifle the Clamour of those whose just Demands upon the Government could no otherwise be answer'd.

If the Objectors have not full Scope given them here in relating their Objections, it is only because the Reproaches and Reflections which they study to set them off with, and which they very plentifully bestow upon the Government, and upon the Persons who they think are the Instruments of it, are left out, as Things which seem not to be necessary at all, either to make their Argument more forcible, or add to the Number of Reasons; and this Omission 'tis hoped they will excuse in an Author who is not writing to reproach any Side, but to calm and quiet the Minds of every Side, and bring Things, if possible, to a clear and right Understanding.

[...]

It remains to enquire, why that, which in a separate Consideration is so clear, and without exception, should fall under such a general Dislike when brought together; that there are some Reasons to be assign'd, which are Invidious, Personal, and which the Author of this cares not to mention, is a Thing rather to be sigh'd for than disputed; but some Reasons other than these may be hinted at.

1. The seeming Force there is in the Act, to make these the Company, and none else, and to oblige these to be the People.
2. The unhappy sorting of the People, in the Consequence of the Act, putting them upon the Trade, who are neither qualified by Circumstances or Genius to it, and who by their Ignorance have brought themselves to dislike it, even because they do not understand.

Both these I take to be Misfortunes to the Proposers of this Affair; and yet both are Things, which, 1. They could not easily foresee. And, 2. Foreseeing they could not easily prevent, without putting all upon a Hazard.

1. They could not easily *foresee* it; for who could have imagin'd that a Thing so generally applauded before, which we had been blam'd so often and so publickly for neglecting, which our Enemies the *French* have made such Infinite Advantage of, should not be esteem'd an Advantage to us? *Or that,* to oblige them all to an equal and proportion'd Subscription would be taken as an Imposition? I must own I'm against all Manner of Force, and think it had been better here left more to Choice; *But how better?* I do not mean better for the *People,* but better for the *Ministry*; that their Work had been easier, and the Popular Clamour less without it; for the Advantage proposed is to the People, not to the Ministry; and the Force then is no more than as you would have forc'd a Child or a Lunatick out of a House that was on Fire; and I rather put it thus upon a Supposition, that there is some Constraint, than argue, tho' the Case might hear it, strictly speaking, that really here is no Force at all.

2. But suppose the Ministry had foreseen that the Notion of a Force, how much soever to our Advantage, is so Irksome a Thing, that it would hazard the bringing the Proposal into a general Dislike. Since Liberty is so Nice a Thing that it should not be touch'd upon, tho' it was never so much to the Advantage of the Person; yet I own I do not see how they could go forward (*viz.*) in joining the Two Proposals, and leave the Thing more to Choice, than they have done.

Liberty is an Invaluable Priviledge, and no Man can in his right Understanding be easily able to be too careful of it.—I remember a Story of Two *English* Soldiers in *Catalonia* this very War.—The General finding that the Liberty our People took in eating Grapes, and other Luscious Fruits in those hot Countries, was very destructive to the Health of the Men, that it threw them into Fluxes and Fevers, and destroyed great Numbers of them, made an Order that none of the Men under great Penalty should eat any Grapes.—Two *English* Soldiers had transgress'd the Order, and carried the Punishment along with the Crime, for they fell into a Flux, and were dangerously Ill.—The Officer order'd them to be brought before him, in Order to punish them: One of the Men answer'd,

'The General may e'en let us alone, for we shall not trouble him long. However, Sick as they were, Orders in the Army must be observed, and they were brought before him, *for go they could not.* The Officer ask'd them how they durst eat Grapes when they knew the Order, the Fellow boldly told him, *That in all his Orders as to the Service they had obeyed punctually, and never transgrest; but in this, what concern'd themselves only, they were* English men *and* Freemen, *and thought they ought to be at* LIBERTY *to Kill themselves whenever they had a Mind to it.*'

Indeed upon these Nice Principles of Liberty here may be some Force alledged, but in the main it cannot be so properly called *Force*; because every Man that does not think fit to come in may remain in the State he was before; nor do I think that State is or can be made *Worse* than before because other Provision than a Parliamentary Fund of Interest could never be made, or be expected to be made; and if I judge right of the Additional Article, which they call the *South-Sea Stock*, which is reckon'd an Incumbrance, it stands upon this Foot, (*viz.*) that it takes nothing from the Subscription which it does not first add to it; because the Interest which is paid by this Subscription upon the Arrear of Interest allowed to be added to the Principal, amounts in Time to much more than the 10 *per Cent.* which is to be called in by the Company to form the Stock for Carrying on the Trade.

[…]

But have we not something then Peculiar in the Fate of this Nation, which an indifferent Man must needs lament, that the Surface of Affairs can so much alter our Temper, and that our Judgments are so over rul'd by our Prejudices, that we cannot approve of that join'd together, which we would so freely embrace if offered apart? I am not writing Satyrs here, nor pleading for a Party, if I were I should take some Freedom on both Sides; I should perhaps reproach those People who will reject Publick Advantages for the Sake of Private Prejudices; and because they cannot go along with the Publick in all their Proceedings, will not therefore go along with them in those wherein the general Good is evidently carried on.—I should, on the other Hand, perhaps say, that the joining these Two Unhappy Happy Thoughts together was no Token of making a right Judgment of the Temper of our Times, and the only Cause of the Disorder that has happened among us upon this Head.

Unhappy Conjunction! That Two Good Things should make One Bad One; Two Things equally Happy asunder, Advantageous, Pleasing and Profitable, apart, but put together pleases every Body the less, and hardly and Body so well as they would do asunder.

If any Man enquires why this is so? Why that, which in itself is Agreeable, Useful, and Profitable, should not be so when join'd with another Thing equally so?

3. From *The Trade to India Critically and Calmly Considered* (1720)

[This essay extends Defoe's concerns about deleterious trade relationships, employing his favored personifying metaphor of the nation as a body. Noting the difficulty of forbidding the importation of popular goods, he revises and broadens the idea of solidarity through exclusion by connecting the cause of Great Britain to that of Europe's larger body.]

Critically and Calmly consider'd, And prov'd to be destructive to the general Trade of *GREAT BRITAIN*, as well as to the Woollen and Silk Manufactures in particular.

AFTER all the Arguments which have been used, on one Side as well as on the other, in the *Callicoe Controversy* now on Foot, have, as it were, been summ'd up, and laid before the House of Commons, and when we thought there had been little more to do than to wait the Resolutions of the House, and receive from thence a conclusive Sentence: I say, after all this is done and over, we are attack'd a-new with powerful Applications, I do not say powerful Reasonings, drawn from the Usefulness and Advantages of the *East India Trade*.

This is the more surprizing, because they say 'tis done in Behalf of the *East India Company*.[1] Many People really think there is so little to be said on that Head to the Company's Advantage, that it was always thought they would have been wiser, and had known their Interest better, than to bring that Dispute upon the Stage, especially on this Occasion of the *Callicoes*. It is surprizing I say also, because in all the Disputes about the *Callicoes*, the Weavers and Manufacturers have let the *East India* Company alone, as to the Consideration of their own Conduct, or the Trade in general: In short, they have never attack'd either the Company or the Trade, 'till these Men even forc'd the Discourse of both into the Controversy, by insisting upon the Merit of both, and that in a Manner, which no People, *that had really so little to say for it*, would have ventur'd to do, unless they were under some Infatuation, or the ill Influence of some Star, which pointed against them, and makes their being expos'd inevitable.

Nay, so far the Manufacturers have been from designing to concern the Company, or their general Commerce, in the present Dispute, that in the first Book which was publish'd in this Cause, entitl'd, *A brief State of the Question*; and in the very Introduction to that Book, it was laid down among the general Maxims, as a Fundamental, that the Trade to the *East Indies* was less concern'd in the Dispute than was generally imagin'd; that the Company might go on and flourish, though all that the Manufacturers ask'd were to be granted. In a Word, the *East India* Company, or their Trade, seem'd unconcern'd in the Dispute, unless we must suppose the Jobbing of their Stock to be call'd the *East India* Trade, and the Brokers to be the Company, which I cannot admit; I repeat it therefore again from the Book call'd *The brief State of the Question, &c.* the Words are these:

That the total Prohibiting the Wearing and using of Printed or Painted Callicoes in Great Britain, *is not ruinous to or inconsistent with the Prosperity of the* East India *Trade; or*, to put it into an Affirmative, that may be more capable of Evidence, *the* East

1 The East India Company (1600–1874) was an English, later British, joint-stock venture. Formed for trading with the Indian subcontinent and Southeast Asia (later East Asia as well), the Company ultimately constituted a major colonial enterprise as the world's largest corporate body. The Company traded for commodities such as dyes, spices, tea, cotton, silks, salt, sugar, and saltpeter (and, in the later period, opium), and was the driving force for imperialism in India. For an introduction and an analysis of Defoe's relationship to the Company, see Markley, "Defoe."

India *Trade may and would remain in a very thriving and flourishing Condition, and be carry'd on to the Profit and Advantage of the Adventurers, tho' all the Subjects of* Great Britain *and of* Ireland *were effectually limited from and prohibited the Wearing and Using of Printed and Painted Callicoes.*

'Tis remarkable, and deserves to be taken Notice of here, that in all that is said of or for the *East India* Trade, the Advocates for it rather apply themselves to answer and clear up the Objections continually rais'd against it, than to advance any Thing new or substantial in its Favour: This proves that the present Case is not the only Occasion there has been to complain of the injurious Effects of this Trade.

The great Question is plainly laid down thus, Whether the Trade, as now carry'd on to *India*, or to the *East Indies*, is profitable to the Nation, or whether it is not.

But, before I enter upon the Question, I must openly and professedly distinguish upon the Thing we are talking of; for I am certain, if we do not agree upon the Subject, we shall never agree upon the Argument; and, I believe most of our Wrangling is for Want of determining first what it is we are talking of: My Distinction is this:

I say, we must *distinguish* here between the *East India* COMPANY and the *East India* TRADE: The Mistake here is the Foundation of all that Cavil and Talk, to little Purpose, which we have had on this Occasion; the Difference is plain; the *East India* TRADE is one Thing, the *East India* COMPANY *tradeing* is another.

I grant what was formerly voted by the House of Commons in 1694, That *it is most for our Interest that the* Trade *to the* East Indies *be carry'd on by an exclusive Company*: But this has no Relation to the main Question, *viz.* Whether *Trade itself*, whether with a Company or without a Company, *is an advantageous Trade?*

Again, we must distinguish between the Trade in Callicoes and Wrought Silks from *India*, on the one Hand, and the whole *East India* Trade, consider'd complexly.

But the officious Advocates for the Callicoes, will not suffer the *East India* Trade to be so passive or neutral in this Case as they ought to be; but as an Argument to support the Use of Callicoes, they bring the Company into the Debate, and, at last, they have petition'd to be heard.

It will be, as it were, but by Accident, that we embark the Cause of the Callicoes and *East India* Silks in this Debate: That the Callicoes are destructive to our Woollen and Silk Manufacturers, have lessen'd their Consumption, beaten several Sorts of their Goods quite out of Trade; and that the Broad Cloth and Stuff Trade, in particular, are still more and more declining upon that Account, *has been prov'd at the Bar of the House*, and at the Board of Trade; and the Report of the Lords-Commissioners of Trade makes it out farther, thus:

It being therefore self-evident, that Printed and Stained Callicoes and Linnens are used and worn, by almost all Sorts of People in this Kingdom, and that every Piece so worn prevents the Consumption of the same Quantity of our Woollen and Silk Manufactures, we must conclude, that the Complainants have been and are exceedingly discouraged, and their Trade prejudiced thereby.

But 'tis the Trade to *India* in general, not the Callicoes, that is now the Question, and whether it may pass under that Title of a beneficial Trade to the Nation, or not.

If my Answer to this might distinguish rightly of the Company's Circumstances, I should, after some Regulations, vote in Favour of the Trade; and I will not doubt, but, with necessary Limitations, it might be allow'd to be an advantageous Trade: But without those Limitations, I cannot venture to call it so, by any Means; but, on the contrary, a Trade destructive to the Prosperity of our Country, not only in the Woollen and Silk Manufactures, but many other Ways besides. What those Limitations are, will appear in the Consequence of this Discourse.

There are but two Things, which, in this Case, can denominate a foreign Trade gainful to the Nation.

I That it exports that which it is the Advantage of the Kingdom to export.
II That it returns, or imports, something of which we consume little at Home, and export much.

The *East India* Trade, *I fear*, will be able to claim neither of these Qualifications; but, on the contrary, it exports, or sends out of the Nation, that *which answers all Things*, and brings back that which amounts to *little* or *nothing*; and it is in this Particular that the Merit of the whole Cause will lye.

[...]

[I]f they carry'd out all they brought in, what Gain could they be to the Publick, which is the main Question in Hand: Indeed, then they would plead the Merit of all the Manufactures which they export, as above, besides that of bringing Home several useful Things for our Home Consumption, which we cannot well be without; such as, Salt Peter, Pepper, Drugs, Dye, Stuffs, Coffee, Tea, Raw Silk, *&c.* This, I think, is the full of what they alledge.

But I shall answer this two Ways, and, I think, both shall confute them effectually[.]

[…]

Some have computed, that the Quantities of *East India* Goods, run in upon us from *Holland*, and consum'd here, are not only equal in Value to all the Goods of our Company's exporting from hence, but much superior to them: Where then is our Bullion procur'd? In short, the Bullion is then only bought with Bullion; that is to say, is taken away from the Balance of other Branches of our Trade, which are advantageous, and which supply it: But as to the *India* Trade, it does nothing for us.

If ever the Use and Wearing of Callicoes and Silks comes to be prohibited, all this Mystery of Iniquity will be discover'd, or will discover it self. It is impossible it should be then hid; for no Body will import the Goods which no Body will buy; and no Body will buy the Goods which no Body will wear.

But this is not all; for if *this Trade* does nothing *well* for us, it must do much *ill* against us; for there are no neutral Trades which do neither Good or Hurt. The Character of this Trade is, in short, what was printed of it near 20 Years ago, by an Author that examin'd it to the Bottom, (*viz.*) That it carry'd out that *which answers all Things*, and brings back that which evidently *proves the Destruction of our own Manufactures.*

These are short but pungent Arguments against the Benefit of the *East India* Trade in general, and are drawn up thus.

[…]

Nor is this Custom of running Callicoes the only Mischief of the *East India* Trade; for 'tis the same in the Tea, the Coffee, and the Pepper; the Examples are most flagrant; if the Quantities of Tea enter'd for Exportation were calculated in any single Year, by the Custom-Bills only, and that discounted out of the Quantity of Tea imported, it would not leave a Proportion equal to the visible Expence in *Great Britain*, by a prodigious Quantity: Whence then can it be supply'd but by foul Practices?

The Coffee ('till a late Engrossment of Coffee, has alter'd

the Case, and rais'd the Price) was to be bought cheaper of the Druggist, by the Bale or Hundred, than the Duty and the Price cost at the Candle amounted to, and that by 40 or 50 *per Cent.* and how should this be done, but by clandestine unfair Trading.

Pepper, since the high Duty of *1s. 6d. per* lb. has wholly disappear'd, as to the Duty; the Exportation has been as great as the Importation, within a Trifle; and the Home Consumption has been reduc'd to about four Bags of Sweepings, or thereabouts, in a Year; that is to say, there has not about four Bags paid Duty at the Custom-House in a Year; and yet we had no Want of Pepper in *England*, but have consum'd as much as ever; and how has this been done, but by the Arts of Shipping and Relanding, *&c.*

The Article of *foreign* East India *Goods*, (I call them foreign, because not imported by our Company, but by Stealth) has also another Thing in it, which overthrows all the Merit of the *East India* Trade; for, you must note here, that I am talking of the *East India* Trade in general; that is to say, the Trade in *East India* Goods, no Matter by whom imported, whether by our Company, or a foreign Company.

[...]

It is impossible, indeed, to make exact Calculations of the Value of Things that are thus done by Stealth, and in private; but the Sum is incredible, and exceeds all our Calculation.

A certain Draper, learned in the smuggling Trade, and whose Importations of foreign *East India* Goods, if Fame belies him not, have borne a great Share in this Over-balance, has been pleas'd to say, at the Bar of the House of Commons, that the Number of People in *England* who wear printed Callicoes, is very inconsiderable, in which he is pleas'd to differ strangely from the Opinion of the Lords-Commissioners of Trade, who judge them to be a Million.

I have heard a judicious Observer of these Things say, that he has calculated, that 320000 People were cloth'd in printed Callicoe and Linnen in the County of *Middlesex* only, exclusive of the Cities and Liberties of *London* and *Westminster*: Whether this Gentleman or the modest Pleader about were nearest the Point, I leave to the Judicious.

[...]

And here we sensibly feel the Damage sustain'd by the Publick from this Trade, namely, the Lessening and Consumption of our current Coin. Whether they melt it down or no, I will not enquire here; that is a dark Trade by itself, which deserves to be enquir'd into; and which, if enquir'd into, may easily be laid open. But does any Silver, (that's the Question that will try it all) go to the Mint? The common Accidents of the World, and the ordinary Occasions of Trade and Travelling, will necessarily diminish the Coin if there is not a Supply. *And why are we not supply'd?* Why no Silver sent to the Mint? But because of the immense Quantities sent away to the *East Indies*.

And here, if we cou'd dilate and extend our Thoughts to consider not our own Trade singly, but the general Trade of the World, we shou'd find the *East India* Trade ruinous and destructive to the general Trade of all this Part of the World, as well as to ours in particular.

To judge of this, you must consider *Europe* as one Body, one Nation, or one general Interest in Trade, and set the *East India* Trade against it as another. The *East India* Trade exhausts the whole Treasure of *Europe*, and destroys thereby their Trade; carrying every Year such immense Sums of Mony in Specie out of *Europe* into *India*, that the whole Body feels the want of it very sensibly. In Return of which, they bring their chief Manufactures and their Growth, and fill these Parts of the World with Gaiety and Trifles, and rob them a second Time of the Employment of their People. Some Part of *Europe* indeed have been wiser than we are, and have prohibited the Use and Consumption of all these *East India* Goods for the very Reasons that indeed all the rest of *Europe* ought to do the same; namely, because they rob them of their Coin, and starve their Poor. This carrying the Mony thus away into *India* from *Europe* in general, is evident in the different Parts of *Europe*; for there are more Channels than this one, tho' by all the Channels it runs into the same Place.

[…]

Thus, in a Word, *Europe*, like a Body in a warm Bath, with its Veins open'd, lies bleeding to Death; and her Bullion, which is the Life and Blood of her Trade, flows all to *India*, where 'tis amass'd into infinite Heaps, for the enriching the Heathen World at the Expence of the Christian World.

From this great Cause of *Europe*'s Poverty come all the Shifts and Projects of *Europe*, for raising imaginary Wealth in the room of real Wealth; substituting Credit, which indeed is but Air, instead of Bullion, and Paper instead of Money; and they do indeed supply the Want of the Species, or else *Europe*, which is a trading Nation, *if we may, as above, speak of it all as one Body*, could not carry on her Commerce. Her Product and Manufactures wou'd not circulate for want of Money to assist that Circulation, and to circulate with it; for, in short, Money is the Stream of Trade which carries *the Product and Manufactures*; that is to say, Merchandise along with it. And if the Merchandise did not thus float upon the Water, that is Money, 'twou'd be a-Ground, stand and stagnate, and wou'd never be carry'd from Place to Place.

The Good go out, the Money comes in; more are carry'd out upon the Strength of that Money, and the like. But here the Order of Trade is inverted; for in the Trade to *India* the Goods do not go out; the Product and Manufacture does not go out to fetch in the Money, as is the natural Course of Trade, but the Money goes out to fetch the Goods in; and this, in Trade, is letting out the Blood, and with it the Life.

There is an Evidence of this past Contradiction in the ordinary Affairs of Trade in *Europe*. For Example, if by the Interruptions of War, or any other Accident of the Sea, or Pyrates, or whatever it be, the Galloons from *New Spain* are prevented coming to *Europe*, by which the Quantity of Bullion is supply'd and kept up; we immediately feel the Loss; Trade, like the Belly, misses its Food; a Scarcity appears, like that of Corn in the Markets after a bad Harvest; and the Price advances 'till a Supply comes.

What is the Reason, but this, that the Trade to *India* exhausts the World, the Money drains all away insensibly, and grows scarce?

The other Trade of *Europe* does not do thus: If the Money goes out of one Country into another, it passes from thence into a Third, and thence again into a Fourth, and so back again from whence it came, and round again; ever circulating like the Blood in the Veins, and carries with it the Spirits, which nourish the whole.

But *India*, like the Grave, swallows up all, and makes no Return; *that is*, the Money never returns: What they send us back, *is nothing*; 'tis consum'd here, and so vanishes and dies away; serving only to amass more Bullion to be carry'd away; till, in a Word, it impoverishes not *England* only, but all *Europe*. And was Gold as good a Commodity in *England* as Silver, we shou'd not have Mony left to carry on the common Course of Trade.

Thus, I think, 'tis clear, That the Trade to *India* is a disadvantageous Trade, in its own Nature, not to *England* only, but to all *Europe*.

[...]

1. I cannot close this Work, without observing how effectually all this might be prevented, how easy a Stop might be put to it, and to what infinite Advantage to Trade, by this only Method; namely, of forbidding the Use and Wearing of printed Callicoes and Linnens.

2. That no other Method but this can do it, no Prohibitions, no Penalties, no Forfeitures; no, not if Running them were to be punish'd with Death, or Transportation, which is worse than Death.

But once forbid the Use and Wearing, the Work is done; what no Body can wear or use, no Body will buy; what no Body will buy, no Body will bring to Market; what no Body will bring to Market, no Body will fetch from Abroad. And thus the Trade will be at a full Stop at once.

It has been too plain, that all Laws for preventing clandestine Trade, where the Gain of it is so high, are in vain. The Running of *French* Brandy is a Proof of this, which is done so openly, that *French* Brandy is now to be bought, upon the Coast of *England*, as cheap, within a Trifle, as at *Calais*; and so of all other Goods, for *10 l. per Cent.* Men will contract to Run in any Kind of Goods that come from Abroad; and ensure them into our Shops, such as Pepper, Coffee, Tea, Callicoes, Chints, *East India* wrought Silks, *French* Brocades, *Dutch* Blacks, Linnens, Fine Hollands, and, in a Word, almost every Thing.

But once prohibit the Use of these *East India* wearing Cloths, and you effectually stop it all.

'Tis a Particular to the Callicoes and *East India* Goods, that they are chiefly used for upper Garments: If they were less expos'd, 'twou'd be more difficult to restrain them; but as it is, 'tis easy to do it.

It remains to show, that if this was done, the chief Grievance of the *East India* Trade wou'd be over; not but they would be an advantageous Trade even then, but they would do much less Harm than now, and yet wou'd drive a very great and profitable Trade to themselves: And with this Note shall close this Work, reserving the Explanation of it to another Time.

Works Cited and Select Bibliography

Biographies

Backscheider, Paula. *Daniel Defoe: His Life*. Johns Hopkins UP, 1989.

Novak, Maximillian. *Daniel Defoe, Master of Fictions: His Life and Ideas*. Oxford UP, 2003.

Works Cited, and Select Bibliography of Defoe Scholarship 2000–24

Austin, Michael. "'Jesting with the Truth': Figura, Trace, and the Boundaries of Fiction in *Robinson Crusoe* and Its Sequels." *Eighteenth-Century Novel*, vol. 5, 2006, pp. 1–36.

Borsing, Christopher. "Re-Humanizing Robinson." *Digital Defoe: Studies in Defoe and His Contemporaries*, vol. 12, no. 1, 2020, pp. 23–29.

Clark, Steve. "'Le coeur fou robinsonne à travers les romans': Crusoe's *Farther Adventures* in the French Robinsonade." Clark and Yoshihara, *Robinson Crusoe in Asia* 137–58.

Clark, Steve, and Yukari Yoshihara. "Introduction." Clark and Yoshihara, *Robinson Crusoe in Asia* 1–22.

Clark, Steve, and Yukari Yoshihara, editors. *Robinson Crusoe in Asia*. Palgrave Macmillan, 2021.

Cole, Lucinda. *Imperfect Creatures: Vermin, Literature, and the Science of Life, 1600–1740*. U of Michigan P, 2016, pp. 143–71.

Davis, Leith. *Acts of Union: Scotland and the Literary Negotiation of the British Nation, 1707–1830*. Stanford UP, 1998.

Defoe, Daniel. *The Farther Adventures of Robinson Crusoe*. Edited by W.R. Owens, *The Novels of Daniel Defoe*, W.R. Owens and P.N. Furbank, general editors, vol. 2, Pickering & Chatto, 2008.

——. *The Farther Adventures of Robinson Crusoe: The Stoke Newington Edition*. Edited by Maximillian E. Novak et al., Bucknell UP, 2022.

——. *A History of the Union of Great Britain*. Edited by David William Hayton, *Writings on Travel, Discovery and History by Daniel Defoe*, W.R. Owens and P.N. Furbank, general editors, vols. 7–8, Pickering & Chatto, 2001–02.

——. *Memoirs of a Cavalier*. Edited by N.H. Keeble, *The Novels of Daniel Defoe*, general editors W.R. Owens and P.N. Furbank, vol. 4, Pickering & Chatto, 2008.
——. *Mere Nature Delineated*. London, 1726.
——. *Robinson Crusoe*. Edited by John Richetti, Penguin, 2001.
——. *Satire, Fantasy and Writings on the Supernatural by Daniel Defoe*. Edited by G.A. Starr, vol. 8, Pickering & Chatto, 2005.
——. *Serious Reflections during the Life and Surprising Adventures of Robinson Crusoe*. Edited by G.A. Starr, *The Novels of Daniel Defoe*, W.R. Owens and P.N. Furbank, general editors, vol. 3, Pickering & Chatto, 2008.
——. *A Tour thro' the Whole Island of Great Britain*. Edited by John McVeagh. *Writings on Travel, History and Discovery by Daniel Defoe*, W.R. Owens and P.N. Furbank, general editors, vols. 1–3, Pickering & Chatto, 2001–02.
Didicher, Nicole E. "(Un)Trustworthy Praise and (Un)Governed Passions in *The Farther Adventures of Robinson Crusoe*." *Relocating Praise: Literary Modalities and Rhetorical Contexts*, edited by Alice G. den Otter, Canadian Scholars, 2000, pp. 75–85.
Dowdell, Coby. "'A Living Law to Himself and Others': Daniel Defoe, Algernon Sidney, and the Politics of Self-Interest in *Robinson Crusoe* and *Farther Adventures*." *Eighteenth-Century Fiction*, vol. 22, no. 3, 2010, pp. 415–42.
Faller, Lincoln. "Captain Mission's Failed Utopia, Crusoe's Failed Colony: Race and Identity in New, Not Quite Imaginable Worlds." *Eighteenth Century: Theory and Interpretation*, vol. 43, no. 1, 2002, pp. 1–17.
Free, Melissa. "Un-Erasing Crusoe: *Farther Adventures* in the Nineteenth Century." *Book History*, vol. 9, 2006, pp. 89–130.
Gildon, Charles. *The Life and Strange Surprizing Adventures of Mr. D— DeF—, of London, Hosier [...] with Remarks Serious and Comical upon the Life of Crusoe*. London, 1719.
Harada, Noriyuki. "*Robinson Crusoe* in the Context of Travel Narrative of Early Modern England on Asia." Clark and Yoshihara, *Robinson Crusoe in Asia* 67–86.
Hunter, J. Paul. "Serious Reflections on Daniel Defoe (with an Excursus on the Farther Adventures of Ian Watt and Two Notes on the Present State of Literary Studies)." *Eighteenth-Century Fiction*, vol. 12, nos. 2–3, 2000, pp. 227–38.
Hutchins, Henry Clinton. Robinson Crusoe *and Its Printing 1719–1731: A Bibliographical Study*. 1925. AMS Press, 1967.

Joseph, Betty. "Capitalism and Its Others: Intersecting and Competing Forms in Eighteenth-Century Fiction." *Studies in Eighteenth-Century Culture*, vol. 45, 2016, pp. 157–73.

Knox-Shaw, Peter. "Defoe and the Politics of Representing the African Interior." *Modern Language Review*, vol. 96, no. 4, 2001, pp. 937–51.

Loar, Christopher. *Political Magic: Fictions of Savagery and Sovereignty, 1650–1750*. Fordham UP, 2014.

Ma, Ning. *The Age of Silver: The Rise of the Novel East and West*. Oxford UP, 2017, pp. 139–66.

Markley, Robert. "Aesthetico-Constructivism: Farther Adventures in Criticism." *Philological Quarterly*, vol. 86, no. 3, 2007, pp. 291–314.

——. "Defoe and the Problem of the East India Company." Clark and Yoshihara, *Robinson Crusoe in Asia* 23–46.

——. *The Far East and the English Imagination 1600–1730*. Cambridge UP, 2006. [See esp. chap. 5.]

——. "'I Have Now Done with My Island, and All Manner of Discourse about It': Crusoe's *Farther Adventures* and the Unwritten History of the Novel." *A Companion to the Eighteenth-Century English Novel and Culture*, edited by Paula Backscheider and Catherine Ingrassia, Wiley-Blackwell, 2005, pp. 25–47.

——. "Teaching the *Crusoe* Trilogy." *Approaches to Teaching Defoe's* Robinson Crusoe, edited by Maximillian Novak and Carol Fisher, Modern Language Association, 2005, pp. 96–104.

Min, Eun Kyung. *China and the Writing of English Literary Modernity, 1690–1770*. Cambridge UP, 2018.

Novak, Maximillian E. "Crusoe's Encounters with the World and the Problem of Justice in *The Farther Adventures*." *Robinson Crusoe after 300 Years*, edited by Andreas Mueller and Glynis Ridley, Bucknell UP, 2021, pp. 167–82.

——. "'The Sum of Humane Misery'? Defoe's Ambiguity toward Exile." *SEL: Studies in English Literature, 1500–1900*, vol. 50, no. 3, 2010, pp. 601–23.

Nowka, Scott. "Building the Wall: Crusoe and the Other." *Digital Defoe: Studies in Defoe & His Contemporaries*, vol. 2, no. 1, 2010, pp. 41–57.

Orr, Leah. "Providence and Religion in the *Crusoe* Trilogy." *Eighteenth-Century Life*, vol. 38, no. 2, 2014, pp. 1–27.

Pauley, Benjamin. "Crusoe's Rambling." *Robinson Crusoe after 300 Years*, edited by Andreas Mueller and Glynis Ridley, Bucknell UP, 2021, pp. 151–66.

Pearl, Jason H. "Desert Islands and Urban Solitudes in the *Crusoe* Trilogy." *Studies in the Novel*, vol. 44, no. 2, 2012, pp. 125–43.

Peh, Li Qi. "Fragile Communities in the *Crusoe* Trilogy." *Studies in Eighteenth-Century Culture*, vol. 51, 2022, pp. 175–91.

Ricci, Matteo. *China in the Sixteenth Century: The Journals of Matteo Ricci.* Translated by Louis J. Gallagher, S.J., Random House, 1953.

Richetti, John. "Eurocentric Crusoe: *The Farther Adventures of Robinson Crusoe*." *Études anglaises: Revue du monde anglophone*, vol. 72, no. 2, 2019, pp. 213–24.

Rogers, Pat. *Defoe's Tour and Early Modern Britain: Panorama of the Nation*. Cambridge UP, 2022.

Seager, Nicholas, editor. *The Cambridge Edition of the Correspondence of Daniel Defoe*. Cambridge UP, 2022.

Starr, G.A. "*Robinson Crusoe* and Its Sequels: *The Farther Adventures* and *Serious Reflections*." *The Cambridge Companion to Robinson Crusoe*, edited by John Richetti, Cambridge UP, 2018, pp. 67–83.

Stuchiner, Judith. "The Death of Friday: A Precursor to Crusoe's Failure of Enlightenment in Defoe's *Farther Adventures*." *Digital Defoe: Studies in Defoe & His Contemporaries*, vol. 12, no. 1, 2020, pp. 49–54.

——. "Family Instruction in *The Farther Adventures of Robinson Crusoe*." *Studies in Eighteenth-Century Culture*, vol. 51, 2022, pp. 193–217.

Swenson, Rivka. *Essential Scots and the Idea of Unionism in Anglo-Scottish Literature 1603–1832*. Bucknell UP, 2016. [See chap. 1, esp. pp. 51–58.]

——. "*Robinson Crusoe* and the Form of the New Novel." *The Cambridge Companion to Robinson Crusoe*, edited by John Richetti, Cambridge UP, 2018, pp. 16–31.

Thell, Anne M. "The Aesthetics of Mental Illness in Defoe's *Crusoe* Trilogy." *The Review of English Studies*, vol. 71, 2020, pp. 709–28.

Traver, John C. "Defoe, *Unigenitus*, and the 'Catholic' Crusoe." *SEL: Studies in English Literature, 1500–1900*, vol. 51, no. 3, 2011, pp. 545–63.

Turley, Hans. "The Sublimation of Desire to Apocalyptic Passion in Defoe's *Crusoe* Trilogy." *Imperial Desire*, edited by Philip Holden and Richard J. Ruppel, U of Minnesota P, 2003, pp. 3–20.

Wheeler, Roxann. *The Complexion of Race: Categories of Difference in Eighteenth-Century British Culture*. U of Pennsylvania P, 2000.

Williams, Laurence. "Religious Conversion and the Far East in the *Crusoe* Trilogy." Clark and Yoshihara, *Robinson Crusoe in Asia* 109–36.

Wood, James Robert. "Robinson Crusoe and the Earthy Ground." *Eighteenth-Century Fiction*, vol. 32, no. 3, 2020, pp. 381–406.

About the Publisher

The word "broadview" expresses a good deal of the philosophy behind our company. Our focus is very much on the humanities and social sciences—especially literature, writing, and philosophy—but within these fields we are open to a broad range of academic approaches and political viewpoints. We strive in particular to produce high-quality, pedagogically useful books for higher education classrooms—anthologies, editions, sourcebooks, surveys of particular academic fields and sub-fields, and also course texts for subjects such as composition, business communication, and critical thinking. We welcome the perspectives of authors from marginalized and underrepresented groups, and we have a strong commitment to the environment. We publish English-language works and translations from many parts of the world, and our books are available world-wide; we also publish a select list of titles with a specifically Canadian emphasis.

broadview press

The interior of this book is printed on 100% recycled paper.